THE BOOK

BIHA

LITERATURE

'This is a magnificent and engrossing tribute to the vigour and vibrancy, the sensuality, the philosophical depth and the stylistic sophistication of Bihari literature. The voices and narratives resonate across a slew of languages, across prose and poetry, from classic to contemporary, through centuries and millennia.'

—Namita Gokhale, writer, editor, publisher

'An extraordinary collection of Bihari poetry and prose. Who could resist the charms of "The Goon"?'

—Shobhaa Dé, author, journalist

'Abhay K. is a poet, translator, anthologist and scholar, apart from his day job as a diplomat. This book, apart from being a tribute to his multiple skills, reveals the amazing history of the many languages and cultures that have flowered over the centuries in Bihar and created its incredible literature. Poetry, fiction, sacred text, history, travelogues, fascinating tales that interweave to introduce us to a culture that is breathtakingly rich in its range and diversity. This is the Bihar that will tell you what India is.'

—Pritish Nandy, poet, journalist, filmmaker

'Anthologizing is a complex task, riddled with issues of inclusion, exclusion, representation, discovery, balance, and so on. And when it involves multiple languages, histories and cultures, the task is harder. Abhay K. has taken on this task, and brought together writers and translators from eleven languages to give us a feast of Bihari literature.

From meditations on the art of kissing and the meaning of love and desire to experiences at the sharper edges of life marked with loss and want, from men and women caught in the sucking mud of oppressive traditions to those who soar into freedom, this collection spans centuries of Bihari literature in all its linguistic and cultural diversity. A must-read for everyone interested in the literary evolution of a region.'

—Jayasree Kalathil, author, translator

'What a glorious, delightful medley of Bihar's languages and literary traditions! From classic to contemporary and original works to translated ones, this diverse collection spans many time periods, forms and genres to reveal a richly layered, storied, and forever evolving region. This isn't merely a book of Bihari literature; it's an unmissable and enduring Bihar state of mind.'

—Jenny Bhatt, author, translator

'Spanning a gamut of emotions and experiences—from wisdom to sensuousness, romance to reflection, history to contemporary politics—this anthology attests as much to the brilliance of the works as to the judgement of its editor. This volume is an able representative of the region it derives its name from.'

—Hansda Sowvendra Shekhar, author

'From the wisdom of the ancient to the tumult of the present, *The Book of Bihari Literature* presents the voices of this glorious land in all their richness and variety, sourced from a bouquet of familiar and obscure languages.'

—N. Kalyan Raman, translator

THE BOOK OF
BIHARI LITERATURE

edited by

ABHAY K.

HarperCollins *Publishers* India

First published in India by HarperCollins *Publishers* 2022
4th Floor, Tower A, Building No. 10, Phase II, DLF Cyber City,
Gurugram, Haryana – 122002
www.harpercollins.co.in

2 4 6 8 10 9 7 5 3 1

P-ISBN: 978-93-5629-147-8
E-ISBN: 978-93-5629-150-8

Typeset in 11.5/15.4 Minion Pro at
Manipal Technologies Limited, Manipal

Printed and bound at
Thomson Press (India) Ltd

For
the warm and industrious people of Bihar
and
my mother, who taught me Magahi

Contents

Contents

Editor's Note

Bihar has a long history that dates back to the foundation of the Mahajanapada (great kingdom) of Magadha in southern Bihar, with its capital first at Rajgriha, present-day Rajgir, and later at Pataliputra, modern-day Patna. Over the centuries, several dynasties ruled Magadha and gave rise to two of India's great empires—the Maurya empire and the Gupta empire. Both empires witnessed great advancements in mathematics, astronomy, literature, philosophy, science and statecraft, and saw the emergence of new religions such as Buddhism and Jainism.

Bihari literature, spread over two millennia, consists of literary works produced in the various languages of Bihar. These include Magahi, Bhojpuri, Maithili, Angika, Bajjika, Hindi, Urdu, Persian (Farsi), English and classical languages such as Sanskrit and Pali.

Magahi is derived from the ancient Magadhi Prakrit, which was spoken in the ancient kingdom of Magadha, the core of which was the area south of the Ganga and east of the Son River. It is believed to be the language spoken by Gautama Buddha to deliver his sermons. It was also the official language of the Mauryan and Gupta courts, and the language in which the edicts of Emperor Ashoka were composed.

Pali is also identified with Magadhi Prakrit. Written in Brahmi script, it was the sacred language of Buddhism.

Bhojpuri is chiefly spoken in western Bihar. The language is also spoken in Fiji, Guyana, Mauritius, South Africa, Suriname, and Trinidad and Tobago.

Maithili is spoken in the states of Bihar and Jharkhand, and is one of the twenty-two languages listed in the Constitution of India. It is also spoken in the eastern Terai region and is the second most-spoken language in Nepal. Tirhuta was formerly the primary script for writing Maithili.

Angika is mainly spoken in the Anga region, which includes Munger, Bhagalpur and Banka districts of Bihar, and the Santhal Pargana division of Jharkhand.

Bajjika is spoken in eastern India and Nepal, mostly in the north-western districts of Bihar and the adjacent areas of Nepal.

Persian was the court language during the Mughal reign. Hindi and Urdu, meanwhile, are spoken across the state. English newspapers are printed and read in the capital city of Patna and distributed in the large urban centres of Bihar every day.

This book is the first-ever attempt of its kind to present a glimpse of the rich world of Bihari literature in English translation, drawn from the many languages spoken across Bihar. Many of these works have been translated for the first time, making these accessible to the English-speaking world.

This anthology also brings to the fore literature from some of the lesser-known languages of Bihar, such as Magahi, Angika and Bajjika, making them available to both Indian and international readers, enriching Indian as well as world literature. It also highlights the original English writings of Bihari diaspora writers.

The Bihari diaspora is spread across the world. Countries such as Mauritius, Seychelles, Suriname, Trinidad and Tobago, Fiji, Netherlands, the United States of America, the United Kingdom, Australia, Canada and New Zealand have a significant Bihari population that continues to speak and read in various languages of Bihar. This book will hopefully act as a bridge in connecting them with their roots.

Editing this book has been a transformational journey for me. I was born in Nalanda district of Bihar. My mother spoke to me in Magahi, while my father spoke in Hindi. I remember finding a copy of *Rashmirathi* by Ramdhari Singh Dinkar at home when I was in class 3 or 4. I started reading it and fell in love with the sound of its words. Since then, I haven't stopped reading or reciting *Rashmirathi*.

When I came to study at Delhi University, people asked me if I spoke Bihari. This was strange because there is no language called 'Bihari'. So far, I had only heard of Bhojpuri, Maithili and Magahi, besides Hindi, Urdu, Farsi, Pali and Sanskrit. I realized, then, that most people consider Bhojpuri to be Bihari.

In fact, in the school syllabus we had a number of Hindi stories and poems—even English was a compulsory subject in high school and I had to learn by heart William Shakespeare's 'All the World's a Stage', and William Wordsworth's 'Daffodils'—but sadly there was no mention of Magahi, Bhojpuri, Maithili, Angika or Bajjika poems or stories. I studied Sanskrit in high school and learnt about the literature of ancient India, but I was not aware of the literary treasures in my mother tongue Magahi and other Bihari languages.

The idea of editing *The Book of Bihari Literature* was conceived in the first week of November 2020, while I was trying to learn more about the works of writers from Bihar. Despite being from the state, I had very little knowledge about the written literature in the various languages spoken in Bihar. In fact, my ignorance was so profound that I thought there was no written literature in Magahi as I had never come across a single book written in this language. The following poem I wrote in June 2020 reflects it:

A Poem in Magahi

Surprised to learn that there is no written poem in Magahi,
I run here and there, then sit down to write a poem in Magahi.

I listen to the people in the street talking in Magahi,
paying attention to their sounds and tones in Magahi.

They twitter like birds, day and night, in Magahi,
even their abuses sound sweet in Magahi.

Thik hai is *thik hako*, *accha aa gaya* is *accha aa gelhu* in Magahi,
khana khaye is *khana khailhu*, *chai piye* is *chaiya pilhu* in Magahi.

I go around the town looking for books in Magahi,
I return home without finding a written word in Magahi.

At home I hear my mother say her prayers in Magahi,
hamar betake buddhi dehu bhagwan, he wants to write a poem in Magahi.

Here, 'thik hai' means 'all's well', 'accha aa gaya' means 'well, you have arrived', 'khana khaye' means 'did you eat', 'chai piye' means 'did you drink tea' and 'hamar betake buddhi dehu bhagwan' means 'God, give my son sense'.

My ignorance was dispelled soon after writing this poem, when many people made me aware of the rich Magahi literature. It was another year before I set out to find Magahi folk tales, short stories and novels. The treasures I unearthed left me spellbound. Talking to various Magahi writers and poets, I was surprised to learn that the works of Magahi literature had never been translated into English.

Immediately, I started gathering and translating poems and short stories from Magahi into English. I began with a Magahi short story, 'Today's Yudhishthir' by Ravindra Kumar. It is a remarkable story of five brothers whose names are eponymous with the five Pandavas from the Mahabharata, and provides a rare peek into the mind of today's Yudhishthir and his relationship with his brothers and the world.

Similarly, I came across deeply moving poems and short stories in the other languages of Bihar, none of which I had read before. Sake Dean Mahomed, the first Indian to publish a book in English, titled *The Travels of Dean Mahomed*, was born in Patna, while Avadh Behari Lall, a noted poet of the late nineteenth century, who wrote in English, was from Gaya. His poem 'An Epistle to the Right Hon'ble Alfred Lord Tennyson, Poet-Laureate, England' is worth a read for the insight it offers on the impact the colonization of India had on its literature. One of the finest Persian poets, Abdul-Qādir Bēdil, whose poems are still read with great reverence in Afghanistan and the Central Asian countries, was born in Anisabad, Patna.

This book begins with the poems of Buddhist nuns Mutta and Sumangalmata, who were active around 600 BCE. Written in Pali, these poems speak about the drudgery of life and the emancipation of women. Kautilya, the author of *Arthashastra* and *Chanakya Niti*, shares some nuggets of wisdom on the art of living, while Vatsyayana explains the art of kissing and the significance of nail marks and love bites. Dharmakirti, the famous monk from Nalanda, meditates on the dilemma of human desires and the quest for nirvana. Sarhapa, who is considered to be the first poet of Magahi and Angika, as well as of Hindi, reveals the secrets of bliss and suffering in his dohas (couplets) from *Mahamudra*.

Vidyapati's two sensuous poems, 'My Body' and 'My Love, Bathing', delicately bring out the charm of shringar rasa in Maithili poetry.

Abdul-Qādir Bēdil, who is considered to be one of the finest poets in Persian, brings out the richness and beauty of Indian poetry in the language.

The Bhojpuri poems of Mahendar Misir, Bhikhari Thakur and Raghuveer Narayan open up a world of emotions ranging from a wedding song to the call of a migrant abroad, asking people there to visit Hind by describing its beauty and glory. Heera Dom is considered to be the first Dalit writer whose poem, 'An Untouchable's Complaint', highlights the miseries of the untouchables in Indian society. The writer weaves a complex poem around caste-based exploitation and stereotypes.

In his profound short story 'The Key', Acharya Shivpujan Sahay describes the secret of relationships and the harsh reality of the world struggling between the quest for worldly riches and liberation, while 'Budhia' by Rambriksh Benipuri tells the story of a beautiful village girl before and after her marriage, painting a poignant sketch of life in rural Bihar.

The illuminating couplets of Bedil Azimabadi offer the reader a taste and flavour of the finest Urdu poetry.

The selected stanzas from the third canto of the Hindi classic *Rashmirathi* showcase the brilliance of Dinkar's poetry and its undiminished beauty, decades after publication.

Poet Nagarjun, in his haunting poem 'Famine', evokes the landscape and the condition of humans and animals during a famine.

'The Messenger' by Phanishwar Nath Renu makes the reader witness the drama of life unfolding in the remote parts of northern Bihar.

'The Invisible Bond' by Surendra Mohan Prasad is a profound and memorable Angika story about love and loss in a rural setting.

In his poem 'The Business of Donation', well-known Magahi poet Mathura Prasad Naveen examines the prevalent custom of collecting donations in Bihar, while Surendra Prasad Tarun describes the sweetness and tenderness of a full moon night in his beautiful shringar rasa poem 'The Night of Full Moon.'

Known Maithili writer Rajkamal Chaudhary, in his short story 'Fish', narrates the tale of the love between two young men from Mithila and two ravishing young women from south India, and the power of love to overcome differences of culture, language and food habits.

In his short story 'Babu', Kalam Haidari tells the story of a young man living in a shack, whose fortune changes overnight when a person with a gunshot wound leaves a suitcase full of money with him, only to reappear suddenly after twenty years.

Lalit's 'Deliverance' recounts the story of an ailing man from Mithila and his young wife, who elopes with another man, while they are travelling to Baidyanathdham in Deoghar.

'Bereavement' by R. Ishari Arshad and 'A Song of Sorrow' by Harishchandra Priyadarshi give a taste of Magahi poetry along with Arun Harliwal's poem 'Dashrath Baba', which is a homage to the legendary Dashrath Manjhi, also known as the Mountain Man, who carved a path through a mountain using a chisel and hammer when his wife died after falling from the mountain and could not be taken to a doctor because of the lack of a proper road.

'A Hindu Parrot' by Surendra Pandey is a story in which a wounded parrot is saved by a Muslim family. They find that the parrot speaks the names of Hindu gods, taking them back to their own past that had been kept hidden from the world.

'Chilled to the Bone' by Mithilesh is one of the finest stories in this collection. This Magahi story recounts the plight of an old couple during a chilly winter and their tender love for each other.

'A Bowl of Sattu' by Chandramohan Pradhan tells the story of a thief who is offered a bowl of sattu by a kind teacher. This act of kindness is never forgotten.

'Nameless Relationship' by Mridula Sinha is the story of a woman who decides to donate the heart of her husband, who is in a coma, to save the life of a stranger.

'The Dressing Table' by Shamoil Ahmad is the story of Brijmohan, who robs a prostitute of her dressing table during a riot and later finds himself transformed into a pimp.

Ramdhari Singh Diwakar, in his short story 'Through the Prism of Time', explores the changing power equations between the upper-caste and lower-caste communities in Bihar after the advent of grass-roots democracy and reservations.

Usha Kiran Khan, in her short story 'Cover Me in a Shroud', highlights the miseries of poor land labourers in rural Bihar who are exploited not only by their landlords but also by the religious heads of their own communities.

In his poem 'Girls on the Rooftops', poet Alok Dhanwa casts his sharp eye on love blooming in the streets of small towns in Bihar.

'A Twist of Fate' by Hussain Ul Haque tells the story of Bibi Izzat-un Nisa who faces an uncertain future after the partition of India, the abolition of the zamindari system and her husband becoming a cripple.

'Damul' by Shaiwal is the story of a bonded labourer who is forced to steal oxen for his landlord. It highlights the rampant oppression of the lower-caste communities in rural Bihar through the institution of bonded labour and collusion between the politicians and the police.

In the Angika short story 'The Turning,' Aniruddha Prasad Vimal shows the reader the power of a woman to choose, against all odds, whom she wants to love.

Abdus Samad's 'Journey in a Burnt Boat' tells the story of a woman who elopes and returns to her village after several years, thinking she would never be forgiven by her family.

'Jugaad' by Prem Kumar Mani tells the story of a poor family that finds contentment even with meagre resources, exemplifying how less can be more.

'Deception' by Maithili writer Ashok explores the bonds of childhood friendship and the interwoven lives of Hindu and Muslim communities in Bihar.

Nagendra Sharma Bandhu's Magahi short story, 'The Whirlpool', highlights the damage caused by annual floods in Bihar and the sheer will power of the protagonists to survive year after year.

In his poem 'The City of Gaya,' Arun Kamal meditates on life in Gaya, a place of Hindu pilgrimage where people make offerings to departed ancestors.

Narayanji, in his Maithili short story 'Kosi', which is also known as the 'sorrow of Bihar', draws a compelling portrait of rural life in northern Bihar.

In 'Fellowmen' by Avdhesh Preet, the dead reflect upon their lives and the curse of communalism that afflicts our society.

'The Witness' by Maithili writer Vibha Rani tells the story of a young girl who is widowed as soon as she gets married and how her life progresses after that.

Anamika's prose poem 'Amrapali' recounts the life-changing event of legendary Licchavi courtesan Amrapali when she meets the Buddha and invites him home for dinner.

Savita Singh takes a nostalgic trip to her place of birth in the poem 'Self Exile' and dwells upon the life of a farm labourer in her poem 'Chaitram's Afternoons'.

Ashwani Kumar's poem 'Pablo Neruda in Gaya' makes for a delightful read where the poet imagines the famous Latin American poet performing the funeral rites of his ancestors in Gaya.

'The Rat's Guide' by Amitava Kumar takes us to Patna and his ancestral village in search of the Musahar community of Bihar who eat rats.

'The Goon' by Dhananjay Shrotriya is a story of transformation, of an innocent young man into a goon, and once again into a gentleman, conveying the powerful message that only love and kindness can save us from self-destruction.

'The Scam' by Tabish Khair takes some journalists on a journey from Jantar Mantar in Delhi to Tikri village in Bihar, in search of a case of alleged caste atrocity. However, they find something else when they reach the village.

'A Night As an Orphan' by Kumar Mukul narrates the story of a man who leaves his home and family and spends a night roaming at the Patna Junction railway station and the nearby Hanuman temple.

Ratneshwar's 'Lieutenant Hudson' is the story of poor migrant labourers from Bihar during colonial times. Their plight only comes to light when their skeletons are unearthed during the construction of a new housing complex in Delhi.

The Magahi story 'You Too Must Forgive Me' by Kiran Kumari Sharma is the tale of a housemaid, Laxmi, and her employer, and the emotional rollercoaster ride of their relationship.

'Transformation' by Kavita is the story of an aged mother who wants to remarry because she feels lonely, but faces vehement opposition from her children, except her daughter who supports her decision.

Pankhuri Sinha's poem 'A Rainy Day at Jhapsi Mahto's Tea Stall' reflects upon unplanned and unmindful construction, and the environmental consequences it has.

'Nalanda Poems' by Abhay K. tell the story of the fall of the famous Nalanda University in the twelfth century CE and its rise in the twenty-first century.

In this book, a majority of the pieces have been written by men and cater to a male audience, mirroring the times they were written in. However, I've been able to source the writings of quite a few women writers too, from Bihar down the ages. In fact, this book begins with poems by two female poets, dating back around 600 BCE.

While editing this book, I came across a rich world of literature in the various languages spoken in Bihar. I have only been able to include a very small fraction of it because of space and time constraints, and the lack of good-quality translations. I think many more such books celebrating Bihari literature deserve to be published in the years to come.

I hope you'll relish this delicious potpourri of Bihari literature.

September 2022
Antananarivo, Madagascar

Free, Fabulously Free

Mutta

(Translated from the Pali by Abhay K. and Gabriel Rosenstock)

Free, fabulously free,
free from three trifles—
pounder, pounding bowl and my wicked lord—
free from endless births and deaths,
the chains that fettered me down
are suddenly no more.

Peace at Last

Sumangalmata

(Translated from the Pali by Abhay K. and Gabriel Rosenstock)

A woman set free at last, how free,
how gloriously free I am from drudgery
of the kitchen, harsh hunger pangs,
the sound of empty pots,
free from that whimsical man,
spinner of yarns,
peace at last,
lust and hatred have gone,
I rest under the shade of sprawling trees
and cherish bliss.

Selections from *Chanakya Niti*

Kautilya

(Translated from the Sanskrit by Abhay K.)

One should not trust one's enemy,
one should not trust even one's own friend,
because when angry or upset
even a friend spills the beans.

★

A true friend is one who helps us,
when we are sick or surrounded by enemies,
in performing state duties
or by cremating us after death.

★

A son is one who obeys his father,
a father is one who nourishes his children,
a friend is one who is trustworthy,
and a wife is one who pleases the heart.

★

Well-thought plans should be kept a secret.
Like a well-guarded mantra,
one should work on them secretively.

★

He who rushes to the uncertain,
leaving behind the certain,
loses the certain,
the uncertain is woefully uncertain.

★

These should be treated
as one's own mother—
king's wife, guru's wife, friend's wife,
and wife's mother.

★

Knowledge is the friend in foreign lands,
one's wife is one's friend at home,
medicine is the friend when one is sick,
and good deeds are friends after death.

★

Big or small, whatever task it may be,
one should do it wholeheartedly,
one should learn this from the lion.

★

The learned should learn from the heron,
to succeed in one's mission
by assessing the time, strength and place
and keeping one's senses under control.

★

A wise person should learn three things from a donkey—
to achieve one's goal without procrastination,
to work without paying attention to the changing seasons,
and to continue towards one's goal being content,
as a donkey continues carrying the load even when it feels tired
and is content grazing here and there.

Selections from the *Kama Sutra*
Vatsyayana

(Translated from the Sanskrit by Abhay K.)

Kissing

Among the lovers, whatever is done
by the one, the same should be done in return—
if a woman kisses him, he should kiss her in turn,
if she strokes him, he should stroke her, too, in return.

[Book Two, Chapter Three]

Nail Marks and Love Bites

Seeing the nail marks
on her private parts—
even though old and worn out,
a woman's love is kindled,
but fades
in their absence—
nothing to remind her about their
sweet love duels,

just as not making out
for long
extinguishes the flame
of love,
even a stranger looking
from far at her breasts,
full of love bites,
is in awe,
and a man carrying teeth marks
on his body, swoons a woman's mind,
nothing fuels the fire of love more
than the nail marks and love bites.

[Book Two, Chapter Four]

Biting

A woman bitten by a man
should bite him angrily,
twice as hard,
a 'point' should be returned
with a 'line of points', and
a 'line of points' with a 'broken cloud'.[1]
And if extremely annoyed,
she should start a love
quarrel at once, catching
hold of her lover by the hair,
pulling his head down to kiss
his lower lip,

1 As per the *Kama Sutra* by Vatsyayana, a small part of the skin, bitten with two teeth only, is the 'point'; a small part of the skin bitten with all the teeth is a 'line of points'; and the biting resembling unequal risings in a circle, because of the space between the teeth, on the breasts, is known as the 'broken cloud'

closing her eyes,
drunk with love,
bite him everywhere.
Even during the day, in public,
she should smile looking
at her love bites on his body
and give him an angry look,
showing the marks on her own body.
When two lovers love
each other this way,
their love will never diminish,
not even in a hundred years.

[Book Two, Chapter Five]

Two Poems

Dharmakirti

(Translated from the Sanskrit by Abhay K.)

Making Love to Her

Making love to her lasts only moments,
like a dream, illusion, ending in regret.
I reflect upon this truth a hundred times,
yet my heart can't forget the gazelle-eyed girl.

The Moon and Your Face

Every month, the moon attempts
to capture the beauty of your face,
and having miserably failed
erases the work to start afresh.

Selected Dohas from *Mahamudra*

Sarhapa

(Translated from the Prakrit by Pandita Vairocanaraksita)

Just as the insane are possessed by demons
and helplessly experience meaningless suffering,
beings possessed by the great demon
of conceptualization and belief in reality,
create nothing but meaningless suffering.

[1.2 Beings are Deluded]

Just as in the forest a lion's roar
terrifies all the weak animals,
while the lion cubs joyously run towards it,
teaching this primordially unborn great bliss
terrifies the ignorant and the mistaken,
but raises goosebumps of joy on the worthy.

[1.3 The Realisation of Savara]

Just as a crow flies away from a ship,
circles in all directions and returns to it,
the desiring mind, even though it pursues thoughts,
returns to the natural primordial mind.

[2.1.3 Gaining Certainty]

Don't hold your breath, don't bind the mind;
leave the uncontrived mind, be like a baby.
If memories and thoughts arise, look at them,
don't think of the water and the waves as separate.

[2.2.2 The Supreme Meditation]

Just as animals that are afflicted with delusion
run towards a mirage of water,
ignorant individuals who are afflicted by desire,
however hard they try, move further from the truth of life.

[3.2. The Delusion]

Two Poems

Vidyapati

(Translated from the Maithili by Abhay K.)

My Body

When my love returns home,
I'll turn my body into a temple of joy,
an altar of pleasure, and sweep it
with my hair.
My pearl necklace
will adorn the altar,
my voluptuous breasts—the water jars,
my sensuous hips—the plantain trees,
the jingling bells of my girdle—
freshly sprouted mango shoots.
I'll put the ancient art of beauty to use,
to shine brighter than a thousand moons.

My Love, Bathing

What a joyous day for me,
I saw my love bathing—
a draught of water falling
from her hair, as if clouds
raining strings of pearls.

Selected Poems

Abdul-Qādir Bēdil

(Translated from the Persian by Nasim Fekrat)

Whoever left us, ailed us
and left a wound in our hearts,
like the soft ground
reflecting the footprints.

★

O, the consumer of imagination's residue, blessing is something else,
you are being vain with illusion; the truth is something else.
The paradise that is adorned with gems and gold,
it reflects your avarices—the paradise is something else.

★

Across ages, we are being amused at expressing worthlessness,
and we are the opener of pages of the stories of nothingness.
You could expect nothing from us, but name,
we are the messengers of the world of nothingness.

★

You cannot sip the ocean, except as a whale,
you cannot sprint the mountain, unless a tiger.
The sea of time and place, for you, is but one gulp,
limit not your boundless imagination.

Excerpt from
The Travels of Dean Mahomed
Sake Dean Mahomed

I was born in the year 1759 in Patna, a famous city on the south side of the Ganges, about 400 miles from Calcutta, the capital of Bengal and seat of the English Government in that country [India]. I was too young when my father died, to learn any great account of his family; all I have been able to know respecting him, is that he was descended from the same race as the Nabobs of Moorshadabad (Murshidabad). He was appointed Subadar in a battalion of Sepoys commanded by Captain Adams, a company of which under his command was quartered at a small district not many miles from Patna, called Tarchpoor (Tajpur), an inconsiderable fort, built on the side of a little river that takes its rise a few miles up the country. Here he was stationed in order to keep this fort.

In the year 1769, a great dearth overspread the country about Tarchpoor, where Raja Boudmal (Budhmal) and his brother Corexin (Kora Singh) resided, which they took an advantage of by pretending it was impossible for them to remit the stipulated supplies to the

Raja Sataproy (Shitab Rai), who finding himself disappointed in his expectations, sent some of his people to compel them to pay: but the others retired within their forts, determined on making an obstinate defence. My father, having received orders to lead out his men to the scene of dispute, which lay about twelve miles from the fort he was quartered in, marched accordingly, and soon after his arrival at Taharah (Telarha), took the Raja Boudmal prisoner, and sent him under a strong guard to Patna, where he was obliged to account for his conduct. My father remained in the field, giving the enemy some striking proofs of the courage of their adversary; which drove them to such measures, that they strengthened their posts and redoubled their attacks with such ardour, that many of our men fell, and my lamented father among the rest; but not till he had entirely exhausted the forces of the Raja, who, at length, submitted. The soldiers, animated by his example, made Corexin a prisoner, and took possession of the fort.

Thus have I been deprived of a gallant father, whose firmness and resolution was manifested in his military conduct on several occasions.

My brother, then about sixteen years old, and the only child my mother had besides me, was present at the engagement, and having returned home, made an application to Capt. Adams who, in gratitude to the memory of my father, whose services he failed not to represent to the Governor, speedily promoted him to his post. My mother and I suffered exceedingly by his sudden yet honourable fate in the field: for my brother was then too young and thoughtless, to pay any great attention to our situation.

I was about eleven years old when deprived of my father, and though children are seldom possessed of much sensibility or reflection at such immature years, yet I recollect well no incident of my life ever made so deep an impression on my mind. Nothing could wear from my memory the remembrance of his tender regard. As he was a Mahometan, he was interred with all the pomp and ceremony usual on the occasion. I remained with my mother some time after, and acquired a little education at a school in Patna.

In a few months after my father's fate, my mother and I went to Patna to reside. She lived pretty comfortable on some of the property she was entitled to in right of her husband: the rest of his substance, with his commission, came into the hands of my brother. Our support was made better by the liberality of the Begum and Nabob, to whom my father was related: the Begum was remarkably affectionate and attentive to us.

The Raja Sataproy had a very magnificent palace in the centre of the city of Patna, where he was accustomed to entertaining many of the most distinguished European gentlemen, with brilliant balls and costly suppers. My mother's house was not far from the Raja's palace; and the number of officers passing by our door on their way thither, attracted my notice, and excited the ambition I already had of entering on a military life. With this notion, I was always on the watch, and impatiently waited for the moment of their passing by our door. One evening in particular, as they went along, I seized the happy opportunity, and followed them directly to the palace, at the outward gates of which there are sentinels placed, to keep off the people and clear the passage for the gentlemen. I however got admittance on account of the respect the guards paid my father's family. The gentlemen go to the palace between seven and eight o'clock in the evening, take tea and coffee, and frequently amuse themselves by forming a party to dance; when they find themselves warm, they retire to the palace yard, where there are marquees pitched for their reception; here they seat themselves in a circular form, under a semiana, a sort of canopy made of various coloured double muslin, supported by eight poles, and on the ground is spread a beautiful carpet; the Raja sits in the centre; the European gentlemen on each side; and the Music in the front. The Raja, on this occasion, is attended by his aid-du-camps [aide de camps] and servants of rank. Dancing girls are now introduced, affording, at one time, extreme delight, by singing in concert with the music, the softest and most lively airs; at another time, displaying such loose and fascinating attitudes in their various dances, as would warm the bosom of an Anchoret: while the servants of the Raja are employed in letting off the fire-works, displaying, in the most astonishing variety, the forms of birds, beasts, and other animals, and far surpassing anything of the kind I ever beheld in Europe: and to give additional brilliancy to the splendour of the scene, lighted branches blaze around, and exhibit one general illumination. Extremely pleased with such various entertainment, the gentlemen sit down to an elegant supper, prepared with the utmost skill, by an officer of the Raja, whose sole employ is to provide the most delicious viands on such an occasion: ice-cream, fowl of all kinds, and the finest fruit in the world, compose but a part of the repast to which the guests are invited. The Raja was very happy with his convivial friends; and though his religion forbids him to touch many things handled by persons of a different profession, yet he accepted a little fruit from them; supper was over about twelve o'clock, and the company retired, the Raja to his palace, and the officers to their quarters.

I was highly pleased with the appearance of the military gentlemen, among whom I first beheld Mr Baker, who particularly drew my attention: I followed him without any restraint through every part of the palace and tents, and remained a spectator of the entire scene of pleasure, till the company broke up; and then returned home to my mother, who felt some anxiety in my absence. When I described the gaiety and splendour I beheld at the entertainment, she seemed very much dissatisfied, and expressed, from maternal tenderness, her apprehensions of losing me.

Nothing could exceed my ambition of leading a soldier's life: the notion of carrying arms, and living in a camp, could not be easily removed. My fond mother's entreaties were of no avail: I grew anxious for the moment that would bring the military officers by our door. Whenever I perceived their route, I instantly followed them; sometimes to the Raja's palace, where I had free access; and sometimes to a fine tennis court, generally frequented by them in the evenings, which was built by Col Champion, at the back of his house, in a large open square, called Mersevillekeebaug [Mir Afzal ka Bagh]. Here, among other gentlemen, I one day discovered Mr Baker, and often passed by him, in order to attract his attention. He, at last, took particular notice of me, observing that I surveyed him with a kind of secret satisfaction; and in a very friendly manner, asked me how I would like living with the Europeans. This unexpected encouragement, as it flattered my hopes beyond expression, occasioned a very sudden reply: I therefore told him with eager joy, how happy he could make me, by taking me with him. He seemed very much pleased with me, and assuring me of his future kindness, hoped I would merit it. Major Herd [Heard] was in company with him at the same time: and both these gentlemen appeared with distinguished eclat in the first assemblies in India. I was decently clad in the dress worn by children of my age: and though my mother was materially affected in her circumstances, by the precipitate death of my father, she had still the means left of living in a comfortable manner, and providing both for her own wants and mine.

My mother, observing some alteration in my conduct, since I first saw Mr Baker, naturally supposed that I was meditating a separation from her. She knew I spoke to him; and apprehensive that I would go with him, she did everything in her power to frustrate my intentions. Notwithstanding all her vigilance, I found means to join my new master, with whom I went early the next morning to Bankeepore [Bankipur], leaving my mother to lament my departure.

(This is an extract from the first book published in English by an Indian.)

An Epistle to the Right Hon'ble Alfred Lord Tennyson, Poet-Laureate, England

Avadh Behari Lall

Gya, 22 July 1892

The Sun shines on all things good or bad;
    And you might have, our Poets' laurelled King,
In long experience which you sure have had
    In your eighty years, seen (to say nothing
Of poets' gradual strides in verse-making,)
    Verses of all kinds—even the 'prose-verse',
Or 'prose run mad' of some weak brains' rhyming:
    Now a much youngster poetaster worse,
    A simple scribbler—who, artless, does dare rehearse,

In simple strain, the long and glorious Rule
    Of fifty years of our great Sovereign,

And also in low tone (being in no school
Of Poesy taught laws how to maintain
The dignity of verse,) describe in plain
And unaffected words the season prime
Of his own country—begs with a heart fain
To greet the great Lord Tennyson sublime,
The great acknowledged Fount of Poesy of his time,

With verses these and two books herewith sent,
Himself half-convinced that all are worthless.
But, thou great Poet! Lend me a moment
Of thy precious time and but deign to bless
My lines with a glance: 'twill be happiness
Supreme to me if in one place thou find
One single verse that may seem to possess
A thought high-flying on a sense refined;
Oh! then, my Lord! 'twill be a solace to my mind.

Or else think these attempts a school-boy's fun,
Like many doggrels [sic] that you must have seen,
Destined in Time's great course no race to run,
And to be hidden 'neath Oblivion's screen.
But 'tis custom, illustrious Lord! I ween
For the good old verses to teach the young,
To find a joy in lines e'en when they mean
Almost nothing; to rectify the wrong,
To help the rising spirit and t'inflame the tongue.

So let me hope—it is a pleasing thought—
    That though un-English I'm by birth and race,
The English Poets' King (for so you ought
    To be styled justly) does read, nay does bless,
The English rhymes of one who may be less
    E'en than a rhymester bad. One spark is fire,
And stim'lus is almost itself success:
    So if you think my hopes worth to inspire,
    One good word from your Lordship is all I desire.

An under-graduate I, who long ago,
    (Some eight years have past since) ill-health compelled,
Gave up at early age my studies; so,
    Thought oft I have, with books, communion held,
My knowledge is but too confined, unswelled.
    For my own amusement's sake my soul I fix
Upon verse-making—not by gold impelled.
    'Practice makes perfect,' bids me in heart mix
    Some hope with much despair—I am but twenty-six.

The mellow judgement of the mellow years—
    Ready to give the praise where justly due,
To prune the faults when such the need appear,
    Or to encourage and shew the path true—
Is the great boom this Epistle craves of you.
    In Gya town, in Province of Bengal,
Lives ever praying, with pray'rs ever new,
    For your health, happ'ness, and prosper'ty all,
    Your Lordship's servant true, Avadh Behari Lall.

My Feet Are Tired of Walking

Mahendar Misir

(Translated from the Bhojpuri by Abhay K.)

O my sister-in-law,
my feet are tired of walking,
yet I have not found what I seek,
neither has my beloved come himself,
nor has he sent any message.
He has sent the palanquin with carriers,
I'm a stranger now,
all my friends left behind,
I'm scared going away alone.
Neighbours and the village folks
have all come out of their homes
to bid me farewell,
they have seated me in the palanquin,
and have pulled the curtain down,
my parent's home is left behind.

Bridegroom

Bhikhari Thakur

(Translated from the Bhojpuri by Abhay K.)

Sieved, winnowed, termite-eaten bridegroom,
band playing at the door (to welcome him).

Solemnized by fire, scrubbed with burnt brick,
branded with a ladle, a runaway from the land of fools.

Mother-in-law's eyes blinkered, darkness reigns,
let's steal a glance at the groom chewing betel leaves.

Groom ripe as a mango, banished from the village,
such a foolish groom, a darling of the flashy god.

Wearing the crown and ceremonial attire,
Bhikhari says Rama himself has built the fire altar.

Batohiya[2]

Raghuveer Narayan

(Translated from the Bhojpuri by Abhay K.)

The glorious land of Bharat, O traveller,
my soul lies in her snowy abode,
one side guarded by the Himalayas,
three sides guarded by the deep sea.

O brother traveller, go and see Hind,
where cooing cuckoos sing,
where the wind is fragrant from the sandalwood,
where my beloved sings songs of parting.

Magnificent endless clouds, in the luxuriant orchards,
champak flowers shine bright,
banyan, peepul, kadamba, neem, mango trees,
ketaki and rose blossoms glitter.

Parrots and drongos sing blithely,
The papiha's singing pierces the heart,

2 Traveller

from the glorious land of Bharat,
my soul lives in the Ganga's currents.

The sparkling waters of Ganga and Yamuna,
Sarayu flows making sonorous sounds,
Brahmaputra blows his five conches every day,
Sonbhadra sings her sweet songs.

Above, many rivers dance flowing, overflowing,
fireflies' magic awakens us,
Agra, Prayag, Kashi, Delhi, Calcutta,
my heart is on the Sarayu's banks.

Go, traveller, go and see Hind,
where saints chant all the four Vedas,
like Sita's beauty, like Ram, like Krishna,
is the story of my ancestors.

Vyas, Valmiki, Gautam, Kapil
awaken the sleeping immortals,
Ramanuj and Ramanand, with luring faces,
bumblebees of the forest of great enchantments.

Nanak, Kabir, Shankar, Shri Ram and Krishna
tell the glories of Alakh,[3]
poets Vidyapati, Surdas, Jayadev
and Tulsidas tell delectable tales.

Go, traveller, go and see Hind,
where paddy sways with joy in the fields,

3 Almighty

Buddhadev, Prithyu, Vikramarjun, Shivaji,
their memories come to me again and again.

Our country is better than other lands,
my Hind is the soul of the world,
the glorious land of Bharat, O brother,
Ragubir bows his head to her.

The Untouchable's Complaint

Heera Dom

(Translated from the Bhojpuri by Abhay K.)

We suffer day and night,
we pray to the ruler.
Even the Lord is indifferent to our pain,
when will the burden of our sorrows be lessened?

We will go to the clergyman's court,
we will renunciate religion and turn English.
Hey Ram! Changing our religion will do no good,
how shall we meet our eyes in the mirror?

You saved Prahlad by tearing apart the pillar,
you rescued Gajraj from the claws of the crocodile.
When Dushasan tried to strip Draupadi,
you appeared and offered her a saree.

You killed Ravana and protected Bibhisana,
lifted the mountain on your finger.

Where are you asleep now callously,
are you afraid of touching us Doms?[4]

We toil day and night
and receive two rupees for a month.
The Thakur sleeps sweetly in his home,
we plough the field and make ends meet.

The lord's men descend upon us
and enslave us to work for free.
We bear the pain silently and serve,
we'll report this to the government.

We'll not beg like the Babhans,[5]
we'll not wield lathis like the Thakurs,[6]
we'll not cheat like the Sahus[7] while weighing,
we'll not steal cows like the Ahirs,[8]
we'll not go to the court wearing turbans.

We'll earn shedding our own sweat and blood,
we'll eat sharing meals at home.
Even the Babhans have bodies of flesh and blood,
but they are worshipped in every home.

In all directions they are hosted well,
we can't even go near the well.
Churning mud, our hands and legs are broken,
why is our condition so miserable, why are we forsaken?

---

4 A caste primarily engaged in handling burial and cremation
5 A caste of land-owning Brahmins in Bihar
6 A warrior Hindu caste
7 A caste of traders
8 A caste of cowherds

The Key

Acharya Shivpujan Sahay

(Translated from the Hindi by Mangal Murty)

Had the taxi not been available at the last moment, I would have missed the train. Charging an exorbitant fare, it did bring me to the Howrah station right on time, but then the porters started haggling. First, they swooped upon my luggage like vultures, and then they started bidding—a rupee, a rupee and a half, almost like the priests pouncing on a pilgrim for donation.

Meanwhile, a monk appeared and lifted my suitcase. 'Take your bedding and hurry up before you miss the train,' he said, leading the way as I ran after him with my bedding, leaving the porters astonished.

The moment I got into an inter-class[9] compartment with the monk, the train began chugging. The monk asked, 'A young man like you should be self-reliant. Why should you opt for a porter? Can you be happy if you depend on others? Or is it a sign of being rich? In fact, you should be ready to serve others. But if you yourself need help, how will you help others?'

9 Equivalent to today's non-reserved compartment

'My luggage was heavy and the train was about to leave. That's why I wanted to engage the porters. By God's grace, if you hadn't come to my rescue, I'd be sulking in the waiting room at Howrah.'

'Where are you going?'

'To Kashi. Somebody I know is ill. He went to Kashi to breathe his last. I got his telegram only today. Had I missed this train, I'd have been ruined.'

'Really? But why?'

'The person who is dying is a big merchant from Bombay. I'm his accountant. If I reach before his death, I might get a share of his riches.'

'And how much would that be?'

'Even in the worst case scenario, I will get at least two lakhs.'

'So you're going for two lakhs, not for your employer.'

'For both, if you please.'

'But mainly for the two lakhs, isn't it?'

'You're an ascetic, a monk, but we're all worldly creatures. For us, money is everything.'

My words made the monk brood. Taking a deep breath, he said, '*Bhaj Govindam, Bhaj Govindam, Govindam Bhaj Moodhamate*.'[10]

He looked up into emptiness, and with closed eyes and folded hands, bowed his head. He then looked at me again.

I asked him, 'Maharaj, what were you doing?'

'I was praying to the Almighty who has his mysterious ways.'

'What mysterious ways?'

'What could be more ironic than this show of unabashed selfishness?'

'But is there nothing else in the world except selfishness?'

'Why not? Is selfishness not the most palpable? The rest is only a vast emptiness. That invisible divine way cannot be seen with these mortal eyes.'

10 Pray to God, pray to God, O foolish being!

'But has God given us the third eye, besides these two, for us to be able to see that?'

'Yes, the eye of wisdom, which opens when these two close.'

'Then does man become blind?'

'No, after sunrise the lamp becomes useless.'

'Well, but when does that eye of wisdom open?'

'When God showers his mercy.'

'When did the first shower of God's mercy fall on you?'

This again turned the monk silent and pensive. After a short spell of meditation, he looked at me and said, 'The God who made the swan white, the parrot green, the koel black, the thrush orange, the champa yellow, the rainbow many-hued and painted the peacock's tail with resplendent colours, the same God overspreads a thick layer of selfishness on this world. Just as we cannot take away heat from fire, light from the sun, moonlight from the moon, fragrance from the earth, coldness from water, flash from the lightning, darkness from the cloud and fragility from the flower, we cannot separate selfishness from this world.

'Just as penury and pain are inseparable, the world and selfishness are inseparable. Being a sloth is the cause of all diseases; similarly, this world is the playfield of all selfishness. If this world was not scorched by the raging fire of the conflict of self-interests, it would be far lovelier than paradise itself. Every single atom of this wondrous world is full of the might of selfishness. If selfishness were to go from this world, all its marvels would lose their mystery.

'One who breaks the shackles of selfishness can get freedom from this world-prison. He can conquer the world. The world will bow at his feet and, in turn, he will offer blessings to the world, making it free from all fear. But selfishness, like a rootless creeper, engulfs the world-tree completely. It's not easy to slash this tangled mesh.'

'Then how did you slash it?'

'I haven't been able to, yet. But I hope I will. The flame of that hope was ignited by the fire of my father's blazing pyre.'

'Hearing this makes me curious about your story. Could you please tell me more?'

'If it does you any good, I can tell you in brief.'

'I'm sure your inspiring life story will be beneficial for me. Nothing is more valuable than the company of saints. Your story will quench my curiosity and also bring me valuable counsel.'

'So be it. I was the son of a very rich zamindar in Madhya Pradesh. He had four brothers. When my father was on his deathbed, I was blinded by passion; no worldly worries ever bothered me. Often, I would sit by my father's bed and wipe the tears trickling down his cheeks. He would time and again kiss my hands. When I saw the final surges of his love, my heart churned. The pious stream of his filial love still fills my heart and flows out of my eyes.'

As he said this, his eyes welled up. Tears came to my eyes, too. I impatiently asked, 'Why did you become a monk?'

'That's the story. The day my father died, he was fully consciousness. He was staring at the charming picture of Shri Radhakrishna on the wall in front of him. Moments later, his eyes became still. The whole house started wailing. My harmonious world turned into chaos. My mother consoled herself looking at my face. Embracing me, she forgot her own grief. My wife, too, shedding some false tears, said, "Please take care of yourself. Don't grieve too much."

'That was alarming for me. My mother affectionately wiped my tears with her saree and, lifting up my chin, said, "I, too, am living only for you, otherwise what's the point of my life." I felt a thump in my heart, but even that couldn't break the pitcher of my delusion. Even earlier, when my uncle sat beside my father and whispered to him about various money transactions, I saw my father, who was in great pain, unable to answer his queries. I became extremely upset. But even that turmoil of the heart couldn't break the spell of delusive slumber.'

I interrupted him to ask: 'Did you flee from home because of the iniquities of your uncle?'

His response was sharp. 'Why do you interrupt me? Listen patiently. When my father's bamboo bier reached the burning ghat, I had to help his body on to the pyre and perform the final rites. My heart felt like a stone as I did so. Soon, the pyre was ablaze. Suddenly, my elder uncle shouted, "Oh god, the string around his waist wasn't broken. The key to the safe is still tied to it. Alas, we are ruined!"

'On hearing this, my younger uncle hastily scattered the burning logs. My father's half-naked body slipped out from the pyre. The string around his waist was already burnt, and the red-hot key was lying in the smouldering fire. Picking it up quickly, my younger uncle covered it with ash.

'That key, that same key, yes, that very key was able to open the lock of my ignorance. It was there that I saw the true face of this world. Then and there my third eye opened. I was enlightened.'

Saying this, the monk lapsed back into meditation. I, too, sank into a strange and intense stream of thought.

Budhia

Rambriksh Benipuri

(Translated from the Hindi by Mangal Murty)

A baby goat was frolicking around, nibbling on the soft, supple leaves of the chameli[11] plant. By then, I hadn't developed the aesthetic sense to be totally entranced by the merry prancing of that little beauty, joggling its long ears as it nipped and munched on the lush leaves, looking hither and thither with its large black eyes and occasionally bleating, as if calling out to its mother. Rather, that day I felt great pity for the delicate chameli sapling, which I had brought with great care from the neighbouring hamlet. I had planted it with my own hands, watered it and felt delighted to see its tiny leaves budding forth each day. But this little rogue had undone it all! Furious, I tried to hit it hard. But like a swift doe it leapt away, even as I gave chase.

'Don't hit it, Babu!' called out Budhia, a little girl of hardly seven or eight years. A red rag with several patches was wrapped around her waist, barely covering her knees. Her body was otherwise bare, covered with dust; her face was dark; her hair was tousled, dusty and full of lice. Yellow snot trickled down her nose, which she tried to inhale now

11 Jasmine

and again. Hearing her words and looking at her grimy face, I felt like slapping her until I looked at her feet. My child's heart was riveted.

'Oh, what's all that you have made?' I peered closely at the clay figures spread around her small, muddied feet—toys that she had freshly made from soft, wet clay from the nearby pond, artfully decorated with little flowers of mustard, gram and peas. The toys did not have properly carved faces, but they had limbs like humans and were bedecked with flowers of varied colours, each imbued with their own charm.

'What's all this?' I asked.

She felt shy. 'You won't beat me, will you? I'll tell you then.'

'Surely, I'd have beaten you. But you're pardoned.'

She smiled. 'Please sit down here.'

But how could I sit in that mess? So, I simply bent down for a closer look. And she started.

'This is the bridegroom with the wedding crown,' she said, pointing to the mustard flower stuck on its head. 'And she is the bride, with her colourful skirt made of gram and pea flowers. They are getting married. With all the marriage music, of course.'

She tapped her belly and whistled with rounded lips before continuing, 'With the drum and the pipe. And this is the kohbar.'[12] She pointed to a walled square, also made of clay. 'And this is their marriage bed,' she gestured to a few green mango leaves sprinkled with tiny pink flowers. 'Here, they will sleep. And I'll sing the wedding songs for them.'

She started crooning, singing and swaying. I was under a spell for a while. Then I suddenly remembered my chameli sapling and ran to it, counting each torn leaf and lamenting, swearing that I'd devour the cursed baby goat and showering abuses on Budhia.

★

12 A chamber where the newlyweds spend their first night

'Babuji, will you kindly help me lift this load of grass?' I heard a voice as I was on my evening stroll north of the village, looking downward, lost in my own thoughts. I raised my head.

The day was waning into evening. Down in a field beside the road stood a young girl. A big bundle of grass lay at her feet. I got irritated by her temerity. A city man in clean clothes, I was keeping myself away from the filth of the village folk. After all, I wasn't a herder or a grass cutter to help others lift bundles and place them on their heads. *Who in the village dares ask me such a thing! But look at this young girl...*

'Kindly help, Babuji!' she implored.

I gazed at her face, sizing up the face and the voice. *Budhia! A full-grown lass? Grown up so fast?* I looked around. There was no one and it was getting dark. *Who else would help this poor, lonely girl here?* Out of sympathy, I helped her raise the bundle and place it on her head. Soon, swaying rhythmically, she walked away with it.

Just then a loud laughter burst forth. The next moment, I found Jagdish by my side.

'So now she has a new fish in her net!' Jagdish had an impish twinkle in his eyes and raillery in his voice. He started his long recital of Budhia's story.

'Budhia is no longer the girl in a patched skirt. She now has a flowing chunar[13] that is ever colourful. And her choli[14] is now stitched by the Sewaipatti tailor. True, you'll find her carrying loads of grass on her head every day, but her palms aren't calloused or dirty. Her skin is still dark, but not like the dark waters of the stagnant pool. It now bears the rippling music of the Kalindi River, with many gopals[15] playing their flutes on its banks and many other nandlals[16] dreaming of a romantic union with her. Wherever she walks, life surges and sways.

---

13 Scarf

14 Bodice

15 Cowherds; Gopal is a term of endearment for the young Lord Krishna

16 A term of endearment for the young Lord Krishna

Her black hair is now set with fragrant jasmine oil, and her forehead is adorned with a resplendent tikli.[17] Instead of one gopal in Vrindavan with a thousand gopis[18] around, you now have one gopi surrounded by a thousand gopals. Even that one gopal wouldn't have derived so much pleasure in slinging the thousand-headed Kaliya serpent and dancing on its hoods, which this Budhia now does by making so many gopals dance to her tunes. As if Radha of the Dvapar Yuga[19] is avenging herself through Budhia in this Kali Yuga.[20] Radha forever kept pining for Krishna's love, and Budhia makes all the gopals crave her.'

Damned wretch! My virtuous soul cried out. In the growing darkness, I slowly made my way back home, with a bent head. Jagdish, too, went his way. Hardly had I walked some distance when I felt the electrifying touch of someone rushing past me. Instinctively, I turned around.

'Kindly forgive me for this second fault,' she said and stood still. It was Budhia. Fuming, I shouted, 'Wicked girl!' *I'd almost called her a slut!*

Instead of blushing or looking bashful, she burst into laughter. Coming closer, she giggled. 'Do you remember, Babu, my baby goat ate your chameli plant?' Her pearly white teeth shone in the dark.

'Get lost, naughty girl!' I said, my face probably burnished like red coal.

'And that bridegroom and his bride, that wedding night chamber, that flower-bedecked bed? And that song! Should I sing it again for you, Babu?'

---

17 Decorative mark or dot worn by some women on their forehead; also called bindi

18 Female cowherds; friends and companions of Krishna, the cowherd/Gopal

19 In Hindu mythology, the Dvapar Yuga is the third and third-best of the four yugas (cycles of time that span millennia)

20 The age of decadence in Hindu mythology

Not waiting for a response, she started singing: 'The wedded bride goes to her husband's home, and yet she trembles in fear as she goes…'

Singing tunefully, she ran away, swinging and laughing. 'Oh, how shameless, how brash indeed!' I muttered to myself. But her giggles and laughter kept echoing as she fled.

★

The wheat harvest was in progress. My brother said, 'Bhaiya,[21] there'll be many labourers around today. They might try to steal. Come to the fields with me. You'll only have to be there. The work will go on smoothly.'

It was probably the farmer's blood in my veins that made me walk to the fields just to have a new experience. The harvesting had already begun in the wee hours to ensure the ripe corn would not fall off the stalks. The pale moon on the horizon was still casting its fading light on the fields. It was already over—the harvesting—by the time we reached. The labourers were tying up the bundles. The womenfolk and children were picking up the stray, fallen corn ears. I had been deputed to watch lest they steal some of the harvested stalks instead of the fallen corn. I stood there keeping an eye, when, at a little distance in a corner of the field, behind a labourer, I spied a middle-aged woman and her children hastily picking up corn, and perhaps indulging in 'foul play' as well.

'Aye, you there, that woman! What are you doing there?'

She seemed to be completely oblivious to my loud call. The labourer, her husband, appeared to be warning her. Once, twice, thrice—all my calls went unheeded. Seething with anger, I proceeded towards them. Seeing me approach, all four of her children—well within six years of age—stood closer to their mother. The youngest one, just a year and a half old, hid behind her. From a distance, I shouted again: 'Aye, what are you doing?'

---

21 Elder brother

Her body still bent, her hands still working, she just turned her face towards me and said, 'Salaam, Babuji.'

'Oh, Budhia?' It was her, the same Budhia, the little girl who wore the red rag wrapped around her waist. The Budhia whose chunar never faded in her youth. *Uff! What happened to that merry childhood, that blooming youth ... This is an old woman in a torn saree. The choli is gone, the hair all dishevelled, the face shrunken, the cheeks and eyes—all sunken. And, oh, those two well-rounded, proud blossoms of her youth, which once maddened the young men of the village as she bent down to work, hang like the udders of an old goat—lifeless and cold!*

'Budhia?'

'Yes, Babuji.'

Turning her pale face, she gave me a faint smile and continued working. Her husband, who had by then tied up his pile, called out to her: 'Hey, give me a hand.' Budhia straightened up, gave me another wan smile and proceeded to help him with heavy steps. As she stood straight, I noticed a pregnant belly.

'Wait, Budhia, let me help,' I blurted out.

'No, Babuji. I wouldn't ask you to do it. You may get angry.' Her face glowed with emotion. My heart missed a beat. Old memories cascaded in. I went back to that dark evening, her bundle of grass, her call for help, Jagdish's sarcastic remarks, my exasperation and her frivolity.

Just then, her youngest child started crying. She turned to the child, and I went to help her husband lift the pile. The strong, hefty young man walked away in a swaying rhythm with the pile on his head. And Budhia, trying to push her shrunken breast into her child's mouth, kissing and pacifying him, said to me, 'How many children do you have, Babuji? Look at these kids. The wretches are so wicked. They have sucked me dry, spoilt my body and still don't let up. They're pests.'

The other three children stood by her side. She stroked the head of one, patted the other's back, and with her moist eyes poured her love into each one of them, cuddling the one in her lap. And yet, exuding contentment, she kept prattling on about this and that. My gaze stayed fixed on her face. Eyes staring and the mind musing.

The rainy season was over. The river again flowed with a tranquil, serene visage. The floods were over, as was all the brouhaha of life. Even the mud had dried up, the weeds and straw had been washed away. Absolute calm reigned on the river.

And I had an angelic mother before my eyes—only to be revered and worshipped!

Selected Couplets

Bedil Azimabadi

(Translated from the Urdu by Abhay K.)

You're not even loyal to your betrayals,
why should I be loyal my whole life?

★

The mind tells me not to tread on enemy's territory,
the spirit of heroism counsels otherwise.

★

Love itself is pain and is also the balm for the pain,
it is this difficulty that is difficult as well as easy.

Selection from the Third Canto of *Rashmirathi*

Ramdhari Singh Dinkar

(Translated from the Hindi by Abhay K.)

The Pandavas happily returned from the forest
after their long exile,
like gold smelted in fire,
becoming even more valorous,
brimming with a new zeal,
blood flowing faster in their veins.

It's true that when a calamity hits,
only a coward is scared,
the brave are not shaken,
they don't lose courage even for a moment,
they embrace difficulties
and make their way through thorns.

They never heave a weary sigh,
or beg away the trouble,

they endure all that comes their way
and keep toiling night and day,
to uproot the thorns,
to rise and grow over the calamity.

No trouble in the world
can stand in the way of a man;
when he musters all his strength,
even mountains get displaced;
when a man wills,
even stones turn into water.

Many fine qualities
are hidden within the man,
like the reddish tint hidden in henna,
the light hidden in the lamp.

Those who do not light the lamp
don't get the light,
when the sugarcane is crushed,
sweet juice flows out,
henna, when pestled,
becomes the ornament of brides,
when flowers are threaded into a garland,
they adorn the nape.

Who became the leader of the world,
who conquered the earth,
who received unparalleled glory,
who started a new faith?
The one who never rested,
the one who toiled, overcoming all odds.

It's true, when troubles come our way,
they wake us up from slumber,
they sway our minds,
and shake our bodies every moment,
they lead us to the right path,
and leave us only when we're fully awake.

Famine and After

Nagarjun

(Translated from the Hindi by Nalini Taneja)

For days and days, the hearth stayed cold, the hand mill quiet,
for days and days, the one-eyed bitch slept nearby,
for days and days, lizards paced on the wall,
for days and days, rats too were miserable.

Grain came to the house after many a day,
smoke rose above the courtyard after many a day,
the eyes of the household shone after many a day,
the crow scratched its feathers after many a day.

The Messenger

Phanishwar Nath Renu

(Translated from the Hindi by Rakhshanda Jalil)

Hargobin was surprised. *Someone still needs a messenger in this day and age? Now that even the smallest village has a post office, who bothers with a messenger? A man can send a message all the way to Lanka, if he so wishes, and get news from there—all the while sitting at home. Why, then, have I been sent for?*

He crossed the broken porch of the big haveli and entered the mansion. As always, he sniffed the air to sense the message that needed to be sent. Undoubtedly, it required the utmost secrecy. Not even the sun and the moon should come to know of it, nor should the birds and the bees.

He greeted Badi Bahuriya, the eldest daughter-in-law of the house.

She offered him a low stool and, with the flicker of her eye, gestured that he sit quietly for a while. The big haveli was now big only in name. Where once a horde of maids and servants milled about, today, Badi Bahuriya sat winnowing the wheat with her own hands. At one point, the village barber's wife could feed her entire family merely by applying henna on these hands. But those days were a thing of the past now. Hargobin drew a deep breath.

It was as though the last act of the play had been enacted with Bade Bhaiya's death. The remaining three brothers had started squabbling over the division of the property after that. The tenants had begun to lay claim over the lands. The three brothers had ultimately left the village to live in the city. Badi Bahuriya was left behind—*where else would the poor thing have gone? God always gives good people a hard time. Why else would Bade Bhaiya have died so quickly, in a matter of just a few hours?* The spectacle of division came to an end only after the very last ornament had been snatched from Badi Bahuriya. Hargobin had witnessed himself the disgrace that had befallen her, as it had upon Draupadi. Those heartless brothers had torn Badi Bahuriya's expensive Banarasi sarees into three equal parts. *Poor, poor Badi Bahuriya!*

The village grocer, an old woman, had been sitting in the courtyard for God knows how long. She was muttering to herself, 'It is all very well to buy on credit, but when I come to ask for my money, my words sound bitter. Today I will go only after I get my money.'

Badi Bahuriya did not respond.

Hargobin drew another long breath. He knew Badi Bahuriya wouldn't say a word till the grocer sat there. He couldn't stay quiet any longer. He said to the old woman, 'Have you learnt these wicked methods of extracting money from the Kabuli moneylenders?'

Hearing the word 'Kabuli', she flew into a rage. 'Keep quiet, you whiskerless rascal!'

'What can I do if God didn't give me a moustache or beard like the venerable Agha Sahib from Kabul?'

'If you say the word "Kabul" again, I will pull your tongue out.'

Hargobin stuck his tongue out, as though challenging her.

Five years ago, a certain Gul Mohammad Agha used to come to the village and sell cloth on credit from a shack outside the grocer's shop. Agha was a sweet-talker when he was selling cloth, but when it came to collecting payments, he turned into a heartless tyrant, extracting more than his money's worth from the hapless villagers. Finally, some of his creditors got together and beat him up so badly that he was never seen in the village again. But, from that day on, the old grocer had become a termagant. Even the mention of Kabuli almonds was enough to make her lose her cool. Such was the situation that the village dancers had staged a play alluding to her plight. They had mimicked a phoney Afghan accent and sang: *If you come to my land, I will feed you almonds, pistachios and walnuts, O dear grocer-woman...*

The old woman left the haveli muttering curses and obscenities. Badi Bahuriya turned to Hargobin and said, 'Brother Hargobin, you have to take a message for me. You must go today itself! Will you?'

'Where?'

'To my mother's.'

Giving in to Badi Bahuriya's tear-filled eyes, Hargobin agreed. 'Tell me, what is the message?'

Badi Bahuriya began to cry with great rasping sobs as she narrated her message. Hargobin's eyes welled up, too. He could see the Lakshmi-like goddess, who had once ruled over the big haveli, break down in front of him.

He said, 'You must steel yourself, Badi Bahuriya.'

'How much more can I steel myself? Tell my mother I will serve my brothers and their wives. I will eat the leftovers from their children's plates, but I will not live here any longer. No, I will not ... tell my mother that if she doesn't send for me, I will tie a pot around my neck and drown in the pond. How long can I survive on leaves and grass? Why should I? For whom?'

Every pore of Hargobin's body twitched. *How heartless were her brothers-in-law and their wives!* In the month of Aghan, when the rice was harvested, the brothers-in-law would show up from the city—wives and children in tow—stay for ten or fifteen days, work up a huge debt and return with mounds of freshly harvested rice and home-made chewra.[22] They would turn up in the mango season as well, pluck the semi-ripe fruit, stuff it into sacks and go away. Not once would they bother to check on Badi Bahuriya. *The beasts!*

Badi Bahuriya untied the knot at the end of her pallu and took out a dirty, crumpled five-rupee note. 'I have not been able to put together enough to cover the expenses for the journey. Take the return fare from my mother, and I hope my brother returns with you.'

'You don't have to give me money for the journey. I will arrange for it.'

'But where will you get the money from?'

'I shall leave by the 10 p.m. train tonight.'

Badi Bahuriya sat there, holding the five-rupee note and looking at Hargobin with an expressionless gaze. Hargobin left the haveli with Badi Bahuriya's words clear in his head: 'I will wait for you to return.'

★

Hargobin—the messenger, the one who carried messages back and forth! It was not a job for everyone. A man was either born a messenger, or he wasn't. It wasn't easy to remember every single word of the message, the tone and manner in which it was spoken, and to convey it in exactly the same way. People in the village harboured a common misconception that an idle, good-for-nothing glutton ended up becoming a messenger. What else would you call one who neither had a boss nor an underling, who went from village to village without charging a single paisa as fee … a woman's flunkey? They thought a woman only had to talk sweetly to cast a spell on him and make him do her bidding. According to them, could you call such a person a man? Yet, there wasn't a single mother, sister or daughter-in-law in the village for whom Hargobin had not carried a message. But this was the first time he was carrying a message of this nature!

---

22 Flattened rice

Hargobin sat in the train and was swamped by memories of the old days, of the countless messages he had carried. A half-remembered fragment of a poignant folk song echoed in his ears:

I fall at your feet, O messenger,
take my message, O messenger…

Every word of Badi Bahuriya's message had pierced his heart like a thorn: 'How will I live here?', 'There was one servant left; he, too, ran away yesterday', 'The cow, tethered to her post, whimpers with hunger all day long. For whom shall I carry on like this?'

Hargobin asked the passenger sitting beside him: 'Does the mail train stop at Thana Bihnpur station?'

The passenger snapped. 'All trains stop at Thana Bihnpur.'

Hargobin figured that his co-passenger was the surly type, not one to indulge in small talk. So, he went back to going over Badi Bahuriya's message, memorizing each word. But how would he control himself while narrating it? Would he also cry at the exact moment that Badi Bahuriya had wept while conveying the message?

He reached Katihar station and found that a great deal had changed in the last fifteen–twenty years. Now there was no need to get off the train and make inquiries. The moment the train halted, a voice announced over the loudspeaker: 'All passengers going to Thana Bihnpur, Khagadia and Barauni, please proceed to platform number three. A train is waiting at the platform.'

Hargobin was pleased. At Katihar, you could tell that the country had truly made progress since gaining freedom. In the past, he had missed connecting trains simply because he had lost a lot of time making inquiries about which train to board and from where.

He boarded the connecting train. Once again, Badi Bahuriya's sad face appeared before his eyes. 'Brother Hargobin, tell my mother that God has turned His eyes away from me, but I still have my mother.'

Hargobin's heart grew heavy as the train approached Thana Bihnpur. He had come here before—sometimes carrying good tidings, sometimes doleful ones—but he had never felt like this before. His feet refused to move towards the village. Soon, Badi Bahuriya would take this path to reach her village. She would leave that village. Forever.

Once again, Hargobin's heart began to flutter. What would be left in the village if Goddess Lakshmi herself forsook it? How could he carry such a message? How could he say that Badi Bahuriya had been living on leaves and grass? Anybody who heard it would spit at the mention of his village! What sort of village was it where the goddess-like Badi Bahuriya had to suffer such ignominy?

Unwillingly, Hargobin reached the village. People recognized him instantly. They knew it was the messenger from Jalalgadh. They wondered what message he had brought.

'Ram Ram,[23] brother! Is all well?'

'Ram Ram, brother! By the grace of God, all is well.'

'Have you had any rain there?'

*

Badi Bahuriya's elder brother didn't recognize Hargobin, but when he introduced himself, the first thing he asked was: 'How is my sister?'

'She is well, by the grace of God.'

Hargobin was summoned to the women's courtyard after he had freshened up. Once again, he began to tremble. His heart began to beat furiously. This had never happened to him before. Badi Bahuriya's tear-filled eyes, her message, her sobs and whimpers came back to him. He feebly greeted Badi Bahuriya's mother.

The old lady asked him, 'Tell me, son, what message have you brought?'

'All is well there.'

23 Among Hindus, a way of greeting when two people meet

'Is there any message for me?'

'Huh? Message? No, there is no message. I came to Sirsiya village yesterday, so I thought of paying you a visit.'

The old lady looked sad. 'So, you have not come with a message?'

'No, there is no message, but Badi Bahuriya did say that if she finds the time, she might come to see you during Dussehra.'

The old lady didn't utter a word.

Hargobin continued. 'But when will she find the time? The burden of running the entire household is on her.'

The old lady said, 'I have been telling my son to go and fetch his sister. She can live with us. What is left for her there? All the land and property is gone. All three brothers-in-law have settled down in the city. They never bother to inquire after her. My daughter is there, all alone...'

'No, no. There is still enough land and property left. It is more than enough. Though it is a tumbledown haveli, it is still a mansion. While it is true that she has no children, the whole village is like her family. Badi Bahuriya is like Lakshmi in our village. Her brothers-in-law keep insisting that she moves to the city with them, but how can a goddess leave her village?'

The old lady served him refreshments with her own hands. 'Eat a little first, son.'

The sight of food reminded him of Badi Bahuriya, sitting in her courtyard and waiting for him, hungry! As he was served dinner, it felt as though Badi Bahuriya was sitting in front of him. Her words haunted him: 'No one gives me credit worth a penny', 'Even a dog can find enough to fill its belly, but I ...', 'Tell my mother...'

Hargobin looked at the platter before him: rice, lentils, three types of vegetables, ghee, papad, pickle. Badi Bahuriya must be boiling leaves and grass for dinner.

The old lady asked, 'What's the matter, son? Why aren't you eating?'

'I ate so much at teatime.'

'A young man can eat any number of snacks and still consume a plate full of rice.'

But Hargobin didn't eat anything. He couldn't.

It is said about the messengers that they eat their fill and sleep: What had he done? What had happened to him? Had he forgotten why he had come? Why did he lie?

In the morning, he must give the message to the old lady. He must tell her everything, word for word. He must tell the old lady about her daughter's dire situation. That she should send someone to fetch her post-haste. If not, she may do something terrible. After all, why should she undergo this hardship any longer, for whom? Also, Badi Bahuriya had said she would eat the leftovers from her nieces' and nephews' plates and keep to a corner of the house.

All night, all Hargobin could picture was Badi Bahuriya, sobbing and wiping her tears. In the morning, he hardened his heart and resolved to tell her mother everything. After all, he was a messenger. His job was to carry a message and convey it accurately. He sat beside the old lady.

The old lady asked, 'What is it? Do you want to say something?'

'I must catch the next train. I have been away for several days.'

'What's the hurry? Stay here for a few days. Be our guest and enjoy our hospitality.'

'No, no. You must excuse me for now, but I will come with Badi Bahuriya for Dussehra. Then I will enjoy your hospitality for a good fifteen days!'

The old lady complained. 'Why come if you were in such a hurry! I was thinking of sending some dahi-chewra for my daughter. I won't be able to send the dahi, but there is some chewra made of basmati rice. Take that.'

As Hargobin left the courtyard with a bundle of chewra tucked under his arm, Badi Bahuriya's eldest brother called out, 'Do you have enough for the train fare, brother?'

'Yes. By the grace of God, there is no shortage of anything.'

★

Hargobin reached the station and took stock of the money he had. It was just enough for a ticket till Katihar. And if the four-anna coin turned out to be fake, only till Saimapur. He could not even think of travelling without a ticket. The blood in his body just dried up with terror.

He felt worse when he sat in the train: Why had he come here? Why was he returning without accomplishing his mission? What would he say to Badi Bahuriya?

Had a blind beggar singing nirguna[24] songs not entered his compartment, who knows how far his condition would have deteriorated? He took heart from the words of the beggar's song:

The happiness of my father's home appears like a dream now,
the palanquin leaves for my husband's home,
don't cry, brother, for this is my fate…

When the beggar left, Badi Bahuriya was back in front of Hargobin. Her sobs and words rang in his ears: 'For whom should I undergo these hardships?'

He reached Katihar at 5 a.m. There was an announcement over the loudspeaker: 'Passengers travelling to Bairgaddi, Kusiar and Jalalgadh should proceed to platform number one.'

Hargobin had to go to Jalalgadh, but how could he head towards the platform? His ticket was valid only till Kathiar. Jalalgadh was twenty kos[25] away. *Badi Bahuriya must be waiting. What is twenty kos, after all? I can walk.*

---

24 Songs about formless God, who has no attributes

25 One kos is nearly three kilometres

Hargobin remembered Lord Hanuman and set off. For the first ten kos, he cruised along. He reached a small town and quenched his thirst. He sniffed the bundle of chewra under his arm—the fragrance! Chewra made from basmati rice! A mother's gift to her daughter! No, he could not eat even a handful. *What would I say to Badi Bahuriya?*

His feet trembled, but he couldn't stop. Not now. He had to walk, he had to reach his village. Badi Bahuriya's tear-drenched eyes were tugging at him. 'I will wait for you to return,' she had said.

Fifteen kos! *Tell my mother I can't take it anymore.* Sixteen … seventeen … eighteen. He could now spot the signal at Jalalgarh station. Before long, he could see the tall palm tree, sitting under which, Badi Bahuriya must be keeping a silent vigil, waiting for him with her eyes glued to the door, hungry and thirsty.

I fall at your feet, O messenger,
take my message, O messenger…

But what is this? Where am I? Which village is this? Why is there the dense darkness of a moonless night when it is time for twilight? A river? Where did the river come from? No, no, it isn't a river. These are fields. And is that a cluster of huts or a herd of elephants? Where did the palm tree go? Have I lost my way? There's not a trace of light anywhere. Whom shall I ask? Doesn't anyone live in this village? Why is there no light? Wait, is that light or are those someone's eyes? Is that person standing or moving? Am I in a train or on the ground?

'Brother Hargobin?'

Is that Badi Bahuriya's voice, or is it the loudspeaker at Katihar station?

'Brother Hargobin, what is the matter with you?'

'Badi Bahuriya?'

Hargobin felt around him with his hand and discovered that he was lying on a mattress on the floor. He touched the faint shadow in front of him. 'Badi Bahuriya?'

'How do you feel now, Brother Hargobin? Here, take another sip of milk. Open your mouth, drink … have some more!'

Finally, when he came to, he fell at Badi Bahuriya's feet. 'Forgive me, Badi Bahuriya. I could not convey your message. Don't leave this village, don't go away. I promise you will know no more hardships. I am your son. Badi Bahuriya, you are my mother, you are the mother of the entire village. I won't sit idle, I will find work. I will run all errands for you. Tell me you won't leave the village. Promise me!'

Badi Bahuriya added a handful of chewra into the warm milk and stirred it. She had been regretting sending the message ever since the messenger had left.

The Invisible Bond

Surendra Mohan Prasad

(Translated from the Bajjika by Abhay Kumar, Jay Ram Singh and Chaitali Pandya)

Keuli trembled as she arrived on the outskirts of the village. *Will anyone recognize me*, she wondered. She had not thought about this before leaving her home. But today she had felt this sudden urge to see her mother's village and had set out without thinking twice. Her middle daughter-in-law had tried to stop her. She should not have come here. Her feet lumbered now. Whom could she visit? She told herself that if no one recognized her, she would simply wander about the village and return. *But it would be foolish to return after coming all this way!* She walked slowly, contemplating how times had changed. All the people she once knew had probably passed away. She had learnt from her paternal family that Aunt Kabutri, Aunt Agni and her sister, Golahiya, had all passed away within a year of each other. Even her mother-in-law and father-in-law were no more. *Yes, Ma shouldn't have left the village. At least there would have been some hope, had she been here.*

Her mud house once stood next to a big mango orchard. Next to it had been Uncle Baon's cowshed. But there were no traces of them any more. It was just a flat land. *What had happened to the big mango orchard?*

Gone was the shade it offered; the blazing sun scorched it now. Earlier, the orchard blocked the view of the temple pinnacle, but now it was clearly visible. *Men are ordinary mortals, but trees and gardens should not be destroyed*, she thought. The roads, too, seemed narrower. The litchi garden next to Dharam Gachhi had become old. She remembered playing dol-pati[26] on the branches of the litchi trees. She recalled the day Uncle Baon had hit her with a stick. He did not like girls climbing the trees. She had been caught that day. The memories made Keuli laugh.

Just then, she sighted someone. *Oh, she seems to be Lolwa's mother. The place is the same, but the house is now made of bricks*. Keuli surely had a good memory.

Her face is sagging. She's old now! Her hair is completely white and she's picking out white lice eggs with a comb. At least I found an acquaintance. How I wish to hug her! Ignoring these thoughts, Keuli stood at the doorway and asked loudly, 'Do you recognize me, Aunty?'

Lolwa's mother tied her hair up and squinted, staring at Keuli, as if she were searching for something in her fading memories. She said, 'I can't see properly now. Tell me your father's name.'

Keuli's enthusiasm spilled forth. 'I am Keuli.'

The darkness that had gripped Lolwa's mother's memory was pushed aside. 'Ah! You are Prabhu's daughter … come and sit. You are coming from your in-laws' house, aren't you? Listen, daughter-in-law, look who has come!' she called out to Kaniya, her daughter-in-law.

Keuli faced a series of questions from Lolwa's mother until Kaniya joined them. Her questions popped up like bubbles in boiling rice. 'Well, tell me, how did you come? Your mother was impatient to marry you off. She did not even wait till your father's first death anniversary. I am seeing you here for the first time since the day you left.' Then, taking a deep breath, she added, 'It wasn't your fault. Your husband, your children … is everyone fine?'

---

26 A game played around a tree

Keuli was puzzled by this volley of questions. She spoke timidly about her home, her three sons and two daughters, and her grandchildren. All her daughters were living with their in-laws and her sons were engaged in agriculture along with her husband. The daughters-in-law took care of all the household chores. The youngest daughter-in-law was pregnant. Thus, Keuli patiently answered every question, all except why she was visiting after ages.

Kaniya and Keuli had got married in the same year. Kaniya suddenly seemed to remember everything clearly. She hugged Keuli and took her to the courtyard. *How time flies when you talk to someone your age!*

Of course, there was no question of returning the same day. Keuli did not even mention it.

Memories of her childhood came flooding like the monsoon rains. While walking towards the northern street and chatting with Kaniya, Keuli noticed that the road, the embankment of the pond … everything had changed. Everything showed signs of ageing, even the eastern land where she used to take her cattle for grazing and the fields where she went to pick the snails in the months of January and February. Keuli remembered how she would lift her saree and tuck it at the back before secretly heading to the paddy fields to catch garai and chenga fish. Soaked in mud, she would resemble a ghost. Now, a brick kiln stood there, its chimney emitting smoke. There were hardly any straw houses; most of them were made of bricks, thanks to the kiln.

'What if there are so many houses made of bricks? Even now, the only house with a concrete roof is the bungalow, and it will remain the same,' said Kaniya.

Bungalow—the word seemed to draw some memories out of the abyss of Keuli's mind. Calming herself, she said, 'I heard the owner is dead.'

Having had the privilege of once being the Brahmani, the family priest's wife, at the bungalow, Kaniya explained everything in detail.

According to her, the wealth of the residents of the bungalow hadn't decreased, but the money was no longer safe. The master's manager had been shot by a thief. There was a rumour that the manager had two bags full of currency notes. These notes were believed to have been scattered in every corner of the house. His mother had wept so bitterly that even the police inspector had been moved. Crying, the old woman had cursed many people. The police had caught several people and tied them here in the bamboo field, but they had not found any evidence. Soon after the older master's death, the younger master had arrived in the village and performed the rituals in a grand manner. Men from ten villages, and people from his own village, had been invited for a feast. Many gifts had been handed out, including two beds and a lot of grain that her family had received. However, the older master's mother and his wife had both died within a span of one year after the rituals were performed.

Keuli was startled. 'Oh! What happened?'

'Well, it has been more than ten years since they passed away. Maybe more. The younger master married off his daughter, too. I have heard his younger son studies in Bombay.'

'Who looks after the farm work?' asked Keuli, lost in a state of reverie.

'The servants take care of it. Every Saturday, the master comes to supervise. He stays till Monday morning. He will come tonight because it is a Saturday. On the occasion of Shravani puja,[27] his son, daughter and the others come once a year. But that's just for a day or two. Oh yes! You used to live in the bungalow before. Now, I think Kaari Kaka will be the only person you will recognize there. That effeminate man! He still talks with hand gestures. Once he starts talking, it's difficult to get him to stop.'

---

27 A ritual performed in honour of Lord Shiva during the holy month of Shravan, which is the month of August as per the Gregorian calendar

Keuli was getting more inquisitive after hearing this. Hearing Kaari Kaka's name seemed to make her feel better. She said, 'Let me meet him once. God knows when I will come next.'

On arriving at the bungalow, Keuli tried to notice the changes that may have set in over the last thirty years. The land looked the same, as did the pond. There was a big hole in the trunk of the gulmohar tree. Its thick branches, gazing up at the sky, seemed to be narrating their own story.

And there was Kaari Kaka, seated on a high porch with red flooring. Only his face looked sunken owing to his age. She could easily recognize everything else there. A buck sat on a muddy patch with its legs folded, face turned and eyes closed … perhaps it was sleeping. A shaggy dog was trying to catch a gadfly. It did not bark on seeing Keuli, but it did howl because it detected an unfamiliar smell.

The women of the village did not have to be in purdah before Kaari Kaka. His head covered with the edge of his dhoti, a gamcha[28] on his knee, Kaari Kaka was rubbing tobacco between his palms. On seeing Keuli, he asked, 'Kaniya, who is she? She seems familiar.'

On hearing these words, Keuli felt like an eleven-year-old girl. She said gleefully, 'Oh, Kaka! Don't you recognize me? You have held me in your lap many times. Kaniya, promise me that you won't speak!'

Kaari Kaka's face muscles tightened; he started racking his brain. Laughing, he said, 'Yes, I recognize you. You are Keuli, Prabhu Mahto's daughter! You are married in Talimpur. Once, I went to Ganj market to buy oxen for the bungalow. There, some people told me that your house was on the banks of the Bagmati. First, tell me, what made you visit the village? How many children do you have? What do they do?'

Keuli answered bashfully and spoke about her house and her children. She even added that her youngest daughter-in-law was pregnant.

---

28 A thin, coarse cotton towel, often with a checked design

After inquiring and feeling assured about everything, Kaari Kaka asked, 'Tell me, how did you venture out to this village? I thought you must have set out in search of some relatives. Although your mother fled from this village, it cannot be denied that you were born here. Your brothers, do they meet you?'

Keuli shook her head. 'Their whereabouts are unknown. Along with my mother, all other bonds were also broken. When my mother did not bother, why would the brothers?'

Kaari Kaka's mind was filled with compassion. 'Forget about them! Aren't we here for you? You grew up working in this bungalow. What if the mistress of the house is no more? I will not let you go without a good meal. And you must stay here for a day. The master will be coming today. Meet him. Now even you are well-off. Let's see if he recognizes you.'

Keuli felt as if someone had thrown her into a storm. 'Master? You mean Basant Babu? Will he recognize me?'

She felt as if someone had thrown a big clod into the calm pond. She went back in time.

'Keuli, fetch me a glass of water,' Basant Babu had called out from the eastern wing of the house. As always, she was about to rush to his room, but stopped short. Something had come over her that day. Why had she got cold feet? Sitting on the porch, Basant Babu's grandmother had flung sharp words at her: 'Look at her! Her youthful spirit has taken over her so much that she deliberately refuses to take a glass of water to my grandson.'

Eventually, Keuli took the glass of water to him. After all, whom could she tell that this was not thirst for water. Living in the same house, having played and grown up together, they hadn't realized they were adolescents now. As Keuli had stood with the glass of water in her hand, Basant Babu had stood admiring her figure. She had trembled in fright. 'Have the water. You will again call for me to take the glass back and I will get a scolding,' she had said to him.

Staring at her face, Basant had said, 'You remember I made you swear on me, don't you?'

★

Sitting there in front of Kaari Kaka, Keuli was soaked in sweat. To her it seemed like yesterday. That evening, too, had been like this one. Even today, the courtyard was visible from the front gate. Keuli was curious to go inside and see the courtyard.

Kaari Kaka, not paying heed to the way Keuli was looking towards the courtyard, kept talking. 'Master reads books day and night because he has become a sage now. He wears such thick glasses that you can use them to light a fire by harnessing the sun's rays.'

Keuli once again remembered the past. Once, Basant Babu had set fire to some dry leaves using the senior master's magnifying glass. On another occasion, he had focused the heat on Keuli's hand. 'Ouch! Maa!' she had exclaimed then and run away rubbing her hand.

Keuli came out of her reverie and focused on Kaari Kaka's words again. 'This courtyard here … you certainly must not have forgotten. Why don't you go there and see it yourself? Tears will come to your eyes. This time, before Shravani puja, the courtyard was cleaned and coated with a paste made of cow dung and mud. They were going to come to see my son for marriage. Who else will look after this courtyard if I don't?' Then, getting up, he said to Keuli, 'Why don't you take a stroll and look around while I go and feed the oxen?'

After Kaari Kaka went away, Keuli, who was ill at ease, went to the well and lowered a bucket into it. Although the well had been there since her childhood, today it seemed to be asking a lot of questions, intrigued about her absence all these years. *Everyone is bound by time. Why am I shuddering when looking back at my past?* Right in front was the bamboo field and adjacent to it was the dung-cake house. Her lame mother would stuff nearly four- or five-hundred dung cakes there.

Now, in its place, was a room made of brick and cement, electric wires running overhead. It appeared to be the motor room for the borewell.

Back then, on that quiet afternoon, a magnetic force had pulled her towards the dung-cake house. She hadn't known that Basant Babu had hid himself there. Unaware, she had calmly entered it to get some dung cakes when he had come from behind and held her tightly in his strong arms. Before she could scream, Basant Babu had placed a hand over her mouth. Luckily, she had managed to escape because Jhapsi Kaka, who was supposed to be visiting a relative, was secretly drinking toddy behind the dung-cake house. 'Let me go!' she had said in a hushed tone, glowering at him.

'I haven't caught you to let go of you,' Basant Babu had gasped, his heart thudding against her back. 'Now I shall never let you go. I will hold you like this forever.'

Keuli had mustered up some courage and said, 'Which master has ever spent a lifetime with a maid? You will get married and the very next day I will be driven out of the house with my own broom. Let me go! What if someone sees us?'

'I am letting you go now, but promise me that you will come to meet me at midnight,' Basant Babu had said, loosening his grip but continuing to stare at her.

What has happened to Basant Babu? This is some other person speaking from within his body, she had wondered. Just to set herself free, she had said, 'Okay, I promise. Now let me go. Your tight grip is hurting me.'

'No, swear on me and then I shall let you go,' Basant Babu had said, holding her more tightly.

Keuli had caught a look outside as she had tried to wrench herself free from his grasp. 'Oh my god! Look, Mohini Dai[29] is coming! Let me go. No harm will come to you, but they will surely throw me into the hearth.'

29 Midwife

Basant Babu had not fallen into her trap. Ultimately, Keuli had to give in by placing her hand on his head. 'I promise you!' she had said. Later, she had thought to herself, *Do such promises matter*?

★

The bucket had taken a while to fill. Keuli pulled it out, its weight drawing her out of her thoughts. She washed her face and hands, and wiped her face with the pallu. Then, she decided to take a look around.

There used to be a kathari champa[30] plant next to the well. It was still there, smelling like ripe jackfruit. Basant Babu used to say that her body, too, exuded the same smell. This thought often made her feel intoxicated. Not even her husband had said such rousing words to her. She had given birth to his children, but he had never said something that made her feel besotted.

What had happened to her? Had she come to the village to think about all this? She had her own family. Today, why were these surreptitious thoughts rendering her defenceless? Are the forgotten memories of the past burying their fangs like a cobra into every corner of her mind? It seemed as if the poison had already spread before the cobra could bite.

It was not that she had not been wise enough at that age. There had been no dearth of women in the village who would time and again instil into her mind that she was a young woman who should cover her body well. She herself had experienced changes in her body, that too at a fast pace. *The body can be kept in check, but what about the mind?* That was why she was unable to understand what they told her. Even after thinking hard, she couldn't understand what lay hidden in her mind. Whatever it was, she could feel it floating like semal cotton in the air, transporting her to her childhood days – changing her, crushing her.

30 Jackfruit Champa (*Artabotrys odoratissimus*), jackfruit frangipani or jackfruit plumeria

As children, Basant Babu and she used to play together in the courtyard. Many times, in anger, he would punch her. She would bite him in retaliation, making his fair skin turn black and blue. They had learnt to swim together in the same pond, during the month of Chaitra–Vaishakh,[31] when the water level wasn't very high. They would bet on who would touch the pillar in the centre of the pond first. They would compete to get a catch of the fish in the shallow waters.

One day, upon hearing the sound of kettledrums playing in the street, she had rushed to the corridor. She hadn't noticed Basant Babu approaching and had bumped into him. Had he not saved her from falling, her head would have hit the doorpost.

He had asked her, 'Why don't you walk with your eyes open? You would have hurt your head.' At that time, she had been desperate to hear the band, so she had run away hurriedly. In the quietness of the evening, when she had recalled the incident, she had almost burst into tears. Her entire body had squirmed when she lay on the mat that night, just like a fish out of water. She could only sleep after the watchman started patrolling the streets and calling out into the night.

The next afternoon, on Basant Babu's elder sister's order, she had gone to get a picture book from Basant Babu's room while he was asleep. She had picked up the book and turned, but the edge of her saree had got entangled in the leg of the bed. She had jerked and fallen on Basant Babu's legs. He had woken up and stared at her for a while before saying, 'This has happened a second time.' Keuli still remembered the glint in his eyes. Women are well aware of what that look means; these signs need not be taught. She remembered how Basant Babu had suddenly stopped laughing. In a choked voice, he had said, 'Give me a glass of water. Why is my throat parched?'

It appeared that Basant Babu had been really thirsty. He had gulped down a full glass of water in one go, but his eyes had stayed fixed on

31 April–May

Keuli's face. While handing over the glass to her, he had grabbed her hand and made her sit on the bed. Keuli had lowered her gaze and kept looking at the glass. She had been trembling; she couldn't meet his passionate gaze. He had held on to her hand tightly, making her weak at the knees. Basant Babu's hand, that had been caressing her hands until then, had moved to her cheek. Every pore of her body had frozen. She closed her eyes. Her body seemed to be swirling, flying. Basant Babu had been gasping for air. Just like a diver who, upon coming to the surface, breathes amply, Basant Babu too had breathed out and whispered to her, 'Your people, why do they keep you so confined? Why can't we play together any more?'

Keuli had felt something stuck in her throat. 'We are no longer children. People will mock us if we, grown-ups, were to play together like before.' And then, instinctively, she had added, 'When you get married, play with your wife.' There had been something about this innocent remark that had filled Keuli with embarrassment. She had got up and left.

That day, Basant Babu had remained in the house till nightfall. Although Keuli had been doing her work in the courtyard, her ears had been trained in the direction of Basant Babu's room. For several days after that, Basant Babu had wandered here and there in a sullen mood. Not once had he asked her for water or even looked at her.

Had it been the same as before, she would have entered his room unhesitatingly. But now, whenever she glanced at it, she breathed like Kaltu Thakur's furnace. She had begun to feel restless. She wondered what had upset Basant Babu so much. Soon after that, the dung-cake house incident had taken place. *Why had he made me promise*, she had thought. *He could have said the same thing by summoning me to his room instead of catching me unawares. Being bound by someone's swear, how does it matter? Unless the person chooses to be bound by it. The tongue can either bind you or liberate you.*

After the ritual lighting of the evening lamp and supper, everyone went to sleep. But Keuli lay awake on the floor, next to Basant Babu's grandmother's cot, thinking what the consequences would eventually be. After all, they were wealthy people. At worst, Basant Babu would be sent to Patna. As for her, she could only imagine what would befall her behind closed doors. She had already heard of many such incidents. What was her relationship with Basant Babu? Only growing up and playing together? Is that what sanctified the promise and bound them to it? *Well, we can't be bound by it*. She had tried to sleep by covering her face with her pallu.

This was not fire but the lava simmering beneath the surface. Everything seemed normal, but what about the mind which, at one moment was convinced and the next moment soared skyward like smoke. It was this weakness that had made her helpless. Feeling suffocated, she had uncovered her face.

What kind of match would it be, between a master and a maid? What was the joy of living a life like a used pattal?[32]

Grandmother took opium to sleep soundly. Bhajan's mother had been snoring in the verandah like a frog in the month of Bhadra.[33] She used to breathe in through her nose and out through her mouth, quite noisily. *Everyone is asleep. Why am I awake?*

A long ray of light had appeared from the eastern room. It had crossed the verandah and passed over the porch, covering half of the courtyard. Had it settled in the middle of the courtyard to remind her of her promise?

Opening the main door, Basant Babu had gone outside the house. After a while, there had been a thud on the main door, as if the cat had run into it. The flood of light had continued to spread. Watchman Maanchand's call could be heard from the southern street. He had set

32 Plate made of dried leaves
33 August–September

out after the second pahar[34] of the night. Within no time, he would be at the bungalow and call out the name of each servant to wake them up.

Someone had poured water from the pitcher. It had been Basant Babu. Keuli had listened to the sound attentively with her eyes closed. The flood of light had continued to cover the courtyard, shining like a well-tilled farm on a moonlit night.

Keuli, too, had felt the urge to drink water. But she had been unable to get up. Such was the faith and confidence in the power of a promise. *What kind of a man is he who lives in the hope that an unmarried girl would go to his room stealthily in the middle of the night to honour a promise!* She had been angry at herself. She shouldn't have promised. And if she had done it, she should have bit her tongue or spat immediately after, so that the oath would be negated. At least he wouldn't have been hopeful. These were all childhood games. Basant Babu only appeared to be mature; he was actually still a child.

The main door had opened again. Ghooran Singh had coughed loudly. She had turned to her side and gazed at the patio. The bright light had still been radiating on to it. She had cursed the light, which had rendered her sleepless. She had got up hastily, walked to the verandah and gone straight to Basant Babu's room. The frosted glass of the imported lamp had been emitting powerful light. To hide herself, she had squeezed her body behind an almirah. The wood on the eastern side had been moonwashed. The bare gular[35] tree at the edge of the pond had resembled a ghost. Her body had shaken involuntarily. And then she had heard Basant Babu closing the door. Now there was no escape. Unaware of Keuli's presence in the room, a dejected Basant Babu had closed the door. The light by the side of the closed door had looked alluring.

---

34 Traditionally, night and day are divided into four pahars each, with each pahar spanning three hours; the first pahar of the night sets in after sunset

35 Cluster fig

She had wondered if she should frighten Basant Babu like she used to when they were children. But here someone was trying to gag childhood. She had stood holding her breath. When Basant Babu had turned around to dim the light, he had seen her. 'I was confident,' he had said in an attempt to try and feel at ease.

With lowered eyes, Keuli had tried to search for something on the floor. She had whispered, 'Why did you make me promise?' How could she have told him that not believing in the promise is the truth and believing in it is a lie. That had been the tradition ever since. Could she tell all this to her childhood friend? Did it matter? Silently, she reminded herself how his childhood friend had been ready to break the promise which he had deep faith in. Perhaps in the future someone would bind this innocent mind. She had come in the middle of the night only to ensure that the new tender buds springing in her mind should not wither away as a result of betrayal.

All these years, she lay lost in her love for her family, and now her loneliness was bringing her dormant emotions to the fore. The unrelenting emotion that had lain like a dormant seed in the earth of the past had now begun to sprout. Could that night ever be forgotten? Like a beautiful story heard a long time ago, the sensation was still so fresh that even if she wanted to forget it, she couldn't.

That night, whose pearl had been stolen? Hers or Basant Babu's? In reality, probably nobody's! Justice would be done only in the court of God. She did not regret that night then, and she did not regret it now. She was not ready to call it a sin even if someone else did so. If deeds of affection undertaken to celebrate the reason why God has granted us this life are termed as sins, then so be it. When a wrong deed is committed knowingly, only then can it be termed as a sin. She had not gone there out of greed or with any selfish motive. She had gone to give something, and by giving she had felt liberated. In fact, that night she had felt a love blossom in her heart, one that she had never felt even for her own children. Her husband considered her to be his Kamadhenu, his cash cow, rather than his wife or beloved. Did she ever experience the same pleasure afterwards as she did that night? What is a sin? To rob or be robbed?

That night, resting his head on her chest and calling out her name again and again, a mature child had been born. From the mist of inexperience had risen a new sun—bloodstained and trembling. In his view, Keuli had been his realization, his self-realization. With much reluctance, she had left, just like a mother leaves her children when when she has to go to work. Even today, she remembered that expression on Basant Babu's face, like that of a child whose toys were being snatched away. *I wonder how he looks now!*

After that night, she had never gone to Basant Babu's room. The two had kept their distance. Whenever they saw each other, Basant Babu teased her, but she remained silent.

On another day, there had been no one in the courtyard. Everyone had gone to the temple on account of Lakhauri puja.[36] She had come to the courtyard for some work. As if Basant Babu had anticipated that she would come there, he had wrapped her in his arms and said, 'Today you must tell me why you are running away from me. What is my fault?'

She had released herself from his grasp and said, 'Don't block my way. That particular night cannot be repeated in our lifetime.'

Basant Babu's innocent face had borne an expression of mistrust. He had kept staring at her.

She had continued. 'That day you were childlike, full of innocence, but today you are a grown-up man. Tell me, did you hold me in the hope of seeking the same pleasure of that night? Now it's a sin, for both you and me!' She had seen a spark in Basant Babu's eyes, which seemed to suggest that vice and virtue were merely ideas that held no value. 'I am a maid. You can beat me, torture me, overpower me. But I will not

36 Worship of Lord Shiva

allow you to commit the sin deliberately,' she had added and then kept her gaze fixed on him. Basant Babu had looked shocked for a brief moment and left after letting out a sigh.

She still remembered that look on his face, which had emanated sadness, as if he had lost something. But how was it possible to regain it? Would she be able to give herself to him like she did before? *That moment can neither be repeated, nor recreated. Do auspicious moments repeat themselves?*

These twenty-five years seem to have rushed past in the story of this village, at the speed of a spinning top. On the other hand, her own life had gone on like a squeaking bullock cart crossing a wide, deep and dark path. What had made her come to this village today? She had no answer.

Kaari Kaka came to sleep just then. He said, 'The master has arrived. He is a little tired, so I did not inform him about you. Meet him in the morning.' She did not speak a word, and she knew she could not discuss it with anybody. *This night is so different from that night*, she thought. That night, she had had the courage. Today it seemed every drop of her blood had been drawn out. She was too weak to even turn to her side and sleep. This was the same place where, twenty-five years ago, two innocent souls had dreamt together. After having gone through the long tunnel of life, after overcoming the ups and downs, the two of them now stood at opposite ends.

Basant Babu, then a child showered with affection by his parents—the master and mistress of the house—was now his own man not bound by any bond. Even then he lay awake, gazing at the stars the whole night.

In the morning, a voice was heard from the upper room. 'Kaari...'

Lifting a bucket and walking towards the well, Kaari Kaka replied, 'I will be there.' He then turned to Keuli, 'He still has the habit of drinking water after waking up. Today, why don't you take a glass of water for him while I finish some other work?' He then handed her a glass and a lota filled with water. 'Take it right away, otherwise he will keep calling out my name.'

Noticing that Keuli was hesitant, he said, 'Are you feeling shy at this age? Make haste!'

Holding the lota and the glass in her hands, Keuli climbed up the stairs to Basant Babu's room. She wondered whether this part of the house was built later. Balancing the lota carefully and holding her pallu between her teeth, she entered the room.

There he was, a tall and slim body on the bed. Basant Babu's hair had turned white. Resting his head on the headrest, he was looking downward. On hearing the tap on the door, he extended his hand to take the glass of water. Keuli was trembling all over. Without looking up, he took the glass. His thumb touched Keuli's bangles. Startled, he got up and sat upright, his gaze fixed on Keuli. She watched a dreamy Basant Babu with the glass of water shaking in his hands. He could barely utter his next words: 'When did you come?'

Keuli stood rooted to the spot. Kaari Kaka, who had come upstairs, replied from behind: 'She came yesterday. You came late and were tired, so I did not inform you.'

'Did you offer her food last night?' Basant Babu's gaze was still fixed on Keuli.

'That goes without saying. Don't I know her? I was there when she got married. She now lives in Talimpur. She has a family … children, grandchildren. Her youngest daughter-in-law is pregnant. Look, she insists on returning today itself. I requested her to stay for a couple of days, but she wouldn't agree. Why don't you tell her, maybe she will agree?'

Once Kaari Kaka started talking, he went on continuously. While Basant Babu was soaring high in the sky of his imagination, just like a kite, Keuli was bobbing like a spool. The kite string had run out. And just like the kite and the spool, Keuli and Basant Babu quivered from within. Looking at Keuli's face, Basant Babu could only ask her this: 'Are you fine?'

Keuli didn't know whether she nodded or not. But an unexpected reply did come from her. 'Why shouldn't I be? I own three bigha[37] land, buffaloes and a pair of bullocks—'

Basant Babu couldn't hold back. He interrupted, 'Are you leaving today itself?'

Though this question was for Keuli, Kaari Kaka spoke. 'I entreated her several times, but her daughter-in-law is expecting, so she insists on going. God forbid if something goes wrong, she will have to live with the stigma her whole life. She will depart soon.'

Basant took the glass of water and drank it in one go. Getting up from the bed, he said, 'If she must leave today, then at least pack some chewra and jaggery for her.' He glanced at Keuli once again and walked away.

Keuli was leaving. Running her hand gently over the packet of chewra and jaggery, she fondly remembered Basant Babu's touch. Should she consider this a gift from her mother's house? Basant Babu was standing on the verandah. She stood before him with folded hands. Stooping, she muttered, 'I touch your feet.' But she herself couldn't hear her own voice. She felt a lump in her throat as she went down the stairs.

The one-way road turned to the right after one crossed the pond. Keuli had her back towards Basant Babu. Upon reaching the bend of the road, she stopped for a while and then turned to see him still standing on the verandah. He stood there motionless, looking at her. Everyone has to leave their past behind and move on. The one-way road before her was her present. In spite of that, the past was so powerful that her legs felt heavy. What sort of tiredness was this? Like some invisible bond trying to drag her back in time. The one-way road went past the bamboo field, from where the mansion was no longer visible ... just like the dark past.

37 A traditional unit of measurement of the area of land, commonly used in India

The Business of Donation

Mathura Prasad Naveen

(Translated from the Magahi by Abhay K.)

This business of donation too is a duty
to grab the seat of power.

There is no shame, no grace,
there is nothing new, nothing old.

Everyone says, the rich and the poor
are God's creations.

You must think who says it,
who are these people?

All dispute is about this,
caste and religion continue to flourish!

The Night of Full Moon

Surendra Prasad Tarun

(Translated from the Magahi by Abhay K.)

Every part of the body, intoxicated with memories,
is burning without smoke.
This fragrant night of full moon,
Tonight is the night of the full moon.

Adorning the hair bun with the buds
of tuberose and night jasmine,
all are busy playing hide-and-seek
in the mango orchard.

Youthful and alive tonight,
in the sky the moon,
even her moon-like face looks dull.
Tonight is the night of the full moon.

Seeing the crowd of revellers,
music has gone missing,

priests are drowned in devotion,
poets are busy writing sweet lyrics.

Wine is flowing everywhere,
it is raining dew drops.
Tonight is the night of the full moon.

Far and wide in the fields and furrows,
paddy panicles are swaying,
the earth's forehead is glowing
with the blossoming flowers
of linseed and mustard.

An army of swinging
toddy palms is marching
in the winter of life.
Tonight is the night of the full moon.

Fish

Rajkamal Chaudhary

(Translated from the Maithili by Vidyanand Jha)

Kanhaiyaji broke into hysterical laughter and then spoke in an affectionate tone, just as Lord Hanuman spoke to Sita while giving her Lord Rama's ring in Ashok Vatika, 'Gadadhar Babu, no matter what, you can't find anything more beautiful than a Maithil[38] woman in any place, in any form. There is something special about the Maithil beauty and grace. Maithil freshness is not to be found elsewhere. I have travelled across India. I have seen Punjab; I have seen Kerala—'

Now, Gadadhar liked to argue. If you praised Malda mangoes before him, he would praise the Sinduria and Gulab Khas varieties. So, he cut Kanhaiyaji off and said, 'You have never been to Doctor K.K. Nambudiri's house, that's why you are talking rubbish like this. There is no comparison between the Maithil women—smelly, smeared in kajal, turmeric and vermilion—and Nambudiri's three daughters. The eldest is called Surbala, the middle one Madhubala and the youngest Jayabala. Come with me, Kanhaiyaji! All your presumptions about beauty will meet a grievous end when you see these three goddesses!'

38 People from the Mithila region of Bihar

Surbala, Madhubala, Jayabala—what poetic names! Kanhaiyaji was quiet after this.

The songs kept playing on Vividh Bharti radio channel. It was the month of January, but it was raining heavily that morning. People said that rains at this time were beneficial for the rabi crops. This would mean that the fields would turn green and a high yield of wheat crop could be expected. But what this rain meant for Kanhaiyaji and his bosom buddy and confidant, Gadadhar Jha, was that they had not gone to the college to teach that day. Instead, they were sitting in their shared apartment in Rajendra Nagar, Patna, discussing the physical attributes of Maithil women.

★

Gadadhar was married off when he was still in class eight, to fulfil the last wish of his father, who was suffering from complications related to opium consumption. He completed his bachelor's degree in English with a first class from Darbhanga and came to Patna. He sought admission at the university there and started staying in a hostel. Kanhaiyaji had been staying in the same hostel for the last three years. Friendship blossomed between the two. Around this time, Gadadhar was informed through a letter from his in-laws that his wife had passed away after drowning in the Kamla River during a flood. Gadadhar was untouched by this news. He was neither happy nor unhappy. There was neither joy, nor sorrow. But that day, for the first time, both the new friends bought a small bottle of whisky for five rupees and thirteen annas, and locked themselves in their room, guzzling the entire bottle after diluting it with some water. In the resulting exuberance both the friends took a vow: 'We will never ever, under any condition, get married.'

Kanhaiyaji was a bachelor anyway. Timid but academically bright, he always had some money on him and so he was quite popular amongst his friends. Kanhaiyaji and Gadadhar Jha, like a couple, were together most of the time. Both the friends loved movies and always sent congratulatory fan mails to their favourite heroines. Whenever they received a reply, they would go from one hostel to the other with the letter in their pockets.

Kanhaiyaji was extremely shy, like a touch-me-not (*mimosa pudica*) plant. He could talk about anything and everything with Gadadhar, but in the presence of others he became a saint who had taken a vow of silence. Gadadhar was the complete opposite. He was quite forthcoming in his interactions. Given his sense of humour, Gadadhar was well liked by women.

★

There was another reason, a special event, for Kanhaiyaji being an introvert. While studying as an undergraduate, Kanhaiyaji had been attracted to a female classmate, Gayatri Jha, who was unmarried. She was the daughter of Pashupati Jha, an advocate at the high court. Finding some excuse or other, Kanhaiyaji had visited Pashupati Babu's residence at Boring Road a few times. He would pay his respects to Gayatri's mother and take some Cadbury chocolates and lozenges for Gayatri's younger brothers. During one such visit, Gayatri had even told Kanhaiyaji, 'Why do you remain so serious? Do say something.'

But Kanhaiyaji hadn't said anything. Even his friends had tried to coax him into inviting Gayatri out for a movie, or to take her to Golghar, or to go for a long walk towards the airport road. But nothing had helped. Then, when Kanhaiyaji had gone to Patna again to seek admission in the master's course, he had found out that Gayatri had been married to a budding advocate from Patna High Court and that currently the newlyweds were visiting Darjeeling.

That was how the widower Gadadhar Jha and the unsuccessful lover Kanhaiyaji reached a point where they vowed to maintain ample distance from snakes, elephants, the police and women. Together, they had completed the two years master's programme and one year as lecturers.

These details were necessary to set the context and acquaint you, the reader, with the protagonists. It was also necessary to tell you how the two friends depended on each other when it came to their social and professional lives. Gadadhar Jha, of the English department, and Kanhaiyaji, of the Economics department, were always together. Be it choosing the members of the college senate, or participating in the processions taken out in honour of the principal or dignitaries visiting the college. All other lecturers were part of some clique based on religion, caste or political affiliations. The ones who didn't participate would either not get promoted or not be entitled to fringe benefits!

Gadadhar's and Kanhaiyaji's students had named their apartment in Rajendra Nagar 'bachelors' home'. The two had employed a maid called Patia, who visited twice a day to do the dishes, and a helper called Biltu. For some time now, Kanhaiyaji had been secretly studying the romance budding between Biltu, who was in the last of his teenage years, and the mature and jaded Patia who was in her early thirties. Gadadhar kept telling him, 'This is not appropriate. You shouldn't get involved in the affairs of the servants.'

'This is the topic of my study. I want to see how romantic feelings develop between illiterate people and between people from the lower castes. The aesthetic sense of the country bumpkins—' Kanhaiyaji had barely completed his sentence when he saw Patia coming towards them to serve tea.

Gadadhar got angry. In a serious tone, he said, 'But you are not a scholar of aesthetics. You are a teacher of Economics. You study how Patia looks after her five children and her drunkard husband by working in five houses from morning till night!'

Kanhaiyaji, meanwhile, would keep spying on Biltu, taking note of how he stowed away two pieces of meat and a bowlful of rice for Patia, how Patia had suggested to him that if he felt so cold, why didn't he ask the masters for an old coat? Kanhaiyaji would derive pleasure by tracking all these happenings. Lying under the quilt with a silk cover, listening to songs on the radio, reading an entertainment magazine or a book, he would spend most of his time in his room, lost in reverie.

★

One day, Gadadhar decided to take Kanhaiyaji to Dr Nambudiri's house. He hoped that all the preconceived notions—about beauty and talent, modernity and fashion, courtesy and affection—that were enjoying a comfortable existence in Kanhaiyaji's mind would disappear at the first glance of Surbala, Madhubala and Jayabala.

Why Gadadhar Jha was doing this now was because he wanted to break the vow of remaining a bachelor. He had realized the relevance of the saying: 'A house is incomplete without a woman.'

Gadadhar was of the opinion that young women from the southern part of the country were like the famous product from those parts: cardamom, which was called 'dakshini' in Maithili (or perhaps a 'yakshini'), beautiful and fragrant, better than the best.

But Kanhaiyaji said, 'My elder sister-in-law is from Krishnapur village in Darbhanga district. If at all I get married someday, it will be to a beautiful, angelic and polite young Maithili woman like her! If I can't get Gayatri, then some Savitri, Manorama, Kalyani, Nirupama...'

★

20 January 1966
7.00 p.m.

Pandit Ravi Shankar was playing sitar on the radio and Kanhaiyaji was sitting on one end of the sofa. Mrs Nambudiri had been there for some time, but she had now gone inside. Doctor Sahib was in Calcutta with his eldest daughter, Surbala; he was to return after a week. Gadadhar, with full attention, was trying to demonstrate his knowledge of music to the doctor's third daughter, Jayabala, by comparing the way Ravishankar and Vilayat Khan played the sitar. Madhubala, the second daughter, was looking at Kanhaiyaji. Ravishankar's sitar continued to provide background music; it was raag Malkauns. There were dreams in Madhubala's eyes, dreams in Kanhaiyaji's eyes, poems in their dreams and Mandakranta chhand[39] in the poems.

'*Chhand jodi mile jay, jibane thake dukh ki aar*?' The heroine of Rabindranath asks: 'If you find the metre, will there be anything missing in the poem of life?' There would be nothing lacking, no sorrows, no fears. Kanhaiyaji was creating a metre in his heart. It was a metre of the Maithili language, an unknown metre of an unknown body, with which he was trying to get acquainted with for the first time. And he was trying hard.

Never before in his life had he had a chance to hear the music of the beating heart of a coconut beauty from the distant land of Kerala. Never before had Kanhaiyaji received an invitation to gaze into the eyes of a rohu fish at such close quarters, with such clarity. He was quite young and inexperienced, too. Gadhadar Jha, meanwhile, was happy with his victory, seeing the amorous atmosphere and seeing Kanhaiyaji give an enchanted smile under the charm of these celestial maidens—a smile a person would have when standing on the crown of the hundred-headed Kaliya snake in an overflowing Yamuna.

Ali Akbar Khan's sarod started playing after Ravishankar's sitar. Another round of tea followed, after which Kanhaiyaji took out 555 cigarettes and a matchbox from his pocket. He was not a regular smoker, but he kept some in his coat pocket for special occasions—the costly cigarette came in handy to impress a senior professor, to establish his presence in a meeting.

Jayabala asked him, 'Do you like this cigarette a great deal?'

'No, not so much. But sometimes, to distract myself, I smoke one,' Kanhaiyaji replied, lighting one up, speaking bashfully as if responding to his elder sister-in-law. Jayabala was planning to appear for the

39 A slow metre

masters in Economics examinations next year as a private candidate. Kanhaiyaji was an Economics lecturer. So, to get to know him closely could prove useful for Jayabala. Shifting her attention from Gadadhar to Kanhaiyaji, she asked again, 'So what do you like to eat? And drink?'

If a question was posed, it must be answered. With this thought in his mind, Kanhaiyaji started to think about his favourite things. Gadadhar, meanwhile, replied, 'As a beverage, we like green tea, the one served at Prince Hotel.'

Kanhaiyaji replied shyly and said in a diffident tone, 'Nothing better than Coca-Cola for me! I end up drinking eight to ten bottles every day. But nowadays you don't get it very easily in Patna.'

Hearing this, Madhubala was quite excited. 'Even I am a fan of this drink! I, too, have had ten bottles in one go a few times. My mother gets quite angry, but for me there is nothing better than Coca-Cola. Not tea, nor sherbet.'[40]

Gadadhar and Jayabala, however, were tea lovers.

Kanhaiyaji kept blowing the scented smoke of the cigarette. Jayabala found more and more stories praising tea. Their conversation ranged from Coca-Cola to the wines of France and Italy. Sitting on the sofa, the four of them became quite close to each other. Gadadhar started planning in his head. If Kanhaiyaji would agree to get married to Madhubala, he would offer a varmala, the marital garland, to Jayabala. He was sure Doctor Nambudiri or his wife wouldn't have any objection. They were Brahmins from Kerala and the grooms were Brahmins from Mithila. Once again, there would be a meeting of souls between the families of Shankaracharya and Mandana Mishra. Gadadhar was seeing an old dream.

⋆

40 A drink made of sweetened fruit juices, diluted with water and served chilled

Due to the politicking among the doctors of Patna, Doctor Nambudiri's practice was almost non-existent. He was a gentleman, kind and modest. The patients, however, didn't look for proper treatment alone, they also looked at the paraphernalia of their doctor. Even if the doctor did not have any knowledge or experience, he needed to have a good car, a grand mansion, felicity in talking, two nurses and four compounders. But our Doctor Sahib was not adept at the art of advertisement and promotion. He was somehow making a living, managing to hide the holes of a tattered life. What would be more joyful for him than Jayabala and Madhubala getting married into good families!

Gadadhar was a practical person. He calculated that Jayabala had already finished her graduation and would complete her masters the following year. After that, she would get a job at any college. Both Jayabala and he would earn at least a thousand rupees a month. What else would they need? What else did one want from life? A beautiful wife, a well-furnished house, and a gainful and prestigious job. Nothing else. Gadadhar kept these calculations going in his mind while talking about food and drinks.

Then Madhubala said, 'We have talked enough about beverages! Tell us what is your favourite food? I mean, what dishes do you like the most?'

It seemed Jayabala had anticipated this question. She spoke out, 'Yes, Gadadhar Babu, tell us your favourite dish. One day we will have you over and serve the same dish. I like to cook and feed people. That's why my mother also calls me Draupadi—the wife of the Pandavas—who was a good cook. In our part of the country, people say that she was the one who first made Madrasi upma and Marathi shrikhand.'

Kanhaiyaji was delighted at hearing Draupadi's name. The wife of the five Pandavas, daughter of Drupad, protected by Lord Krishna, destroyer of Duryodhan and Dushasan. But Madhubala was not Draupadi, not from any angle. She was Radha Rani of Raslila, the celestial dance. He remembered the famous Vidyapati song: '*Dheere sameere Yamuna teere vasati vane vanamali*', which meant 'in the slow breeze, on the banks of the Yamuna, Vanamali[41] resides in the forest! Kanhaiyaji was overcome with emotions as a result of his fantasy of a job worth seven hundred rupees a month, including dearness allowance, a small bungalow in Rajendra Nagar and Madhubala cooking for him, making arrangements for tea and snacks, hosting friends, singing melodious songs like "*Radha Rani of Raslila*" … He had forgotten that he had vowed to not get married at all, or to marry only a Maithil girl. Gadadhar had been right, it was impossible to remain unaffected by Madhubala's charm. But, like the climactic deflection of all dramatic events, when Madhubala started talking about food for the third time, Gadadhar said, 'I love Bengali rasgulla the most!'

'I know how to make rasgullas! I shall serve you all next Sunday,' said Jayabala with childlike enthusiasm, clapping her hands as she stood up. All this while, Kanhaiyaji was contemplating what he should mention his favourite food item. *Should he tell the truth?* Kanhaiyaji loved the pieces from the middle fleshy portion of the rohu fish. In fact the primary reason for his visits back home during vacations was the fish cooked at home. He did not like the fish available in bazaars or restaurants. He only liked the rohu from the pond in his village, fried after being marinated in curd and turmeric paste, served with mustard curry!

★

'I like fish. There is no dish better than the rohu fish in this transient world. I am a Maithil Brahmin. For us, fish comes first and then comes chura-dahi.[42] There is no third thing!' Kanhaiyaji exclaimed.

Hearing this, both Jayabala and Madhubala looked at him with their eyes wide open, just like that of a rohu fish. Gadadhar Jha, dismayed at this turn of events, prompted Kanhaiyaji to change his decision. He hoped his friend would say something like rasgullas, shrikhand,

41 Another name for Lord Krishna
42 Curd and beaten rice flakes

upma, uttapam, sandesh or any other vegetarian dish. But Kanhaiyaji did not understand the entreaties of his friend. He was not aware that non-vegetarian food was considered a big taboo for south Indian Brahmins. And no matter how modern or fashionable Jayabala and Madhubala might be, they were daughters of a Brahmin from South India; they had probably never even heard about rohu!

'You may not know, but the cultural symbol of Mithila is the rohu fish! There is nothing more auspicious. If you happen to catch a glimpse of a rohu when you set off on a journey, you are bound to succeed. Both ancient and modern Maithili poetry have so many similes on the fish. Often the eyes, the body, or even the nature, of the female protagonist is compared to that of a fish!' Kanhaiyaji had launched into a non-stop discourse in praise of the fish.

Jayabala was staring at her sister. Madhubala was listening intently to Kanhaiyaji, looking at him with dreadful disbelief. Gadadhar Jha, totally devastated, was plotting how he could turn things for the better, how the camel could change its side. But no, the camel refused to budge. When talking about fish, Kanhaiyaji remained unmindful of everything else.

★

That day, after returning from Doctor Nambudiri's place, the first thing Kanhaiyaji did was to call Biltu. 'Go to Machuatoli and get a kilo of rohu. Tonight, I will have roti and fish. Where is Patia? Has she left for the day?'

Kanhaiyaji loved the fish Patia cooked. Whenever there was fish in the house, Patia would do the cooking. Only after eating four fried pieces of rohu separately and another eight in the curry would Kanhaiyaji feel satiated.

Gadadhar said, 'My great friend Kanhaiyaji, today's evening was in vain, absolutely futile due to your idiocy. What was the need to sing praises of the fish?'

Gadadhar's despondency had not ebbed. His heart was beating faster because of anxiety. He was worried that Jayabala would become disinterested in him just because of that incident.

Kanhaiyaji seemed to be unaffected. He answered, 'Between a fish and a lady, I would always put the fish first, Gadadhar Babu! You can get a woman to love even after death, in heaven—Urvashi, Menaka, Rambha, Tilottama, each more beautiful than the other. There will be many Madhubalas, each better than the other! But you won't get rohu fish there! That's why, all I desire in this life is fish and not a damsel with eyes like a fish!'

In the throes of his persisting anger and mental agony, Gadadhar Jha didn't eat any fish that night. Despite Kanhaiyaji beseeching him, he just had roti and alu sanna, a mash of potatoes, and went to sleep. Before falling asleep, he decided that he would inform Jayabala the very next morning that he had given up non-vegetarian food.

The next day, Gadadhar got ready before Kanhaiyaji and went to college alone. Kanhaiyaji felt hurt because of his friend's unexpected behaviour. Every day, both the friends shared an autorickshaw to go to college. They would have tea and samosas together at the Regal Hotel. Saddened, Kanhaiyaji didn't go to college that day. He sent his leave application through Biltu. He ate his meal all by himself—rice with the leftover fish from the previous night, and an alu-gobi[43] gravy—and fell asleep.

Kanhaiyaji had a divine dream during his afternoon sleep. He saw that he was in the midst of a deep sea, sitting on a swan-shaped boat with two beauties. Both the women were mermaids, their bodies below their waists resembled rohus!

★

43 Potato and cauliflower

After he woke up, Kanhaiyaji told Biltu, 'Please bring me a cup of tea quickly.'

Sometime later, Biltu brought a letter along with the tea. 'A servant of some Doctor Sahib just brought this.'

It was a letter from Madhubala, stating that she was learning to cook rohu from her neighbour, Chaudhariji's wife. She had invited Kanhaiyaji over the next Sunday to have the fish. After reading the letter, Kanhaiyaji closed his eyes. He dreamt the same dream again.

Babu

Kalam Haidari

(Translated from the Urdu by Syed Sarwar Hussain)

I finally returned home after being out since 7 a.m., feeling tired to death. Though the anxiety constantly weighing on my mind had nearly eased, the one that had now started pinning me down was stronger than what had been troubling me till now.

Well, it might just have been my foolishness.

Night had taken over. A quick glance at the watch told me it was past eleven. As I entered the house and called for the help, my wife woke up. A quick wash later, I settled down at the dining table.

When my wife asked me why I had returned home so late, I simply told her that it had been a hectic day. I did not mention the real reason and continued to eat.

Later, I couldn't get myself to sleep, despite turning and twisting several times in bed and being awfully tired.

To my great relief, the man had been caught! The crime for which he had been sent to jail would never allow him the freedom to set foot on my land again. He would be deported, if and when he was released. With his arrest under the Foreigners Act, I had finally managed to get rid of a huge load, which a chance encounter with him had suddenly put on my mind.

What horrible luck! I shuddered at the recollection. *Chance!* I had never imagined that after having spent a calm and respectful life of twenty years in the town, I would be left so horrendously shaken in a flash, that too by a mere trespasser.

A beautiful house with a well-tended lawn, a loving wife, three sons and a daughter, and the biggest garment factory in town—it had seemed as if all would be wiped away in one stroke. This had been an unexpected upheaval, especially after having lived a life of uninterrupted pleasure and contentment for twenty years!

The external signs of ageing had started showing in the white strands around my temples. No, I was not in the least willing to let anyone jolt my smooth life and steal my peace. Not now, not ever. So, I had fired my driver of ten years, because … because…

Well, it had all started with him, the driver. Not long ago, while driving me to the neighbouring town for an important assignment, he had asked for a week's leave as he was expecting his brother suddenly after a gap of almost two decades.

'Where is he coming from, this brother of yours?' I had asked him.

'I don't know, sir. He sent me a telegram from Calcutta, by the way.'

'Who is this brother who is suddenly coming now to see you after all these years?'

'I know nothing more about him, sir, except that he lived in Calcutta until I was ten years old. He was much older. I remember his wedding. And then he had suddenly disappeared. I never knew where he went and where he is coming from now.'

When I returned from my tour, the driver had already left.

A week later, having finished my breakfast, I was flipping through the morning newspaper on the verandah, when I saw him coming in with a stranger.

He saluted me. The stranger followed suit.

'Sir, this is my elder brother, Yaseen!'

I felt the driver's brother staring hard at me.

All at once it dawned on me that I was looking at a familiar face. In a matter of seconds, myriads of faces danced before my eyes and clouded my brain in confusion. And then, from that multitude emerged a face, slowly but clearly.

But ... but how ... how could it be possible?

I shifted uneasily in my chair and tried to remove from my eyes the face that was quite clear. I tried to fault my memory.

Yaseen! No, no, it can't be him.

'I have recognized you, babu,' said Yaseen.

I looked up at him. Yes, it was undeniably Yaseen. Whether I liked it or not, the face was there, in front of my eyes. It bore all the signs of ageing, but it was the same face.

A thought slithered into my mind. *What if he has recognized me*? I decided to vehemently deny knowing him. I was afraid I might have to pay a huge price if I recognized him. His startling appearance stirred unpleasant memories that were buried deep within the very fibre of my being, covered by the sands of time.

Yaseen's dramatic appearance summoned up those unfortunate days when I was living in a kholi[44] in a far-off corner of a big town. It is best to let it go unnamed. It was my second month in that locality, which was largely inhabited by the urban poor.

I was neither a rich globetrotter nor a freelance journalist who had agreed to live in a slum for the sake of the experience, only to leave the place after my short stint to write articles on the life there to earn a lot of money or fame.

The appalling adversities of life had compelled me to find lodging in that despicable shanty town. I had otherwise been living comfortably in a college hostel, enjoying pleasant dreams of a bright future. A fixed

44 A room or a small apartment

sum of money would reach me every month from home, and I had led a normal hostel life. I had completed my graduation and was pursuing my masters, dreaming passionately of a better life when … I was shocked to receive the news of my father's untimely death. Though the death was sudden, its general aspects were not entirely unusual. Many parents die as suddenly as my father did. And many people are forced, like me, to live the rest of their lives in chawls or slums.

My father had been an ordinary government servant. After he died, my mother started to live on her widow's pension. But there is a considerable difference between salaries and pensions, and you have to provide for the difference, which my father had not. Therefore, I had to move from the hostel to a kholi. The dull reality of the future of my two brothers and the marriage of my sister nested in my mind, where once golden dreams flitted.

Often in my kholi, I lay awake at night, lost in thoughts. *Where has life brought me*? *Where is it going to take me from here*?

I got up early every morning and looked out of the bedroom window to see people from my block crowding around the roadside municipal water tap, which was used as an open bath. A row of buckets and pitchers lined the place. *Who would fill his pitcher or bucket first?* Spats and quarrels arose from every direction. In the midst of that verbal mayhem, I would often appear with my lungi and towel. The moment the squabbling creatures saw me, their fights and sneers would magically disappear. They would stand on one side and clear space for me.

'Make way! Babu is coming to wash himself!'

'Babu gets first priority!'

I do not know who first gave me the honorific title of 'babu', but that was how I was mostly addressed there. I was honoured with that epithet every day when I visited the public bath. I could not think of responding to their respectful greeting in any other way except leaving after a quick bath. And the moment I left, the brawls and abuses that had halted momentarily resumed with renewed speed and vigour.

I have always followed certain lifestyle habits, which was why I was considered a serious and humourless fellow among my friends. The insolent among them considered me asocial and unwise.

My father's death had added another layer of seriousness to my disposition. In such a stressful situation, I regarded the kholi as the most suitable place to disengage myself from all worldly temptations and lead a sequestered life.

In the beginning, I felt that I could not stay among those people for long. But the respect and admiration with which they treated me convinced me that they would not be an obstacle for me.

I, nevertheless, had to pay for that respect and admiration in a different manner. Most of the inhabitants of that locality came to me to get their postcards, letters and money order papers read and written. Starting with one or two, it grew into a fairly large number queuing outside my room every day. Distressed by their unannounced appearances without any care or concern for my time, I fixed one day in the week for them: Sunday. In keeping with the schedule I had set, on Sundays, my neighbours would patiently queue outside my room, as if standing outside the government ration shop.

I read their letters and wrote their replies, one at a time, and it never took me less than two hours to finish the entire business.

On one such Sunday evening, after finishing my weekly community service, I had my dinner and went off to sleep early. I don't know how much time had passed when I was suddenly awakened by a loud knock. I jumped out of bed, half asleep, and lurched forward to open the door. A young man, one of my regular Sunday visitors, shot into the room like an arrow.

'Babu!' he exclaimed and turned towards the door to latch it from inside. He then pushed the suitcase he was carrying under my bed.

'I have a gunshot wound … here!' He bared his left shoulder. A thin, ragged gamcha was tied around it.

'A gunshot! Arey! How did it happen, Yaseen?' I asked him nervously.

'Don't worry, babu! It's only a pellet or two. I'm afraid I will get caught if I stay here longer.'

'What's the matter?'

'I'm in a great hurry, babu. I can't tell you anything now. Please keep my suitcase. I'll come and take it away tomorrow. No one will bother you.'

And then, before I could think or say anything, he dashed out of the room.

I returned to my bed and was on edge for the rest of the night. Sleep evaded me.

Who could trust people like Yaseen? He might have burgled a house. Or he might have quarrelled with someone and had now gone into hiding for fear of reprisals. Or…

What I knew about him was only this: he worked in a lock-manufacturing factory and lived in a kholi in the same block as mine with his wife, to whom he was only recently married.

The suitcase under my bed was worrying me. I tried to push all alarming thoughts out of my mind and sleep. But between me and my sleep were two impenetrable barriers: Yaseen and the suitcase.

And then, I don't know how and when, I drifted into deep sleep. When I woke up in the morning, it was 7 a.m.

The suitcase under my bed suddenly suggested itself to me. I came out of my room, looked around and walked ahead. I could see Yaseen's kholi just a few feet away. The door was ajar, wide enough for me to see inside. It was empty. Outside, men and women had gathered and were talking about the mysterious disappearance of Yaseen and his wife. Some said he had crossed over the border on the east, looking for better opportunities in the country of his co-religionists. Others said he and his wife had been eliminated by a dreaded mafia boss.

I rushed back to my room, pulled the suitcase from under the bed and opened it. My eyes flew open in shock and surprise. It was filled with bundles of hundred-rupee notes. Three, four, five lakh, and more…

I quickly resolved to leave the kholi quietly with all my belongings and the suitcase. I moved to another town, the place where I am now living.

Deliverance

Lalit

(Translated from the Maithili by Vidyanand Jha)

It's not like my strong streak to wander aimlessly does not exasperate me. It does. I do get angry. But that's that. The good sense returns afterwards. I can't sit quietly; it makes me feel as if I am sick. Whenever I get a reprieve, I desperately want to go out somewhere. I can't resist the temptation of spending a week or a few days in a far-off place, usually at a place of pilgrimage. *Why a place of pilgrimage?* I get a great sense of joy from spending time in the midst of a variety of people, people with myriad faces, people from peasant families from remote places. It gives me a sense of freedom. There's no hurry to start at ten thirty in the morning. There's no anxious wait for four in the afternoon.

Under the influence of this wandering streak, I found myself at the Baidyanathdham Temple during the Durga puja holidays. I was staying at a local priest's house. Like a tree offering shade by the roadside, they are the only refuge in a place of pilgrimage. They are almost duty-bound to provide boarding and lodging to pilgrims.

I didn't have anything to do; so I just wandered around the whole day. In the morning, the sun was tolerable even as late as 8 or 9 a.m. with strong and slightly chilly westerly winds. All around, the undulating landscape of the rocky earth was decorated with trees and creepers. It filled me with a sense of abandon. With no specific purpose, I went about aimlessly. When I got tired of walking, I returned to my temporary dwelling. The thought of spending time in solitude, away from the noisy atmosphere of my joint family, filled my heart with happiness.

That day, when I returned to where I was staying and lay down on my bed, I felt like I would die of exhaustion. Then I detected some movement from the neighbouring room, which had been vacant since I had come. *Must be some new pilgrims.* But I was so tired that I didn't get up to meet my new neighbour. After a little rest, I felt hungry. Locking my room, I turned around and saw a young woman sitting in the verandah. She had a wheatish complexion and big eyes. Her hair was tousled from the journey. She was gazing at the white clouds in the sky, floating like the autumn leaves with the westerly wind. A shadow of despair was visible on her face. She was beautiful and healthy, with long arms. Dressed in a blue blouse with simple sleeves and a plain coloured saree without any print or border, she didn't look any less than a goddess. She may have been around sixteen or seventeen and was married. It was a grave sin to even steal a glance at a married woman, but driven by desire I couldn't control my temptation to look at her longingly. Her attention was drawn to me. The sadness vanished from her face when she saw a stranger staring at her. She looked at me with a frown. Then she got up and went to her room, glaring at me with her brows knitted. I was embarrassed. While going back to her room, her ear studs glinted. I also caught a glimpse of her pointed bosom. Lost for a while, I started going down the stairs with my head bowed. At that moment, I heard the light coughing of a sick person from that room.

When I was near the gate, the doorman, Chaube ji, called out to me, 'Going for your meal? Have you got some chewing tobacco?'

'No, I am going to eat right now.' I was quite irritable. Chaubeji was the caretaker of the house; fair-complexioned with a muscular physique and a well-kept moustache. He was around thirty years old, a philanderer, and fluent in Bangla, Hindi and Maithili. He belonged to some place near Mathura and had come all the way, leaving behind his family, in search of a livelihood. We often used to share chewing tobacco.

The woman's forehead with the black tikuli,[45] her glistening ear studs and pointed bosom kept lingering in my mind. Sometimes I would get angry with the wayward depravity of my mind, but so what? *Does the mind accept restraints easily?*

When I returned after having my meal, I sat down with Chaubeji. After chewing some tobacco, I felt lighter and asked him, 'Who are these neighbours of mine?'

'Oh, they are also from your district. That young woman's husband is sick. They came for a change of weather.'

'Who all are there?'

'Just three of them. The couple and a servant. See, that is the servant.'

When I followed his gaze, I saw a well-built man of around fifty climbing the stairs carefully, balancing a small bucket of water.

After some idle chatter, I headed towards my room. When I got there, my eyes automatically went towards the next room. On one side was a bed on the floor. On it, an ailing young man with a pale pallor was sitting cross-legged. The young woman was passing peeled oranges to him. For a moment, our eyes met—the young man's and mine—and the next moment he beckoned me with his eyes and a nod.

Before I could decide what to do, I was standing in the middle of that room. The young woman pulled at her saree to cover her head a little more and kept peeling the oranges.

Pointing towards one portion of the bed, the young man said, 'Please sit.'

The mattress was quite thick and seemed costly. The way the man was dressed—the leather suitcase in the corner, some books on the

45 Dot

suitcase—indicated that they surely belonged to a well-to-do, if not wealthy, family. The young man was good-looking but had a pallid complexion and also seemed to carry the weight of extreme weariness on his face, one that was borne out of long illness.

Puckering his lips, he spat out the orange seeds and calmly asked me in Maithili, 'Where are you from?'

I was surprised that he even knew I was a Maithil.

'Chanpura.'

'Basaith Chanpura?'

'Yes. And what about you?'

'Dadhia Manikpur,' he said, spitting out some more seeds in a corner. 'Sometime back, I fell ill. I still am. The doctor has advised me a change of weather. I thought, what could be a better place than the shelter of Lord Mahadeva.'

Which disease? I thought to myself. *I hope it's not phthisis. That's quite contagious. And how close am I sitting to him!* I started to breathe slowly, my panicky nature surfacing.

Seeing me stare at him strangely, he perhaps figured out what was on my mind. He said, 'It's a sickness of the digestive tract. Sometime back, I had a bout of dysentery. I took a lot of care, but the disease turned chronic—'

'Why do you lie, Beeso? Would we have landed in such a far-off place like this, leaving our home, if you had taken care of yourself?' For the first time, the servant spoke from the corner while rubbing chewing tobacco on his palm.

The next moment, deterred by the fiery gaze of the young woman, he went back to his tobacco.

When the young man turned to the other side to drink water, I stole another glance at the young woman. She was listlessly looking at the emaciated body of her lanky husband. Suddenly, she looked at me. For a moment, her eyes looked impenetrable. But the next moment, the same frown and the angry eyes returned!

After drinking water, Beeso Babu felt some relief. He spoke to me. 'She wants me to get myself admitted to a hospital, but I don't feel like it. To be around your own people is more reassuring. And on top of that, I have never stayed in a hospital before.'

He looked at me, as if seeking succour.

I, too, offered him encouragement. 'Yes, why should you get hospitalized? You are healthier among your own people. You have the freedom to be on your own. You can move around—'

'That's what I say,' Beeso Babu said with a bit of excitement.

His wife stared at me, as if chiding me for speaking out of turn.

The servant, giving final touches to the chewing tobacco, said, 'But here you aren't following the regimen.'

'Kunjia, please bring a paan for sir,' Beeso Babu told the servant.

'Why? We already have some chewing tobacco,' I said.

'Oh, you have chewing tobacco?'

I nodded and took my share of the tobacco. I noticed some of the books and monthly magazines kept on the leather suitcase. They included *Paro* by Yatri, *Shesha Prashna*, *Vipradasa*, *Pather Dabi* and *Charitraheen* by Sarat Chandra Chattopadhyay.

I took their leave and lay down after returning to my room.

The next day, I came to know that Beeso Babu had been admitted to a hospital. Only the wife and the middle-aged servant Kunjia were around.

I was looking out of my window in the evening, when I saw the young woman in the same squatting posture, with the same shadow of despair on her face. But this time her eyes were a bit restless. When I followed her gaze, I saw that she was looking below at Chaubeji. He was sweeping the verandah in front of his room. He wasn't wearing anything above his waist and had only a narrow towel wrapped around him. His fair exercised body, his shapely thighs and thick calf muscles were on display. *Was she checking him out?*

At that moment, I don't know why, she turned towards my window. Her face reddened when she saw me looking at her, as if she had been caught. But within a moment, her frowning brows returned. She gave me a look of disdain and went into her room.

I felt ashamed. *Am I worse than even a caretaker? Don't I look good?* I examined my face in the mirror. It looked fine to me.

Over the next few days, I became close to Kunjia due to our shared habit of chewing tobacco.

One day, the young woman went to seek darshan of Lord Mahadeva. Kunjia told me about the family while preparing chewing tobacco. A habitual talker, he spilled the beans. 'I have served three generations of this family. I first began by looking after their cattle when Beeso Babu's grandfather was alive. I looked after his father, too, when he was a child. And then I brought up Beeso Babu. He was only twelve when his father passed away. As he lay dying, he told me, "Kunjia, please look after Beeso."

'Since then, I have given my life for this family. I am one of the few people Beeso listens to. The family has plenty—fifty acres of land, a pond, a bamboo grove and an orchard. By God's grace, nothing is lacking. But they don't have anybody to enjoy these with.'

Taking a deep breath, he continued, 'Now I only wish to hold Beeso's child in my arms before I die. But it is solely in the hands of Bhole Baba.'[46]

'What afflicts him?' I asked.

'He has been sick since the time I have known him. He has always had poor digestion. When he was five years old, he had to be put on a fruit diet for two years. Later, his condition improved. But then he went away to Muzaffarpur to study. He didn't eat properly there and again fell sick.'

'Is he educated?'

46 Another name for Lord Shiva

'Yes. He was studying for his Bachelor of Arts degree. But when his condition worsened, I brought him home.'

'And his wife?'

'Oh, sir, didn't you notice those books? They belong to her. She is addicted to them. Sometimes even the master reads them, but mostly it's her.'

Extending a pinch of chewing tobacco towards me, Kunjia said, 'But, sir, she doesn't have any of the airs of an educated person. None. She is alone in the household. No mother-in-law or sister-in-law to help her. She looks after all the affairs of the family, the food regimen of the master and everybody else.'

'So, tell me, if she has so much self-control, do they get along well?'

'Don't even talk about that, sir,' the servant took his tongue out and nodded. 'She does everything single-handedly and still doesn't leave a single ritual or fast for the well-being of the master. Today is Tuesday, isn't it? She is fasting again.'

'That's commendable.'

'And, sir,' he stretched to spit in the drain and then spoke, 'it has been three years since they got married. But what good does marrying a sick person do?'

Saying this, the servant hesitated a bit, as if he had said something untoward. He immediately changed the subject. 'She comes from a very poor family. They are sustained by my master's family.'

By this time, the young woman had returned, freshly bathed, with her hair untied. She was wearing a white saree and holding the ritual water vessel in her hand.

The servant got up in a jiffy. For the last ten days, I had only had uncooked food. I felt like eating some cooked food. The terrible desire to cook myself sprang up within me.

When I started lighting the hearth after organizing all the ingredients, I felt it was too much. I felt angry at my idiocy. *I could have just eaten at a restaurant by paying twelve annas. But what's the use of that thought now?*

At that moment, the woman came and stood in the doorway and told me with a bemused smile: 'Why do you want to burn your hands? I am going to cook. You can come and eat.'

She went away without waiting for an answer. I had seen her smiling for the first time. For a moment, I felt exhilarated. But then I remembered her words, 'Come and eat.' As if I were a low-category Brahmin who went around eating everywhere. Such an ill-mannered woman! I got very angry. *Oh, I wouldn't eat her food.*

After almost an hour, when Kunjia came to fetch me for the meal, the word 'no' refused to come out of my mouth.

When I reached her room, I saw a small mat spread out on the floor for me. Scrubbed clean, a bell-metal lota and bowl were laid out for me. I washed my feet and sat down. The lady of the house gently placed the thali in front of me with aromatic kanak jeera rice, alu dum,[47] parwal bhujia and rahari lentils seasoned with hot ghee. My ten days' worth of hunger for cooked food was awakened.

After eating two or three morsels, I looked towards the bed. *Shesha Prashna* lay open.

I was curious. *What fine taste must this woman have to read such books? Does she understand their deeper meaning, or does she read them only for their intriguing plot?*

To initiate small talk, I asked, 'Do you read all these books?'

'Yes, when I get time.'

'How did you like *Shesha Prashna*?'

'Very nice,' her answer was quite short.

'And the character of Kamal?' I asked without any premeditation.

She stared at me as if I had humiliated her. I froze. To save myself further embarrassment, I asked, 'He … how long has he been sick?'

47 Potato curry

But that question made things worse. A shadow of despondency clouded her serious face. After remaining motionless for a moment, she asked, 'Shall I give you some more parwal bhujia?' And then she dropped a handful in my thali.

After that, I finished my lunch without any more conversation.

When I got up after eating, the servant was standing with long pieces of artistically cut betel nut, cardamom and saunf in a small plate. I took some of that, and also some chewing tobacco, and went back to my room.

After this incident, I had hoped that I would get another chance to further my acquaintance with my neighbour. But the opposite happened. It wasn't that we didn't cross paths. We did—at the ghat, in the temple, in the bazaar—but she wouldn't even look at me.

I noticed another change. Chaube, the caretaker, was often with her. In the temple, at the ghat, in the bazaar. He even accompanied her when she carried food to her husband.

Chaube also started avoiding me. I knew that womanizer quite well, and was perturbed. I started to worry. *How long could Savyasachi of* Pather Dabi *or Kamal of* Shesha Prashna *save this cursed goddess?*

One day, when I was returning after my wanderings from Karainibad, I saw that Chaube and the young woman were seated in a tonga and going somewhere. Chaube didn't look into my eyes, but my gaze met hers. Suddenly, I asked, gesturing with my eyes, 'Where are you going?'

She gave me a look of disgust, as if asking me how I could be so bold as to enquire about them.

Humiliated, I returned to my room. I was quite tired … and deeply hurt … and full of many ill thoughts. But as soon as I lay in bed, I almost instantaneously fell into a deep slumber.

When I woke up, it was quite late in the evening. My body felt quite weak. Suddenly, I heard hushed voices from the next room. Given the accent, it seemed it was Chaube. I was astonished. I put on my chappals and came out of my room. As I reached the other room, Chaube came out.

Seeing me, Chaube's face turned pale. In a dry voice, he said, 'I had a message from the lady's husband. I came here to give it to her.'

I was enraged at Chaube. I felt like taking him into my fist and crushing him to dust. I gave him a little shove on the right shoulder. He winced.

'Chaube, you are too proud of your well-built body. Don't forget that you won't be able to bear another jab. You know this well,' I said. Chaube stood like a lifeless statue for some time and then went away.

I am not a wrestler, but I am strong and tall. One day, looking at my body, Chaube mistook me for a wrestler. He challenged me to a contest. I pulled my dhoti up a bit and stood firm. He was changing stances. I didn't think too much, just held him tightly, lifted him up and dropped him with a thud. He was hurt. He kept lying down for a long time. For a whole week, he applied a poultice of turmeric and lime on his knees.

After impressing Chaube, I looked at the young woman, overjoyed with my victory and thinking that even she would have been impressed. There was a lantern burning in the room. She was looking at me with eyes bereft of any emotions.

'All this with a stranger!' I said to her, the words tumbling out of my mouth.

'You shouldn't get too involved in others' problems, take this lesson from me,' she said.

'Indeed.'

'Uncouth man.'

And then she slammed the door shut. I was lucky that my nose got saved. Had I not been watchful and moved back a little, my nose would have been flattened. *Think of it, how proud my sharp nose looks! Now, imagine me as a person with a flat nose.*

I was angry at myself. *What is it to me? Let her run away with anybody. I don't give a damn. I am getting humiliated for no good reason by getting into this mess.*

Angry, I headed out to eat. The servant met me on the road. Blocking my way, he said in a tone of urgency, 'Sir, my master would like to see you at the hospital immediately.'

Still enraged, I turned him away with a wave of my hand. 'I don't care for any master of yours. You should stop your master's wife, the way she is so shamelessly indulging in an affair with Chaube. This family has done you so many favours. You must be true to your salt.'

I walked ahead, but the servant didn't leave me alone. He followed me, saying, 'That's why I am here. I can't tolerate this. I don't know what has happened to the lady. It is as if that bastard has done some black magic on her. I have never seen anything like this before. I have surely grown old, but even now I am capable of tackling four people like Chaube all by myself. God has ordained his ruin through my hands. I couldn't tolerate such shamelessness unfolding before my eyes any longer, so I told the master everything. But he doesn't believe me.'

'What did he say?'

He said, 'Kunjia, if somebody becomes bed-ridden owing to prolonged illness like this, how long can you stop her?'

'He has a point.'

'No, sir, no. We can't figure out his emotions, whether he is happy or sad. He keeps things to himself. When I kept on cajoling him to do something, he asked me to call you.'

'Listen, Kunjia, I don't want to put myself in an unpleasant situation by interfering in the affairs of your master and his wife. It's up to your master, whether he wishes to keep her locked in a snuff box or leave her free to enjoy the hill breeze. It's his wish. I don't want to get embroiled in this mess.'

'Please, sir.'

'You may go back, servant.'

I didn't feel like returning to the room after dinner. I thought of watching a movie. *Awaara* was playing in the cinema hall. I had seen it before and got bored watching it. By chance, the projector developed some snag around the interval. I got irritated and left. I came back to my room, found the bed in the darkness and fell asleep.

I got up quite late the next morning. Once my eyes opened, I saw that the sunlight had spread on the roof. But, in the next room, people were talking loudly.

Out of curiosity, rubbing my eyes, I went to the other room. I saw an exhausted Beeso Babu sitting in the middle of the room. The local priest was saying something very loudly. Beeso Babu beckoned to me. I went inside and sat on the bed. Kunjia was squatting on the ground with a look of weariness on his face.

'So, you woke up just now?' Beeso Babu asked me with a hint of a smile.

'Yes, I returned a bit late last night.'

'Give him some chewing tobacco, Kunjia.'

The priest started talking again. 'Sir, where can they run away to? I will send somebody immediately to Jasidih railway station. And we will report it to the police.'

'Panditji,' Beeso Babu said, 'I detest all this. You can go.'

'But, sir,' the priest seemed to beseech Beeso Babu.

'You may go, please.'

The priest left.

I had already caught a whiff of the scandal. Lightning had struck. A shocked look on his face, Beeso Babu pointed towards the servant. 'Please take some chewing tobacco.'

I turned around. The chewing tobacco was ready. Kunjia's palm was stretched out towards me. I didn't feel like taking the tobacco, yet I took a pinch and placed it between my lower lip and tongue.

'Beeso, why didn't you let the police register a complaint? We have been disgraced.' Kunjia's eyes were full of tears.

Lying flat on his pillow, Beeso Babu spoke with his eyes closed. 'Kunjia, your mistress got deliverance from the duty of looking after me, a lifelong patient. Why would you become an obstruction in somebody's deliverance? The first need of a woman, more than anything else, is a healthy man.'

Then he looked at me and asked, 'Don't you agree?'

I was speechless. *This person's wife ran away last night with the caretaker. And with such great calmness, he is propounding philosophical precepts. He is smiling such a beatific smile.* I couldn't get over the cheer on his colourless face.

He took out a folded chit from under the pillow and held it out towards me. When I opened it, I saw some lines written in a feminine handwriting:

My master!

It's true that I am leaving you right now … but if I get restless at any point to come back to you, then I hope you would still be open to taking me back.

Shefali

I kept the letter down. Beeso Babu spoke quietly, as if responding to the letter, 'You know me so well. Then what was the need to write all this? Yes, I may not be there till that time, though.'

Then, as if he had escaped his thoughts, he said, 'Kunjia, please pack our things!'

The servant said with great unease, 'So you will go … and your health?'

'Health, huh? The one for whom I wanted to get well is gone. But it's impossible for Chaube to hold back such an intelligent person for long.

She will surely return, but then I will still be sick.' After this, he became quiet. A dark smile played on his pale face.

He looked at me and said, 'Please get on with your morning rituals. And please come at the time of our departure.'

Without saying anything, I ran back to my room and crashed on to my bed. I felt like crying. I don't know why I was so distressed. I started counting the beams of the roof. Around 10 a.m., Kunjia came. With a mournful voice, he said, 'My master is leaving. He has called for you. No one knows what Lord Mahadeva ordains.'

When I went out, Beeso Babu was already seated in a tonga. He was wearing a green shirt. When I went near him, he took my hands in his own and spoke softly. 'I don't know why, but I have started feeling as if you are my friend. I am going now. Though life is very short, just a long step from cradle to grave, it seems endless because people don't know the time of their death. It's possible that we will meet again. If you feel like having alu dum made by her, please come over after six months. My village is just by the side of the railway station.'

Then he became quiet and spoke after a few minutes. 'If she misbehaved with you in any manner last evening, I am sorry for that.'

I was surprised. *How did he know about that incident?*

Probably taking note of my expression, he said, 'Sick people's bodies are weak, but all the inactivity during sickness makes their imagination sharper! What other reason could there be for you not turning up last evening despite me calling you? Well, goodbye, friend.'

The tonga went away.

I didn't even have the presence of mind to respond to his goodbye. I kept looking at it as the tonga rode away into the distance. Then, when it took a turn, he waved once again. That's when I came back to my senses. I folded both my hands in response and touched them to my forehead.

A year has passed since this incident. I have had no news of Beeso Babu. I think I should visit his house during the summer vacation.

Today's Yudhishthir

Ravindra Kumar

Translated from the Magahi by Abhay K.

They were also five brothers like the Pandavas in the Mahabharata. They were even their namesakes—Yudhishthir, Bhim, Arjun, Nakul and Sahdev. Whether these names were given to them by their parents or if they had given themselves these names is not known. All brothers were close-knit. They'd seen better days, but now lived in poverty. They had two-and-a-half bighas of land in all. They were all hard working, and therefore had enough to make ends meet. After much toil, they had managed to buy a buffalo, whose milk earned them a little money. The green revolution had swept over the rest of the nation, but their fields remained dry and barren. If it rained, they would raise some crops; otherwise drought was a regular visitor. Lord Indra decided whether the seeds sown would thrive or if the brothers would be compelled to cut muar.[48]

One evening, the buffalo did not return to her shed. Everybody thought she must have lost her way, and will be back after some

48 Paddy crop without the grains

time. But it was getting dark. Clouds of foreboding began to darken Yudhishthir's mind.

Did some enemy take away the buffalo?

Yudhishthir sent Sahdev to look for the buffalo. It was getting dark. Sahdev did not return.

It was Nakul's turn to go now. He did not return either. It was already late.

Arjun and Bhim were also sent one by one to look for the buffalo. None came back.

Now Yudhishthir started getting restless too. How long could he stay calm? He left home to look for the buffalo.

The first place where he searched was near the pond. He looked carefully but did not find the buffalo there. Perhaps she had strayed into the nearby village…

He kept walking. He must have travelled one or two kos, asking the people he met on the way about his buffalo. None had seen her.

It was a full moon night. There was no difficulty in walking. However, the question was, where should he go? Disappointed, he thought of turning back. But it was his duty to look for his brothers as well. What would people say? With these thoughts coursing through his head, he kept going forward. He was thirsty too.

He came upon a village. He thought of all the free electricity the village enjoyed. He decided to ask the inhabitants for a *lota*[49] of water, and to enquire about the buffalo.

Seven–eight people were sitting on the outskirts of the village. Approaching them, he saw his buffalo sitting with them, masticating. He was shocked! He also spotted his four brothers lying motionless on the ground.

He was not ready for this eventuality. Just then, he heard a voice.

---

49 Jar

'Do you recognize me? Once, my cow had strayed into your village. Perhaps she was grazing in your field. These four brothers of yours had assaulted two of my brothers, and had beaten them black and blue with their lathis.[50] You had finally intervened and let go of my brothers and the cow, saying that my brothers had not set the cow loose deliberately to graze in the field. It was not my brothers' fault that our cow had strayed. You're wise. So, I'm letting you go. Otherwise we also have this ...' Saying this, the man took out a revolver from his pocket and brandished it.

'Even now, your brothers are not dead. They have been dealt with only sticks and whips so far. They bled a little too much and therefore lost consciousness. I will ask you five questions. If I like your answers to four questions, I'll allow you to take the buffalo. And if you can answer all the five questions to my satisfaction, I will get your brothers loaded in the bullock cart too. You can get them treated by the Block's doctor.'

Yudhishthir started pondering what to do. Any show of strength would not work. It was better to take a chance and try to answer the questions. The conversation between the two men went thus:

'First question: who are the people closest to us?'

'People of our caste, who else? Daughter and vote are not given to people of other castes. This is the law of democracy.'

Everyone sitting in the alcove erupted in unison: 'Wah, wah!'

'Second question: which is the heaviest burden?'

'An unmarried young daughter. All our properties may be sold to lift this weight from our shoulders.'

The others shouted their appreciation for the answer again.

'Third question: which is the best game?'

'The game of kidnapping someone. If you kidnap a wealthy person and ask for a huge ransom, you get lots of money. Ninety per cent

50 Heavy, sturdy sticks

players win this game … As they grow, they may even form a gang, then fix a percentage for everyone—from the sentry to the minister. Dare anyone touch you after that? Take a little risk and get rich. Newspapers will get the matter to print news. The government and the police will get a little maligned. The police will issue a statement: "The matter is being actively pursued. The criminals will be apprehended soon." Then some deal making, and the matter will be over soon enough.'

The man proceeded to ask the fourth question. It was evident that the answer to the third question was liked by everyone.

'Yes, now the fourth question: who is the most powerful?'

'The one who does not fear death. Look at Ram Khelawan. He is a minister today. Who was he earlier? A thief. Initially, he kept hiding because of the fear of getting caught by the police. Later, he made a gang and became adept at playing with danger. He took on the responsibility of getting MLAs elected. He ensured their victory with the power of the barrel. He made a lot of money in this pursuit. Then one day he too contested an election and won. First an MLA and then he became a minister. Earlier, he used to be scared of the police, but now the same police protect him. He let go of his fear; that's why he could become a powerful person.'

Evidently, everyone was enchanted by Yudhishthir's explanation.

'The fifth question now: what is the most compelling, *true* nature of man?'

'I hope I've answered the first four questions to your satisfaction.'

Everyone said in unison: 'Yes, brother, yes.'

'I don't wish to answer the fifth question. All of you have given me your word that if you find my answers to your four questions satisfactory, you'll let me take the buffalo.'

Yudhishthir untied the buffalo and left, taking his buffalo with him. Everyone was shocked.

On the way, Yudhishthir pondered over his decision: *I could have answered the fifth question as well. The true nature of man is his own self-interest, what else? If the answer to this question were found satisfactory, I would have been obliged to take back my brothers as well. Then I'd have had to make arrangements for their treatment, which would have meant arranging for lots of money. I would have had to borrow money, and part with my buffalo as well. Who knows if my brothers would have survived or died? If they die, the two-and-a-half bigha of farmland would not have to be divided.*

Bereavement

R. Ishari Arshad

(Translated from the Magahi by Abhay K.)

Bhole Baba, accept the water of the holy Ganges,
take away the pangs of bereavement.
I know why you drink bhang
and take dhatura.
I know why you invoke the ghouls
and wear the necklace of a cobra.

Accept the water of the holy Ganges, Bhole Baba,
take away the pangs of bereavement.
I know why you let loose your hair
and crown the moon on your head.
I know why you sit on the Bash-ha[51] bull
and bear the Ganga on your head.

Accept the water of the holy Ganga, Bhole Baba,
take away the pangs of bereavement.

---

51 Nandi Bull, the carrier of Lord Shiva

I know why you wield the trident
and carry the kamandal.[52]
I know why you blow the conch
and have your phallus worshipped.

Accept the water of the holy Ganges, Bhole Baba,
take away the pangs of bereavement.
Now the Ganges will not be lone,
she will be one with Bharat.
Her locks will interlace with the gods',
she will bless Mount Kailash.[53]

Accept the water of the holy Ganges, Bhole Baba,
take away the pangs of bereavement.
The king of Lanka walks away lifting you,
your brother beseeches you with folded hands.
Don't move even an inch, don't leave Kailash,
the lord of Lanka comes to heaven's gate.

Accept the water of the holy Ganges, Bhole Baba,
take away the pangs of bereavement.
My eyes are thirsty for you,
I have brought the water of the holy Ganges,
don't keep Ishari thirsty now.

Accept the water of the holy Ganges, Bhole Baba,
take away the pangs of bereavement.

---

52 An oblong water pot
53 Abode of Lord Shiva

A Song of Sorrow

Harishchandra Priyadarshi

(Translated from the Magahi by Abhay K.)

Leaving behind everything,
I had come to the banks of the Ganges.

The night was awake,
the currents of the Ganges strong

This side, her bank,
a pyre lit with life's betrayals.

Brimming with love and affection,
a proud married woman.

Away from her friends,
her eyes welled up with tears.

That frenzied night on the banks of the Ganges,
it was pitch-dark, only a circle of fire glowed.

There was no way out, I was lonely
among the crowd, no zeal to live.

Each dream burnt to cinders, each endeavour failed,
that star-crossed night on the banks of the Ganges.

A Hindu Parrot

Pandey Surendra

(Translated from the Bhojpuri by Gautam Chaubey)

Dusk had fallen. A parrot flew on to the verandah and perched on the clothes line. When Reshma saw the bird, she wrapped a stole around her palm, took care to make no noise, and grabbed it with one swift move. A triumphant shriek followed; one that drew everyone at home out to the verandah. The kids were ecstatic at the sight; they pranced all around the parrot. Badi Bi examined it carefully and issued a few instructions: 'Rasool, put some ointment on the bird. The crows have poked at it with their sharp beaks. Rahim, bring down the egg basket. We'll keep it in it till a cage is arranged.'

Muravvat Miyan was sent to the market to get a birdcage. Meanwhile, efforts were made to ensure the parrot was as comfortable as possible in its temporary home. An earthen bowl was filled with water and placed in the egg basket. Salma ran to the backyard and returned with a freshly plucked guava. That, too, was shoved in. Badi Bi's four grandchildren huddled near the basket, intently observing each little antic of the bird. The parrot seemed to be really thirsty. As it drank hastily from the bowl, the kids broke into loud, wonder-filled laughter.

Within an hour, Muravvat returned with the purchase. The bird was transferred to its new enclosure, which was then suspended from the ceiling. A fistful of chickpeas was soaked to feed it in the morning. To the family, it wasn't just another renegade parrot that had escaped from someone's home; they considered it a godsend. Wearied by its harrowing experiences and the day-long starvation, the bird had grown quiet and sickly. It sat still, its head drooping because of the fatigue. Everyone feared that the wounded parrot was slowly dying.

A while later, Muravvat's wife dragged a bed into the courtyard. Although Badi Bi and her grandkids were quick to lie down, no one really slept. They stayed awake till late, their eyes fixated on the cage.

The next morning, the house was once again abuzz with excitement. Awoken by the parrot's screech, Muravvat's wife had run excitedly to the cage. Perhaps the bird was trying to mimic a song. 'Parrot, speak. Say "Allah, Allah,"' she entreated, holding on to the cage.

The bird immediately sprung to action and trilled. 'Say, parrot; say "Sita Ram". Bring me Shiva's swig.'

'Haye Allah!' exclaimed Muravvat's wife, visibly shocked. She released her hold on the cage and took a step back, as if recoiling in horror at the sight of a snake.

'Ammi Jaan! Ammi Jaan!' she shrieked.

Alarmed at the noise, Badi Bi and the kids woke up. 'What happened? Is the bird dead already?'

Muravvat's wife dashed towards the bed. 'Ammi Jan, this parrot is Hindu. What to do? Should we set it free?'

'So what? Don't release it,' the kids protested fervently. But Badi Bi suddenly seemed unmindful; she was lost in deep thought. She, too, had once tended to a Hindu parrot. She thought of the time she had eloped with Raghunath Misir, severing ties with her entire world—parents, relatives, community, village and her home—leaving all of it behind. Rechristening Raghunath Misir as Rahmat Miyan, she had devoted her entire life tending to him, just as one tends to a pet parrot. The runaways had settled in a new place and lived a life of obscurity, distant from the people they once called their own. Like a devout Muslim, Rahmat Miyan used to pray five times a day. He was well-regarded in the community. Over the years, he had made a fortune as a doctor of homoeopathy. He had built a house, educated Muravvat Hussain, his only son, and made him capable of leading a respectable life before peacefully exiting the world. No one other than Badi Bi knew his story. But, sometimes, Badi Bi suspected that her son had caught a whiff of their secret. *Only Allah can tell if my suspicion is right.*

Rahmat Miyan's last day flashed before Badi Bi's eyes. He had asked everyone to leave and had spoken to her in private. 'Biwi, till this day, I have asked no favours of you. But today, I beg you for something. Won't you oblige?'

Tears had rolled down her cheeks. She could merely nod in agreement.

'There is a bottle with sacred Ganga water in my trunk. Before I die, please pour a little of that in my mouth,' Rahmat had urged.

When Rahmat Miyan had eloped with Badi Bi, he had first taken her to Haridwar. She had vivid memories of that trip: she remembered how he had bathed in the Ganga, discarded his holy thread in the stream and filled a bottle with the river water. When Badi Bi had sought an explanation, he had promised to do so at an opportune moment. True to his promise, he had clarified it all when the time came. That day, Badi Bi had poured a spoonful of the Ganga water in his mouth, making certain no one saw her. She also recalled that Muravvat, too—knowingly or unknowingly—had poured a little water into his father's mouth from the same bottle. At the time of his death, Rahmat had softly chanted 'Hey Ram, Hey Ram.' How could she ever forget that!

One day, while rummaging through Rahmat Miyan's trunk for a paper, Muravvat had stumbled upon an old photo. It was the portrait of a tonsured boy in his loincloth. He was wearing padukas[54] and held a bamboo stick over his shoulders, tiny bundles tied at both ends. Muravvat had stared at it for a while and then offered his pranam with folded hands before returning it safely to the trunk. Since that day, as far as Badi Bi knew, Muravvat had never felt the need to open the trunk.

'Of all the homes here, the wretch decides to come to ours. I'll release it at once,' averred Muravvat's wife.

By now Badi Bi had composed herself. 'No, bahu. I will not have it chased away; if it has come to us, it will stay with us,' said Badi Bi, her voice firm.

She spoke with such conviction that Muravvat's wife did not have the courage to defy her. Instead, Badi Bi turned to Muravvat and said, 'Muravvat, yesterday it was put in that profane egg basket. Take it to the Ganga for a holy dip.'

---

54 An ancient form of footwear in India, consisting of little more than a sole with a post and knob, which is engaged between the big and second toe

Chilled to the Bone

Mithilesh

(Translated from the Magahi by Asif Jalal and Abhay K.)

Shivering because of the cold, the old woman walked into her small mud hut stealthily, so that her husband would not see her. However, the moment she entered, he cursed her: 'Arrogant woman! You went out and left the door open. May both your worlds be ruined!'

Throwing down the sack slung over her shoulder on to the straw-covered floor, she groped for the money she had hidden in it. She mumbled to herself: 'I saved some money from his prying eyes. If he comes to know, he will run to a liquor shop with all the coins. He does not earn a penny, good-for-nothing fellow, but he always keeps an eye on my earnings.'

In the dim light, the old woman turned the sack upside down and scattered everything on the floor. She separated three cow-dung cakes. *This fellow keeps peering. He has gone to piss now. Son of a bitch. If he sees money in my hands, he will talk to me sweetly. Even if I abuse him after that, shout insults at his mother and sister, he will laugh. He should be thrashed. He should be thrown out into the icy storm.*

The old woman, Chikni, earned money by begging the whole day and sometimes stealing in the locality. Back in the hut, she warmed her shrivelled body with the fire from the borsi.[55] She picked a half-smoked beedi with her shaky hand from the side of her ear, lit it and puffed. Then she started crying. 'Whose unlucky face did I see this morning that my first glass of tea spilled? After so much pleading, Kishorewa had given it to me. But that hefty Pasiya pulled the jute sack from underneath me in such a way that not only did I tumble down, but the whole glass of tea spilled over my feet. May divine wrath fall on his son! Let a witch chomp on his liver.'

'Oh! What will she chomp on, Chiko?'[56]

The old man, Garo, sat curled up against the wall of the hut. He dragged himself near Chiko's borsi, which was glowing with fire, and put his hands over the blue flames. He then brought his warm palms to his freezing ears.

Seeing the old man near the fire, Chikni stood up. 'With time, you have become senile. Stay away from me.'

'Oh! Chiko, you are acting as if you are a young bride. If you permit me, I will tell you something.'

'Will you tell me what happened, or should I go?'

'Softly! Even walls can hear. Let me tell you something. Every morning, I go to relieve myself close to a mound near the village, but today I rambled in the direction of the tube well. And see what a coincidence it was … as I was washing my face, I heard Operator Sahib's voice on a loudspeaker. He was announcing: "Blankets at the Block". I could not believe what he was saying. Hurriedly, I sprinkled water on my face and rushed to inquire about the offer. I invoked the grace of Mother and the blessings of Dak Baba.'

He paused for a second and then continued sheepishly, 'But why would the mukhiya tell others about the blankets? He would rather invite his relatives and friends, isn't it? Did you see what happened

55 An earthen firepot
56 Chikni's pet name

to the roadwork? He said the contract was for a Harijan, but like a fat cat he gobbled up all the cream. There's loot and corruption all around here.'

The fire from the paddy straw was dying out. Chikni fanned the dying flames with her hand and murmured, 'I have not seen such an atrocious cold wave in years. Heavens! Dense fog and biting cold since the last fifteen days! The market is deserted. I can hardly walk ten steps before I have to look for a borsi. Only a woman like me can stay alive in such a terrible winter. People keep irritating me, but I do not care. I keep going. The boys have a telephone connection it seems; as soon as I set foot in the bazaar, the whole town is out there to poke fun at me. If I am hassled, I abuse them and throw stones at them. Even then they don't desist. Cursing them makes me feel I have avenged the insults.'

Looking at Garo, her husband, she said, 'Why are you sitting here like this? Let the fire glow in the borsi. Till then you go outside, under the banyan tree, and warm yourself there.'

Garo got up, lost in thought, dragged his feet and went outside.

Chikni started to find something to eat. Since the fog had enveloped the plains, she had not lit her clay oven. She had survived on the few bites of bread that she had got by begging. Tomorrow was Tilsakrat.[57] Chikni had already bought two hundred and fifty grams of maska[58] from the bazaar. She opened her torn motari[59] to see if she had all the items required for celebrating Tilsakrat at home. She thought she would ask someone in the village for chewra. Only dahi[60] had to be arranged, and it was sold in every street. If she could not arrange it somehow, she would buy it.

She opened another motari and found two biscuits. Chikni was peeved looking at these, which looked more like sticks than regular

57 A harvest festival celebrated in north India on 14 January

58 A sweet made from jaggery

59 Sack

60 Curd

biscuits. She grumbled and threw them down on the floor. She got up, brought out an aluminium thali and opened another motari. She counted: 'One … two … three … four … roti … rice … mixture. Oh!' Everything was mixed up. 'What a mess!'

Chikni took out five potatoes from a clay pot and placed them in the borsi. She sat down on a thin mattress and covered herself with a genra.[61] Thoughts started racing in her mind. *Today seemed more difficult than other days. The sun seemed to have lost its strength, a thick cloak of fog covered its beauty and brightness. The frost was biting. It feels as if somebody has thrown icy water on my body.*

Chikni sometimes saw the whole bazaar dancing before her eyes. She imagined running through it helter-skelter, her legs numb, ears frozen, water dripping from her eyes and nose, her heart racing and her breath out of control, like a panting dog's. She imagined lakhs of people running after her—old, young, children—and chasing her.

Breaking away from these agonizing thoughts, Chikni sneezed. She got up and lit the dhibri[62] kept in a hole in the wall. She picked a beedi from behind her ear and lit it with the dhibri's flame before filling her chest with smoke.

Garo came back trudging. 'Chiko, today I think I am going to die of this biting cold. Please sleep early after supper. When dawn breaks, I plan to go without having breakfast. Nobody will notice me leaving. If somebody asks about me, tell them I have gone to my daughter's place, that I was invited there,' he said and pulled the borsi closer to himself. Chikni pulled it back immediately.

'These potatoes, when roasted in the borsi, will be delicious,' said Chikni.

'Will you make chokha,[63] Chiko?'

'For you?' Chiko smirked.

---

61 Cotton sheet

62 Lamp

63 Mashed potatoes

'Look, Chiko. I'm seriously telling you, let the straw burn. I will feel comfortable. Otherwise, my heart may stop beating.'

'Should I scorch the paddy I brought home as wages?' Chiko's remark transported Garo back to the past. He used to bring home ten bundles of paddy stalks from the farmland on his head. Then the whole winter would pass in comfort. Those days, Chikni, who used to sneeze frequently, was a gorgeous young woman. But nobody dared to eye her curvaceous figure. Today, both wife and husband were the butt of all kinds of jokes for the whole village. She sneezed incessantly, leading people to call her a sneezing old hag. Once upon a time, she was a hard-working woman. After working in the field, she would pluck a basket of spinach and cook delicious food. They would have a bowl of hot rice soup, red rice and spinach on a sunny winter afternoon. Life was beautiful and satisfying. But now her charm and wit had vanished.

Chikni's attention was drawn to Garo's paralysed leg. She said, 'Had you hurried up, you would not have met such a fate. All efforts to save you failed.'

'Garo is dead, Chiko. I am just an old man who lives on the alms his wife brings. You are right, Chiko. I will also start begging from tomorrow. I will beg for myself,' saying this, he curled up in the bed.

Chikni got upset. 'Why will you beg? Am I dead?'

She took the last puff of the beedi, crushed its top end and planted it back over her right ear. She stirred the borsi a little, thrust some straw into it and lit up small pieces of wood arranged in one corner of the hut. As she blew at the wood, flames leapt out of the dense smoke. She rubbed her eyes to get rid of the irritation.

Dragging herself, she moved closer to the borsi. A cloud of smoke covered her whole body; it felt as if she was at the Brahma Kund[64] in Rajgir. She remembered the sugar mill of Warisaliganj. Her friend

64 Hot springs

Tarengna had taken her to see the place. *Baap re baap*![65] She was so stressed then that she was sweating even during the winter as she stood near the machine. Tarengna must be enjoying it there.

'Even smoke gives warmth, isn't it Chiko?'

'The cold wave is like the sting of a black scorpion. Don't you see? For neutralizing the venom, a person is treated with smoke.'

Garo could feel the strong venom coursing through his veins. Snake poison and a scorpion's venom were the same. Now, the broken wood pieces were burning. Garo felt like cradling the flames in his arms. Chiko would be on one side and the wave of flames from the borsi would stand between both of them. Holding each other, they would dissolve into the flame. It would be their agnipariksha,[66] just like the one Mother Sita had to undergo.

Garo wondered if he ever needed a borsi to warm himself when he was young. Winters used to pass merely with a gamcha. Nothing stung him like the cold did these days. What else did he have? Just a bed of straw. His thoughts meandered towards Chikni. For him, she was not the old, sneezing Chiko. She was a young maiden, her body chiselled like a white marble sculpture.

'Why are you silent, Chiko?'

'Should I speak to the wall?'

Garo felt like somebody had hit him. *Am I a wall to her? Can she not speak to me? Isn't a man really a wall that confines a woman from all sides?* He looked at his legs. *Oh!* Garo realized he was a broken wall, a dilapidated one. He put his head between his knees. Chikni picked up a few dry leaves and kept throwing them in the borsi, so that she continued to feel warm and the potatoes kept roasting. Things looked surreal: a borsi between the two of them, blaze from the straw, red flames, a momentary spark and smoke rings. Chiko figured the

---

65 My God!
66 Trial by fire

potatoes must be roasted by now. If she left them longer, they would get burnt. She knew that straw smoke was not fit to roast potatoes. They required wood, charcoal, saw-dust and a glowing fire.

She remembered the last paddy harvest. At home, she used to add fuel to the clay stove and sit on a stool, picking lice from her hair, which resembled a sparrow's nest. She used to steam rice by continually adding paddy husk into the mouth of the clay stove, which resembled that of a clay pitcher. *Oh! How time has passed. Everything has slipped out of Chikni's beautiful hands.* Just then, the blow of an easterly wind broke her backbone. Chikni shivered and moved closer to the borsi, extracting the potatoes.

When Garo escaped his thoughts, he saw Chiko mashing the potatoes. 'I do not feel like eating,' he said and slipped into the straw spread on the floor, dragging his feet. Chikni kept staring at him. *It is not possible that he will sleep without eating.* Usually, Chiko's arguments were as piercing as that of a lawyer, but today she did not have anything to say. *What is the matter? Hey Goddess Surusabita Meera! Save our lives.* The icy wind howled outside. It was like the wrath of the goddess, like her destructive rage. Chiko got up, readied the bed and turned off the lamp. On other days, she slept on a different bed, but tonight her feet turned towards the straw bed where Garo lay silently. She moved gently. The straw crackled as Chikni dragged herself close to Garo's back. She put her arms around him. God was raining distress on them. Chikni, too, was feeling low. Garo, once a mountain-like man, was now in terrible shape. His entire body was in Chikni's embrace. She remembered how, once upon a time, her arms could embrace only half of him, or perhaps a quarter.

'Only this night is frightening, Chiko. From tomorrow, we will have a blanket from the block,' Garo said, his voice trembling.

'Why didn't you eat?'

Garo stayed quiet. He did not know what to say.

'I will give you mashed potatoes wrapped in paper tomorrow morning. God knows when you will return. This festival comes once in a year. The government had to choose the day of Tilsakrat to distribute the blankets?'

She fell silent for a while. And then she said, 'Well, do you really think we will get a blanket?' Chikni was not able to believe it. She had heard such rumours several times. She had travelled to Delhi and Patna with a flag, a banner, but…

'Sleep, Chiko. Wake me up early,' Garo said and closed his eyes. He was lost in the dream of a blanket. He did not know the quality and colour of the blanket he would get. The shepherd of Dhanpura wove blankets too, but of questionable quality. They were bristly like palm leaves, and dirty like pigs. However, if one covered one's body with it, one was sure to feel warm and slip into slumberland. People called it the quilt for the winter. In his dream, he blabbered, 'But the blanket said you first cover me, then I will guard you from the cold. First, place a genra over a blanket and then both the wife and husband can sleep carefree. Covering myself with straw, I feel suffocated. I have to take my head out of the straw to breathe. The noise it makes disrupts sleep at night.'

The block office, where the blanket was to be distributed, floated before Garo's eyes. He had gone there many times with Chiko. Inquilab zindabad![67] Employment, food, clothes! He had raised so many slogans there. *Wasn't a blanket like clothing too?* If people did not get food or employment, they should at least get cloth. One required only four metres of cloth. After all, even the son of King Harichanar[68] wore a shroud of blanket.

But both winter and a blanket? Alas! This was not to be in Garo's destiny. He dreamt that Bada Sahib himself was distributing blankets.

67 Long live the revolution!
68 Another name for legendary Indian king Harishchandra

Garo grabbed one and dashed towards his hut. He moved his hand over the blanket to feel it. He was lost in the reverie of owning a blanket. He unfolded it, measured it and found it to be wide enough. *Oh, how wonderful!*

Immersed in his dreams, Garo felt a terrible pain in his chest. He wanted to wake Chiko up, but he could not speak. He lost consciousness within minutes.

The storm in the night had cleared the dirt from the lane outside. In the morning, shivering men came out into the streets to warm their bones. Hearing the clang of metal buckets at the well, Chiko woke up. *Good*, she thought, *sunshine has finally descended on the village.*

'Oh, ji! Are you listening?'

Chikni held Garo's head and shook him. But Garo, covering himself in a dream blanket, had gone out in the cold, in the bitter cold.

A Bowl of Sattu

Chandramohan Pradhan

(Translated from the Hindi by Ram Bhagwan Singh and Chaitali Pandya)

On that last day of November, as the wind blew fiercely, Bhagirathji tied the muffler tightly around his neck and closed the window. Night had fallen. However, the wind still had the crevices of the old dilapidated tiled roof from where it could creep in. Wrapping a shawl around his body, he sat down in an easy chair. He slid the oil lamp to the side of the table and picked up a book to read.

Someone knocked on the door. It was 8 p.m. by the table clock. *Who could it be at this hour!* He opened the door to find some people standing in the moonlight.

'Master Sahib…'

Bhagirathji recognized the voice of Mukhiya Ramsumer. 'Mukhiyaji? What's the matter? Please come in.'

His personal room behind the school's office felt cramped thanks to the presence of the six or seven people. Bhagirathji was surprised to see that they had brought in a young man of a stout physique, with his hands tied.

'Who is this man? Why have you brought him here with his hands tied?'

Mukhiyaji responded, 'Masterji, he is the infamous rogue, Masta; you must have heard of him. He sometimes comes here secretly to meet a woman. Today, laying an ambush, we caught the rogue.'

'Oh!' Bhagirathji's eyes widened. Masta was a notorious criminal, a terror in the locality. He had a small gang of his own. Whenever he wanted, he would rob a traveller, commit a dacoity, snatch motorcycles on the highway. There were several cases of rape registered against him. He had been caught after all.

'Why have you brought him here? The police station—'

'Sir, the daroga has gone to sleep in his quarters and the jamadar refuses to wake him up. He is also not ready to keep him in the police station without the daroga's order. So, we have brought him here for the night. Early in the morning, we will hand him over to the police.'

'In the school?' Bhagirathji was in two minds.

'Masterji, it is just a matter of one night. Tell us, where else can we keep him? No one is ready to help. We will keep him in one of the classrooms with two of our men. In any case, tomorrow is Sunday.'

It had to be done. The class seven classroom, which was at the end of the corridor, was opened and, along with two young men, Masta was deposited there. The school peon, Dinu, had gone home in the evening, so Bhagirathji took a lantern and unlocked the room himself.

He had no home of his own here. This room behind the office had perhaps been built for the headmaster who lived without a family. After all, transfer was a regular affair in government service.

There was also a library on this floor. In the daytime, the peon prepared food for him; in the morning he would have tea, biscuits and bread; at night he only ate sattu.[69] Dinu ensured he bought the sattu for the headmaster during the day from the vendor in the village.

---

69 A type of flour prepared by grinding roasted gram

He felt like having tea. Given the cold weather, he decided to offer some to the others too. Since he was fond of the drink, he had made arrangements for a stove, tea leaves, sugar … all the necessary ingredients. He, however, preferred tea without milk.

At times, when he had an informal meeting of teachers here, he would serve them tea, too. He owned five to six glasses and cups in all. He made some tea and took three cups to the classroom where Masta had been kept.

'Here, have some tea, brother.'

The two villagers happily accepted the hot drink. When Bhagirathji offered a cup to Masta, they said, 'Why do you serve tea to this rogue?'

'Let him have it. It is cold. After all, he is also a human being. Just untie one hand.'

The villagers cautiously untied Masta's left hand and ensured that his right hand and legs were tied. Masta took the cup.

'It seems he has been belaboured.'

'Masterji,' one of the villagers laughed. 'He has not been beaten enough. He will be thoroughly dealt with at the police station. In fact, he deserves to be killed, but the law will take its own course. We will hand him over to the police.'

Bhagirathji's teacher's instincts prompted him to convince Masta that the path he was following would directly lead to jail or a death sentence; that he should mend his ways and live a gentleman's life. But he was also aware of the fact that it was practically impossible to bring about a radical change in a person with a criminal disposition. Some people are simply after making quick money.

At 9 p.m., putting down the book he was reading, Bhagirathji yawned and decided to eat sattu. When he was pouring it from the bowl into a dish, he paused. *The two men probably ate supper at home, but what about Masta? Why worry about that ferocious rogue, though? Let that bastard die! But he looked like he had been badly beaten. Who knows when he ate last? If someone lies hungry here, how can I sleep with a full stomach?*

*

Yawning, one of the two men said, 'Because of this devil, we also have to stay awake the whole night.'

The other one, crushing khaini,[70] said, 'I suggest we sleep by turns, for two hours each.'

The door opened just then. Masterji appeared in the dim light of the lantern with a bowl, a dish and a mug. He said, 'You two must have already eaten, I assume.'

Both of them laughed, 'We ate at home before coming.'

'Did you give him something to eat?'

Puzzled, the villagers said, 'What are you saying, Masterji? Now this scoundrel will eat only in jail.'

Bhagirathji emptied the bowl of sattu into the dish, put the jug of water down, opened a packet, put some salt, chilli and onion in front of Masta and told him, 'Here, eat this sattu.'

As if the villagers were pained, they spoke in a choked voice, 'What are you doing? Feeding milk to a serpent?'

Bhagirathji said, 'Whatever it may be, who knows for how long he has been hungry? And he is sure to be beaten at the police station. The police send the matter to court only after beating a person mercilessly … but he is also a human being.'

'Masterji,' one of them protested, 'we know you eat only a bowlful of sattu at night. What will you eat?'

'Don't worry about me. I have some biscuits. However, it is not possible that he who comes to me at night goes hungry while I sleep having my fill. Take it, eat.' He pushed the dish towards Masta.

*

70 Tobacco

After a few days, Bhagirathji came to know that Masta had been sentenced to seven years rigorous imprisonment. The people of the area heaved a sigh of relief.

Years passed. Having served in several schools, Bhagirathji retired from Mirganj Gram Panchayat school and settled in his village, Gauripur. Since he was physically and mentally fit, he found it difficult to sit idle. He started conducting classes at home. He was a well-read scholar, his style of teaching was good, and so the students started coming in. Soon, he was running a coaching institute that operated in two shifts.

Many in the village cultivated flax and people were largely well-off. The road passing through the village connected it to the state capital. Plenty of vehicles plied on it.

A market as well as some hotels and restaurants had sprung up on either side of the road. Travellers would stop for tea and refreshments; the market would be busy till late in the night.

Masterji also acquired wealth. His house was built with brick and cement. At first, he thought of constructing an upper floor, but then he hesitated. Only four people lived in the house: his old mother, he and his wife, and their young daughter. Soon, the daughter would be married off; why bother constructing an upper floor?

Crime was growing. Dacoity, murder and abduction cases were on the rise. The rich often experienced sleepless nights. Masterji, however, remained largely unperturbed. There were several shopkeepers and money lenders around. *Why would anyone lay a hand on a teacher?* There was a vast difference between the riches of a teacher and of a money lender. But in his heart of hearts, he had a lurking fear. Like everyone else, he too was worried and remained on guard. There was a police station in the village, but people had no faith in the police at all.

In the last days of November, a bitter cold had set in. The shops in the main market were still open. As the night progressed, the crowd thinned. The pucca house on the fringe of the village was somewhat different from the others. A little distance away from it, behind the trees, a jeep waited in the darkness.

There were two men in the jeep. The man in the driving seat said softly, 'That is the house. We have finally found it after searching for fifteen kilometres. Here the job is easy, the two of us can easily handle it.'

'Hmm,' said the other man.

'We have found something better than what the customer wanted. He will be pleased to see her, and may pay us thirty in place of twenty.'

'Hmm,' the other man responded again.

'Sardar,' the first man said again, 'besides the old man and woman, there is only that girl. I have been watching them for two days. The old man goes to the market daily at 6 p.m. for a walk, buys essentials and returns in two hours. Just as he goes out, we will get in. We will load her in no time and...'

Here, he paused to watch the old man leaving for the bazaar, walking stick in hand. Just then, a young girl came out and turned on the light in the verandah. She went back in.

'Did you see, sardar, isn't she ravishing?'

In the dim light of the jeep, seeing the distressed look on the face of the second man, he said, 'Sardar...'

'Stop!' the second man growled. 'Is he the man?'

'Yes, boss, he is...'

'Turn the jeep. We must return.'

The first man failed to understand the sudden change in the demeanour of his boss. Nonplussed, he spoke, 'What do you mean?'

'No arguments. You won't understand. For now, let's just leave.'

Sensing disgust in his tone, the first man silently reversed the jeep, the parking light still blinking. The jeep moved slowly on the main road. A little distance away, the first man couldn't help but ask, 'Sardar, why did you say we need to turn back?'

On getting no response from his boss, he ventured again, 'Are you thinking about something?'

'Yes, I'm thinking … about a bowl of sattu…'

Nameless Relationship

Mridula Sinha

(Translated from the Hindi by Ram Bhagwan Singh and Chaitali Pandya)

Chitraji began to read between the lines of the request written in hand, sent along with the invitation card, and gauge the underlying sentiment. She read it several times and thought about the questions people would ask at the wedding ceremony. *Who am I? What relationship do I have with Shaligramji? What reply shall I give? What reply will Shaligramji give?*

She had never chalked out on the slate of her mind the relationship she shared with Shaligramji. Giving it a name was another matter altogether. Even after repeatedly shrugging off that unknown, unspoken and nameless relationship, it had felt familiar and immensely intimate. At times, she would feel threatened by its formlessness. Then, in order to give that relationship a name, she would riffle through thousands of words in her vocabulary. But she never found one. *And when I have no name for it, how do I address him?*

So, it was true that she never made any mention of that relationship. Neither at the time of the initiation of the relationship, nor when she ceased living her own life. Not even during her fierce struggle for survival. She never remembered Shaligramji. It was he who took the initiative to continue this nameless relationship.

After much thinking, Chitraji finally decided to go to Bhopal. It was a long journey. First by bus and then by train, that too in the summer. Shaligramji had assured her over the phone: 'You will have no problem. While arranging the accommodation, I have considered the weather. I have ensured that our guests face no trouble, and you are a special one.'

Chitraji had said nothing. When she had decided to go, there was no question of trouble or comfort. At the Shimla bus stand, she boarded a bus. Her mobile phone rang. It was Shaligramji. He said, 'When you arrive at the Delhi bus depot, you will meet Rakesh. He will have your train ticket.'

Chitraji did not respond. She did not even tell him that she had already booked her ticket. As soon as her bus arrived at the Delhi depot, a young man entered the bus. His searching eyes recognized Chitraji. He unloaded her suitcase and said, 'If you have any train ticket, please give it to me. I'll get it cancelled. Here, take this AC II-tier ticket. The train leaves in the evening from Nizamuddin station. I'll also travel with you.'

Chitraji gave Rakesh her sleeper-class ticket. In an autorickshaw, she went to a friend's house located near Gol Market. In the evening, they took the train to Bhopal.

The next morning, the train stopped at Bhopal Junction. A young man came to her and touched her feet. 'I am Deepak. My father's name is Shaligram Kashyap.'

Chitraji blessed him and followed him. They got into a car that was waiting for them. There was complete silence. Nobody spoke at all. Chitraji wanted to talk to Deepak, but she did not know how to start a conversation.

She did not know anything, neither about the location of the house, nor the number of people living there, nor their traditions and customs.

She had no idea at all. As she was about to initiate a conversation by asking about Bhopal city, Deepak spoke. 'Can I call you "auntie"?'

'Yes!'

'Auntie, the baraat will come this evening. It is a local baraat; so it will arrive on time. I have heard that you are returning tomorrow. You have little time. Father said that since you have come to Bhopal for the first time, you might want to see our beautiful city. Please get ready immediately. My cousin will take you around.'

'All right,' Chitraji managed to utter. She wanted to express her gratitude to Deepak for being so considerate. But she said nothing.

Deepak said, 'My father admires you very much. He says you are the living incarnation of a devi. But I don't know why you neither came to Bhopal nor invited us to Shimla before. He told me about you just a few days ago. Naturally, a strong desire to see you arose within me. That's why I came to the station to receive you myself, notwithstanding all the wedding preparations!'

While Chitraji was fumbling for words, the driver pulled up in front of a guest house. Taking out her luggage from the boot of the car, Deepak came forward. She followed. Leading her to her room, he said, 'Auntie, breakfast will be served at home. After that you can go to see the city. You will be back home for lunch, after which you can take some rest. And, as you know, the wedding is in the evening.'

Chitraji said nothing. She saw him off till the door. When he was out of sight, she returned to the room, fastened the latch and sat down on the bed. She began to think. *Deepak is such a responsible man. He must be nineteen or twenty years old. So responsible and devoted to his father. Society is unnecessarily worried that the younger generation has gone astray. Having spent just a few moments with me; but this young man has left a lasting impression on my mind. But all the credit goes to his father, Shaligramji.* Remembering him, Chitraji sat up. To divert her attention, she started preparing herself.

Naresh, one of Deepak's friends, reached just as Chitraji got ready. While driving her home for breakfast, he asked, 'Are you Deepak's aunt? I have already met two of his aunts, but I am meeting you for the first time. I'm Deepak's friend.'

★

Shaligramji hurriedly reached the gate. He greeted Chitraji.

Naresh reported, 'On the way, auntie saw the city. She liked the three ponds.'

Had Naresh not elaborated so much, perhaps Chitraji would not have recognized the man standing before her. Something stirred in her heart, but she controlled herself. Responding to the greeting with folded hands, she smiled. Breakfast had been arranged in the verandah of the house. Hardly two minutes had passed when Shaligramji joined Chitraji.

'Who is she?'

'Never saw her before!'

The questions popped up. People were curious.

Nobody had an answer. Shaligramji's wife, Mala, also came there. She went around asking the relatives whether they relished the food, and urged them to have more. Someone asked her, 'Who is she? That beautiful lady in the Kota saree?'

Mala looked around. Somebody spoke in a hushed tone, 'Shaligramji himself served breakfast to her. Look!'

Mala, too, noticed her. Shaligramji was standing holding a cup of tea in his hand. *A serene face, about my age, decorously eating breakfast. Who is that lady? Shaligramji has never mentioned her before.* Mala had also read the invitees' list. There was no name on it that she was not familiar with. *Who was she?*

Mala knew it was not the right time to ask her husband. However, the same question kept tossing between the guests throughout the day.

Chitraji came back for lunch after the sightseeing. One of Shaligramji's sisters-in-law approached her and asked, 'Where have you come from?'

She was about to ask another question: 'How do you know my brother-in-law?' Just then, Shaligramji came there and busied his sister-in-law with serving another special guest.

Later, while resting at the guest house, Chitraji's mind was preoccupied. After a long time, the memory of the incident that had taken place twenty-five years ago came flooding back. Her family of four—husband, wife and two children—had set out from Shimla for Kullu–Manali in a car. After covering a short distance, the car had fallen into a ditch. Her husband had been injured on the head and had lost consciousness. A doctor had been called in. He had advised a helpless Chitraji to take the decision at the earliest. Helpless, Chitraji had stood there with her two children snuggled up to her. Friends, family, relatives ... no one had been there by her side. She had to make the decision alone. Everything had been lost. She had been asked to give whatever was left, too. Chitraji had agreed to give even that. Then, a life had been saved.

It was all still alive in her memory. But Chitraji prevented the memories from coming back on this auspicious occasion. Besides, she lived by the dictum of 'let bygones be bygones'. She must think about the well-being of the girl who was getting married. That was the need of the hour and the occasion.

The baraat was at the doorstep. The men and women who stood there to welcome the guests continued to give Chitraji a sidelong glance. Everyone had the same questions: *Who is she? What relationship does she have with Shaligramji?*

At the main gate, Shaligramji introduced Chitraji to his samdhi.[71] His two sisters-in-law had been standing there, too, along with their

71 The father of one's son- or daughter-in-law

husbands. He did not introduce them. This news spread among the crowd very fast.

After both parties—the bride's side and the groom's side—had eaten, the marriage rituals started. The pandit called Shaligramji for the kanyadan.[72] Before sitting in the pavilion, he looked around. His eyes did not find the face he was looking for. His sisters and sisters-in-law gauged his search. Two or three of them spoke together: 'Your guest, there she is.'

Mala also noticed that. Out of irritation, she said, 'Now be seated and perform the kanyadan with a quiet mind. Everything is being taken care of by the guests present here. You please be seated!'

Shaligramji called out loudly. 'Chitraji! Please come here and take a seat in the pavilion. My daughter needs your exclusive blessings.'

Chitraji was shaken from within. People's eyes, like arrows, pierced through her. She was already nervous. Standing in her place, she said, 'You people have assembled here for an auspicious work. Please perform your daughter's kanyadan. I want to sit here. I am a widow. Society forbids such a woman from wishing marital happiness to a bride. I wish for your daughter's well-being from the core of my heart. Let me sit apart. You please accomplish your sacred work. Don't worry about me.' Then she sat down.

'I don't accept such a code. For my family, for my daughter, nothing will be more auspicious than you. Had it not been for your kindness, neither me nor my daughter would have been alive. Please come, I request you to perform my daughter's kanyadan.'

The pandit was embarrassed. He said, 'Shaligramji! Your guest is right. You perform the kanyadan and have your wife seated by your side. All ladies in the pavilion have their husbands alive.'

---

72 A ritual in which parents give away their daughter's hand in marriage to the groom

By now, Shaligramji was agitated. 'All of you have been anxious since morning to know about Chitraji. You have been encouraging all kinds of gossip. While I was busy with work, I too was subjected to your questioning arrows. Unless and until I introduce her, you people will not concentrate on the rituals. Please listen. Twenty-five years ago, in an accident, Chitraji's husband was injured. He was declared brain-dead. I was lying on the operation table of the hospital he was in. My heart had stopped working. The doctors had decided that if an active heart became available, I would get a transplant. People know about eye donation or kidney donation after someone's death, but heart donation is possible only when the organ is active and the person is alive. Then, you might ask, why will anybody donate his or her heart? Chitraji's husband's heart was still beating, but his brain had stopped working. Dr Sharma had requested her: "Your husband can't be saved. But if you agree, his heart can be transplanted into another person's body and that person will get a new lease of life."

'I don't know what Chitraji must have felt after hearing the doctor's advice. And I wonder whether anyone even tried to know her state of mind at that time. Chitraji gave her consent. My heart, which has been beating for the last twenty-five years, is not mine. It is her husband's. But during the last twenty-five years, she never burdened me with any obligation. She did not know me then, nor had she seen me. I, too, had neither seen her nor known her. She never tried to find me. But I was very anxious. I could not even express gratitude to my life-giver. Two years ago, I went to her city. I met Dr Sharma by chance. Unfortunately, I could not meet her, but managed to get her contact number from Dr Sharma. I introduced myself to her over the phone. She has come to grace my daughter's wedding at my request. I met her for the first time this morning. Now you yourself decide, panditji! Who can be more auspicious for my family than her? I owe my marriage and children to her.'

Hearing Shaligramji, people gazed admiringly at the kind lady. Tears rolled out of everyone's eyes, though the kanyadan ceremony was yet to happen. Mala stood up and went straight to Chitraji, touched her feet, and sought her blessings.

Naming the relationship was no longer required. The courtyard was full of relatives. Shaligramji and Chitraji's relationship was greater than all others. So what if it was nameless!

The Dressing Table

Shamoil Ahmad

(Translated from the Urdu by N.C. Sinha)

Even the prostitutes had been targeted during the riots.

Brijmohan had managed to lay hands on Naseem Jaan's dressing table. It had a full-length mirror encased in an ivory frame. His three daughters took turns to look at themselves in this mirror from different angles, even though it was cloudy, and the hair oil, nail polish and lipstick stains on the frame gave it a run-down look. Brijmohan was a little uneasy noticing this change in his daughters. They had stood on the balcony in the past, too, but not quite in the same way. Now, even Chhoti, the youngest one, plastered her face with talcum powder and lipstick and giggled and laughed as she stood on the balcony.

That day, too, the three of them were out on the balcony. Standing across the road, Brijmohan watched their antics. Suddenly, Badi, the eldest one, stretched out her arms provocatively, displaying the contour of her breasts. Manjhli, the middle one, bent over to look down and then scratched her back. A young man standing near the cigarette stall smiled and looked up at the balcony. Chhoti nudged Manjhli and the three of them broke into laughter. Brijmohan's heart began to sink. His premonitions were coming true.

He had had this fear since the day he had robbed Naseem Jaan of her dressing table. There had been a veritable pandemonium when the rioters had entered the prostitute's kotha.[73] Brijmohan and his companions had barged into Naseem Jaan's quarters and grabbed whatever they could. As Brijmohan had picked up the dressing table, Naseem Jaan had screamed and shouted. She had fallen at his feet: 'Brother, this is an heirloom. Please don't take it; let it be. Brother!'

'Get lost, you whore!' Brijmohan had yelled and given her a mighty shove with his leg. As she fell, her saree rose up to her hips, but she quickly pulled it down and grabbed Brijmohan's legs again.

Brijmohan had extricated his feet with violent force. 'Move aside, you whore!'

'Brother … this is a memento from my grandmother. Brother, leave it!'

Brijmohan had pulled his leg free and kicked her hard on the waist. Naseem Jaan had rolled on to the floor. The buttons on her blouse had burst open, exposing her breasts. Brijmohan had flashed his knife. 'Shall I chop them off?'

Terrified, Naseem Jaan had covered her breasts with her hands and huddled into a corner. Brijmohan had gone down the stairs, carrying the dressing table, immensely pleased that he had robbed Naseem Jaan of an heirloom. It was obviously a prized possession. Her great-grandmother, grandmother and mother would have dressed up before it to entice their clients. *Naseem Jaan might buy a better dressing table, but she would never get this one back*, thought Brijmohan. Like the other rioters who had indulged in plundering and looting, he also felt a sense of great satisfaction in the knowledge that they had succeeded in robbing a community of its heritage.

When he reached home, his wife took an instant liking to the dressing table. The mirror, however, looked somewhat hazy. She began

---

73 Brothel

to clean it with a piece of wet cloth. There were far too many stains all over it, mainly oil stains and dust. After she cleaned the mirror, it began to sparkle, delighting her. It gave her pleasure to stand before a full-length mirror and watch herself from all possible angles. The daughters also took turns to view themselves from angles they had never seen before.

Brijmohan, too, admired himself in the mirror. Looking at his own self, he felt there was something special about his reflection. He wanted to go on looking at himself, but it was difficult to stand face-to-face with it for long.

Each time he would look into the mirror, Naseem Jaan's image would appear before his eyes. Her pleas would ring in his ears: 'Brother, don't take away the dressing table! It's a memento from my grandmother…'

Brijmohan had installed the dressing table in his bedroom. Everyone seemed to have fallen in love with it. No one cared about the old dressing table. At any given moment, some or the other member of the family would be standing in front of the new one. Brijmohan often wondered what secret lay behind the whore's dressing table, which drew every beholder to it. His daughters were glued to it, and his wife spent even more time in front of it, looking and re-looking at herself … even he…

But it was always difficult for him to keep standing in front of the mirror for a long time because Nasim Jaan's wailing image would soon make an appearance.

Brijmohan noticed a subtle change in each of his family members. His wife now swung her hips as she walked; she used missy powder to tint her teeth. His daughters began to wear anklets and to spend a lot of time dressing up in new ways. They began to put on lipstick, line their eyes with kohl, apply vermilion marks on their foreheads and draw artificial moles on their cheeks. Soon, a betel box was purchased and, every evening, fresh flowers and garlands were ordered. Early in the evening, Brijmohan's wife would sit with the betel box, cracking open betel nuts, and indulge in light-hearted banter with everyone. Brijmohan watched it all like a spectator. He was baffled. *Why don't I say anything! Why don't I chide them?*

One day, when Brijmohan was in his room, Badi came and parked herself in front of the dressing table. She examined herself from the right and then the left, and then began to loosen her bra. She lifted her left arm and touched her hairy armpit. Then she took out some lotion from the drawer of the dressing table and began to apply it to her underarm. Brijmohan was in shock. He observed his daughter without a word. Meanwhile, the second daughter appeared, followed by the third one.

'Sister! Give me some lotion, too,' the second daughter said.

'What do you want it for?' the eldest one asked with an air of exaltation.

'She will use it in the bathroom,' the youngest said.

'You rogue!' the second daughter pinched her youngest sister's cheeks. The three of them burst into laughter.

Brijmohan's heart began to beat faster in alarm. His daughters had changed completely. They didn't seem to care that he was in the same room. He stood in a way that his reflection would be visible in the mirror, but even that had no effect on them. The eldest continued to apply the lotion while the other two stood beside her, making faces in the mirror. It occurred to Brijmohan that he had ceased to exist in the house. Just then, Naseem Jaan's face made an appearance in the mirror.

'I reign over your house now,' she said.

Brijmohan was stunned. It looked like Naseem Jaan had entered his house through the mirror and would soon get out and take over every nook and corner. He wanted to go out, but his feet seemed to be frozen. He couldn't budge from his position and kept staring at the dressing table while his daughters laughed heartily. For a moment, in the midst of the playful girls, he felt as though he wasn't their father but…

Brijmohan was afraid of the dressing table. Naseem Jaan seemed to be laughing. She laughed when the eldest tinkled her bangles or when the youngest jingled her anklet. And now Brijmohan…

Even today, when they were standing on the balcony and laughing, he was merely watching like an onlooker, his heart thumping with the dread of something unknown. Brijmohan realized that even passers-by were looking up at his daughters. Suddenly, a young man standing at the cigarette shop made some signs towards the balcony. Upon getting a response from his daughters, he smiled.

Brijmohan thought of asking the young man his name. He took a few paces towards the shop, but could not say a word upon reaching there. It dawned on him that he, too, was taking the same kind of interest in the young man as his daughters. He was not surprised at being unable to ask the young man his name. *What were his intentions? Would I take him to my daughters?* A mischievous smile spread across his face. He crushed the betel nut under his teeth, took out a comb from his pocket and straightened his hair standing before the mirror at the betel shop. This act of combing gave him some relief. Once or twice, he looked askance at the young man. He was talking to a rickshaw-puller and occasionally looking up towards the balcony. Shoving back the comb into his pocket, Brijmohan realized that he was actually interested in that young man. *Does that mean I am … a pimp? What is happening to me? What kind of upbringing did I get that I robbed a whore? Of all people, a whore? Oh, how she had entreated me to stop and called me 'brother'!* Brijmohan's ears began to ring with Naseem Jaan's wailing. In sheer exasperation, he violently shook his head and threw a quick glance towards the balcony. He paid for the betel nut, crossed the road and disappeared into the house.

Brijmohan entered his bedroom and stood before the dressing table. He could see his transformation. His face revealed wrinkles in many places and dark circles under his eyes. For once, he loosened his belt and fastened it back before running his hand over the wrinkles.

He felt a sudden desire to apply collyrium under his eyes and tie a red handkerchief around his neck. He continued to imagine himself like this, all the while looking into the mirror.

Just then, his wife made an appearance. She had loosely wrapped herself in a saree, with just her bra on. As she stood in front of the mirror, the pallu of her saree slipped. She threw a seductive smile at Brijmohan and gestured with her eyes, telling him to fasten her bra. Brijmohan looked at the mirror. The sight of her breasts behind the bra was tempting. In the process of fastening it, his hands crawled up to her breasts.

'*Oi daiya*!' Brijmohan's wife turned and his passion rose to a crescendo. He cupped her breasts with full force.

'*Haye Raja*!' She erupted with passion, making Brijmohan want her even more. With a swift jerk, he took off her bra, threw it away and pulled her to the bed.

Kissing him all over, she rolled on the bed with him and began to giggle.

Brijmohan took one look in the mirror. Seeing his wife naked, his passion grew even more intense. He quickly undressed himself, as his wife passionately whispered into his ears.

'Haye Raja! Plunder this kingdom.'

Brijmohan had never heard his wife use such expressions before. It seemed to him that these weren't words but notes from a sarangi flowing out from Naseem Jaan's kotha. And then ... the mirror became clouded, the sarangi kept playing.

Brijmohan got up from the bed, took the kohl out of the drawer and lined his eyes with it. He tied a garland around his wrists, fastened a red handkerchief around his neck and went down. Leaning against the wall near the landing, he puffed at his beedi.

Through the Prism of Time

Ramdhari Singh Diwakar

(Translated from the Hindi by Chaitali Pandya)

From the culvert nearby, seventy-five-year-old (or maybe seventy-six) Babu Chandradev Singh turned and gazed at his so-called haveli, with its old, weathered tiles and its equally old foyer. Then he looked intently at the culvert, which had collapsed from the middle. During the monsoon, this culvert, which had been constructed decades ago, was rendered useless. It was built with bricks, but the middle part was dilapidated. For the past few years, bamboo logs were being laid across this patch during the rainy months, to keep it connected with the main road. However, this problem affected only Babu Chandradev Singh and four or five other families of the rajput community; the others did not use the culvert as they lived on the other side.

In the past five or six years, several applications had been sent to the Block Development Officer (BDO). Babu Chandradev Singh had run from pillar to post with his applications, right from the president of the gram panchayat to the office of the zilla parishad, but to no avail. The culvert remained in a state of disrepair. He came to know that some funds had been allocated to the gram panchayat to carry out such public works. However, the fact that Ramsaheli Devi, the president of the gram panchayat, happened to be a woman from the dhanuk khawas[74] caste, left Babu Chandradev Singh in a dilemma—whether or not to meet her and seek help.

But then how was the culvert to be repaired? Even the BDO had said that the gram panchayat would carry out the repair work and that the village head had to decide on the same. The culvert was in such a state of ruin that laying bamboo logs would be futile this monsoon.

Babu Chandradev Singh mustered the courage to meet the village head. His priest, Pandit Jagdambi Jha, said encouragingly, 'What's wrong in that? On the occasion of Chhath puja,[75] we need wicker baskets and winnowers. Don't we go then to the doms and dharkars?[76] If you wish, I can accompany you.'

When Babu Chandradev Singh walked towards the dhanuk khawas basti,[77] he felt as if he were going to drown in a pit of his own making.

Many years ago, in his heyday, he used to go to the dhanuk khawas basti. He even used to walk towards that one house. In those days, the heart had been full of passion. At the epicentre of desire had been Sukhdeva's mother. It happened before Sukhdeva was even born. Several times in Sukhdeva's mother's home … and in the dark and secluded corner of the cowshed in front of his own mansion…

By a twist of fate, today, Sukhdeva's wife was the village head. The government had hurled the upper castes into the abyss. They no longer enjoyed any honour or respect. These days, not even adolescent boys from the raad-solkan caste[78] bowed to people from his caste in obeisance. Only a few old men greeted them upon meeting, either willingly or out of habit. The government had passed a new law, under

---

74 A backward caste

75 A Vedic festival dedicated to the Sun god, celebrated on the sixth day of the Hindu month of Karthika

76 A scheduled caste community

77 A settlement

78 A socially and economically deprived community

which certain seats were reserved for people from the backward and scheduled castes in the gram panchayat elections.

Whether Babu Chandradev Singh damned the times or himself, he did often wonder if the lightning had to strike this gram panchayat only! Babu Shridev Singh had twice been elected the village chief. But this culvert had not collapsed then. Now, when a dhanuk khawas's daughter-in-law was the village head, the rajput community had been affected. He knew there was no alternative. Finally, after having crossed several impassable culverts of internal conflict and self-pity, Babu Chandradev Singh arrived at the village chief's house.

It was a sultry morning in the month of Vaishakh.[79] Four or five people from the nearby basti were seated on a broken bench on a thatched verandah and were chatting. One of them, an old man, greeted Babu Chandradev Singh: 'Salutation, master!'

Upon hearing himself being addressed as 'master', Babu Chandradev Singh's slightly bent spine, a sign of ageing, became taut. 'Who are you? … Sajivan?'

'Yes, master! Sajivan from the fishermen's village.'

Of the remaining four, Babu Chandradev Singh knew three, but one young lad was an unfamiliar face. The four men extended their respect to him by merely vacating the bench and somehow accommodating themselves on a cot nearby. The broken bench had two legs intact, while the other two legs had been replaced by stacked-up bricks. Babu Chandradev Singh inspected the bench closely. There was a vacant chair, too. Just as he was about to sit on the chair, the young lad remarked, 'Don't sit on that chair. It's for the village head.'

Embarrassed, he went and sat on the opposite bench. At that moment, he did not feel like Babu Chandradev Singh but just an ordinary man who had been made to get up from a dhanuk khawasin's[80] chair.

---

79 April/May as per the Gregorian calendar

80 A woman belonging to the dhanuk khawas caste

Sakaldeva, an intermediate-level student and the son of the village chief, saw Babu Chandradev Singh sitting on the verandah. His mother was making chapatis. He informed his grandmother: 'Grandma, Babu Chandradev Singh is here.'

His grandmother informed her daughter-in-law, and stood up, adjusting her saree. She examined her bodice from all angles, ran her fingers through her unkempt hair and came to the front door.

Seated there, on a broken bench, was Babu Chandradev Singh. Sukhdeva's mother kept staring at Babu Sahib. They both kept staring at each other, completely speechless. They shared a piece of the past that lay frozen in time. Perhaps, the memories of this house, of Sukhdeva's mother's house, came flooding back to Babu Chandradev Singh's mind … the secluded corner of the cowshed in front of his house! Apart from the memories of sweeping and mopping, cleaning and scrubbing, doing the dishes at the mansion, Sukhdeva's mother, too, reminisced about the past that she had shared with Babu Chandradev Singh.

It took some time before Sukhdeva's mother realized that Babu Chandradev Singh was sitting on the broken bench. She instructed her grandson: 'Sakaldeva, get a chair for the master from the courtyard.'

Sakaldeva returned with an old chair. As Babu Chandradev Singh settled in it, he looked at the young boy standing in front him and the group of four men sitting on the cot. It was as if he was saying to them: 'Look at you and look at her, Sukhdeva's mother, … see how respectful she is towards me!'

It took nearly thirty to forty minutes before the village chief came out all dressed up. Babu Chandradev Singh looked at Ramsaheli in the hope that she would greet him first, but the village chief had hoped Babu Sahib would do the same. While taking her seat, Ramsaheli commented: 'You have never come to our house!'

Gazing at Sukhdeva's mother's face, he replied, 'I used to come here! I used to!' There was a sparkle in his otherwise dull and sunken eyes, which only Sukhdeva's mother could see.

He turned his gaze back towards the village chief and said, 'The culvert in front of my house has collapsed ... if only it could be repaired before the rainy season. It becomes very troublesome, especially during the monsoon. I have come to know that some funds have been allocated.'

'Yes, the funds have been allocated. You can give an application in writing, get it signed by eight to ten members of your basti, and I shall put it before the committee.'

Grinning, Sukhdeva's mother looked at her daughter-in-law and said, 'It should be built at the earliest. He is our patron.'

Ramsaheli laughed and said, 'Not *is*, mother-in-law, you should say *was*.'

Sakaldeva, the son of the village chief, laughed out loud at his mother's measure of time. Others, too, joined him. Sukhdeva's mother covered her face with her pallu like a newly-wed bride. She preferred to see the world through the old prism, while her daughter-in-law did so through the new prism.

Cover Me in a Shroud

Usha Kiran Khan

(Translated from the Hindi by Ram Bhagwan Singh and Chaitali Pandya)

With a 'hau-hau', Kokai stopped the oxen. He had already straightened the plough coulter. The oxen stood like statues. Kokai took off the towel from around his head, wiped his sweat-soaked face, arranged his dense moustache and then stroked the oxen's back. 'Isn't it too hot? You are foaming at the mouth. Alright, sons, now we are homeward-bound. You can leisurely drink water, devour the grains and husk in the trough and ruminate and masticate till tomorrow.'

The oxen seemed to nod. The master's hand felt comforting on their backs. Standing in a corner of the plot, Kokai looked at the freshly ploughed land. *How beautiful the furrows look! Not even a single one is out of place.* It was his miracle. The senior master used to say: 'Kokai is the master of ploughing; he is skilled in sowing seeds. When the paddy plant is just eight to nine inches, it is a marvel to see the beauty of the land. What a natural artist Kokai is!'

The master's words boosted his morale. *Oh, what a kind man the senior master was!* It was said that Kokai's father had left the world when Kokai was still in his mother's womb. He was taken care of by his uncle and aunt. He grew up in his uncle's lap. When he was five years old, an ox had hit him in the eye with its horn. The senior master had taken him to Patna for treatment, but his eye could not be saved. Since then, he had been living with only one eye. *What is the point of thinking about it now?* He had lived without it for so long and would continue to do so for the rest of his life. Kokai being the son of his old servant, the master had bequeathed a piece of land in his name. Had he not written it to him, it would have been acquired by the government under the land ceiling act.

⋆

In the past, the villagers would go east to earn money. Now they went west. Back in the day, in his youth, Kokai had gone east with his companions during the monsoon to earn money, but he had not liked it. While washing flax there, something sharp had pierced into his sole. It had taken a long time to get it treated. There had been no money coming in. On the contrary, it had affected his health. Kokai, who could walk with a load of sixty kilos on his back, had been unable to lift even five kilos. He vowed to never go to Dhaka, Bengal,[81] to earn a livelihood.

Later, when his sons Phenkna and Budhna headed west, they tried to convince him. 'Baba, the west is totally different. The work is better. What will you do at home in the lean chaumas?[82] There, you can at least sow paddy. You will see another province.'

'No dear, east or west, it does not suit me. I will not go anywhere. What will I do here, you ask? Is there any dearth of work here? There is lots to do during chaumas. There is roof thatching to be done and I am the only artisan here. All you men go away, leaving behind only five

81 The story is based in pre-partition days
82 Monsoon

of us men in the village. We have bundles of straw to place on to the thatch, and you say there is no work!'

Kokai would keep on prattling. The boys would think that their father was right. There was no shortage of work in the village. When there was enough rainfall and the sowing of the paddy was over, Kokai would spin rope on his spinning tool, the terua. When the rope was ready, he would make girdles for the cows and bulls for Govardhan puja in no time. During the rainy season, Kokai would make nets from the rope, which would be fastened on the oxen's mouths during threshing. People would just hand him some flax and ask Kokai to make it, and he would oblige, never charging any fee for it. But if someone called him to their house to spin rope and make the mouth net, they had to pay him.

'Actually, there's barely any time left after work, and these fools wonder what I will do at home during chaumas?' Kokai would say. 'Stay at home and see what needs to be done!'

Every year, the field and barn were submerged in the flood. Would the lone woman of Belsandi cut the grass for cows and bulls? How were the recently calved cows to be kept healthy, without green fodder? Were the daughters-in-law to be sent to cut grass? They were also breast-feeding mothers. Preoccupied with such thoughts, Kokai did not leave the village. That's how he was. When, during the all-devouring flood, it became necessary to leave the village, Kokai accompanied animals, women and children on boats to the embankment. He shivered when he recalled that scene even today. It was a deluge! Doomsday! All the young men had gone to far-off places. Only the women, children and old men had been left behind. *Would a sensible man leave his village?* The new blooms were lending fragrance to others' gardens, leaving behind their own.

★

Suddenly, there came a gust of cool breeze. Kokai liked it. He looked up at the sky. Dense, dark clouds had gathered. 'How wonderful! Clouds at the onset of Rohini. A very auspicious sign. If it rains today, it will rain throughout the year. It will bring good crops, and a feast for saints can be arranged,' he said to no one in particular. Kokai wanted to throw a community feast from his own earnings. After all, he was a follower of the Kabir sect. He was his own master. Both his sons came running towards him, breathless.

'Baba, Baba!'

'What is it?'

'Baba, let's go home. A storm is approaching."

'All right, release the oxen's yoke. Lay the plough down. Hurry up!'

The boys ran hurriedly. Kokai laughed. 'No, it's not a storm. It'll only rain. During the storm, the sky looks grey, but now it is jet-black.' He knew his sons had little experience in this regard. *They will understand when they grow up. For now, I am their sky*, Kokai thought to himself.

'Hey, Kokai! Run! Come to my hut. It's the first rain. If lightning strikes, you may ...' Manijra called out from beneath his scaffolding in the field.

'Coming, coming! It has been too hot, just let me feel the cool breeze.' Now, lightning usually strikes black objects, which is why buffaloes and elephants remain hidden during storms. And there was Kokai, pitch-black. On many occasions Kokai's aunt would joke: 'Hey, Kokai, don't go to the fields during the rains. You're black as granite, lightning may strike you.'

'Untie the oxen quickly and release them. I am also going home. The raindrops of Rohini will refresh the body.' Collecting the basket and mattock, and passing them to the younger son, Kokai chased his elder son away. The air was humid, the heat was terrible. Mother Rohini had come to relieve the earth suffering from scorching heat.

*

Nobody knew what deadly disease Kokai's mother suffered from. She had died on the very day of Kokai's gauna.[83] Kokai had become an orphan. His bride from Belsandi, already an orphan after her parents died of cholera, never saw her mother-in-law's face. She had been brought up by her maternal uncle and aunt. At least Kokai had the privilege of experiencing the bliss of his mother's nurturing. Being a mother's son, he possessed a deep knowledge of the household. He became a typical cultivator and frugal family man. Being a follower of the Kabir sect, he was a maverick from outside and a clear stream of water from within. His wife from Belsandi gave birth to two sons, one after another. She could not conceive again. Kokai wanted a daughter, but that was not to be. On many occasions, he fulfilled his desire by buying colourful clips and frills for the little girls in the village.

A stickler for customs and traditions, Kokai would change his oxen every year. He would buy a new pair for every sowing season. Whatever he got from the sale of his old oxen, he would add some money to it and buy new ones. Three years ago, he had sold an ox. Its buyer was heard complaining that Kokai had sold him a spent ox that was not capable of doing agricultural work, and that he planned to sell it. Kokai did not pay heed to it. In November, when Gosain Sahib, a guru, came to the village, Kokai also went to pay his respects to him with gifts. The moment he reached, the guru admonished him.

'Kokai, you sold your ox to a butcher. You will have to atone for it,' he ordered.

'No, Gosain Sahib, no! I sold my ox to a farmer from Newla village.'

'It's a lie! A score of people have seen the butcher taking away your ox. Tell me, who among you has seen it?'

Some people sprang up to say that they had seen the ox with the butcher. Kokai was left flabbergasted. He said that he would find out

83 A ritual after a wedding ceremony, when the bridegroom goes to his in-law's house and brings home his bride

from the farmer to whom he had sold his ox, but he was punished without being given a hearing. No one from the Kabir sect could object as the punishment was pronounced by Gosain Sahib.

'This year the crops have failed, Gosain Sahib, but you must certainly punish me,' he implored.

'Pay a penalty when you have good crops. The time limit is until you depart from this world to reach the Great Master. Will you go with a tarnished image?' Sahib told Kokai who lay at his feet.

★

The black sky, the drops of Rohini, instilled hope. Kokai gazed at the sky with his one good eye. He saw the gleeful face of Gosain Sahib and his hollow mouth with a lone tooth. There was a sudden flash of lightning and thundering. Phenkna, Budhna, Manijra inserted their fingers into their ears. With their faces downward, they began shouting: 'Take care! Take care!'

The panic-stricken pair of oxen that had begun to run, stopped. Thick raindrops fell down to the earth. The oxen came and stood next to their ploughman.

Phenkna, Budhna and Manijra came running. Kokai lay fallen like a scorched tree, a large pit near his feet. His open eyes were staring at the sky; his body had turned grey from black. He was lying unconscious, motionless.

'Baba', 'Baba', 'Kokai Ka!' The piteous cries stirred nothing in the body. More villagers came running from their fields and scaffoldings.

Old Yadu said, 'Lightning struck here. Kokai was trapped in it. Why are you waiting? Bring in a cot; take him to the courtyard.' Half an hour of rainfall had changed the weather, turning it stuffier and more humid.

After Kokai's funeral, as it usually happens, his sons arranged for a community feast by buying things on credit. Since it was a feast for the sadhus, the menu consisted of halwa,[84] puris made of pure ghee[85] and boondi raita. During the cremation ceremony itself, the representative of the sadhus had asked the elder son, Phenkna, 'How can you light the funeral pyre? After all, you are a Kabir Panthi. First don a kanthi,[86] then only will your ascetic father attain salvation.'

Weeping like an ignorant man, wearing a kanthi, Phenkna sat down to perform the rites. The ritual feast on the twelfth day was over. With a towel around their necks, Phenkna and Budhna stood before the sadhus. 'Are we free from debt?' they had asked. Their ears were impatient to hear the word 'debt-free'.

The sadhus were soaked in the aroma of ghee. The holy chanters were singing and playing the cymbals and drums to the tune of '*How can I approach you wearing a soiled shawl?*'

'No, Phenkna, you are not debt-free yet. Gosain Sahib had pronounced a penalty of a feast to be organized for seventy-five sadhus. The poor man could not fulfil it. Now you must honour it after him. If you want to be debt-free, you will have to do this,' said the representative of the sadhus.

'Seventy-five sadhus! What do you mean? We are already ruined. Who will give me a loan now?' Phenkna began to weep.

'What? Then how will your father's sin be washed away?'

'You people are being unjust. Kabir Das was against all conventions. In his name, you have climbed to the top of orthodoxy,' said a boy pursuing his matriculate.

'Who asked you? It is about Phenkna becoming debt-free. Don't compel him to be liable to sin by misleading him.'

'Do you claim to be a great scholar?' More boys came forward in retaliation. There was a huge furore. Phenkna fell at the feet of the head

84 A type of Indian dessert

85 Clarified butter

86 A sacred neck string, usually made of dried twigs of holy basil

of the sadhus. Budhna was weeping beyond control. Kokai's wife from Belsandi fell unconscious.

'O mortal, call your mother. We will ask her where she wishes to place her man in the other world.' The sadhu's fearless roar instilled courage in Phenkna. He turned towards the villagers, wiped his tears and stood with folded hands.

'Tell me, uncles, brothers! Will you help us destitutes?'

'No need to say anything. We are going to the village grocer and will give him the list of our requirements. The work will start right away,' said an experienced old man. The grocer came in no time and delivered all the provisions required. The confectioners came, too. Starting from the twelfth day until the thirteenth day, seventy-five sadhus were fed.

The holy chanters sang: *Cover me in a shroud, it is time to leave.*

'Dear Phenkna, sign this list. It shall remain with me. You and your brother can keep paying out of your earnings. Read it carefully,' the grocer said.

Phenkna read falteringly, 'Interest two per cent.' With tearful eyes, he looked at the people present there and signed the bill.

'Ah, the father's last rites were performed. The penalty was also met. Well done, son!' remarked the old man. Gradually, the guests began to leave. Phenkna walked with heavy steps and stood before his semi-conscious mother. He sat down quietly as his mother looked on feebly.

'Ma, tomorrow morning I must leave the village. Please don't lose heart. Budhna will manage the field and help you. So long as we don't pay off the debt of Baba's last rites, how can we cover him with a shroud? Baba's spirit won't attain salvation.'

Holding her son tightly, she wept her heart out, never to return to her senses again.

★

Pulling a rickshaw and working a double shift in Benaras, an exhausted Phenkna slept at the Kabir crossroad like a dog. The sad tune of the holy song continued to resonate in the air: *Cover me in a shroud...*

Phenkna pedalled his rickshaw vigorously. He was yet to pay back some of the debt.

Girls on Rooftops

Alok Dhanwa

(Translated from the Hindi by Anonymous)

Still the girls come to the rooftops,
their shadows fall on my life.

The girls are here for the boys,
downstairs, amidst bullets, the boys play cards.

Sitting tea, a boy on the stairs above the drain,
lazing on benches outside the footpath tea stall.

Sipping tea, a boy plays the mouth organ sweet,
the timeless tunes of *Awara*, *Shree 420*.[87]

A newspaper-wallah spreads his wares,
and some young men read the early edition.

---

87 *Awara* and *Shree 420* are popular Hindi films

Not all are students, some are unemployed,
some small-timers, some whilers, lumpens.

But in their veins, bloodstreams,
they await a girl.

A hope—that from these houses and rooftops,
one day, some day—love will arrive.

A Twist of Fate

Hussain Ul Haque

(Translated from the Urdu by Huma Mirza)

Bibi Izzat-un Nisa was busy winding up her daily chores as quickly as she could. When she leaned out of the kitchen window, she realized that though the evening was drawing closer, her errands didn't seem to end. An afternoon siesta had turned her schedule upside down. After she was done with the utensils, she remembered the pile of clothes, full of filth and faecal matter, that needed to be washed.

With the children growing older, she had thought that she would be relieved of this laundry routine at least, but who can predict the misfortunes destined to befall us! Her husband had been struck with paralysis and was bedridden. All he could utter was 'food' and 'water', that too with much effort. Any minor ailment could make a man irritable, and Izzat-un Nisa's husband's ailment was a serious one. While he was hale and hearty, he kept up to his name; he never let anything or anyone take him for granted. There was absolutely no chance of him tolerating anything outside his comfort zone. Nobody could dare solve an issue without consulting him—be it at home or in the neighbourhood. From perverse to debased language to abuses, he could go to any length to pamper his ego.

Izzat-un Nisa was taken aback by this bestial demeanour when she got married and came to live with her in-laws. Her sisters-in-law, her friends and relatives, all advised her to ignore his behaviour for a while, as it was typical of the landlord lineage that he belonged to. He was the proverbial spoilt nawab of an influential family, they said. With perseverance and generous caring, she would be able to bind him in her love. His sharp tongue and authoritarian ways could be tamed according to her will, they advised.

Following these suggestions, Bibi Izzat-un Nisa started experimenting with her affection. She believed that her usual meticulous and impeccable mannerisms alone would not suffice if she had to gain his attention and kindness. Jalaluddin had this monster hidden inside him that, leave alone the usual times, would emerge even at the time of lovemaking. His use of brute force made the act of making love rather gruesome. Whenever she would be in the mood for tenderness, he would find an excuse to pick a fight with her, which would then result in slaps and violence, after which he would drift into a peaceful slumber. Izzat-un Nisa never dared to improve his mood by trying to entice him. By the time Jalaluddin would tame his boorish ways to some extent and get drawn to her, it would be time for her menstrual cycle. She would expect some relief in this period, but those few days would turn out to be the most terrible ones. Every month, during that week, he would pinch and assault her not just in his usual bestial ways but with all the characteristics of a maniac. The entire exercise would be nothing but sheer torment. She would try to escape the ordeal but would fail. To add to it, during those days, there would be a river of desire rising within her. Despite all the violence, the meeting of two bodies would ultimately result in heightened emotions. Despite her tired body, and blinded by the emotional turmoil, she would quietly lie down with her eyes closed and let the tornado take over her senses.

All three of her children were beautiful reminders, conceived in and around those cruel days.

This continued for about seven or eight years of their marriage, till her husband had a paralytic stroke. Doctors ascribed it to high blood pressure. Izzat-un Nisa wasn't surprised. It wasn't difficult to figure out the cause of such high blood pressure. It was a natural fallout, given Jalaluddin's nature. But the cause of this high blood pressure did not take a toll on him alone, it managed to cripple the entire household.

It wasn't just Jalaluddin's anger that was sustained by the lands he owned; the entire household depended on the revenue coming in from those lands. All their acquaintances vanished over time, along with the landlord's power. His brothers, too, shifted to other cities when the lands were taken away. Later came the news that they had migrated to Pakistan. The only people left in his family were his parents, who, unable to bear this fury of fate, departed from this world one after the other, within a year. Her own family, too, had left for Pakistan. Her entire universe now centred around her three children and paralytic husband.

Her life had become like a lacerated wound on the head of a dog that was already suffering from rabies. It was during one of these days that Lala Harihar Prasad visited her house.

Lala Harihar Prasad was the younger brother of Jalaluddin's family accountant, Munshi Lala Bansidhar Prasad. Bansidhar was the same age as Jalaluddin, but he would never sit in front of or beside Jalaluddin. As soon as he began climbing the steps of the haveli, he turned into a pliant pet wagging its tail. He would take off his shoes the moment he entered the house, adjust his dhoti and sit on the bench placed on the verandah. He would keep sitting there calmly even if nobody showed up for an hour or so. When somebody did step out and saw him sitting on the bench, he would ask them to inform the master about his arrival. But in spite of that, there was no guarantee that Jalaluddin would acknowledge Bansidhar's presence and meet him. His job was to sit and wait, and to leave only when Jalaluddin allowed him to.

All the household necessities, from groceries to jewellery, were managed by Bansidhar. Nobody gave him any money, nor did he ever ask for it. Jalaluddin himself never asked Bansidhar for accounts of income or expenditure. Bansidhar handled all issues related to the farm and the land given for tenancy. Every deposit and withdrawal, buying and selling of land, was handled by Bansidhar. After all, he was in charge of all the finances.

But when the zamindari system came to an end, what task could be assigned to Bansidhar?

That orchard would have definitely been left intact, Izzat-un Nisa wondered. *But whom can I ask*? Definitely not Jalaluddin. Living corpses are never in a position to ask questions or answer them. She could have asked Lala Bansidhar, but no one knew where he was. Bansidhar, who would be in attendance at the haveli every day, had not visited once in the last six months. Earlier, at the onset of Jalaluddin's paralysis, he used to visit them regularly for about two months or so. But once he gathered from the doctors that the paralysis would plague Jalaluddin for the rest of his life, and his consequent incapability to share any details with anybody, his daily visits had dwindled to a routine absence.

When Lala's absence was finally established and the household items were being sold to fulfil day-to-day needs, for the first time since her wedding, Izzat-un Nisa crossed the threshold of the haveli.

Putting on her veil and wearing her burqa, she reached the front gate. Immediately, the family's palanquin bearer, Ghooran, came to her.

'Maalkin,[88] are you planning to go somewhere?'

'I am thinking of going to Lala Bansidhar's house.'

'Why are you going there? I will go and call him.'

She gave a cynical laugh, 'Those times are gone. Now I will have to go on my own.'

---

88 Mistress

'Okay, if you insist. Please stay here, I will bring the palanquin.'

'Don't bother, I will walk down.'

Ghooran pleaded in an emotionally charged voice, 'Till I am alive, I will never let this happen.'

She laughed with a hint of authority. 'Okay, go and get the palanquin.'

There was an instant buzz in Lala Bansidhar's house when Izzat-un Nisa arrived. Ghooran announced her arrival the moment they reached.

'The palanquin has come from maalkin's house.'

Bansidhar's old mother immediately came to the front door to greet her, stunned by her sudden visit.

'Maalkin, you took the trouble of coming here yourself?'

'Yes, mataji, I thought I should visit you,' Izzat-un Nisa answered with a smile as her eyes swept over the house.

The accountant's haveli was bigger than theirs. It was surrounded by magnificent fort-like walls. One part was cordoned off for the servants' quarters, a stable stood on the other side, and a cow shed occupied the third corner. There was a small temple on the side, adjacent to the well; the haveli towered in the centre. There was also an outhouse and an inner space. Stretching through the expanse and connecting the two was a small courtyard. Through the same courtyard, Bansidhar's mother took her inside the house.

All the family members were there except Lala Bansidhar! The first person she saw was Lala Harihar Prasad. He was undoubtedly handsome, with a clear and fair complexion, sharp features and average height. He was impressive at first glance. Immediately, a thought crossed her mind: *He is younger than Bansidhar, might be a year or two older than me.*

She had not crossed thirty-two yet.

After some polite small talk, she came to the point. 'Mataji, where is Lala Bansidhar?'

'Don't ask me his whereabouts. I might have borne him, but he has turned into a stranger. We could have never imagined. Three months ago, he left for Delhi with his wife and children. Had Harihar not been with us, we would have been devastated by now.'

'Any idea of his whereabouts there?' Izzat-un Nisa felt her voice drowning in a sea of hopelessness.

'None at all, bibi. The only thing he said before leaving was that he doesn't want to stay in this city any more. We know nothing besides that.'

Izzat-un Nisa could see that Bansidhar's mother did not want to talk about him. She also understood the implications of this knowledge on her fate. Her heart sank.

'Okay, mataji. I will take your leave now.'

She cried to her heart's content all the way back home. She was lost in a reverie of the time gone by—her childhood, the courtyard of her parental home, the flowers and fruits in her backyard, friends and relatives, all those games she played as a child, a distant cousin who would stare at her at every opportunity and how she would run away, giggling at his absurdity. Bibi lived through many decades as she sat in the palanquin that day. She found her home in utter chaos when she got back.

Her husband had soiled the bed and the children were crying. Her elder daughter was trying her best to handle the mess, but her father was not easy to handle with such utter confusion all around. Izzat-un Nisa first cleaned up her husband, then tended to the children and then turned her attention to the kitchen. It was dark by the time she finished all her chores. When she finally hit the bed after feeding everyone, her senses were in disarray. She could not think of any consoling balm that could be applied in these circumstances. Let alone her husband's treatment, even arranging for food and clothes would be a challenge. She racked her brains, but she could not think of anybody who could come to her rescue in these turbulent times. There was this utter mayhem of 1947, followed by the abolition of the zamindari system. All her near and dear ones, on whom she could have depended to ease her towering burdens, had migrated to Pakistan. Had this tragedy not befallen Jalaluddin, a tragedy that rendered him disabled for the rest of his life, they too would have moved to Pakistan.

In the six months that followed, life took a completely different course. The golden era of abundance and prosperity under the zamindari system had already come to an end. The household items had been sold. Izzat-un Nisa's stature had altered from a maalkin to a tutor. When this, too, proved to be insufficient, she started stitching clothes for children and reading the Quran in people's homes. Despite all this, there did not seem to be any silver lining behind the dark cloud of her existence. There seemed to be no way to alleviate her suffering and leave her with some time to relax. The local doctor had advised her to give her husband the juice of pigeon's meat; Maulvi Sahib's fees were yet to be paid. The new academic year had begun and the expenditure of buying new books for the children was adding to her pile of woes. While she could somehow manage to face the day-to-day challenges, the ones looming over the future filled her with dread. She sometimes felt as if her head would burst.

It was during these testing times that Lala Harihar Prasad visited her house.

The month of Sha'ban[89] was almost nearing the end, and it was the last phase of the moon, too. Darkness was pouring in like cloudbursts on the haveli. Fog had enveloped the entire neighbourhood, even though the night hadn't yet descended. The door had not been shut yet. That was when she had sensed that someone was standing at the threshold.

---

89 The eighth month of the Islamic calendar, the last lunar month before Ramadan

Izzat-un Nisa couldn't imagine who could have come at this hour, on a cold and dark night such as this. She raised the wick of the dim lantern and moved towards the front door with her daughter, Ruqayya.

She could see a silhouette in the light of the lantern. Lala Harihar Prasad was at the door.

'Lalaji?'

Lala Harihar Prasad stood with folded hands. For a moment, she stared at him, unable to figure out what she should do. But, in a flash, she regained her composure.

'Please wait a moment, Lalaji,' she said and dashed inside to open the door of the sitting room. She swiftly dusted the two chairs and the table—the only furniture that remained—and leapt back towards the door. 'Lalaji, please come in!'

Lalaji entered the sitting room with reluctant steps. When she asked him to sit down, Lalaji folded his hands and pleaded, 'Excuse me, but I cannot sit unless you do, too.'

She sat down with a smile. With humility, Lalaji sat down on the edge of one chair, as if on tenterhooks. A desert of silence stretched between them for some time. Izzat-un Nisa felt that Lalaji was hesitant to initiate the conversation.

'What brings you here today?'

'I am most embarrassed,' he said with folded hands. 'I wanted to come earlier, but somehow couldn't muster the courage. Today I was passing by here and felt a strange compulsion.'

Izzat-un Nisa looked at him with a bemused expression and listened intently. There was a strange mixture of hesitation and confusion in Lalaji's voice. She remembered her distant cousin who was crazily in love with her. He had met her once after she had got married, and had asked her in a dull voice: 'How are you? My eyes have been deprived of your sight.' Later, whenever his voice had reverberated in her mind, she had felt as if it had been a dying man saying his last goodbye. It always made her shudder.

It was uncanny that Lalaji's voice reminded her of that love-crazed young man from her past.

That day, Lalaji stayed for a very short time. He made some small talk and left. One day ... two days ... four days, and then the entire week passed. Izzat-un Nisa forgot about his visit. As usual, her days were hopeless.

And then, on an idle and empty day, Lala Harihar Prasad visited again. He inquired about the children as soon as he sat down.

'They have slept,' Izzat-un Nisa answered quietly.

'Ruqayya?'

'No, she is studying.'

'Will you please call her?'

Izzat-un Nisa went inside and called Ruqayya to the sitting room. Lalaji touched her chin and kissed her. He caressed her head and handed her a packet. 'This is for you and your siblings.'

Ruqayya's hand unconsciously moved towards the packet, and then she suddenly stopped. She looked at her mother.

'What's the need for all this, Lalaji?'

Lala simply folded his hands.

'This is for the children. I came across a sweet shop on my way here and thought they would enjoy them.'

'Take it, Ruqayya. It's rude to not accept presents.' Her eyes dimmed with tears as she said this, trying to recall the last time her children had a sweet treat, but her memory refused to come to her aid.

'Get some tea,' Izzat-un Nisa said in a soft voice when Ruqayya was about to leave.

'It's quite late now, please don't bother,' Lalaji spoke, his hands folded yet again.

'Lalaji, this was the time the merrymaking started in the haveli once upon a time.' Izzat-un Nisa could not hide the soft lament in her voice.

From that moment, Izzat-un Nisa started opening up to Lalaji. He would visit every alternate day, and always bring something for the children.

Then one day Lalaji came, sat for a while and got up to leave early. He stopped at the door just before leaving, turned towards Izzat-un Nisa, and gave her a handkerchief pressed between his palms. His demeanour was extremely humble and his voice had a pleading and fearful tone. 'Please don't refuse this.'

Izzat-un Nisa could not discern what it was. It was a dark night. There was a sharp breeze and chaotic emotions. *How will I protect the candle in the wind? How will someone as weak as me stay upright in these storms?*

Before she could decide what to do, Lalaji pressed the handkerchief in her hands and stepped out. Izzat-un Nisa closed the door behind her and leaned against it. She opened the handkerchief. It was the night of the new moon. She peered at the small bundle in her hand. There were five notes of hundred rupees tied neatly into the handkerchief. She sat there at the door and cried her heart out.

Lalaji did not come for almost two weeks after that. Those days proved to be a kind of testing period. The house was in absolute chaos. The money was lying at the bottom of her trunk, waiting for the warmth of her touch. During those times, the children cried several times; she herself broke down umpteen number of times. She felt overwhelmed as the realization hit her that there was nobody to inquire about her welfare. In one such desultory moment, she looked at her husband and found herself in the grip of mixed emotions—anger, hatred and sympathy, all at the same time.

In those exhausting moments, the question which consumed her was: *This man is being punished for his deeds. Fine. What was the indiscretion for which my children and I are suffering*? It was beyond her comprehension.

Sometimes she would get tired of the daily rigmarole and mentally explore possibilities. She would think: *It is impossible that Lala Harihar is unaware of Bansidhar's financial control over my household, and he certainly must be familiar with all the transactions regarding my husband's assets. It is possible that Harihar had informed Bansidhar and he had sent the money.* She would run towards the trunk with these seductive thoughts in her head. But, as she would unlock it, she would again be rocked by a dilemma. *Mataji had made it very clear that they had no idea about Bansidhar's whereabouts. They didn't even have his address to send letters to. Then where could this money have come from*? She would stop, shake her head, wipe her tears and walk away from the trunk.

Life is made up of myriad shades of colours and moods. Spring takes over autumn, there's humidity over fresh breeze! Izzat-un Nisa's life was akin to somebody trapped in a whirling tornado. *But where is the rapture, Izzat-un Nisa*?

In one of those penetratingly crushing moments, Lala Harihar Prasad knocked on the door. After some light conversation, Izzat-un Nisa asked, 'Did you receive any letter from Lala Bansidhar?'

'No, I don't know anything about him.'

'And don't you plan to look for him?'

'I wanted to, but Mataji did not let me.'

'Why does she not want to know about him?'

'Please, let's leave it here. I don't want to go into the details.'

'But, Lalaji … this detail is essential to my survival. Please don't hide anything.'

Lala Harihar relaxed and answered in a dull voice. 'He had a fight with Mataji. She advised him to return all the remaining property, of which he is the guardian, to the real owners.'

What is left to ask now? She understood everything that Lalaji was trying to hide. And he knew her concerns and questions. There was some kind of supernatural transmission. The dark night, hurtling down the corridor slowly but deliberately, was busy forming a network of strong emotions. Izzat-un Nisa wanted to break this network, but she felt trapped in a labyrinth.

Suddenly her house seemed to be suffering a paralytic stroke.

She felt like a woman, but in that moment, she was a housefly whom some demon had pinned to a wall. She looked at Lala Harihar Prasad penetratingly. Was he that demon?

Lalaji's face was angelic, pure and innocent. He got up and said, 'I will take your leave now.'

'Lalaji, just a minute, please!' she uttered in a trance-like voice and quickly went inside. She took the handkerchief out of her trunk and came back to the sitting room. She stretched out her hand towards Lalaji. 'You entrusted me with this.'

For a minute, Lala Harihar Prasad looked at her intently. He gently took the money from her and, bending down, kept it at her feet. He knelt down, took her right hand in his, raised it to his eyes and started sobbing silently, uncontrollably. Her hand was drenched with his tears.

This was a very unusual and peculiar situation, not to mention unwanted. Izzat-un Nisa tried her best to not drown in the fast-flowing river of emotions, even as she felt the presence of an unseen sea inside her, like an impending storm. In those dreadful moments, that boy, whom she had met only once after she got married, and whose voice seemed as though it was coming from the depths of the ocean, rang in her ears. *How are you? My eyes have been deprived of your sight.*

Lalaji stood bewildered for a few minutes and then quickly left. That night, a compelling juxtaposition of colours enveloped Izzat-un Nisa. Blue, yellow, red, purple, pink, turquoise, ivory, beige, black, pistachio, mauve, grey, lime, rose and blue—all the hues of life were bathed in blissful fragrance, merging into infinite space as the weather submerged into a wintry fog. The birds encircled her fragile persona—parrots, sparrows, bulbuls, koels, swans, pelicans, peacocks and falcons. All night, she drowned and rose in that turbulent sea.

The waves tossed her into crests and troughs as if she were a tiny boat. She could feel the presence of somebody flinging her from a forlorn desert to a gushing river, back and forth. When she woke up, she could clearly recall the colour black, some birds, the turbulent waves of the ocean, and the scorching afternoon of a desert.

Something else, too, happened that day. When she sat in front of the mirror after a bath, she noticed her own reflection and was startled at her appearance, her perfection. Neither the testing times nor the travails of life had impacted her beauty—the long tresses, the pinkish complexion and the sharp, refined features. The smile that adorned her face was self-conscious and apprehensive.

'Bibi, please wear these earrings. They suit you.' The distant cousin took over the mirror.

'I am going crazy,' she laughed uninhibitedly.

'Do you have any idea how the entire universe forgets to breathe when you carelessly push those tresses off your face and laugh?' the cousin's voice was still there.

Ho chukein Ghalib balaayein sab tamaam,
ek marg-e naagah aani aur hai…
(All misfortunes have passed, Ghalib,
just one deathly disaster is yet to come…)

As this long-forgotten couplet crawled into her mind and her consciousness reached the second line, the mirror started to form a glittering image of Lala Harihar Prasad.

Allah, save me from these depraved thoughts. She moved away from the mirror. But then, in a strange move, she took out a hundred-rupee note from the trunk, put on her veil and left for the market.

Another strange thing was her deviant thoughts that constantly flew towards Lala Harihar Prasad, more so when she was cleaning Jalaluddin. She would be seized by an image … the image of a man sitting on his haunches, holding her hand and crying. A handsome, dashing man! A gentleman!

She would try her best to dismiss those thoughts by focusing on other tasks, but they refused to let go, keeping up a constant game of hide-and-seek with her.

This time, Lala visited after a gap of twenty days. He did not knock. He entered the haveli at sunset and quietly stood behind the doors. Izzat-un Nisa was busy preparing dinner. She did not hear any sound, but her sixth sense alerted her. She felt a queer emotion taking over. Leaving behind her work, she came out. Everything was as usual. Jalaluddin was on his bed, the children were doing their homework in the dim light of the lantern, and her youngest son had fallen asleep. She was relieved and went back to the kitchen.

But within a few minutes, she again felt uneasy. She was unable to figure out the cause of her heightened nervousness. Something drew her eyes to the door. She took a couple of steps towards it. It wasn't fully dark, yet she recognized him. *Lala! Standing quietly!*

'Oh, since how long have you been standing? Why didn't you knock?'

'I didn't have the courage.'

'You are one of a kind, Lalaji. Please come in.'

He followed her into the sitting room in the outer part of the haveli and sat down.

'I will be back in five minutes. The vegetables are simmering on the stove,' she said, and hurriedly walked towards the kitchen.

She quickly placed the kettle on the stove, put together some snacks she had bought from the market earlier that day on a plate and placed the tea mugs on a tray. She took the tea and snacks to the sitting room.

'Oh! Why did you take the trouble?' Seeing the tray in her hands, Lalaji stood up with folded hands.

'Lalaji!' she said with a laugh tinged with sadness. 'This was the least of my troubles,' she added, stressing on the word 'least'.

'Bibi, you can punish me whichever way you want to, but it was never my intention to hurt you.'

Izzat-un Nisa laughed again. For a moment, it felt like the dark clouds of her tribulations had cleared up. This was the first time that Lalaji had stayed for long, almost an hour and a half. This was the first time the conversation had swayed towards her own folks, her parental home. And it had swayed in a way that she had completely lost track of how she travelled from the desolate desert of her present surroundings to the soft and cool shade of her past. The conversation took her back to her parental home, where she ran recklessly into long-forgotten rooms, verandas and courtyards. She saw a monkey dance with fierce abandon in the alley. The memories of her loving mother, adoring sisters, friends, relatives, neighbours and her doting brothers took her into the realm of euphoria. The time and place she encountered during that conversation was calm, entering her very being with a peaceful tranquillity, like the light and cool drizzle of an early monsoon on the parched earth … Izzat-un Nisa poured her heart out and Lala listened, his eyes not once moving away from her face.

The muezzin's call from a nearby mosque for the isha[90] prayers jolted her out of her reverie. 'Oh, so much time has passed!'

Lalaji stood up with folded hands. 'I am so sorry for taking up so much of your time.'

No, Harihar, you have released me from the clutches of time after decades, she thought, but did not say anything.

Lala slowly walked towards the door. Izzat-un Nisa was waiting to bolt the door for the night after he left. As Lalaji stepped on to the threshold, he stopped, stepped back a little, and came closer to Izzat-un Nisa. She noted his proximity with incredible wonder.

'Can I say something?' Lalaji's voice was tense, laboured.

90 Since an Islamic day starts at sunset, the isha prayer is technically the second prayer of the day; if counted from midnight, it is the fifth prayer of the day

'Say it, please,' she said with wonder and anticipation in her voice.

'You will not mind, I hope!'

`Have I taken offense at anything you've said until now?'

'Promise me that you won't stop me from coming to your house.'

'Who else comes here otherwise?'

'Should I say it?'

'Yes, please do.'

'I want to see you, to my heart's content, in the brilliance of the sun!'

'But how is it possible?'

'Why? What's wrong with it?'

'You must try to understand. It is true that no relatives from my parents' side or my in-laws are left to inquire about my welfare, or to even hold me accountable for any digression, as they have all migrated to Pakistan. But the houses in the neighbourhood have been handed over to refugees. It is also a fact that all our old acquaintances, familiar with Jalaluddin's rage and atrocious behaviour, have distanced themselves from us, with a certain enmity in their hearts. Now that we are in this sorry state, it is quite obvious that they will be waiting for a chance to seek revenge. In spite of this, there are some poor houses left in the alleys. Their daughters come to study at my house. Sometimes their sisters and mothers also visit in the daytime because they are scared of the refugees. How can I ask you to come during the day?'

Suddenly, Lalaji went down on his knees. He was facing Izzat-un Nisa and both his hands were pressed together. 'Bibi! I will die. I need a breath of fresh air.'

In the symphony of his tone, there was a powerful and unmistakeable blend of tears. Izzat-un Nisa felt that the man on his knees was not Lala Harihar Prasad. He was a thirsty bird longing for a sip of water in the scorching afternoon sun. She felt like … for the first time she felt like…

She bent over Lalaji's forehead in a trance, as though she was intoxicated. Both her hands were eager to cup his face. She felt herself bending, shivering with anxiety.

In that kneeling posture, Lalaji's eyes were focused on her face in a manner that suggested the yearning in the eyes of a farmer upon sighting a cloud after long months of extreme drought.

Izzat-un Nisa's face leaned towards Lalaji's and his craving eyes. This sight was witnessed by the glittering darkness, by the encircling haveli, by that corner of the sky whose imperceptible tent had stretched over them. But the spectacle changed within a moment.

Izzat-un Nisa suddenly stopped, even as she was bending towards Lalaji's forehead. With tremendous effort, she slowly stood up and pleaded piteously. 'Lalaji, please don't make it more difficult for me. I already have enough on my plate.'

Lalaji stood up with urgent anxiety. Izzat-un Nisa's tears were glistening on his hands, sparkling like gems. He lifted his hands towards his parched lips and kissed her tears. His voice reached her, traversing an infinity, 'Bibi, may your enemies be doomed to death. Why should you burden yourself with so much responsibility?'

'Please leave now. I can't bear it anymore,' Izzat-un Nisa pleaded with folded hands.

Lalaji looked even more distressed. 'It's okay, bibi. I am leaving.'

He took a few steps, stopped and then turned. 'Please take this,' he said slowly, and extended a packet towards her.

'What's this?'

'I was confident you would not reject my devotion.' There was a tinge of softness in his tone.

She smiled quietly. 'Okay. Khuda Hafiz!'[91]

Bolting the door, she came to a room where neither her children nor her husband were present. She opened the packet. There was a saree, some clothes for the children and an envelope with five hundred

91 A common parting phrase originating in the Persian language, meaning 'God protect you'

rupees. All of a sudden, she remembered that a month had passed since Lala gave her the money last time. *Oh god! What should I do*?

Izzat-un Nisa never found an answer to this question.

However, Lalaji came back after a week. She opened the door to let him in, but he kept standing at the threshold.

'Why are you standing here? Why aren't you coming in?'

'No, I will not come inside. Please read this letter.'

Lalaji extended an envelope towards her, turned around and, with quick long strides, merged into the darkness.

Izzat-un Nisa brightened the flame of the lantern upon entering the room.

> I feel like a culprit. I have no right to take advantage of your vulnerable position.
>
> I want to serve you, and that I will do till I am alive. Your happiness alone will be the reward of this service. I just need some fresh air.
>
> —Lala Harihar Prasad
> Peeli Kothi
> Bypass Road
>
> Last house on the second street after the first left turn.
> Available hours: 11 a.m. to 2 p.m. (Wednesday and Sunday)

The next day was Sunday. Bibi Izzat-un Nisa returned home around three in the afternoon. She was wearing the saree that Lalaji had gifted her.

When she entered her house, she saw a neighbour waiting for her. She had come to invite her for milaad shareef[92] after the evening prayers.

92 A religious holiday celebrating the birthday of Prophet Muhammad

Izzat-un Nisa took out an old saree Jalaluddin had bought for her to wear for the milaad shareef. She got ready and reached there slightly before time. The moist eyes of the listeners were proof of her passionate and intense recital. Her own eyes welled up; her tears were unstoppable. She was crying and singing in exhilaration…

Please save me from the wrath of God on
the day of judgement…
I am most miserable and unfortunate,
O prophet of Allah!

Damul

Shaiwal

(Translated from the Hindi by Ram Bhagwan Singh and Chaitali Pandya)

On the other side of the river, on its sandy bank, Rajuli sat helplessly, feeling run-down. She wiped off the sweat on her face with her pallu. Her whole body felt stiff. She felt as if her legs had hardened into logs.

She knew why she was feeling that way. This was not the fatigue you felt when you walked a lot. This was another kind of fatigue, the kind she felt while coming out of Jehanabad court, as if there was no life left in her body.

Standing in the witness box like a statue, Sanjiwana had kept staring at her. The police asked him to step down, but before he could do so, Rajuli exited the court. Perhaps she knew that there was nothing else to be done; there was no way to save Sanjiwana.

Mukhiya Madho Pande walked past her, lecturing someone. A few people followed him. Rajuli had moved to the other side of the road. Standing under the banyan tree at Lali's tea stall, she had had a cup of tea. From the position of the sun, she guessed that the day was coming to an end.

Trudging along, she reached the Jehanabad dak bungalow. From there, she took the adjacent lane. By the time she reached the bus station through the bazaar, it was 4 p.m. She took the Ekangarsarai bus and got to Telhada. She bought two annas worth of roasted puffed rice. *Now even getting food will be a challenge. Sanjiwana will come back after serving twenty years in jail. Until then, the children … who knows*? She shuddered at the thought. She then strode off, down the unmetalled road, lumbering forward on her seemingly lifeless legs.

By the time she reached, the sun had already slumped like a man who had had an epileptic fit.

The chirping of the crickets could be heard from behind the karmi bushes. Hearing them in the calm atmosphere, Rajuli felt as if Mukhiya Pande was laughing and chortling. He, too, would be there soon. It would be better if the boat reached before he came. The boatman, Triloki, would not refuse to take her to the other side. After all, only a wearer knows where the shoe pinches. His young son, Channar, had also been in jail for the last five years.

During the election, Mukhiya's brother, Baso, had lured Channar by offering him some money. He would take Channar everywhere. He had also arranged a gun for him. And during the booth-capturing at Basopatti, six persons had been gunned down. Channar had been caught and sent to jail. Baso Pande became the MLA, but who cares after one's interest is served! Poor Triloki, even in his old age, toiled for the sake of Channar's wife and his two children.

Rajuli's eyes wandered towards the village across the river. From east to west, from the huts of the Dusadh toli to the mansion of Mukhiya Pande to MLA Baso Pande's well-furnished house to their contractor brother, Ragho Pande's flour mills and two-storeyed house. And then, looking at the silhouette of her unthatched hut, she was overcome with grief. Her children, Rukna and Dulli, would be squatting at the door, expecting their mother to return any moment.

Rajuli felt the packet of puffed rice tied to her pallu. *It's safe*! *It hasn't fallen*. She would feed her children puffed rice and give them some water. She had no strength left to cook. Moreover, there was no rice or pulses at home. When she had gone to Khosi Grocer to beg for rice on credit, she had been humiliated. She realized that all this was Mukhiya Pande's doing. The whole village was a slave to the three brothers. They had a say in every matter. They would often fight amongst themselves, but it seemed to be just an eyewash. The three were each other's spies. Whenever any villager rebelled against any of them, they came to know about it and got him implicated in a case, or had his crops looted.

Suddenly, the sparrows on the peepal tree nearby started chirping, sounding aggrieved. Rajuli was startled. Looking in that direction, she plunged deep into her dark past.

The day Rajuli had come to Sanjiwana's home after their wedding, he had told her, 'Now, let us go to seek Pandeji's blessings!'

Wearing a veil, Rajuli, with Sanjiwana, had gone to the three houses one by one, offering her salutation by touching her head to the ground. In return, she had not heard a single word of blessing. It was only after returning from the three houses that Sanjiwana had taken her to seek the blessings of his ancestral tutelary deity and the other gods and goddesses.

At night, Rajuli had asked him, 'Are the three Pande brothers greater than the gods and goddesses?'

'Why?'

'Because you took me to them first, to touch their feet—'

Rajuli's sentence had remained incomplete. Sanjiwana, either trying to conceal his cowardliness, or out of annoyance, had rained abuses on her. He had then turned to the other side and slept.

The next day, at noon, Rajuli had come to the door after hearing some brouhaha. She had looked outside through the slit in the door. A crowd had gathered outside Mukhiya Pandeji's house. Amid the crowd had been Sanjiwana, holding a rope tied around a buffalo's neck.

Mukhiya Pandeji had said to Baraahilji:[93] 'Runu Babu! Fasten the buffalo in the cowshed and lay this rogue on the ground. Tie his hands and feet.'

An old man standing nearby had been repeatedly touching Mukhiya Pandeji's feet. 'Leave him, babu! He is an orphan.'

'Lachhman, have you become a leader in this old age? This rogue will not mend his ways without punishment. He is an orphan, you say? Does that mean he will turn into a rogue? Don't we exist? We know how to bring these young lads to their senses.' Mukhiya Pande's words had made it seem as if he was the father of the whole village, empowered to reform all and sundry.

'One last chance, master!' Stooping, the old man had touched Mukhiya Pandeji's feet three times. His scraggly beard had been quivering. Mukhiya Pande had moved away. Trembling, the old man had said to Sanjiwana, 'Saala! You scoundrel! What are you standing here for? You shameless fellow! Why don't you fall at the master's feet?'

Rajuli had shut the door tightly. It had been painful to see Sanjiwana rubbing his head on Mukhiya Pandeji's feet. It had been unbearable. With indescribable pain and an extreme feeling of humiliation, she had closed her eyes, as if the same scene was repeating on every wall.

The next moment, Mukhiya Pandeji's voice had pierced through her. 'Bastard! What was the need to get married? That year, during the flood, I saved you from starvation by lending you money, but you did not remember to repay the debt. The moment you had your fill, you started craving comfort and luxury.' There had been a strange melody in Mukhiya Pandeji's voice, as if he were reprimanding his own son, showing him the right path, but there was unmissable and immense bitterness in his intentions.

93 A strongman, usually also the caretaker of the house, cattle and fields

'If you can't repay the money, give me your buffalo or mortgage your house. If you can't do either, tell me right now, you brat! Are you so full of youthful lust that you can't do without a wife?' he had said.

Rajuli had closed her ears at this point and gone to the courtyard. Her heart had been thumping. Her intuition had warned her that something untoward would happen.

Sanjiwana had not returned home the whole day. He had not even turned up at night. The next morning, the police had come searching for him. Rumours were rife that the night before Sanjiwana had stolen a pair of Maina oxen from the cowshed of Babu Sahib of Kadra village.

The police had come to the hut looking for Sanjiwana. They had smashed the pots and clay vessels with their boots. Rajuli had sat quietly in a corner while the police went on a rampage, wondering whether they thought someone could be hiding in the pots and pans. When the police had left, Mukhiya Pande had come to her and whispered, 'Don't fear. I am here. The police are just making a show.'

On the pretext of saying something in her ear, he had brushed his chin against her cheek and said, 'Sanjiwana is with me, inside the house. The police want a bribe; I will take care of it.'

Rajuli had been aghast. She had stared at Mukhiya Pandeji in the face, unmindful of her immodesty. She had been unable to understand what was happening.

Everything came to light later. Sanjiwana had come home at midnight. He had bruises all over his body. For a minute, both of them had just kept looking at each other. Then, clinging to his chest, Rajuli had wept. Sanjiwana had brashly pushed her away. In the light of the oil lamp, Rajuli had seen Sanjiwana's bloodstains stamped clearly on her saree.

Asking her to boil some water, Sanjiwana had laid down on the cot. He had taken out the tube of ointment and some cotton from the fold of his dhoti and placed it on the cot.

After cleaning the wounds and applying ointment on them, and after putting hot packs on the swollen part, Rajuli had just lain beside him when the crow had begun to caw.

Already in a state of shock, Sanjiwana had not said anything. He had just been transfixed with horror. There had been fear in his eyes, as if he had seen a ghost.

Rajuli had bound him in oath and asked, 'Why are you so terrified? Won't you say something?'

Turning towards her, he had closed his eyes. Then he had spoken. 'Mukhiya is the head of all thieves. In the women's quarters in his house is an underground store. The stolen oxen are kept there. A gang of thirty people from the village is involved in stealing oxen when Mukhiya demands it. Ten people are middlemen. They bring in the ransom money …' Sanjiwana's voice had trailed off, as if he had been speaking to himself, as if he couldn't help but speak out what was inside him. Rajuli had gently stroked his hair.

'Mukhiya had told me to steal the oxen for him from Kadra. He said my debt would be squared. I brought in the oxen. But I had no idea that …' Sanjiwana had been unable to say more. Tears had started rolling down his cheeks.

Watching the morning star, Rajuli's eyes were moist from crying. A flock of doves flew past the house, seemingly humming *Visunji eke tum, Visunji eke tum.*[94]

After three days, when Sanjiwana had recovered a bit, Mukhiya Pandeji had once again summoned him. When he had returned, he had had in his hand a bordered saree and a dhoti. Putting them into a wooden box, he had lain down like a corpse.

'What are you thinking?'

'Nothing.'

'Then why are you lying down like this?'

94 God you're one, God you're one!

Hearing her words, Sanjiwana had got angry. Battling both anger and helplessness, he had said, 'What do you say, you despicable woman! What shall I do? Laugh … dance … sing … your mother's … don't you see that I have a noose of slavery around my neck!'

Sanjiwana had kept on prattling about many other things, but Rajuli had not interrupted him. She had thought it would be better if all the pus oozed out of his wound … it would give him some respite!

At midnight, Rajuli had seen Sanjiwana getting up and heading out like a ghost, lost in his thoughts! Rajuli had cupped her face between her palms and wept bitterly. She had been wondering how to extricate Sanjiwana and herself from this snare that felt like it was tightening day by day.

Rajuli knew Sanjiwana went to steal cows and oxen in the dead of night. One day, she had mustered some courage and asked him, 'Can't you leave this job? Can't you tell Mukhiya Pandeji that we have paid back his debt, and that he must set us free?'

'Do you think I am doing this out of choice?' Sanjiwana had mumbled, his mouth reeking of cheap liquor. 'If Mukhiya Pandeji releases me, the police will arrest me. As long as I am doing his bidding, he is protecting me. If I give up, he will get me arrested.'

A deathly silence had settled between the two, sticking out its fangs like a cobra. When the oil lamp was blown out by a gust of wind, they had been gripped with dread.

⋆

Rajuli came out of her past to the splashing sound of the river, the sound of the oars hitting the water, the sound of Triloki chanting quatrains in his broken voice. After a few moments, forming flickering shadows on the sand under the dim light of the lantern, the boat had come ashore.

Rajuli rushed to the boat. Triloki's tired eyes tried to recognize her. 'Who are you, dear?'

'I am Rukna's mother,' she said, balancing herself on the boat.

'Are you returning from Jehanabad?'

'Yes!'

Triloki did not ask further. And what could he ask? He knew that every man of a small stature, who rose against people like Mukhiya Pande, was sure to become a living ghost!

Another shadow joined them from the right side. As it came closer, Rajuli recognized Dahu, the beedi maker. He was probably returning from Ekangarsarai after buying beedi leaves.

'I'm in a bit of a hurry. The children must be hungry,' Rajuli appealed to him in a low tone.

Triloki released the boat. He had started discussing the Ramayana with Dahu. 'Hanumanji had been cursed. Until someone reminded him of his strength, he was not able to use it. When he needed to cross the sea, Jambawan had told him, "O brother! You are powerful. Why are you sitting idle? Crossing the sea is a trifle for you!"'

Rajuli had started thinking about something else. About Madho, Baso and Raghav Pande, about how the three brothers were clawing into the flesh of the villagers, about how nobody protested, about how everyone served them submissively with their heads bowed. They saluted them by touching their feet, by treating them as greater than gods.

'Are all low-status people cursed like Hanumanji?' Rajuli asked herself, but found no answer to her question. Like the current, maybe the question too flowed away.

Do the memories of the past drift away with the currents of time? They are alive in the present, in the form of retribution, and would assume the proportion of a flood in the future. A cold chill ran down her spine. She was trembling from head to toe. The next moment, she was conscious of the dark nights. As Sanjiwana was becoming a seasoned thief, he was getting rid of all guilt. Perhaps he had begun to think that he had no strength to resist whatever was happening. If that was the case, why worry? He had become reckless. His longing for Rajuli had also died out. Not only for Rajuli, he had no desire left for anything. He would eat whatever was served. He would come home drunk. He would sleep next to her like a dead man. Rajuli had begun to feel that she was not sleeping with Sanjiwana but with a stranger. *How can a man change so much*?

But this was the truth. Mukhiya Pandeji's vicious snare had killed Sanjiwana from within. And whatever remained of his original self, did not belong to him. He had become lifeless, a stranger to his own self!

One night, in this frenzied state of mind, Sanjiwana took her to Thakurji's chamber[95] at Mukhiya Pande's house. He said, 'Keep praying until morning and don't fall asleep!'

He then left her there, alone. Instead of hearing the ringing of Thakurji's bell, she heard Mukhiya Pande's voice: 'There is no other vacant place in the house. My aged father is sleeping in the dalan.[96] But don't worry, Thakurji knows it all … everyone's pain and troubles.'

That night, Mukhiya Pande moulded a new idol with the clay of Rajuli's sorrows.

For a few days, life had followed its usual course. There had been no pain, no joy, no regret. *After all, can the idol even feel anything?*

But the day Dulli was born, nobody knew how Sanjiwana turned into a man from a lump of clay. He started weeping, sitting beside her cot.

'What happened?' Rajuli had asked, and had proceeded to rebuke Rukna: 'What will you eat now, you ill-fated one! Chew me up!'

Sanjiwana had started banging his head against the cot; he had started blabbering. 'Verma Babu's clerk died last month. His widow, Mahatmayeen, has come to the village from the town. She does not have any children. She says she will die here. Mukhiya Pande says all this is a mere pretence, that she will register her land and property in

95 Prayer chamber
96 Guest room

the name of some relatives. And who knows when she will die! Until then, Mukhiya Pande will be ill at ease. Moreover, her land is adjacent to his. Her house is the den of Mukhiya's thieves and agents … he has asked them to obtain her thumb impression on a blank paper and then finish her in a clean way.'

'Then?' Rajuli had asked coolly.

'The rascal Mukhiya wants to send me to the gallows. Am I a fool to agree to his demand? When I spoke in favour of Mahatmayeen, Mukhiya Pande got angry with me. I told him to do whatever he deemed fit. I told him I will not serve him any more, and I will ensure that nothing untoward happens to Mahatmayeen.'

'Who is Mahatmayeen to you that you are in her favour?' Rajuli had asked in a feeble tone. Sanjiwana had got up in a fury at this point. He had stared at her silently with bloodshot eyes.

★

The boat came to a halt at the bank. Opening the knot at the end of her pallu, Rajuli placed four annas in Triloki's hand and rushed home.

She crossed the line of palm trees, the plinth of Mahavirji and Sarwan Gossain's cowshed. While passing Mahatmayeen's house, she felt as if she were passing through a cremation ground. Sanjiwana had been deceived there.

Rajuli remembered the sudden uproar in the middle of the night. 'Sanjiwana has killed Mahatmayeen! Catch hold of him! Catch hold of that rascal, that murderer! What enmity did he have against that innocent woman!'

And then she had heard Sanjiwana's terrified shriek, like a bird whose wings had been slashed, '*Maiya ge, maiya!*[97] No, babu, I did nothing. I … I …' and there came the end. When Rajuli had rushed to the spot, she had seen Sanjiwana lying unconscious in the lane. In the

97 Mother, oh mother!

light of the lantern, he looked like an unkempt dog. A number of other wild dogs, like Mukhiya Pande, Baso Pande, Ragho Pande and Runu Babu, were hovering around him.

At daybreak, the police had come. Along with the dead body, they had carried away the half-dead Sanjiwana. When he was being taken away, Rajuli had gone and, without speaking a word, put a tattered towel over his shoulder.

That evening, as she stepped into her house, her two children clung to her. In the light of the oil lamp, Rajuli saw that their faces were shrunken, cheekbones clearly visible. All of a sudden, she was filled with rage. Perhaps she was angry at her helplessness.

'Away, you skunks! Why don't you die?' Her voice pierced the dead silence like a spear. Mercilessly, she pushed them away. Murmuring and abusing, she went into the house. The children stood rooted to the spot in fear.

Filled with rage, Rajuli pulled out an aluminium plate, untied her pallu and put the roasted puffed rice on the plate. Then, putting some salt in a corner of the plate, she shrieked, 'Now devour!'

The children leapt forward. They sat on the floor as Rajuli pushed the plate towards them. They kept switching their gaze between their mother and the plate before them, eating hurriedly. Rajuli sat with her back against the wall.

When the children finished, she rebuked them sternly. 'What are you looking at? Wash your hands and drink some water.'

The children sprang up and quietly went into a corner. Rukna nervously poured water from the pitcher, spilling some on the floor. He looked at his mother stealthily. Seeing her look the other way, he hastily lifted the pitcher to his mouth. Gulping down a lot of water in one go triggered a bout of hiccups and he started coughing. Dulli took the pot from his hand. Taking a gulp or two, she stood silently, too.

'Now will you not go to sleep? What are you doing there? Performing your father's last rites?'

Walking feebly, the children lay down quietly on the mat. Rajuli shut the door. She then blew out the oil lamp and lay down beside her children.

The neighbourhood was quiet. The night progressed. Only the huk-huk sound of the watermill was reverberating. She could see a patch of black sky through the window.

'Hanumanji had a curse ...' Triloki's words played back in her mind. It felt as if Madho, Ragho and Baso Pande were pounding on her chest. Filled with fierce fury, she burst out, 'Coward, why didn't you go to the gallows after killing Mukhiya Pande?'

Rajuli's chest was smouldering like a bonfire. With a firm resolve, she got up. The patch of sky visible from the window had now assumed the size of an ocean.

The Turning

Aniruddha Prasad Vimal

(Translated from the Angika by Vivek Perampurna)

The earth slopes down once you cross Baratikar on Majhauni Road. Right below it, nestled in the small hillocks of Jethaur, is a small settlement of the Kadirs.[98] They call it Jeetnagar. Totally separated from the main community, it has approximately twenty to twenty-five houses. Stricken by poverty, the children of the Kadirs roam carefree and bare-chested, with hardly any piece of clothing on their bodies, in the chilly winter.

Before dawn breaks, they run to the fields with fists clenched under their armpits to take a dump. The westerlies carry the chill—sharp as needles—and all you can hear is the deep howl of the winds. December is on its way out. There are bamboo groves all around and mustard flowers adorn the terrain, swaying with the wind, as if calling out to the spring.

The sun is halfway up and the alley reverberates with the noise of kids squabbling over a game of tipcat. Suddenly, there is a commotion

98 A community of daily-wage earners and land tillers in northern Bihar

in Ramu's house. Loud voices rise, interspersed with wailing. Men, women and kids, the old and the young, run towards his house.

The walls are low and made of mud. The thatching of khus[99] is held together by crumbling bamboo poles. The jambs are broken. The villagers jump over the walls and crowd Ramu's courtyard where Ramu had just given his wife a sound thrashing.

Sonam was spewing the choicest of expletives. 'You low life, may you be infected with leprosy and may you lose the hands that you raised on me. May you have the curse of Rangdhari Baba on you and may you vomit blood till you die.' She was crying and cursing everyone, all in one breath.

Ramu's wrath simmered periodically. His heavy breathing sounded like air passing through bamboo reeds. He was warning Sonam to stop cursing him, but she continued: 'This lazy bugger! Can't feed his family, but he is man enough to hit me every day. The whole day he works for the master, and then he snores through the night like a bloody codger. In the morning, he asks for rice. Where should I get him rice from? Out of thin air?'

Ramu was about to lash out again with his shepherd's crook, but Batesar held his hand. 'Don't hit her,' he said to Ramu. 'Everyday your house witnesses the same fight. She is your wife, not your cattle that you can flog her at will.'

Batesar was like the headman of Jeetnagar. When he said something, neither the village committee members nor anybody else disputed him. His decision was final. Nobody could dare cross him.

Ramu threw his crook into a corner and addressed Batesar vehemently. 'I will stop, uncle, but when will this woman cease cursing me? Look at her viciousness! She has nearly gobbled up my entire clan. If things continue like this, one day I will strangle her to death.'

99 Vetiver

'You thrash her, too. One cannot run a family like this. You are a man; you cannot lose your wits,' Batesar said while leading Ramu out.

Sonam thundered from the patio. 'Uncle Batesar, I can no longer live with this man. I want to separate. My mother is no more, my father is dead. I have lost my whole family. He thinks I have nowhere to go. He thinks I am helpless and therefore he torments me.' With this, she started to wail.

Batesar took Ramu to his own house. He made him sit down on a bed of dried grass and said, 'Do you understand passion? It's a disastrous thing. Love blinds people. Your wife doesn't love you. She is in love with Jeetan. Even if you kill her, it won't extinguish her love for him.'

Ramu was stunned. He was under the impression that nobody in the village knew about this secret that he had kept to himself for over a year now. He had tried to reason it out with Sonam, but when everything failed, he had resorted to beatings a month ago.

'Jeetan is the real culprit. He has ruined my house,' Ramu said, tearful and choking.

'What do you have to lose? Why don't you let her go?'

'How can I, uncle? I got a wife after much effort. It took me years to find one. My days are long. I come back every evening after toiling for the master. The mere touch of her body takes away all my pain. One needs someone to massage one's arms and feet.'

'I hope you remember that she is your second wife. Besides, her hand was almost given in marriage to Jeetan. Your master is influential. This marriage has been solemnised with his blessings. It is out of gratitude that you sweat it out at his house. Sonam needs company, and you don't have time for her. And if you spare your hours at home, you will lose your wages. Age is catching up with you. How long can you work?' Batesar spoke out of experience.

Ramu understood everything but remained silent. After a while, he said, 'I will lodge a case against him, uncle, and then you can pass judgement.'

The truth flashed like lightning in Batesar's mind. *A woman is a man's biggest weakness. Ramu will never relinquish his claim on her. She didn't just fall in his arms. He had paid her father five hundred rupees! Money that his master had lent him. It wasn't something that he would just let go of.*

It was getting late. Ramu had to report for work. Batesar tried to reason with him. 'Son, listen. You must think logically. You go, I will talk to Jeetan.'

By the time Ramu returned home, the clamour had settled down. In the courtyard, Sonam was lying on the paddy straws, basking in the sun. Ramu wanted to have a word with her, but he couldn't. Swinging his cane in his hand, he left for work. Sonam was thinking about Jeetan. In times of grief and hurt, one seeks solace in the thoughts of those closest to one's heart. Sonam felt herself dissolving in Jeetan's thoughts. Now it was only her and Jeetan, nobody else. He was everything for her, as she was to him. He permeated every part of her existence.

She recalled her first days in the village, just a couple of years ago. Jeetan had been teasing Ramu. 'Brother, take care of her. I might elope with her. After all, she is my sister-in-law, so she is half mine. I don't even have to ask,' he had said and sang a local ballad.

The bride and her friends,
  like gourd soup.
And the bride's mother,
  a thief scooped…

She was, after all, Jeetan's sister-in-law as per the customs of the village, which is what had prompted this banter. But Sonam had felt a stir in her heart. She had looked at him from the narrow opening of her veil. There was something in his eyes that had captivated her heart. Ramu, with his short and paunchy figure, ageing and drooping, was an unpleasant contrast to the tall and lanky Jeetan and his cheerful persona.

Sonam had gradually come to know Jeetan; love had slowly blossomed in her heart. One day, Jeetan had approached her on her way back from the grocery shop. 'You were to be my bride. It's unfortunate it didn't happen. But you can still be mine.'

With flushed cheeks, she could only manage to say 'go away' before running home.

A couple of months later, Jeetan came to her house when no one was around. Before she could gather herself, he had held her in a tight embrace. To this day, she had not been able to free herself from his arms. Her body was in Ramu's grip, but her soul longed for Jeetan.

Jeetan worked in a government farm nearby. His days began at eight and ended at five. In winter, the sun set by the time he came home, but in the summer, there would still be an hour of sunlight left. He would head straight for the village from the farm, for the village would be deserted and Ramu would still be at his master's place.

One evening, at Sonam's house, his hands gently caressing her body, he said, 'Sonam, freshen up. Take a look. See what I have brought for you!' He placed a packet of jalebis in her hands and left. Sonam hadn't eaten a morsel that day. She devoured the jalebis one by one. The succour of food refreshed her.

It was getting dark. She knew Ramu would come home any moment. Indeed, he was home shortly after. He put down the provisions and left for Batesar's house. Just like the other days, she stepped into the kitchen half-heartedly to cook, all in order to avoid another quarrel.

Shortly after the day of the commotion, one evening, the village council assembled in Batesar's courtyard, in the middle of an old mango orchard. They had lit a bonfire. Everyone sat around the blazing fire. Lamps were hung from the low branches of the trees. The discussion began, and Jeetan was unanimously found guilty. After all, wasn't it a great crime to steal the affection of someone else's wife! Everyone spoke according to the best of their wisdom at the council meeting. Everyone had the opportunity to say what they hadn't been able to voice so far. Until now, none of them had the courage to stand up to Jeetan and tell him what they felt, but that night they vented out their grudges against him.

Finally, Jeetan was allowed to speak. 'First of all, you shouldn't interfere in the lives of two people who love each other. Before Sonam is someone's wife, she is a woman. And she has every right to love whoever she wants. You should raise your voice against the father who married off his daughter to an older man merely for money. Sonam loves me. What's left to say? You should let Sonam come to me. I give my word that I will marry her right here, in front of this council, and take her home.'

Jeetan's brazen words enraged Batesar. He said angrily, 'What you have said is against the law. You are dishonouring the council.'

'Dishonouring? How so? Is it such an unheard-of incident in our village? Batesar's own daughter left two husbands and married a third one last year. Our village is full of such marriages and you pretend as if I have committed a huge crime! Who is unblemished? As if I don't know what goes on in your homes!' Jeetan's voice was a mix of pleading and anger.

Hearing this, Samar stood up. 'This council meeting has not been called for us to mud-sling each other. This meeting is about your relationship with Sonam. And we have unanimously decided that you will leave this village. Sonam, you'll—'

Before he could finish, Sonam roared, attracting the attention of all the councilmen. She spoke with a burning rage. 'Who is Samar to decide? Doesn't he have any shame? This year itself his own sister-in-law married for the second time. And before the month ends, his brother … How dare he decide our fate? What sadistic pleasure do men derive from blaming others? First look at what's happening in your homes!'

Samar was furious. It seemed as if a fight was about to ensue. An uneasy clamour rose, but Batesar restored peace. After a while, the councilmen allowed Sonam to speak again. This time, she spoke calmly: 'I want to spend the rest of my life peacefully with Jeetan, and that's my only request to this honourable council. I admit that I have murdered my husband many times in my thoughts. Please deliver me from this sin. I told Uncle Batesar this morning that I cannot live with this man any more. Why, then, have all of you assembled here to force me to do something against my will?'

Finally, Batesar proclaimed his judgment. 'It is not for men to pass judgement. Let God decide. There will be a fulais.[100] If it falls, it will mean the sanction of Lord Rangdhari himself. If it does not, she will have to stay with Ramu. Until then, she will stay at my place, under my protection.'

The day for fulais was fixed for Monday, three days later. It was already late by the time this decision was arrived at. The air was becoming chilly. Everyone hurried home. For Sonam, the night was especially hard. She felt like a thirsty person sitting on the riverbank. She coursed through the next day listlessly. Ramu came once and Jeetan, too, was hovering around, but Batesar told them to have patience. It was just a matter of a day more. 'You should trust the will of God! Neither of you can meet her or talk to her,' he told Ramu and Jeetan.

The silence of the night was broken only by the occasional barking of stray dogs. Unable to take it, Sonam sneaked out. The moon whispered through the bamboo groves. Sonam wished she could just run and run and run until she was in Jeetan's arms. Standing in a dark corner,

100 A ritual to please God, wherein a coin is placed on top of a mound made of rice soaked in water and worshippers dance around it; if the coin falls, it is considered that God is pleased

she was thinking of the tale of the princess with golden wings and the sorcerer. She imagined herself flying to heaven.

And she really flew away. She knocked at Jeetan's door. He himself hadn't been able to sleep. They embraced each other as if they were meeting after ages. They lay in each other's arms. After a while, Sonam said in a hushed voice, 'Don't lose hope. Nobody can separate us. I love you.'

The day of fulais arrived. The preparations started in the evening. A small idol of the god was painted with cow dung. Incense sticks were lit and rice grains were crushed to adorn the idol. Now it was time to place the coin. The womenfolk sang local ballads and folk songs, the musicians played the instruments. The songs of the Kadirs filled the air.

Sonam sat in the left corner, opposite Jeetan and Ramu. The air resonated with incantations to Rangdhari Baba. Sonam, Jeetan and Ramu were also chanting:

> Glory be unto you, Rangdhari Baba,
> please take care of this mendicant…

Sonam was praying in her heart. The chants grew louder:

> Rangdhari Baba will come riding from the west soon.
> He will descend on the body,
> redeeming the world,
> the will of fulais will be done.

Rangdhari Baba's spirit was to descend on Shanichara, the village healer. Bathed, he was sitting in wet clothes in the bitter cold, even as the crowd gathered around him. Everyone was waiting. *Why hadn't the spirit descended upon him yet?* Suddenly, he trembled and his body began to sway. He started rolling on the floor, his body contorted and his tongue stuck out. The music grew louder. Everyone stood with bated breath, waiting for the fulais to slip. But strangely, even after an hour of incantations to the divine, the fulais refused to budge from its place. People started to talk. Sonam and Jeetan stood up as if their blood had been sucked out. Disappointment swept across their faces. Ramu's face lit up.

Batesar felt the ardour of the spirit that had descended on Shanichara. He mumbled, 'Please, God, pronounce your will. I can't find a way. Sonam—'

Before he could finish, Shanichara shouted, 'Can't you see? The fulais didn't fall. Sonam will have to live with Ramu.'

An agitated Sonam stood up and hit the fulais with a large stick. It came tumbling down. She roared, 'Uncle Batesar, see, the fulais has fallen. I am leaving with Jeetan. Let me see who dares to stop us!'

She held Jeetan's hand and left. Nobody had the courage to stop them.

Journey in a Burnt Boat

Abdus Samad

(Translated from the Urdu by Syed Sarwar Hussain)

The train belched her out on to a ramshackle station.

She was carrying some suitcases and a lot of stuffed polythene bags. It was only after the porters and fellow travellers helped her that she could unload her luggage. It was definitely not easy, as the train made a very short halt at the station. Shabby passengers rushed in and out of the train, blocking entry and exit points.

She came out of the station and looked around for a taxi, only to realize that it was a quaint village that did not even have a paved road for motor vehicles. On her way home, she had to pass a small rivulet. Since her childhood days, she had heard that it was to be filled up, but it was still flowing freely, as undisturbed as she had left it. Children were still jumping into it from the railway bridge, and people waded through its waist-deep water to catch fish, as she had watched them do in the past.

There was nobody at the station to receive her; no one recognized her either. She hadn't informed anyone about her arrival. She had dispensed with all the customs and expectations that sustain relationships after she eloped from her home some years ago. There were marriages in the family, and some deaths too, but she never sent greetings or condolences. Although she kept meeting her family's needs.

She knew well enough that the mere fulfilment of formalities would hardly endear her to her relatives, and that their non-fulfilment would hardly earn her any reproach. She had no intention of staying for long. She already had a return ticket. Her village was some twenty kilometres away from the station. She was thinking in terms of kilometres, but in her village, they measured distances in kos, yard and baans.[101] People usually walked down from the station with their luggage on their backs, or they took cycle rickshaws. There were a few one-horse carriages, but the fares were very high, and not everyone could afford them.

She sought the help of two coolies to load her luggage on a tonga. The tonga driver stared at her, but perhaps he could not recognize her. She had changed a lot. Her face, her complexion, her dressing style, her mannerisms, nothing betrayed the old Chanda. She wasn't sure whether even her family members would recognize her.

She did, anyway, recognize the old, shrivelled tonga driver. He was Barkan Dada. Prudence, however, pressed her to remain silent. She told him the name of the village she was headed to but did not mention which house, wary of the stories people might have spun about her after she eloped.

Though the road leading to the village suggested that nothing much had changed, the sight was more depressing. The pathways were as rough and uneven as ever. A thick layer of dust covered the road full of potholes, causing the tonga to almost overturn. Had she not held on tightly to the rails on either side of her seat, she would have fallen.

This was the place where the looming, pallid shadows of poverty, penury and an uncertain future had sealed her fate, until she had run away and found freedom.

---

101 A baans or bamboo is a unit of measurement equal to 12.8 metres

Thanks to a stroke of fortune, she had broken free of all that shackles people to their homes, inhibiting them from fulfilling their ardent wishes. Her existence had seemed like a burden. She knew it would not make any difference to anyone whether she ran away, died or met with an accident. At most, her mother would have shed some silent tears, which would soak into her old, discoloured saree.

She never really maintained regular correspondence with her relatives after leaving. The letters that reached her brought tidings of marriages and deaths, but she kept all of them aside, leaving them unread. When they grew into big piles, she quietly consigned them to the dustbin. It was not lost on her that her greetings would not gladden any heart, nor would her condolences heal any wounds.

She had started for her village imagining herself to be the same Chanda who had been born there many years ago. Riding on the tonga, she gazed calmly at the familiar terrain that led to her home. But there was turmoil in her mind. She didn't feel even a remote sign of yearning for the home she was visiting after such a long absence. She had planned for the journey long before she had embarked on it, but even after travelling such a long distance, the flush of enthusiasm hadn't risen in her.

What, then, had compelled her to visit? Why did she always talk with her sahelis[102] so earnestly about her journey? Why would she become increasingly enthusiastic whenever they chatted about her approaching journey? Where had all those conversations gone? And from where did they emerge in the first place?

She felt like she had no feelings left in her.

Barkan Dada was quite old now. Though his body appeared to be stricken by palsy, he still held the whip strongly, cracking it in the air to make the horse go faster. The frightened animal ran headlong, panting.

102 Friends

Barkan Dada turned his lifeless eyes towards her many times, but he said nothing. Perhaps he had not recognized her. She could have cleared up his confusion if she wished to, with just a slight smile, and learnt from him about the welfare of her relatives and every person in the village. She might just have given him a pleasant surprise, but no, she wasn't going to do anything of that sort.

Barkan Dada started humming a folk song. She could hear the tune but couldn't make out the words; even if she did, she would hardly understand anything. The tune, nevertheless, was pleasing. It sent a strange tingling sensation through her body. It seemed to her that the song was urging her to keep moving on like the river. Sheer ecstasy was gradually closing in on her from all sides. She felt a strong urge to close her eyes and imagine the waving fields, the verdant, dancing spikes of corn, the relentlessly bursting rain clouds, the intoxicating winds, the cascades pouring melody into one's ears, the mountains playing hide-and-seek with the clouds, the cool and fresh breeze whispering to the leaves…

Though she could not really appreciate the discordant tune of the song, it was unfolding a stunningly vivid landscape before her closed eyes. It reminded her of her own existence. She had failed to conjure up any reason for returning to her village until she heard Barkan Dada's song.

Now, all of a sudden, a new world lay open before her. She began to realize, for the first time, that there was a life here. Hitherto, she had been travelling from one place to another like a wrapped book. Barkan Dada's song had unwrapped intense feelings.

After a short pause, Barkan Dada resumed his song. She slipped into a trance again. She knew her journey would end soon, yet she wished earnestly that it would not. She would not hesitate to use whatever energy was left in her to keep going. She desperately longed to be lost in the breath-taking scenery created by Barkan Dada's song. She had already seen a good part of the world at a young age. But the world that she now visualized seemed even greater.

The tonga was entering an inhabited area. The surrounding scene, as well as the atmosphere, appeared so familiar—the houses, lanes, gutters, thick piles of rubbish and the cocks and hens playing love games in their shady pens. Some new houses had been built. The old houses had extensions and fresh coats of paint.

Barkan Dada stopped humming as soon as he entered the basti. In a curt and harsh tone, he asked her the address. She was now strong enough to face any eventuality, so she gave him the location. He darted a startled look at her and muttered something under his breath. But she didn't care. She had become indifferent to everything. She was behaving like a traveller who returns home after a very long absence, eager to meet loved ones and ignoring every bitter experience. The beads of sweat appearing on her face were symbolic of her internal excitement.

Barkan Dada drove his tonga through the dusty winding tracks and pulled up at a strange-looking porch. There wasn't a soul in sight. She found herself standing before a house, one that appeared unfamiliar to her.

She looked at the house closely, only to discover that its once-dilapidated walls had been interred with new ones. She felt as if the decaying walls were being strangled, that they were trying to call out to her.

'You're Zamru Miyan's daughter, aren't you?' Barkan Dada asked curiously.

His cracked voice frightened her. She couldn't speak; so she nodded.

A flush of triumph crept over Barkan Dada's face. He blurted, 'Wasn't I right?'

She had no idea what had happened after she had eloped; what the people thought and talked about her. Barkan Dada was a village elder. She didn't know how he and others like him reacted to such an episode.

She examined the house closely once again. It had been extensively renovated. The money that she had sent had been used for renovation and had obscured her intimate association with the house—an association that had been tugging at her heart ever since she had left. She stepped inside, as if walking into one of the many hotels she had visited around the world. Her life was now associated with hotels only. In reality, wherever she looked, she found only hotels, not houses.

She could clearly recall that whenever visitors arrived at any house, the village children would rush to surround the horse carriage. Even old people would stop to look. The moment a newcomer alighted from the carriage, his fragrance would spread all over the village. Children and grown-ups would throng around him till the visitor entered the inner precincts of the house. But that wouldn't happen to her. She stood rooted for quite some time after getting down from the tonga, but not a bird stirred at her appearance.

Sweating and panting, Barkan Dada unloaded the luggage. She took out two one-hundred-rupee notes from her purse and extended them towards him. Barkan Dada looked at her. His face was red with anger.

'Please keep it, dada!' she pleaded.

He grumbled in response. 'Give me just the fare! I don't accept unwarranted money.' A stern expression crossed his face as he drew his hand back.

She tried but couldn't muster enough courage to speak out. What she read in his eyes made her realize how miserably small she had become. She gave him 'just the fare' and he went away without any demonstration of feelings. Leaving the luggage behind, she slowly opened the door. The whole house stood before her.

This was surely not the house she had run away from. She had left a crumbling, dark space, hopelessly stifling and bleak. She could now clearly appreciate the change that the money she had been sending from far-flung nations had brought to the house.

The whole house was roofed. Heavy khadi curtains hung in front of the doors. Low parapets were raised on three sides of the courtyard, decorated with earthen flower pots. A bathroom had been built in a corner. The floor of the courtyard was not plastered, but it had been splattered with a thin coat of cement.

Her parents were radiant at seeing her unexpectedly. They were both astonished and delighted. They were wearing clean clothes, and their ageing eyes radiated comfort and satisfaction. She bowed to them with a salaam; they embraced her with tears in their eyes.

'You should have informed us you were coming, Chanda!' Her father said, his voice full of affection.

'Why should she do that? You, too, never dropped a line to ask about her well-being,' her mother complained to her father, demonstrating her protest against her husband more than her love for her daughter.

Chanda maintained her calm while hugging her younger sisters and said, 'I don't get time, Amma! I have no time even to scratch my head. I just run like a machine…'

'We have gone through so much! We were sick, too. You could have at least written a few words about your welfare.' Her mother had started complaining openly.

No one talked about the circumstances that had forced her to leave, not even casually. *Wasn't it shameful and improper for a young girl to run away from home?* She herself couldn't forget that incident. She firmly believed that they must have, at first, resigned themselves to their fate, after being convinced that she was dead. And if they had even a flicker of hope of her being alive, a runaway girl was as good as dead.

It was only after she started sending money home that she was considered to be alive. But a girl who elopes turns into a living example of disgrace and ignominy, which she had become. She thought about the pain her parents must have felt.

When she had decided to visit them, she had made all arrangements to defend herself from the arrows that might attack her from all quarters. Perhaps that was why she carried a confirmed return ticket, like a lifeline.

To her surprise, she detected no warning signs. She realized that she had needlessly burdened her mind with the fear of defending herself. Both the young and the old were asking her about the distant places that she had toured, all with great curiosity and interest. Their eyes and faces displayed waves of exultation. They didn't, however, ask her two questions: about her elopement and about her return.

She secretly laughed at her unfounded fears. She herself wished that they would ask her those two questions, that they would speak about the two venomous snakes that lay coiled in her heart, biting into it deep and hard. But she restrained herself. She thought it better if some matters were permanently left buried to let people live in peace.

She knew the sensible thing to do was to use her confirmed ticket. It was not that no one tried to stop her when the day finally arrived. They asked her to stay a little longer. Her father asked, though casually, if she could delay her departure. The young ones complained when they heard of her decision. But somehow she strongly felt that all of them were restlessly waiting to bid her farewell.

She smilingly told them that she had enormous responsibilities on her shoulders, and that it was quite difficult for her to leave her place of work even for a day. She also told them that it was their love that had brought her there on such a short visit, but that she must leave now.

'Glory belongs to the Lord of the Worlds that he has blessed us with a daughter who is more precious than a thousand sons! O Lord, bless all sinners with a virtuous and lucky daughter like her! O Truest Provider!' She smiled obediently as her mother prayed for her.

Her return journey was not hectic. She had left all her luggage at home, even her own suitcases, and was travelling with just two bags. She could have done without those as well, had her mother not pressed upon her to take the homemade halwa, khurma[103] and kulchas. Her mother had prepared them with great love. She was forced to take them despite a thousand entreaties.

She didn't allow anybody to accompany her to the station, even though her parents wanted to see her off. She refused to budge from her stand in such a way that everyone had to bow down to her wishes. She departed amidst a heavy downpour of tears, carrying her parents' blessings. She went to the station alone on Barkan Dada's tonga.

During the return journey, Barkan Dada was as rude and unwelcoming. His disapproving looks still sent shivers down her spine. As he drove the tonga through the rough and bumpy village track, he started singing the same tune that had made her journey back home memorable.

The same song was now helping her on her way back. It wasn't the song, but its tune that was enthralling her. She still failed to understand the words, though. Lost in reverie once again, she wished for an affectionate and caring lap where she could rest her head and fall asleep—a long and deep sleep.

None of her wishes had ever been answered. She was like a hapless blade of grass that doesn't drown in the fathomless sea but keeps floating, swaying up and down the crests of the leaping, rolling waves.

Barkan Dada's song stopped as the station arrived. An overwhelming desire to ask him to drive her back suddenly awakened in her, not because she wanted to go back home, but because she once again longed to absorb the tune of the song, down to the depths of her soul. But Barkan Dada swiftly handed her bags over to her and left in a hurry, leaving her startled. Perhaps her father had paid him for the trip.

103 *A* Bihari sweet prepared using cottage cheese and sugar

She stood there thinking for some time. The old, dilapidated building of the station stood before her. She had left the rough and bumpy village road far behind.

A heavy, long-suffering sigh was stifled before it could escape her lips. She regained control of her senses and handed her bags to a coolie. With heavy steps and a bowed head, she walked towards the platform. Her train was about to arrive.

Jugaad

Prem Kumar Mani

(Translated from the Hindi by Bindu Singh)

It was the month of January and the third day of continuous drizzle. It was not cold, but it sure was chilly. Shivering had beset every soul. Spread on the floor was a layer of straw covered with a rug made of tattered clothes. The rising warmth of the burning hearth came from one corner, but the biting cold winds still chilled everyone to the bone.

Binda turned over and gathered the courage to get up. For quite some time, she had been feeling the need to get up. Her mind was buzzing with thoughts. *Surely the bitch living near the hut must have made some arrangements for the pups. God alone knows how they have been surviving in this heavy downpour.*

Binda wanted to get up and wash the utensils, but she was feeling lazy. She returned to her bed.

Her entire family, wrapped in an old and worn-out rug, was sleeping on the floor, on a bed of straw. Her husband, the father of her children Hirwa and Johani, opened his eyes for a moment, only to quickly pull the rug over his head again. When his legs were uncovered, he bent and curled them towards his stomach. Binda sat down. She put her legs inside the rug. On the eastern side of the hut was a thick bamboo grove.

On its branches, the crows were cawing. But their sound appeared low and dull, as if they were also dozing off and preaching to mankind to curl up in a rug.

Binda didn't lie down. After caressing Hirwa's forehead, she covered his bare legs with the rug. She felt like singing hymns in praise of the Nirgun[104] God, but all sorts of nonsense filled her mind. Soon, the thought of singing withered.

It wasn't good for Hirwa's father to sleep for so long. He had to be at the barn before the master reached. Though barely any work could be done in such weather, he had already been paid for ploughing ten kattha.[105] And all said and done, one had to honour the payment. *Among all the householders, there is nobody as kind as his master. Why give him a chance to be angry?*

'Hirwa's father, O Hirwa's father!' she nudged him gently.

He squirmed. His eyes closed, he assessed the world with his ears and turned to the other side. He felt like getting up and smacking his wife. *She is poking me even when it's drizzling outside. She has so much regard for the master that it feels as if she is not my wife but the faithful wife of the landlord himself.* He muttered a foul word under his breath and resolved to wake up only after an hour.

Hirwa and Johani fluttered their eyes open on the first call. Binda caressed Johani's head. Feeling loved, Johani put her hand in her mother's lap. Suddenly, Hirwa threw the rug off himself and stood up. Swiftly, he walked towards the hearth in the corner and started digging out the potatoes from the dying ashes.

'Light the fire, Hirwa,' Binda said.

---

104 Nirgun means without attribute, i.e., God is infinite and endless; the believers of the Nirgun tradition do not worship idols but the recognizable qualities of God

105 Kattha is used as a unit of land measurement in the eastern regions of India; one kattha corresponds to 720 square feet

She was waiting for Hirwa's lovely smile that flashed across his face when he was told to light the fire. It had been only a few days since he had learnt to rub the stick against the matchbox and light it. With much enthusiasm, Hirwa searched for the matchbox. Johani stood up and brought a handful of straw.

Hirwa scolded her. 'So much straw? Give me just half of it. Mai,[106] see how much straw she is planning to burn.'

'If you waste even one matchstick, I will take you to task. Even this much straw will not be sufficient. We will need more, understood?' Johani answered back.

Hirwa and Johani began squabbling. Binda, meanwhile, was lost in her thoughts. When the argument amplified, she scolded them. 'Don't start squabbling like dogs early in the morning. The two of you have started quarrelling at the break of dawn. If I come there, I will slap you both.'

The threat worked. Hirwa lit the hearth. Johani remembered something and murmured in Hirwa's ears. Hirwa listened carefully and then stared hard in his mother's direction. Their mother was still lost in her thoughts. He handed Johani a roasted potato, which she accepted with gratitude. Then he made a gesture, as if trying to say something. Johani understood and quietly walked out of the hut. After some time, Hirwa also stood up and stealthily followed his sister.

Binda was still sitting. Hirwa's father, who was still lying on the floor, realized that the children were not around. He opened his eyes to make sure they were gone and then leapt towards Binda as if he were a crocodile. He started rubbing his face against Binda's, forgetting that he had been babbling curses at her a while ago.

Binda was aroused. Many times, in the thick of the night, she had wanted him to show his affection in this manner. But her husband would keep his distance, lying in one corner like an enemy. Now, in

---

106 Mother

broad daylight, he was showering her with affection. Had he done this a while ago, she would not have awakened the children.

Binda's heart was filled with love. She caressed her husband's head and then gently chided him, 'It's morning now. Don't you have work? There's no ration at home.'

'Ten kilos of rice is already finished?'

'You want an account of ten kilos of rice! Did you count how many days it lasted? It has been drizzling for the last three days. And then your sister's husband came twice to eat. Won't you take that into account? I cooked one ser[107] of rice just for him, a quantity that our entire family consumes. What a glutton!'

'Be quiet! He eats less than your brother. And will you now keep track of how much our guests eat? Are we going through such bad times? I also visit them. Don't you know how much *I* eat? Who knows, your brother's wife may have called me greedy!'

'My family members are not so stingy.'

'Then am I stingy, or are you? Tell me, why do you make such comments?'

'Why would I comment? I cooked for him with great care. I simply mentioned it without thinking much, but he certainly is a glutton. If he gets tasty food, he doesn't even bother to drink water. He kept staring at my face while he ate.'

'Oh! Then you mean to say that he ate so much while admiring your face? If somebody so beautiful is sitting in front, who won't eat twice his appetite!'

'Say nothing. I understand all praise of my beauty is merely a lie. I may be beautiful for some, but you find beauty in others. At the master's house, the one who gives you jaggery. I know it all.'

107 An obsolete Indian unit of measuring weight, roughly equivalent to a kilogram; it is now used in colloquial speech

Hirwa and Johani entered the hut, each carrying a pup. The mother of the pups was peeping from outside the door. The hut filled with their little barks. Binda scolded them, but the children didn't pay any heed to her. They went and sat near the hearth with the pups. Johani tried to feed a roasted potato to the pup she was holding, but the pup turned away its mouth majestically, like a sahib.

'Arey, Johaniya, go to the courtyard and bring some firewood. The fire in the hearth is dying,' Binda ordered her while sitting in the same place.

Johani went out and returned with wet sticks. 'Mai, all the sticks are wet.'

Then, keeping the wet sticks on one side, she sat down again with the pup. Slowly, the smoke billowed from the hearth.

Hirwa's father got up and sat upright. He was thinking about something. Binda, who was washing the utensils, was also lost in thought. They were both wondering about managing the ration. *It is not worth going to the master's house. The scoundrel would only hand out a kilo of grain and ask me to work for the whole day*, Hirwa's father thought. He shared his thoughts with Binda and asked, 'Not even a little rice is left?'

'How will a little rice suffice? It will not be sufficient for even two square meals.'

'Listen, cook something for the children. At least feed them.'

'And what about us?'

'I will make some arrangements.'

He took out some tobacco from the case knotted in his loincloth and rubbed some on his palm. In such weather, he felt like doing nothing at all, not even getting up to attend the call of nature. But some arrangements had to be made for the meals. He put the tobacco in his mouth and crouched on the floor.

Though the weather was chilly and damp, it hardly seemed to matter to Binda who was washing the utensils. Her pallu was wet. Hirwa's father spat out the tobacco and started piling up the wet sticks in the courtyard. *Who knows how long this drizzle will last? The dried bamboo roots are the only saviour in this cold. Nobody seems to care about it, but digging them out requires a lot of effort. You need a spade, axe and hoe, and only then can you pull out these roots.*

After finishing with the sticks, he purposefully tied a towel around his waist, as if mustering up the courage to step out of the house into the cold. Then, holding the hoe in one hand, he walked away.

Binda finished washing the utensils. She swept the floor and lit the fire in the hearth again. Suddenly, she remembered that she had not been paid in full for the massages she had given to landlord Kisnu's daughter-in-law for eight days. She was yet to receive payment for four days.

She muttered under her breath, 'After all, when are they going to pay? When we are dead and reduced to ashes? Oh god! More than three months have passed. If I forget about the payment, should she keep quiet too? I know very well the dishonest hearts of the women in the house of landlords. They withhold payment. And if one forgets to ask, one will never see that money.'

'Arey, Johaniya, go to landlord Kisnu's house. I had massaged his daughter-in-law for eight days. She hasn't paid for four days. Go and ask her if she will pay us in this time of adversity or not!'

'I will not go. The path is slippery. Send Hirwa!'

'Oh! You are acting smart! As if you're the grandmother of the house! Why have you placed that pup in your lap? Is he your husband? Will you keep it down or not? The path is slippery! Why don't you just stuff the rug in your mouth and quell your hunger? Now, if you ask for something to eat, I will force this ladle down your mouth,' Binda said angrily.

Hirwa assessed the situation. Landlord Kisnu's daughter-in-law was very beautiful, like a fairy. She was very lovely to look at, like a statue of Goddess Durga.[108] She had a good heart, too. She would surely give some jaggery and puffed rice. Just the thought made Hirwa's mouth water. He said, 'Mai, I will go there and tell her that Uncle has come to visit us and there's no ration at home. I'll ask her to give me half a kilo of rice.'

'Am I begging for half a kilo of rice? Tell her that my payment for four days is due.'

Before leaving, Hirwa said something in Johani's ear and then swiftly walked out. Getting agitated, Johani said, 'If he gets puffed rice, I will also take some.'

'Oh, really! Look at you! A while back you were worried about how slippery the path is, and now you are thinking about puffed rice. I will smack you so hard that you will fall on the floor.'

Binda, however, had gauged the reason behind Hirwa's enthusiasm. She smiled at her son's intelligence. She told her daughter, 'Let Hirwa return. I will make him give you half of the puffed rice. He is not like you who will gobble up everything on the way, before getting home.'

Johani knew about her brother's habit, and she also believed in her mother's assurance. She asked her mother, 'Mai, should I sweep the floor?'

'You want to sweep the floor? Till now you were busy with the pup. When I have already done the sweeping, you want to sweep. Are you blind that you did not notice me doing it?'

The mother and daughter sat near the hearth. Binda stoked the fire while Johani fed it another wet stick. Billows of smoke poured out.

'Mai, should I also put some straw in the fire?'

'Yes!' Binda also wanted a blazing fire.

108 Durga, the goddess of war, is the warrior form of Goddess Parvati, whose mythology centres around combating evil and demonic forces that threaten peace, prosperity and dharma

Johani brought a large quantity of straw and the two of them started throwing it into the hearth, like purohits[109] performing a yajna.

A while later, Hirwa returned with lots of goods. In the bundle he was carrying rice, potatoes, puffed rice and a piece of jaggery. Hirwa said, 'The new bride gave it to me when nobody was looking. She also asked for you to come this Sunday for another massage.'

Binda looked inside the bundle. Johani said, 'Mai, the potatoes are not less than a kilo.'

Binda snapped. 'How much is a kilo according to you? This is more than two kilos. And the quantity of rice is also good.' She took some grains into her palm and tried to ascertain what variety it was. The rice was clean. 'Her soul is as beautiful as her body!' she noted.

Hirwa took something else out of the bundle and quietly showed it to Johani.

Johani shouted. 'Mai, look! Brother is holding black laddoos.'[110]

Binda lashed out. 'What is it? Bring it here. How many times have I told you to show me what people give you? There are many in the village who practise black magic.'

The very mention of black magic scared Hirwa. Last year, his friend Bangur had died within a day of his illness, all because of black magic. People had said that it was brain fever, but his mother had been sure that somebody had done black magic on the boy.

Hirwa kept both the laddoos in front of his mother. She broke a bit from each and put it in her mouth. 'The laddoos are made of methi.[111] They must have come from the bride's mother's house. Kisnu's daughter-in-law doesn't know how to make them,' she said, and gave one laddoo each to both her children.

---

109 In the Indian religious context, it means a family priest

110 A popular Indian sweet

111 Hindi name for fenugreek; the seeds are a common ingredient in Indian cuisine

Binda knew what she was going to cook. Boiled rice with a curry of beans and potatoes. *When Hirwa's father returns home, he will be so happy. And if he sleeps in the corner tonight, I will not give him anything to eat tomorrow!*

She put the pot of rice to boil on the hearth and told Johani: 'Chop the beans.'

Soon, the rice was ready. The curry was boiling when Hirwa's father walked inside briskly, as if he had conquered the world like Alexander. He looked very happy. He had killed eight mice in the barn and knotted them in his towel.

Johani and Hirwa jumped with joy. 'Rat! Rat!'

The house was filled with the aroma of cooked rice and curry. Seeing the food, Hirwa's father was overjoyed. He asked Binda, 'How did you make the arrangements? I thought in case there wasn't anything else, we can cook these.' He untied the knot of his towel, letting the dead rats fall on the ground.

Hirwa and Johani started preparing to cook the rats. Their stomachs were already filled with the aroma of roasted rats.

Binda looked into her husband's eyes. They reflected love and gratitude. Overjoyed, she smiled at him. Her husband was delighted.

Deception

Ashok

(Translated from the Maithili by Vidyanand Jha)

Bholi Jha, from my village, had come to visit me in Patna.

I was overjoyed. I'm rarely so happy. Bholi was my childhood friend. We had practically grown up together. Interestingly, we never fought. In fact, Bholi never fought with anyone. That's just how he was; he would not let a situation escalate. I had not come across many people with such a good sense of humour. When he arrived at my place, he said, 'Listen, please tell your wife that today I will have cauliflower and peas curry. Damn, I am sick of eating potatoes!'

I felt like giggling at his forthrightness, but refrained. Instead, I said, 'Oh, don't be silly. I will feed you what I can!'

But Bholi was not one to give up easily. He said, 'Throughout the journey, in the bus, I thought of nothing but cauliflower. I thought to myself that today I will have cauliflower and peas curry at Arvind's place. I *have* to have it. It has been ages since I ate the curry your wife makes. Ah, it's so tasty!'

It seemed to me that Rekha, my wife, was listening to this conversation from behind the curtain. Perhaps she was laughing, too. There was little for me to do. Even if there wasn't any cauliflower and peas at home, she would get them from the market and make the curry for Bholi. I didn't need to break sweat over it.

Bholi Jha was three months older than me. Because of this insignificant difference in age, he didn't come in front of Rekha. Both Rekha and I found it strange, but what could be said of Bholi! If he decided on something, he stuck to it. Nobody could make him change his mind.

Bholi started telling me about the happenings in the village and the crop yield during the year. He broached the topic about the problem of procuring quality seeds.

Suddenly, I asked him, 'Tell me, I heard that you were going to contest the election for the post of mukhiya. Why didn't you contest, then? You could have won.'

He laughed and said, 'It's true that I thought of contesting; maybe I could have won, too. The Guar,[112] Amat,[113] Keot[114] and Muslims, all would have voted for me. However, I would have got very few votes from the Brahmins. And then Idris decided to contest. Once that happened, I felt as if I were contesting the election myself. I supported him and he won. I am sure you know all this.'

I nodded. I knew everything about the election. Bholi had worked day and night to ensure that Idris emerged victorious. Idris was also our friend. We had all passed matriculation together. Bholi Jha, Idris, Ramchandra, Harishankar, Teju, Prithvi and Budur, all of us would walk to school together from the village, talking all the way, not realizing the distance we covered. It was a daily routine.

I asked Bholi, 'How did the Brahmins vote for Idris? Wasn't Kali Mishra, too, in the fray? I heard he did not get even two hundred votes. How did this happen?'

Bholi roared with laughter. 'Come on! Whoever had Bholi Jha by his side was sure to win, wasn't he? Idris helps people a lot, without

---

112 Cowherds

113 A cultivating caste of Bihar

114 A caste of boatmen

any prejudice. He is honest, too. People trust him. And he has close relations with everybody in the village. How could he lose? He had to win, and he did. You should know how much he works for the village.'

I had been happy to hear that Idris had been elected mukhiya. I had sent him a letter of congratulations, which he had replied to. Some time back, when he had visited Patna, he had even come to meet me. He had been quite excited, and I had found his energy infectious. I was happy that a good candidate had become mukhiya. He was determined to develop the village. Bholi and I kept talking about him till late in the evening.

When we sat down for dinner, I saw the cauliflower and peas curry served in a bowl. Served along with it was olak sanna,[115] made pungent by using mustard seeds. Rekha knew that Bholi liked it. No matter how pungent the olak sanna was, he still loved it. It never irritated his tongue. Delighted to see the food, he ate with great relish. I was elated. Given the monotonous life that I led in Patna, a visit from such friends helped improve my mood.

While eating, Bholi said, 'May I tell you something? When a plate comes in front of you, you should be happy seeing whatever has been served. If you eat with a happy mind, the body absorbs the food well. I got to know about this when my upanayana, the thread ceremony, was held.'

I stared at him in bewilderment. I couldn't figure out why the upanayana required one to eat with a happy mind. I said, 'You will always remain a garrulous one. Tell me, doesn't everyone know that you shouldn't be nit-picking while eating? That you shouldn't be morose while eating. You should eat whatever you get happily. How does the upanayana come into all this?'

Bholi started smiling. 'True. There is no need for the upanayana to eat happily. But the fact that one should eat with a happy mind is something I learnt after the ceremony. After the upanayana, my

115 Elephant foot yam mash

father gave me a slim book to conduct the evening rituals. It was called *Sadachar Samhita*, a manual for good conduct. It contained all the mantras and chants to be sung daily, right from waking up early in the morning till you finally went to sleep. There were mantras to clean your teeth with a twig, to eat, to wash your hands after using the toilet, for the evening rituals and worship, for sleeping … a mantra for everything. Along with these, it also mentioned which tree twigs are best to use. The twig for cleaning one's teeth should be no thicker than the tip of one's little finger. The same manual also contained the rituals and mantras for the time one sits for meals. It was written that after seeing the food served, you should take some water in your hand and chant a mantra. Now, I don't remember any of those mantras. Also, I have never offered food to the gods, but the idea of being happy seeing the food I am served has remained with me. It has become a habit. Whether or not I like the food, I feel happy seeing it.'

'But the fact that eating with happiness is good for your body wasn't in that book, was it? How did you learn about that?' I was enjoying Bholi's chatter and had decided to tease him a bit. But he didn't get angry.

He told me, 'You have remained a simpleton all your life. Idiot, if one does something mirthfully, one is sure to succeed. But if it is done dispiritedly, the result is bound to be disappointing. What is the purpose of eating? It nourishes our body, mind and soul. Food has even been called Brahma, the creator god of Hinduism. Even eating is an activity. If you do not do it happily, how will you see the desired results?'

Saying this, Bholi started laughing. It was after a long time that I was eating so heartily. Today, the food seemed special. I asked him, 'Now that you have visited me after so long, at least stay for a week. Nothing short of that will do.'

Bholi frowned. 'Why? Don't I have anything to do back home? My work in Patna will only take a day. I will be gone the day after.'

'All right, you can go, but at least stay for three days. Today is the seventh. On the ninth is a general body meeting of our cooperative. Briefcases will be distributed to all the delegates who attend. I feel I should present you a briefcase as well. I haven't given you any gift in so long.'

Bholi again roared with laughter. 'You are right about the gifts. Your wife completed her PhD. You, apparently, have become a big shot in the cooperative department. Despite all these achievements, you have never given me any gift. You certainly should give me one. But how will I get a briefcase in *your* general body meeting? I am not a delegate, nor am I associated with the cooperative.'

I smiled and said, 'Why are you worried about that? I will arrange for it. You should participate in the general body meeting and see the kind of respect I command. You will even get to relish a lavish feast. Above all, there will be the briefcase as a gift. You must show that to your wife. She will like it, too.'

Bholi didn't say anything. He simply kept smiling and looking at me. We talked for some time after dinner and then went to sleep.

More than five hundred delegates were expected to attend the general body meeting. Since briefcases were given as gifts each year, many people enrolled as bogus delegates. Influential people arranged to include the names of their friends and relatives on the list. These bogus delegates listened to the speeches, relished the feast and returned with the free briefcases. *This time Bholi, too, should get a briefcase. There's no harm in it. Many officers and employees make this kind of arrangement.*

Misraji was in charge of the registration. I knew he would surely be able to put one more name on the list. The next day, I spoke to him. He informed me that since it was the month of Ramadan, not many Muslim delegates were likely to turn up. He would put my friend's name down as a Muslim delegate. That way Bholi, too, would receive a briefcase. I was reassured. Misarji was reliable. He wouldn't go back on his word. I told him, 'Please see to it. I have promised Bholi a briefcase. Don't bring disrepute to my name.' He reassured me once again.

Bholi was already home when I returned. He was busy playing with Bunty and Gudia, making a rag doll. He planned to put a red tikuli[116] on the doll's forehead. Then he started to dress the rag doll in a chunri.[117] He was completely engrossed. I sat down on a chair, watching him.

Finally, he looked at me and smiled. Bunty and Gudia were carefully watching the doll being adorned. I said to him, 'What are you busy with? A doll?'

He laughed. 'I am adorning the bride-doll. Today is the day of her wedding, isn't it?' he said and looked towards Gudia.

Gudia looked at me and nodded. Her face was brimming with happiness. Her attention was entirely focused on the chunri. At that point, Bunty spoke out, 'And I will be a part of the baraat, the groom's procession. I will also take photographs of the wedding.' He showed me a toy camera and quickly took a photo of me. Gudia created a ruckus.

'How can you be a part of the baraat? Aren't you the bride's brother? You will have to sprinkle laba.[118] Isn't it?'

We all started laughing. I imagined Rekha was also laughing in the other room. Bunty, however, looked downcast. Perhaps he didn't like this turn of events. He told Gudia, 'Is it your wedding that I have to sprinkle laba? No matter what, I will be a part of the baraat.'

Bholi's task was over. He turned the doll in his hands and was delighted to see how it looked. He asked Bunty and Gudia, 'Where did you two see the brother of the bride sprinkling laba during his sister's wedding?'

Gudia said, 'Why? We saw it last year at Usha Didi's wedding. Wasn't Santosh Bhaiya sprinkling it?'

Seeing the three of them busy talking, I went inside to change. Rekha informed me that Bholi had not eaten his evening snacks yet. When she had suggested that he eat, he had said he would wait for me.

---

116 A decorative mark worn on the forehead, especially by Hindu women

117 A bridal dress

118 Paddy pops

But he had got busy with Bunty and Gudia. The children had grown quite fond of him.

I asked her to serve the snacks and came out to the living room. I told Bholi, 'Leave the doll. The adorning is over. Let's eat something.'

Bunty and Gudia took the doll and went away. We ate greedily. Rekha had prepared sohari,[119] Bholi's favourite dish. Accompanying it were non-tel[120] and kutcha achar.[121] I told him while eating, 'I have arranged for your briefcase, but there is one problem. You will have to become a Muslim.'

'What? Why will I have to become a Muslim?'

'Actually, only Muslim delegates' seats are vacant. It's the month of Ramadan, after all. Nobody will ask you anything anyway. And you already wear kurta-pyjama.'

He remained silent for a while, thinking about something. 'Yes, what will happen? I have played the role of a Muslim so many times in plays. Do you remember when I played the role of Emperor Bahadur Shah Zafar and you were Lieutenant Hudson?'

I remembered it quite well. Bholi had given a first-rate performance. Many women had started to sob as he performed. In one scene, Lieutenant Hudson had brought the severed heads of the emperor's two sons on a plate. He had removed the cloth covering the heads to show them to the emperor. The audience remembered Bholi's portrayal of the emperor's despair and my performance of Hudson's cruelty for a long time.

I told him, 'Yes, that was truly wonderful. For quite some time, your character stayed with the people. In the last scene, you sang that famous ghazal. Which one was it? Do you remember the lines?'

Both Bholi and I tried to recall the ghazal. And then he said, 'I can't recall the whole ghazal, but I recollect a few lines. *Lagta nahi dil mera*

---

119 Thick, hand-shaped chapatis, usually made of rice flour

120 Salt mixed with mustard oil

121 Grated mango pickle

ujde dayar mein.[122] After that, perhaps it was this: *Do aarzoo mein kat gaye, do intezaar mein.*[123] The last line was: *Do gaz zamin bhi na mili ku-ye-yaar mein.*'[124]

Bholi remained silent for some time before saying, 'Do you know something? Bahadur Shah was a great emperor. The last Mughal emperor. The leader of the first war of India's independence. Eighty years old. He fought valiantly against the English even at an advanced age.'

A thick layer of grief seemed to have spread over his face. I tried to change the topic, 'Listen, brother, don't get caught at the general body meeting. You have to look like a real Muslim. Nobody should get to know that you are a Hindu. If anybody gets to know, it will be a disgrace for me.'

Bholi tried to smile and assured me. 'No, I wouldn't let anybody come to know. I will pose as a proper Muslim.'

Sure enough! That day, Bholi certainly looked like a real Muslim. He had been excited since morning. He wore his kurta-pyjama and told me, 'Look, Arvind. I am ready. But I don't even know my name. Never mind. Let's go now.'

There was a lot of hustle and bustle in Federation Hall. People had been congregating since morning. When I took Bholi to Misarji, he laughed and said, 'You truly look like a Muslim. Nobody will be able to figure out that you are not one.' He then handed Bholi a chit and added, 'Please read the name written on the chit and sign with the same name in the register.'

I took the chit from Bholi. It read: 'Muhammad Aslam, Representative, Millat Cooperative, Darbhanga.' I gave the chit back

122 My heart doesn't feel at ease in this ravaged land

123 Two moments were spent wishing for things and the other two were spent waiting for them

124 I didn't even get two yards of land to be buried in the street where my beloved lives

to Bholi. He signed as Muhammad Aslam and took his briefcase. I escorted him to the hall, found him a seat and got busy with my own work. The meeting had started. The secretary of the cooperative had started to read the annual report.

An hour into the meeting, I heard some murmurs from the hall. Soon, it turned into a commotion. I rushed to see what had happened. The atmosphere was heated. Now, the board of directors was to be elected through a secret ballot, unlike other times where a show of hands was carried out. There were many complaints against the current management and I was sure the current board would get replaced. I had assumed the commotion to be related to this election. But upon reaching the hall, I saw Bholi shouting at somebody. Some people had gathered around him. I dashed towards him. As if we were strangers, I asked him, 'What's wrong with you? Why are you shouting? Please be quiet. You are disturbing the meeting.'

Burning with anger, he said, 'Sir, this officer has been saying unacceptable things about my religion. He says that Islam is a fanatical religion, that it runs on the might of the sword, that Muslims eat beef and call Hindus infidels. I have been trying to explain to him why he is wrong. We have been living together since ages, but we have failed to understand each other. We simply run after the crow when someone tells us that it is flying away, without first checking the fact ourselves. But the officer is not ready to listen, and has kept up the rude remarks.'

Bholi appeared to be quite agitated. He continued shouting. More people were heading towards him. I quickly grabbed Bholi by the arm and dragged him out of the hall. Almost pushing him, I took him away. Then I shook him and shouted. 'Bholi Jha?'

He looked at me intently and said softly, 'Yes!' And then he continued to stare at me as if he had been woken up from a deep slumber.

The Whirlpool

Nagendra Sharma Bandhu

(Translated from the Magahi by Vivek Perampurna)

Chanoka was on his way back from the fields, a clay pot of milk on his shoulder. The moment he caught sight of his house, Brahma, a constable dressed in a worn-out khaki uniform, came running and threw himself at Chanoka's feet. Chanoka was taken aback.

'Who are you?' Chanoka asked, startled.

'You are like God to me,' Brahma said in a low, respectful voice, his hands folded. 'With your blessings, I have become a father!'

Chanoka's mind transported him back to an incident of the past.

It had been the peak of the monsoon season. The incessant rain had filled the rivers to the brink. The channels had spread so far and wide that it was impossible to see the riverbanks. River Ganga had found its way into the fields through these channels. The entire harvest of jinar, kauni, narkatiya and cheena had been submerged, just the way a starving ogress gobbles up its succulent prey. In just a few days, the whole village had been underwater. All the farmers had been worried. They had been more concerned about their cattle than themselves. How were they to feed them?

Usually, during the floods, the villagers would move their cattle to Farkiya for safety. Five of the farmers had agreed to move them. But what good was mere intention? There was water everywhere. Who would dare enter the raging Ganges? But they had courage. Fate subdues man, but it also reinforces determination. And what other course was there but to cross the overflowing river? Was it wise, though, to risk one's life to save the cattle?

Patitda had been their best bet to ferry the cattle across the river. Once he made up his mind, even Chanoka, Ramesar, Balesar and Chethru sprang into action. Chethru, the youngest, was a tall, athletic and courageous lad. That evening, they had all met in Patitda's courtyard. A few more had joined them. Finally, around ten of them had agreed to move to Farkiya in the morning. It was decided that five of them would take the train with food and provisions, while the remaining five would move the cattle through the river.

There had been a total of twenty-five buffaloes. The five men who had to get them across were young and muscular and bore bamboo staffs. Early in the morning, all the animals were released from their posts. Armed with well-oiled bamboo staffs adorned with tin foil collars and copper ferrule heels, the people had inched closer to the Ganges. Everyone had been talking about the same thing, about how the cattle would be ferried across.

Gradually, the five appointed people had arrived. The river had appeared to be endless. Trees, settlements, villages ... nothing could be seen. Chethru had felt despair stirring in his heart. 'Good heavens! The water is endless! God, is it our Ganges or an ocean?' he had said.

Walking up to Patitda, he had asked, 'Uncle, will I be able to ferry them across this?'

Patitda guffawed and then encouraged him. 'Hey, you are a young lad. Why are you hesitating? Do men wield any power? It's only the gods who possess it. Mother Ganges delivers us all, my son. At your age, I could swim all the way to the levee. Remember, if you are afraid, you're dead.'

Chanoka remembered speaking to Patitda. 'Here we are. Four days of provisions, packed in a sack. You can hold it on your head. No one except you can cross this river.'

'Goodness! It's quite heavy! No less than twenty-five kilos!' Patitda had blurted. 'Anyway, I will take it.'

Chethru had called out. 'Uncle, my mom has prepared some sweets. I haven't even tasted them yet.'

Patitda didn't respond, but he had mumbled in his head, 'Everything is fate, son.'

The buffaloes had started to plod through the water. Chethru had been holding a gravid buffalo. He hit her on the flanks to push her through the water.

Patitda had shouted, 'Hey! Don't hit her on the back; she is pregnant. Leave her and hold the other one there, otherwise she will get separated from the herd.'

Chethru had immediately held the other one. Suddenly, a river dolphin had sprung up near him. 'Oh god! That's such a big one, uncle! I have heard that if they blow in your ears, your whole body will bloat.'

Balesar had laughed. 'These river dolphins are timid. They usually avoid humans.'

A little ahead had been a huge whirlpool. Patitda had seen his pregnant buffalo heading towards it and had felt his heart in his mouth. Without thinking, he had rushed through the stream like a calf running to its mother.

'Hurry up, Patitda, or she will be gone,' Chanoka had shouted.

Patitda had forgotten about the sack of provisions on his head. The buffalo was more precious than his own life. The animal had almost grazed the rim of the whirlpool, but Patitda was not one to let go easily. He had caught hold of the buffalo's horn and swerved it to the left. The animal had been saved, but the sack of provisions had been lost.

However, neither Patitda nor the others had realized it just then. After saving the buffalo, they were as happy as a needy person stumbling upon a bag of gold.

Before long, both the men and the animals were tired. The shore had been sighted. They raised a shout, 'Long live Mother Ganga! We are almost there!'

Ultimately, they had all made it to the other side and fell, exhausted, on the sand. No one was aware of their aching bodies. Patitda had stood a little distance away, near his buffalo that was sitting calmly. He could feel the anxiety in his throat. He was massaging the flanks, back and feet of the animal with force. After a lot of effort, the buffalo had stood up. Patitda had put his ears to her barrel. He could feel the movement of the foetus. Relieved, he had let out a low cry, 'Thank Goddess Bhagwati!'

The others had soon felt better, but then hunger had gnawed at their bellies. Chethru had called out, 'Hey, Patitda! Where were you?'

'What happened?' Patitda had asked and hurried back to the group.

Chethru, meanwhile, had noticed that the bag on Patitda's head was missing. He had asked, 'Our food? Where is the sack?'

'Oh my god!' Patitda had realized that he had lost it. His face hung. Everyone was famished. Their hunger was subdued so far because they were assured by the knowledge that they were carrying food. With the realization that it was gone, their hunger doubled. Just like a flame rises when the oil is almost running out, the scarcity of food only enhances one's cravings.

Patitda's head had drooped. He had felt the weight of guilt mounting. 'In all my years, this is the first time this has happened. You all have to go hungry because of my fault. Maybe Mother Ganges was also very hungry, that's why she took our food.'

Chanoka had felt Patitda's agony. 'Try not to worry so much. Have patience; it will help us all tide over everything. All will be well. We will eat.'

Chethru, however, had been a little miffed. 'We will eat, but how?'

'The one who gave us hunger will provide food, too. Let's go and find a place to stay first,' Chanoka had replied.

Ramesar had pitched in. 'I am so hungry that I can hardly move. How will I corral these animals through the muck?'

'If you don't, you will perish. Even tigers don't get their prey sitting idle. It's monsoon. We will have to find a place to stay.'

'Okay, let's go. Herd the animals together. I am certain we will find a village in an hour or two,' Patitda had said.

The animals were rallied. The buffaloes moved in a neat queue, followed by the men. The sun had been about to set and darkness had been rushing in. The clouds had also spread their canopy across the sky.

Chanoka had exhorted the group. 'Hurry up! If it begins to rain, it will be a mess!'

An exhausted Chethru had said, 'I can't walk any longer!'

Chanoka had tried to lift his spirits. 'You aspire to join the police? Do you know that as a policeman you will have to endure hunger and fatigue?'

Suddenly, Ramesar had spoken up. 'Hey, look there. I can see lights. Come on, nudge the animals in that direction. See, God arranges for everything!'

'How so?' Patitda had asked.

'Do not worry about that. I will arrange for food and a place to sleep tonight for all of you. Move fast.'

A tinge of glow had returned on everyone's face. They had hurried the cattle along. Their feet had sped up like a bird flying to its nest.

It had been a strange sight when they got there. Four lit petromax had been hanging in the yard. As many as hundred, or two hundred, people had gathered. Men and women, the old and children were assembled in a large circle, engrossed in some performances. In the centre had been a young man, an exorcist, dancing with a staff in his hands, with a few singers belting out folk songs.

Chanoka had said, 'All of you please stay here in the dark.'

Tired, everyone had sat down immediately.

'Do not come until I call out,' Chanoka had instructed. He had then adjusted his loincloth and started dancing on one foot, his staff carefully balanced in his arms. He had gradually eased through the crowd and made his way to the centre. Before the exorcist could understand what was happening, Chanoka had gone for his ankles and given him a sharp knock with his staff. The exorcist had been startled. Chanoka had roared, 'Do you need another blow? Do you recognize me?'

The exorcist had stood stunned. Chanoka had motioned with his staff once again. 'What are you looking at? Do you recognize me, or should I strike you once more?'

Chanoka's fiery face was more terrifying than the staff he held. The exorcist was witless. The crowd had begun to murmur.

The exorcist's intuition seemed to have warned him what to do; he had begun singing with the other singers. 'O Mother, you are Gahilwa. How can I not know you … You are above me, my benefactor, how can I not know you?'

Chanoka had started to shake his head in affirmation. The exorcist had thrown his staff and seized Chanoka's feet. 'Now I do recognize you, master. You are the divine Gahilwa.'

'So, you do recognize me.'

'Who am I to you? You are the embodiment of Mother Gahilwa.'

'Yes, now wash my feet.'

The exorcist had washed Chanoka's feet, dried them with his towel and then timidly stood by his side. Chanoka had sat down and spoke loudly, 'Whoever is grieving or wishes for something can come to me, one by one.'

A ten-year-old kid had come running and said with folded hands, 'Mother, my horse has been missing for the last two days. Please tell me where it is.'

Chanoka had thought for a while. He had noticed that the exorcist had placed a few grains of rice on a flat stone as an offering during the rituals. Mumbling, he had picked up a few grains of the rice and handed it to the boy. 'Put it in your mouth and proceed south. You will find your horse in the bushes there.'

Hardly had the boy put the grains in his mouth when his father shouted from behind the crowd, 'Hey, Sumiran, we found your horse. It was in the bushes.'

The crowd had erupted. They had started to chant: 'Long live Mother Gahilwa!'

Someone had said, 'Mother Gahilwa has arrived in person. Did you see? The moment the boy put the rice in his mouth, his wish was fulfilled! They have divine powers indeed!'

Everybody had been astonished. Shortly, there had been a long queue of people waiting for their wishes to be fulfilled. Some had been waiting to get a job, some wanted a transfer. One fellow had approached Chanoka and begged, 'Holy Mother, please ensure my lineage!'

Chanoka had said, 'Where is your wife? Call her.'

His wife had been brought forward. Chanoka had handed a fistful of rice to the husband and wife and said, 'Every morning, after bathing, both of you have five grains each. And sleep together without fail. Until these grains are finished, do not move out of your house; go nowhere. Your wish shall be granted.'

When everyone had had their turn, Chanoka had said, 'Now I will go. Give me some water.'

Chanoka had stretched his limbs after quenching his thirst. He felt like himself again. The villagers had still been flocking around him and asking all sorts of questions. Chanoka had told them the truth about his journey and then added, 'There are four men with me. First, serve them food, then pack these offerings for their breakfast.'

Everything had been arranged in a jiffy. Everyone had eaten puris and kheer. Breakfast for the next day had been packed and everyone slept peacefully.

The entire story had played out in Chanoka's mind like a newsreel. He said to the constable, 'Now I remember. Tell me, what brings you here?'

'Your blessings materialized. I came to make an offering.'

'Offerings are made to gods. You see that temple there? If you want to offer something, have the pulpit repaired and feed five Brahmins.'

Chanoka blessed the constable, gently patting his head, and proceeded towards his house.

The City of Gaya

Arun Kamal

(Translated from the Hindi by the poet)

The city is choked with shaved heads,
dozing languorously in the sun-sharpened sand,
the leftover water of the Phalgu shimmering under the peepal tree.

A soul, lost and homeless, persistently bangs at the door.
Suddenly flings open the rear door of Bharat Talkies,
a shaft of light falls off, a loud burst of sound, then stillness.

The streets of inns are soaked with the sweat of ryots.[125]
Far away in the pond glimmers the water, the last light
of the eye.

Who are these dead ancestors, unsatisfied still
with all these offerings? Who are these ancestors
who keep coming back to the same burning earth?

---

125 A peasant or a tenant farmer

Raking up the ashes of the hearth for their morsels,
a child is trudging along a long desolate street all alone,
suddenly besieged by dead souls thousands of years old, tattered.

Kosi

Narayanji

(Translated from the Maithili by Vidyanand Jha)

Returning to my village from Supaul, I had taken a bus and completed a journey of around 150 kilometres via Kosi Barrage. It had been difficult. That's why while returning to Supaul I decided to take train to Tharbhittha, walk fifteen kilometres and then cross the Kosi in a boat.

It was my first time; I did not know the route. I was afraid of losing my way. Also, a recent incident of a junior engineer being abducted and killed on this route had added to my fears. Yet, I chose to take this route to fulfil my dream of crossing the Kosi in a boat.

Trying to figure out which way to go, I asked a person coming from the opposite direction, 'Sir, is this the way to the Kosi riverbank, to Nirmali?'

He nodded and went away, staring at me. I was scared. His stare either meant that I had asked a silly question, or it was an indication of danger along that route.

Up ahead, the path was waterlogged. There was no way to avoid it, so I removed my shoes and socks. Turning around, I saw a young, newly wed woman in a printed saree, a box on her head, walking behind me. A young man, possibly her brother, was carrying a bamboo basket wrapped in cloth on his head, probably accompanying her to her in-laws' house.

I felt reassured. I assumed our destination was the same, the riverbank. Also, it meant that I was on the right path. We were three people walking together.

Wading through the water, I saw the reflection of the sky and the clouds in it. Fear makes people hear their own heartbeat, but when one gazes at the sky and clouds calmly, one is sure to be free of such fear.

Crossing the waterlogged stretch, I stuffed my socks in the pocket of my kurta and put on my shoes without them.

I looked at the surrounding fields with enchantment, filling my eyes with the verdant green of the luxuriant wheat crop in the month of Pausha.[126]

The newly wed was now walking closer to me, but not once did my eyes stray towards her. I was spellbound by the endless plains of the Kosi region. Just their presence made me feel more confident. I began to wonder how people, mired in their monotonous lives, became desperate enough to indulge in licentious behaviour, or even commit a crime.

A little distance ahead, the path merged with another. There were two more people walking ahead of me. Now we were five of us. Out of the two, one had a cloth bag on his shoulder, just like me.

The other one was carrying a leather bag. He asked me my whereabouts. When he realized that I was new to this path, he said, 'Don't worry, in the dry season I take this route at least four times a month.'

The man with the cloth bag, Dinesh Babu, worked in the medical department at the block office. He lived on one side of the Kosi and worked on the other. He was going to the office in Nirmali for some work.

---

126 December–January

I asked Dinesh Babu: 'How far is the riverbank?'

'Around two kilometres. You are going for the first time, that's why it seems far.'

The newly wed, meanwhile, had walked far ahead of us.

I told Dinesh Babu: 'It doesn't seem to be very far. The path itself is so picturesque with sand all around.'

'Oh, you haven't seen anything yet! If you come here during the month of Baisakh, you will find it difficult to walk in the sand. If you walk ten steps, it will seem like only eight.'

'How is that?'

'When you put one foot forward, it will feel as if somebody is pulling you from behind.'

I thought to myself that this would be an adventurous journey.

The other gentleman, a jansevak,[127] who was silent all this while, added to Dinesh Babu's narrative. 'On top of that, sand-laden westerly winds fill your eyes and ears.'

By this time, we had reached an inhabited area where there were around five thatched shacks. There was also a handpump and some hay and straw nearby.

On seeing some bottle gourds growing on a thatched roof, I said to Dinesh Babu: 'These bottle gourds are quite strange.'

'These are Punjabi bottle gourds. The people who go from here to Punjab bring back the seeds.'

After that, we started to talk about the failures of the current state government. The others pitched in, too. I shifted my gaze to locate the white-breasted waterhen among a flock of birds when the conversation shifted to the fifth pay commission.

I don't know what crossed my mind, but I asked Jansevakji: 'Let's leave aside the case of Dinesh Babu right now, as he is going from his

---

127 Revenue department official

residence to his office. But you are travelling for official work. What kind of travelling allowance can you claim?'

He said, 'I would claim the allowance for travelling by bus via the barrage. Wait till you reach the riverbank. You will find that it's not just me but many employees of the Bihar government who take this route to Nirmali but claim the travelling allowance reserved for motorized transport through the barrage.'

'Yes, one has to walk a bit, but then you spend less money on this route.'

Dinesh Babu chimed in. 'You don't have to pay any fare at all.'

I was surprised. 'How is that?'

'The boatman doesn't charge us money. He thinks we are local government employees and is scared of us.'

I had got some sand into my shoes, and it was hurting my feet. Once this realization set in, it felt as if my mouth, too, was full of sand. My mind went back to the bottle gourds on the thatched roof. I said to Dinesh Babu: 'People have changed a lot, isn't it? Now one can even find Punjabi bottle gourds being grown in these parts.'

Dinesh Babu asked, 'What do you mean by that?'

'What do I mean by what?'

Feeling attacked, he said, 'In Punjab, terrorists often abduct people and murder them. Don't you know that in a similar incident some months back, in this very Kosi area, a junior engineer of the irrigation department was abducted and killed?'

He continued, 'Marijuana is cultivated in Nepal and reaches Calcutta through this same route on boats. We take this route most of the time, but we can't figure anything out.'

'I don't know what you can or cannot figure out, but this place has become as notorious as the river islands of the Ganges.'

'The river islands are near the capital, that's why there are more crimes there. People say that a state-level politician was involved in the murder of the junior engineer. Criminals were hired from outside,' said Dinesh Babu, as if he were privy to the details of the case.

By now, I could see the Kosi and the long bamboo trees near a hut on the riverbank. I looked towards the north. The river seemed to stretch till infinity. In the south, I could see the river, the backwaters and sand dunes.

There were some people already sitting near the hut. The newly wed woman was among them.

The boat had already started from the other side and was heading our way. The river had strong currents thanks to the easterly winds. The currents were pounding against the bank and eroding it incessantly. I pushed a clod into the river with my right foot. It fell with a thud.

I returned to the hut. There was foam floating in the river. The locals were saying that the water level had increased. Last night, it had rained in the hills.

Three people were sitting together near the hut. All of them looked like labourers. I got to know from them that they worked at Tussar Mill in Bhagalpur and were going home. Their village was quite close if one took this route.

Soon, the boat reached the bank. The people sitting in the boat were alighting in thigh-deep water, which was so bitterly cold that I felt my legs go numb. I balanced my body carefully with both my hands and climbed on to the boat.

When the newly wed woman and an old woman with a girl of six to seven years in her lap climbed the boat, I turned my face away and started looking at the river. The boat was big and the passengers were few.

The boatman started to collect the fare when there was no one left on the bank. He didn't ask Dinesh Babu for the fare, but he stretched his hand out in front of Jansevakji who felt offended. Immediately, Dinesh Babu said, 'He is a jansevak.'

The boatman went ahead. He charged me two rupees.

When the boatman reached the workers from the mill, they gave him only one rupee per person. The boatman insisted that they give him a rupee each more.

'Why should we? Are we crossing these banks for the first time?' one of the three workers asked the boatman.

'We are doing a puja on the full moon day of Pausha. We have installed idols. Therefore, I insist,' the boatman replied promptly.

'Fund that yourself. When we got into the boat after wading through thigh-deep water, why didn't you help by carrying us on your shoulders?'

This had no effect on the boatman who ultimately got them to pay up one more rupee each.

There was no argument in collecting the fare from the newly wed woman.

When the boatman held his hand out in front of another person, he said, 'I work at the court in Supaul.'

I saw the boatman's face become flushed. 'Don't you sirs get a remuneration for your service at the court?' he murmured and went ahead.

The next people were the old lady and the child. The old lady said, 'I live in Aslanpur and give the yearly fare.[128]

Just hearing the word 'Aslan'[129] reminded me of poet Vidyapati, his poem 'Kirtilata' and the invader, Aslan, described therein.

The boatman, meanwhile, insisted on the fare for the child. 'I get the yearly fare only for adults. For the child, I would like four annas as chiraki.'[130]

---

128 The yearly fare consists of portions of agricultural produce, allowing a fixed number of adults to travel free

129 Vidyapati's famous work, Kirtilata, revolves around a battle involving Kirti Singh and Malik Aslan.

130 Extra fare collected in cash for the passengers other than those covered by the yearly fare

Several thoughts were circling in my head. *This old lady gives yearly fare, which means she is a local from the Kosi area. The boatman can't ask for a fare from the government servants, but he insists that the old lady must pay for the child*? But, of course, I didn't say anything.

The old lady gave up in the face of the boatman's forceful insistence. She untied a knot in her pallu and took out a four-anna coin. I saw the disappointment on the child's face.

The boat set off. The passengers shouted, 'May the Rannu Sardar[131] be victorious! May Kosika Maharani be victorious!'

The bank was left behind. I stretched out my arm and took a handful of water from the river, sprinkling it over myself with respect. The boatman saw this and said, 'Sir, please do take a look at the idols after you get down on the other side.'

I was midstream in the Kosi; it was flowing between its two banks. It wasn't roaring to intimidate me.

---

131 A mythical character said to be the head of the Musahars who are believed to have brought the Kosi to this area

Fellowmen

Avdhesh Preet

(Translated from the Hindi by Chaitali Pandya)

'Why aren't you sleeping? Are you unable to?' There was an annoyance and, to some extent, restlessness in the voice.

'Yes, I am unable to sleep. I've tried everything, but sleep evades me,' came the sharp retort. The helplessness in the shrill tone was not concealed.

'What's the matter? You seem to be sad.' This time, there was empathy in the first voice.

'Sorrow and not being able to sleep have nothing to do with each other. That the two must be interrelated is presumptuous.' There was an air of seriousness surrounding the second voice. Perhaps it was due to his experience, by virtue of his seniority.

'You are right! But it's been a while since I have been noticing how restless you are. I couldn't hold back, so I asked you,' the first speaker justified himself.

'It's good that you asked. Perhaps this will help ease the restlessness to an extent. One feels lighter after voicing one's concerns.'

The first voice was assured that the second voice was elderly, about sixty years of age. *Yes, he certainly must be that age.* With this thought, he felt content that at least that voice had lived a full life.

Sensing the silence, the second voice asked, 'What happened? Why are you quiet?'

'Nothing much! I was just thinking about you.'

'Thinking about me! What were you thinking?'

'I was wondering how old you must be.'

'What difference does it make whether I am thirty years old or sixty?' There was a mystical charm in the second voice.

'Why not? It certainly makes a difference! A sixty-year-old is a man of the world compared to someone who is just thirty. He has enjoyed life more.'

'No! In fact, a sixty-year-old has endured more hardships and shouldered more responsibilities.'

'In that case, my assumption is right.'

'Which assumption?'

'That you are sixty years old.'

'Yes, you guessed it right. I am sixty years old. What about you? How old are you?'

'My age! Can you guess how old I am?'

'I am clumsy when it comes to such matters. I am not good with figures.'

'Then how did you go about living a long life?'

'I'm not sure if what I have lived can be termed as "life".' The second voice may not have been a learned man, but he sure was seasoned.

'Well, then what is it that makes you sad? Why don't you sleep well?'

'Forget about me! Why are you not sleeping? Why are you so agitated?'

'Why shouldn't I be?' the first voice snapped. 'It would have been different had I died a natural death. At least I wouldn't be sleeping here in this cramped space.'

'Had you died a natural death, would you have found a place in heaven?' There was sarcasm in the second voice.

Ignoring the sting, the first voice continued. 'I don't know about that. But I am sure that at least I wouldn't be lying here, in this confined space.'

'Then where would you have been?'

'I would have been cremated.'

Suddenly, a deathly silence fell. Everything around seemed to have come to a standstill.

Breaking the silence, the second voice asked softly, 'So, are you a Hindu?'

'Yes … and you?' The first voice was clouded in doubt.

'I am a Muslim.'

'In that case, you have come to the right place.'

'No, had I died a natural death, my final resting place would have been better than this one.'

'Why do you say so? What's wrong with this place?'

'I feel the same way as you do. In this cramped space I can't even stretch out my legs, nor is there any space to turn sideways.' There was a deep sense of pain in the second voice.

'So, this is the reason you are unable to sleep?'

'Yes, my body feels stiff all over. The blood that had oozed out from the wound has frozen and triggered a burning sensation,' the second voice moaned.

'Where's your wound? I mean, where were you wounded?'

'Right in the chest. I was stabbed ruthlessly in the chest.'

'Tsk! Tsk! You must have undergone a lot of pain.'

'That's true.' And then dolefully, the second voice asked, 'How did you end up here?'

'Just because of some skunks. Damn! These nasty government officials! They are capable of *anything*!'

'You are right! Each one of them merely pretends to work, without putting their heart into it. Something similar happened to me as well.'

'Really? What happened?'

'I suffered a similar fate! In the dead of the night, some careless government officials came in with lots of corpses and stuffed us into these pits. Those scoundrels! Couldn't they have dug bigger pits?' There was aggression in the second voice.

'One can never expect anything good from these halfwits. In the frenzy of burying the bodies, they didn't even bother to check who was a Hindu and who was a Muslim.'

'It seems you have been a victim of such a misunderstanding.'

'Yes! I used to work at the cash counter of a shop owned by a wealthy merchant named Suleiman. The rioters set the whole place ablaze. Every single person there was charred to death.'

The terror in the first voice hinted that the heart-wrenching scene had flashed back to his mind. 'Till late into the night, our bodies kept burning. Then the callous government officials came and shoved all the bodies into a truck and buried them here in a rush.'

'They must have thought that all the employees working for a Muslim man must be Muslims themselves,' the second voice spoke harshly. 'You mean you are a Hindu and they mistook you for a Muslim!'

'Who will make those fools understand that Master Suleiman is no more. Who will feed my family?'

For once, there was no reaction from the second voice. Silence fell between the two. Finally, the first voice took the initiative, 'What happened? Why have you gone silent?'

'Nothing in particular! I am just thinking about you.'

'Thinking about me? What about me?'

'I am wondering, how many people are there in your family? Who all are there?'

'My wife and two children. One is five years old and the other is three years old.'

'You seem to be young. How old are you?'

'Nearly thirty years!'

'Tsk! Tsk! Tsk! You have truly been wronged.'

'Why! Only a while ago you were saying whether one is thirty years old or sixty years, it does not make any difference.'

'Usually, it wouldn't make any difference. But in your case, it does!'

'What do you mean by that?'

'Well, I mean to say, who, in your absence, will provide for your family?' There was concern in the second voice.

'The one who has committed this act of sabotage!'

'I don't think so!' the second voice, otherwise empirical, was now curt.

'Then, someday, my children will sabotage them.'

The second voice didn't utter a word. Once again, silence descended.

The first voice waited for a while, but not receiving any response from the second voice, and unable to restrain himself, he asked, 'What happened? Why are you quiet again?'

'Nothing much! The old wounds have reopened. That's why I am unable to speak.'

'Those heartless scoundrels! How mercilessly they must've killed you!'

'Are murderers ever kind-hearted?'

'Who killed you?'

'The killers!'

'But who were they? Hindus? Why would a Muslim kill another Muslim?'

'Brother, a murderer is a murderer.'

'Your words are full of wisdom,' the first voice quipped. 'But tell me how you died.'

'Let's not discuss this further! We have been discussing very depressing things since the time we started talking. Don't you have anything else to talk about besides death, mourning and bereavement?' The second voice dismissed the first voice's question tactfully.

'The dead will talk about nothing but death! Can they talk about life?'

'No matter what life brings to us, nothing is better than life itself. Especially for us, the dead, nothing can be more pleasurable than life.'

'Okay, for once I agree with you. But tell me, what is so special about life that it should be cherished?' The first voice refused to give in.

'There are a lot of things! For instance, the taste of bread, a child's giggles, the magic of love.'

The first voice interrupted the second. 'You seem to be a romantic person.'

'Yes, I fell in love with life,' replied the second voice, once again with an air of mysticism.

'But you were saying that what you lived cannot be called "life".'

'Yes, I did say that. But I was talking in terms of experience. It's life that gives us new hope to live every day. Each day, one hopes that one's circumstances will improve.'

'But nothing changed, did it?'

'Yes, but hope lives on, doesn't it?' There was tremendous optimism in the second voice.

'You're dauntless. You're truly incredible.'

Despite the hearty praise, the second voice did not react. This was unsettling for the first one. *Surely the old man has decided to be silent again.* Annoyed, he called out, 'What happened? Are you once again lost in thoughts?'

'Uh-huh! I was recalling something.'

'You were remembering something, or someone?'

'Oh, not really! There was no one so dear to me whom I would miss,' the second voice sighed.

'Why? What about your wife and children?'

'They died a long time ago. I don't even remember the date or the year when they died.'

'How did they die?'

'Of hunger!'

'Of hunger? Weren't you earning enough?'

'No! I used to live in a village back then. There was a great famine. People had no food to eat. I had come to the city to work as a labourer. Back home, in the village, my wife and children starved to death. Many people had died then.'

'Those who died, were they all Muslims?' the first voice was subdued.

'Come on! How's that possible? Don't you know that only the poor die of hunger?'

'Uh-huh!' The first voice probably felt embarrassed. To hide his embarrassment, he said, 'And then did you marry a second time?'

'I wanted to, but it didn't come about!'

'Why didn't it? I don't see any shortcomings in you!'

'It's because I was a Shia.'

'And she?'

'A Sunni!'

'Damn! This is prevalent amongst you, too?' It seemed that the first voice was not aware of this fact. Stuttering, he asked, 'Having known this, why did you get yourself into this situation?'

'Because of love!' the second voice had a slight tremble.

'Then what happened?'

'Then I vowed never to marry again.' The second voice cracked with emotion.

The first voice realized that he had hit a raw nerve. Before he could grow more anxious, the first voice changed the subject. 'Well, tell me, what did you do for a living? I mean, what was your profession?'

'I was a royal mason.' The first voice's efforts had finally bore fruit; there was spontaneity in the second voice. 'I used to build people's homes.'

'Ah, but you didn't get two yards of land for yourself!'

'Had I died a natural death, this fate wouldn't have befallen me.'

'So how did you die?'

'I was constructing a house for a widow. Just when the construction had reached halfway, the people from the neighbourhood kicked up a ruckus.'

'Why?' The first voice sounded astonished.

'They were pressurizing the widow, who was a Hindu, to not get her house built by a Muslim.' The disgust in the second voice was unmissable.

'Then what happened?'

'Believe me, that day I was so enraged that I felt like immuring each one of them in a wall. But sadly, I broke into tears.' Choking up, the second voice said, 'The widow was a kind woman. She explained to me that I should stop the work for the time being and resume when the situation improved.'

'So, you left the work?'

'I had no choice! We kept waiting for the situation to improve. The wait was long! The thought of the partially constructed house kept haunting me. Her daughter's wedding was approaching. So, one fine day, unable to resist the impulse and not thinking twice about the consequences, I set off from home.'

The second voice had barely caught a breath when the first voice impatiently asked, 'And you went straight to the widow's house?'

'No! While I was on my way, some scum from the neighbourhood surrounded me. They warned me that I must desist from building the house of a "Hinduaani".[132] My silence infuriated them and they further intimidated me, saying, "Dare you go to her house."' The second voice, huffing, added, 'But I did not heed their threat and escaped from there.'

'I must say that you are truly a courageous man! Weren't you scared?'

---

132 A Hindu woman

'I wasn't afraid of those skunks, but I was certainly afraid of the widow.'

'Why? What happened?'

'When I reached the site, I saw that the construction work had resumed at a frantic pace. Masons and labourers were engrossed in their work. I was shocked to see the scene that unfolded before my eyes. Poor widow! She turned pale when she saw me. She apologized to me and said, "Zahoor Miyan, I have to live among them only."'

Once again, a deathly silence descended. The first voice, who thus far had been delving deep into the second voice's past, had also fallen silent. Taking a deep breath, the second voice, too, remained silent.

A sudden sound startled both of them. The first voice said, 'Is someone overhearing our conversation?'

'Who cares! When we were alive, no one listened to us. Why the heck would they care now!'

'You are right! It must be just an illusion.'

'Yes, one always fears disillusionment!' The second voice seemed to be lost in thoughts. 'That day, I too suffered from disillusionment. For the first time, I was overwhelmed with fear. Barely had I reached the neighbourhood where the ruffians had waylaid me, when the angry mob surrounded me. They were enraged because I did not obey their command. They began to beat me up. In self-defence, I too hit them back. That was it! They took out their knives and pierced my chest. Upon reaching the corner of my street, I collapsed.'

Towards the end of this narrative, the second voice grew unsteady. He was exhausted.

After a brief pause, the first voice said, 'So, was it your death that provoked an outrage?'

'Yes, those hoodlums who beat me to death caused a great furore. They blocked roads and set shops on fire. The police then resorted to firing. The vandals fled, leaving behind bodies. The passers-by and onlookers were the ones who got killed in the police firing. And then the bodies were hastily disposed of,' the second voice was dying out by now.

Showing sympathy, the first voice said, 'You seem to be tired now. You must rest!'

'Rest?' The second voice asked sarcastically. 'What rest? In this confined space, is there enough room to rest?'

'You are right! My whole body has stiffened thanks to lying here, squished.' There was a tinge of pain in the first voice's words. Suddenly, he was gripped by the pain that flowed in the conversation. He began to groan.

'It's hurting a lot, isn't it?' There was a sense of disquietude in the second voice.

'Yes, so much that I can't endure it any more.'

'Let's do one thing! The wall that separates the two of us, its soil seems to be a little moist. You scrape from your side and I shall do the same from my end.'

'No wonder! After all, you were a royal mason.' Even though the first voice seemed to be in great pain, the banter hadn't ceased. 'While you lie buried in the grave, all you can think of is workmanship!'

'Dead bodies can be buried but not workmanship!'

'Your words are full of wisdom. They are beyond my understanding,' the first voice said earnestly. 'Explain to me in simple words what needs to be done.'

'You dig the soil from your side of the wall, and I shall do it from my side. Once the wall collapses, there will be a little more space. At least there will be enough room to turn on either side. Besides, who knows, it may be possible to even stretch our limbs freely.'

Not receiving any response, the second voice grew a little apprehensive. Wondering if the first voice had felt bad, he asked, 'What happened? Are you terrified?'

'No, big brother!' replied the first voice twice as loudly. 'I have already started digging from my side of the soil!'

'Well, then I too shall start,' assured the second voice.

... And then suddenly, the most impossible sentence ever came into being. The frozen time started thawing. There was some life-like activity taking place under the ground.

The Witness

Vibha Rani

(Translated from the Maithili by Vidyanand Jha)

Rau Baap, Rau Baap![133] *There has been a dacoity in Bhola and Ramchannar's house. Ha Daib!*[134] *Even one's enemies should not see such a day!*

Barely ten days ago, the whole family had turned up at the ghat for the Chhath puja, a celebration the family attended every year. In attendance had been Bhola and Ramchannar, and their wives Gauri and Gayatri. The lovely Munia had been there, too! How she had shone like a moon among the brothers' angelic children, draped as she was in a red Banarasi saree and adorned with jewellery—a tikka,[135] *a nose stud, a Sita haar,*[136] *a cummerbund*[137] *and anklets—her lustrous hair done up in an elaborate braid with a red ribbon. Barely in her teens, Munia had looked like a winsome child bride, soft and smooth, like new leaves on a mango tree. She appeared to be a grown-up. And today the entire village was*

---

133 An expression of shock
134 An expression of shock
135 Traditional Indian wedding jewellery worn in the parting of the hair
136 A type of necklace
137 A decorative belt adorning the waist

scurrying to their house, filling the front yard and the inner courtyard. What had happened to Bhola and Ramchannar? They were fainting one after the other. When they regained consciousness briefly, they beat their chests with both their hands and let out cries of 'Ha Daib!' before losing consciousness again. Bhola's wife was tearing at her hair, beating her chest and cursing her god: 'Rau Mudai, Rau Mudai! You could not bear to see our happiness even for a single day! Mudaia ...' Ramchannar's wife sat in the other room, surrounded by women, dangerously quiet till she tottered up once in a while, looked around and screamed wildly: 'Baap re baap! Let me go, let me go, let ...' Then her shoulders drooped and she lapsed into a stupor. Oh, such misfortune!

As children, Bhola and Ramchannar helped their father sell balloons, toys and whistles pegged on a bamboo stick. They roamed the city, their usual haunt being the rickshaw stand outside the railway station. Four trains crossed the station every day: the up trains (trains travelling to their divisional headquarters or main terminus) came in at 7 a.m. and 6 p.m., and the down trains (trains departing from their divisional headquarters) came at 9 a.m. and 11 p.m. Bauji never waited for the 11 p.m. train because it would get quite late at night. When it was festival time, say during Jhulan, Janmashtami[138] or other festivals, Bauji would sell balloons at the melas without fail. They would do brisk business there. Of course, Bhola and Ramchannar had to work hard, too, inflating more balloons and making more toys. Once the kite-flying season approached, the father and sons would make kites, grinding glass to make the manjha,[139] applying the abrasive paste on to the kite strings to make them sharper.

Mai had a goat. Both brothers took it out to graze by turns, wishing desperately that they were in school instead, studying. The teacher, Ramnath Babu, used to let them in sometimes, but how much could

138 Jhulan and Janmashtami are festivals celebrated by the worshippers of Lord Krishna

139 Abrasive kite string

one study without a slate, a pencil or books? Bauji had taught them how to count till hundred, to multiply up to twenty times twenty, to calculate fractions and multiplication and some other basic math.

Then Mai's goat gave birth to three chagaris,[140] clean and small. Mai made a pact with God: 'Have my sons settled down, O Bhagawati, and I will offer one chagari to you.' At the Chhath festival that year, she made another maanata[141] to Chhath Maiya, saying, 'I'll offer bamboo baskets to you, Chhath Maiya, please have my sons settled down.'

So, ten days before the festival, Bhola and Ramchannar went out early in the morning and placed a red ekranga[142] in a bamboo basket, to be offered to Chhath Maiya.

Human beings have their own way of planning, while destiny has its own. Fate smiled on Bhola and Ramchannar. Bhola started helping out in Ramasray Babu's grocery store. Ramchannar worked in Baldev Babu's Mithila Cloth Store. Baldev Babu was a Marwari who had quite a range of fabrics in different colours. His clientele ranged from the very poor to the richest. Ramchannar displayed the fabrics to them, dreaming all the time of owning his own cloth shop.

Mai, however, ran the household on the money Bauji brought in. The brothers gave half their salaries to Bauji, which Mai immediately took from him. With this money, she got two nose studs made for her future daughters-in-law, and a pair of tikkas from the money earned from the sale of the chagaris. Mai had sold two chagaris and the brothers insisted on selling the third one as well.

Now, both the brothers dreamt of starting a business with the money that they saved each month. Bhola wanted to start a grocery shop, while Ramchannar's heart was set on a cloth store. Bhola was just three years older than Ramchannar, but he was a great deal wiser.

---

140 Lambs

141 Wish

142 A large roll of a single-coloured cloth

Once, he said laughingly, 'Ram Bhai, with the kind of money we have, we won't get more than ten thaans[143] of cloth, and only a big and well-stocked shop attracts customers. People look at nearly twenty-five thaans before they buy half a gaj.[144] A cloth store is for people with a large capital. If you sit with ten thaans, like a pauper, nobody will come to your shop. Also, cloth is not bought every day, unlike groceries, which are a daily necessity. If somebody needs salt, then someone else needs turmeric. That business will not collapse even with less capital. Let's open a grocery store. We'll not spend the profit. With the increased capital, we'll expand our shop. Once we expand one shop, we may even be able to open a cloth store. But not immediately.'

Munia sits silently in a room. She cannot fathom the terror that has filled the house. Why was everyone crying? Everybody said that there had been a dacoity, but no thief or dacoit had entered the house. Everything was just the same as before. What dacoity were they talking about, and who was the dacoit?

Time seemed to be favouring Bhola and Ramchannar. The grocery shop prospered. Mai ordered two sets of silver hansuli[145] and cummerbunds for her future daughters-in-law. The maanatas made to Bhagawati and Chhath Maiya had been fulfilled. Now she waited for her daughters-in-law to arrive. Mai wished both the brothers would get married on the same day. And then a prospective bride came for Bhola. The bride's father said, 'If you think it appropriate, my younger daughter, Gayatri, is also of marriageable age. If, along with Gauri for Bhola Babu, you accept Gayatri for Ramchannar Babu, then my responsibilities will be over and I'll be able to go on a pilgrimage.'

Such marriages were not common in their family, but both Bauji and Mai agreed. If both brothers were married to sisters, they would

143 Cloth pieces

144 One gaj is equal to 0.9144 metres

145 Necklaces

be fond of each other and there would be no rifts over property and inheritance later.

Munia came out of her room and went into Barki Mai Gauri's room. The womenfolk stared solemnly at her, each with tears in her eyes and a shooting pain in her heart. A sigh escaped every lip. Munia went and sat near Barki Mai and held her hand. Barki Mai looked up, and upon seeing Munia, hugged her tightly and started howling again. Munia also cried. But while Barki Mai cried from the pain of knowing it all, Munia cried in imitation, without any knowledge of the situation.

Gauri and Gayatri were to wed Bhola and Ramchannar, respectively. They looked resplendent in all the ornaments Mai had got for them. Soon, Gauri and Gayatri assumed all the household responsibilities and worked as hard as Bhola and Ramchannar did in the shop. Their household was a happy one. Mai oversaw the daughters-in-law at home and Bauji supervised at the shop. Both Mai and Bauji began to spend most of their time worshipping God and making religious donations. Mai continued observing Chhath. Bhola and Ramchannar still went and collected alms, although now it was merely a token ritual. They bathed in the evening of the penultimate day of the puja and collected alms from five houses each. On the day of the parna,[146] they collected prasad from five ghats.

Munia was still in Barki Mai's embrace. The women seated around were openly shedding tears. One woman started to break the lac bangles on Munia's hands. The red and yellow bangles broke with a crackling sound. The bangles, which she first wore five months ago, broke free of her wrists and fell to the ground in pieces.

What an arduous wait it had been! For fourteen long years, no doctor had been spared. From Madhubani to Darbhanga to Patna, Mai had not missed any healer, vaid, ojha, guni or peer mazar. Gauri and Gayatri had kept all the fasts recommended by all and sundry.

146 The day of breaking the fast

The doctors had said, 'There's no problem medically.' The saints had said, 'Have patience.' But Mai had been impatient. So were Bhola and Ramchannar. *What was the use of working so hard if they had no children to pass the wealth on to?*

Time passed. Mai, completely drained of all energy, handed over the Chhath fast to Gauri. Bhola stood waist-deep in water, doing penance each day. Every year, the same plea was made to Chhath Maiya. Bhola and Gauri wept and wept, Gayatri and Ramchannar pleaded silently. And then Chhath Maiya came to their rescue and answered their prayers.

Gauri and Gayatri became pregnant at the same time and gave birth to a son each. Then, one after the other, both had sons again, with remarkable similarities. The third time round, along with her sons and their wives, Mai prayed, 'Chhath Maiya should bless us with a granddaughter this time. Without one, how will we perform kanyadan, how will we amass punya[147] bathing in the Ganges?'

Bhola and Ramchannar begged Gauri and Gayatri, 'We want a girl this time, we want a girl.' The two sisters giggled in unison, hiding their faces in their ghunghats,[148] asking, 'Is it in our hands?'

Gauri gave birth to a son again. But Gayatri fulfilled everyone's long-cherished dream with the adorable Munia. Everyone forgot about Gauri's newborn son, even Gauri herself.

'She's my daughter.'

'No, she's mine.'

Both the brothers wrangled as Gayatri and Gauri smiled. Finally, Gauri said, 'Don't strangle the child in your fights. Is there anything in this house that belongs exclusively to any single person? Then how can Munia belong to only one of us? She belongs to all of us.'

---

147 The religious merit; in Hinduism, performing kanyadan equates to taking a dip in the holy Ganges

148 Veil

Soon, Munia began to turn on her side, then she started crawling, and day by day she became more beautiful. Every year, people saw her on the Chhath ghat, in her mother's arms or running, the anklets tinkling around her tiny ankles, twirling in a red Dacron frock, her hair tied in two long braids.

Then, one day, Bauji collapsed as he sat at the shop. Mai, too, left for her heavenly abode while offering water to the tulsi. Alas, they both died without seeing Munia getting married!

Bhola, Ramchannar, Gauri and Gayatri were all impatient for Munia to grow up and get married. Had it been up to them, Munia would have crossed each year in a second. Every year, throughout the month of Kartika,[149] Gauri and Gayatri made Munia light the lamp before the tulsi.

The people gathered around said, 'Oh, what sin did poor Munia commit? Far from protecting her through all her seven lives, Tulsi Mai has snuffed out her marriage at such a tender age!'

Indeed, the years passed like seconds and people started imagining Munia wearing a tikka and a nose stud. She was still in frocks and pyjamas, but she looked like a doll! When people saw her, glowing and radiant, they would be filled with happiness.

The whole town gathered for her marriage procession. Excellent arrangements were made. A feast was arranged. There were eleven types of sweets and unlimited puris and bunia.[150] One could eat as much as one liked. The groom was handsome, about sixteen or seventeen years old, with a hint of a moustache. He had a widowed mother and a brother. The family was rich; even if both the brothers just frittered away their inheritance, it would last them seven generations.

Bhola and Ramchannar had made their intentions very clear. 'We will fill your house with all that you desire. But the bride is young right

149 The name of a month in the Hindu calendar; it usually falls in October-November

150 A sweet made of gram flour

now, so we will not send her to you immediately. The bidagari[151] will be only after five years.'

The mother-in-law, however, was adamant. 'How can this be? Will the bariati[152] go back empty-handed? You have to follow the dharma.'

'All right. Please send her back after the chauthari,'[153] the brothers and their wives requested. 'This way you won't lose face. We told you, we got our young daughter married only because we wanted to see her future secure. But we are still responsible for her.'

And so, with her aanchal[154] full of rice, and wearing a saree with yellow lace and an oversized blouse, Munia went to her husband's home like a beautiful gift, warm, delicate and soft like an unbaked diya.[155] The groom was taken aback. He was around sixteen or seventeen; he understood the special relationship between a man and his wife, and the importance of the first night. But he could not muster the courage to touch this fragile diya. He felt as if she would crumble if he touched her. So, he admired her beauty, talked for a while and fell asleep.

On the day of the chauthari, by which time the marriage ought to have been consummated, the brothers reached Munia's new home with the puchhari.[156] The bidagari was performed the next day. Little Munia flew like a bird from the cage, prancing around in a red and yellow saree with golden lace, lahathi[157] adorning her wrists, two braids and sindoor[158] in the parting of her hair. Whoever looked at Munia, radiant in the morning light, could not take their eyes off her.

151 A ritual after marriage when the bride leaves her parents' home and goes to her in-laws' home
152 A marriage party consisting of the bridegroom's family and relatives
153 The fourth day of the marriage
154 Pallu; the loose end of a saree worn over one's shoulder or the head
155 Earthen lamp
156 A request to take the bride back to her parents' home
157 Lac bangles
158 Vermilion

And now, the whole Chhath ghat was numb with grief. Gauri was offering the arghya[159] with a winnowing basket in her hands and tears in her eyes. Bhola stood in the water with his head bowed. People came on some pretext or the other, stole a glance at Munia and went back. Seeing her, a deep sigh escaped their lips. Ha Daib! People were used to seeing her in her tikka, nose stud and Dacron frock. Just last year, she had charmed them all in her red Banarasi saree, her body adorned with ornaments, the parting in her hair filled with sindoor. Newly wed Munia had not known the meaning of marriage, but the unforgettable image of her as a sweet and charming child-bride was still vivid in everyone's mind. It was natural to sigh looking at her now.

Now, Munia was wearing a stark white saree, her wrists were shorn of bangles and the parting in her hair was without sindoor. There was no bindi on her forehead, no smile on her lips. She looked older than her age.

When her mother-in-law had been widowed at a very young age, she had had her two sons—Ramkumar and Ramprakash—by her side. She had yearned for a daughter-in-law as deeply as Bhola and Ramchannar had wanted a daughter.

The groom and his brother had opposed the wedding. 'Neither are we adults, nor is she. What is the point if she will be at her father's house for five years after the wedding?' they had argued.

The mother had reasoned, 'I know, but just the wedding will take place for now. Your father is no more. If I die suddenly, who will arrange the nuptials of two orphans? If you are already married and I die, Ramprakash will not be called an orphan. He will be in the care of his brother and sister-in-law.'

But now the person expected to be his younger brother's guardian was gone. The doctors said his heart had failed. *Such an ailment at such a young age? Whoever has understood the games of destiny?*

159 Offerings made to the sun

Bhola and Ramchannar approached Munia's mother-in-law. 'How will she live as a widow at such a young age? Though remarrying a widow is not a custom, we are willing to take on society for the sake of our daughter. But we want your permission…'

'Permission? I give you my approval. You want me to agree, right? I give you my consent. Who understands the travails of widowhood better than me? I had two sons by my side to help me live. I passed my time watching them grow. She, a poor child, has not even seen her husband's face. I know, we make traditions and norms. But if we break them, they are made afresh, in a more logical and rational manner. You want to get her remarried. If you ask me, I too wish the same. But now that she is the daughter-in-law of this house, how can I let her go to some other house? She'll have to live with me.'

'But how is that possible?' Ramchannar asked, intrigued.

'Why? Why is it not possible? Only Ramkumar has gone away from us. Ramprakash is right here. And may he live long! I, too, am concerned about my daughter-in-law. I need her.'

Bhola and Ramchannar were speechless. They had expected that the mother-in-law would not have much sympathy for them, that her heart would be filled with bitterness after the death of her young son. They had expected that they, including Munia, would get nothing but the choicest of abuses and curses, that for no fault of theirs they would be branded as dishonest, and Munia would be declared an evil, inauspicious witch. But instead of bitterness and rancour, she offered them a gentle balm of sandalwood—fragrant, soothing and cool. Their wounded souls were filled with affection, trust and kindness.

The Chhath ghat bore witness again. All the women made a special detour to see Munia, who stood entrancingly innocent in her finery—a red Banarasi saree, sindoor in her hair, tikka, nose stud and lac bangles. She was coming of age; her beauty was like the sun dancing on water.

It had been a year since Ramkumar's death. The first death anniversary had been observed. Bhola and Ramchannar had reached

Ramkumar's home with all the sarees and ornaments that Munia had received when she got married.

Ramkumar's mother had told them: 'Wait for a year. After that, I will get Ramprakash married to your daughter. But there will be no bariati this time. The wedding will be a subdued affair in a temple.'

And so Ramprakash and Munia started a new life together with the blessings of Lord Shiva and Parvati Ma in the famous Garibsthan Temple of Muzaffarpur. People said: 'If there were more people like Ramkumar's mother in this world, no bride would ever be tormented by her in-laws again.'

The Chhath ghat's story did not end there. The next year, people saw Munia again. She could barely walk, and her face was pale. Everyone's eyes lit up with expectation as she placed the lamps on the arghya. The following year, Munia came again, with a bag full of baby clothes! Ramchannar walked in with a six-month-old infant and handed him to Munia. Whether time is a witness or not, I can't say, but the Chhath ghat surely was. The women lit the lamps and sang:

Aihen ge sugani chhati mai,
hoinhen unhin sahai.[160]

The baby looked in fascination at the swaying flame, clapping his chubby hands and gurgling. People offered arghya. A gentle smile spread across the faces of Gauri and Gayatri.

160 Please come, Chhathi Mai, as a parrot to help us

Amrapali

Anamika

(Translated from the Hindi by Abhay K.)

Once, to the north of my maternal home lived Amrapali,
she is still seen wandering in the ruins of Vaishali,
carrying an empty bowl in her hand.

Without casting a glance sideways,
she walks straight ahead,
talking to herself.

'Just as in autumn, the gourd is left to ripen on the vine
to make a kamandal, my muscle wilts,
my very being is in great turmoil.

My dry, scorched bones strewn like dead pigeons
within me, I wonder—was it me—the royal courtesan
of Vajji, a single glimpse of whom was yearned by all.

My white hair, coarse like hemp,
was once as black as a bumblebee,
and my eyes were blue sapphires.

My sparkling white teeth,
once rows of blooming jasmine,
are now half-broken doors of a fort in ruins.

I met Buddha—my life was transformed,
I invited him home and he readily agreed.
While returning home, my chariot's axle

collided with the chariot of Lichhavi's princes, enraged they bellowed:
"'O Amrapali, how dare you run into our chariot!"
"Excellencies, Buddha and his monks are coming home."

"O Amrapali, take a hundred thousands, invite us too."
"O noble ones, even if you offer me the kingdom of Vaishali,
I wouldn't invite you for this holy feast."

Hearing my reply, they flew into a fit of rage:
"What if we have been outsmarted by Amrapali,
let's go and win over Buddha himself."

They went to Kotigram and prostrated before Buddha,
inviting him home, but Buddha kept my honour, he told them:
"All shall perish but compassion and friendship."

All truly perished in the river of time, my glory too,
I turned into a heap of simmering ashes,
ashen Ichhamati, ashen Ganga, ashen Krishna–Kaveri.[161]

161 Ichhamati, Ganga, Krishna and Kaveri are names of rivers

My body kept floating from one bank to another,
an amber kept flickering, floating in the river of ashes,
bejewelled, bespangled, continuously floating.

Some seeds are safely kept in my bag of wrinkles;
now I keep scattering them here and there,
those falling on stones become birds' feed.

The rest sprout and bloom here and there,
becoming a bevy of greenery.'
I listen attentively to Amrapali,

thinking whatever becomes of life—kamandal, gourd
or seeds, life is life, after all, the dream of a seed is
to sprout, the essence itself is alchemy.

Just as in autumn, the gourd is left to ripen on the vine
to make a kamandal, each muscle in my body wilts, so be it!
How ravishing is the world in all its shapes and forms!

Two Poems

Savita Singh

(Translated from the Hindi by Medha Singh)

Self-exile

Often, when I reached Arrah railway station
a city drowning in the dark depth of night

light only available in pockets
a candle, a lantern

appearing as dimming
country lamps

as though the city is a soul
a low flame, an inner life.

Those were days of studying in Delhi,
when one returned to Arrah for the holidays

mother, father, abroad
grandparents in their place

like mother, father, uncle and aunt
awaiting our arrival home

just as the lychees and mangoes
in our backyard

trees of pomegranate, henna,
flowers—rose, kamini, and night queen.

A few hours later, this time I return
to my village Bakhorapur

her cool breeze still lives
on my breath

I don't know what strangers
my village houses now

just as the ancient Shiv temple on the way
sits as it always did

its ceiling full
of honeycombs

a stranger standing alone,
watching

suddenly a four year old runs up to me
pulls at my sari and asks "who are you?"

and I begin to wonder, really
"Who am I?"

Where have I been so long?
Dragged between so many lies, betrayals

the child speaks again
"I know who you are..."

I say not a word.
Inside, a voice grows

"Child, I am solitude."
...the sort that even God cannot fathom

"I am the solitude
of my country."

Then I gather him up
and place him on my lap,

the child of a mendicant
bathed in dust,

I hug him, kiss him
and begin to weep.

Bakhorapur had always been dearer
than Arrah to me, I'd always known

when I hadn't been so utterly
self-exiled.

Chaitram's Afternoons

Just as yesterday, scorching heat
runs through this afternoon

Chaitram has been plowing
the fields since morning

and now, he returns to the hut
out west; he washes up

and out comes a bag
of sattu from his sack

raw onion, green chillies…
as he mixes salt in the concoction

he begins to wonder
whether one ought to knead it

to eat it, or mix enough water
to wash it down

with his sorrows; abandoned
by his son Ram Gauhar

Thakur's fury
raging against Chaitram.

Can sattu douse
the fire in one's belly?

Let that fire raze all to the ground,
the air scorching today as yesterday,

extreme heat wave
running through the hours,

when will time change,
ponders Chaitram?

He begins, then,
to knead the dough

wondering, if he should eat it
this way after all

erase this world…
remake another?

Pablo Neruda in Gaya

Ashwani Kumar

There were rumours in the holy town—
Pablo Neruda was spotted on the ghats of the Phalgu River,[162]
performing the funeral rites of his ancestors.
He arrived with ships, filled with geraniums,
tyrant flycatchers and hermit crabs for local villagers.
Crowds of women, and labourers from the sand mines,
gathered to catch a glimpse of his tanned handsome looks,
propagating fire and rebellion.

Tapping their feet and jingling their bangles,
they started singing his love poems in chorus
and offered him jasmine rice pudding in a copper vessel.
In the yellow flames of the sacrificial fire,
Pablo shaved his head and hairy chest—

---

162 Phalgu is a sacred river flowing through the town of Gaya in Bihar; it is a famous holy site for Hindus for conducting the rituals of pind daan (a religious service seeking release for one's ancestors from the cycle of rebirth)

weeping in sorrow of losing his friends in the Civil War.[163]
Wrapped in mendicant betel leaves, he
remembered his house in Madrid with crescent balconies

on which the light of June slumbered like lovers in the shade.
Old-timers say—
after he finished all the rituals,
he became one of us,
searching for the secret springs
of the cursed river in summer heat.
I can't tell you everything,
but I often hear Pablo's voice between memory and time.

163 Refers to the Spanish Civil War of 1936

The Rat's Guide

Amitava Kumar

The rats have burrowed under the railway tracks in Patna. I imagine them as citizens of a literal underworld, inhabiting a spreading web of small safe houses and getaway streets. There are places where the railway platform has collapsed. In my mind's eye, I see a train approaching Patna Junction in the early morning, and I see the men sitting beside the tracks with their bottoms exposed, plastic bottles of water placed in front of them, often a mobile phone pressed to their ears. But, at night, the first inhabitants of Patna that the visitor passes are the invisible ones: warm, humble, highly sociable, clever and fiercely diligent.

I have also heard that rats had taken over a section of the stacks in the library at Patna University, and that the library was closed. Also, there were rats—always, in these stories, as big as cats—in the Beur Central Jail. The jail was once home to the former chief minister of Bihar, Lalu Prasad Yadav, who tended a vegetable garden there and issued orders to visiting politicians and bureaucrats. One current inmate is former parliamentarian Pappu Yadav, on trial[164] for the

164 The case was ongoing when the story was written, in 2013

murder of a communist leader, but awarded degrees in human rights and disaster management while behind bars.

For some reason, in the Patna Museum, along with Mauryan art and Buddhist relics, including, some say, the ashes of Lord Buddha, there are stuffed rats nailed to black wooden bases. About fifty feet away stands the magnificent and glistening third-century BC sculpture of the Didarganj Yakshi. A long and heavy necklace dangles between her globular stone breasts. In her right hand, she holds a fly whisk languidly over her shoulder. Running away from her are the stuffed rats, a small procession of them, rotting and seemingly blinded with age under the dusty glass.

One winter, in the middle of the night, during a visit to Patna, I was sitting at the dining table with my jet-lagged two-year-old, watching a cartoon on my computer. I had switched on only a single, dim light, as I didn't want my parents to be disturbed. We must have been sitting there quietly for about half an hour when my little boy asked, 'Baba, what is that?' He was pointing beyond the screen. There were two enormous rats walking away from us. They looked like stout ladies on tiny heels, on their way to the market.

The next morning, when my son told my wife about the rats—he was confused and initially said they were rabbits—my wife was alarmed. But no one else was.

Despite how ubiquitous the rats were in Patna, or perhaps because they were ubiquitous, no one paid much attention to them. I would bring them up in conversations and people would laugh and launch into stories. One person told me that the police in Patna had claimed the rats were drinking from the bottles of contraband liquor seized by the authorities and stored in warehouses. I didn't believe the story, so a link was duly sent to me. In the press report, a senior police officer named Kundan Krishnan was quoted: 'We are fed up with these drunken rats and cannot explain why they have suddenly turned to consumption of alcohol.'

I had hoped to get a professional pest-control agency to come and trap the rats in the house in Patna. The problem had been a pressing one—rats had carried away my mother's dentures. But all I could find was a man who would come and put packets of rat poison in different rooms. People suggested that I buy traps and put food inside; the same people also admitted that the rats were too smart to get caught in these traps. I detected a note of pride in these statements. My sister told me that her hospital had bought some expensive ultrasonic machinery that emitted a high-frequency sound to keep rats away. The sound was inaudible to human ears, and my sister said that things were okay for a while. Then they noticed that a rat had bitten through the device's cord.

I didn't find an exterminator in Patna. Instead, I ended up meeting Vijoy Prakash, the principal secretary in Bihar's Rural Development Department. He had caused controversy by suggesting that restaurants should offer rat meat on their menus. Questions about this proposal were raised in the Bihar legislature, and the papers had reported it with some relish. I met Prakash in his office in the Old Secretariat. He was a kind-looking man, quiet and dark-skinned, his eyebrows flecked with grey. In the spacious, air-conditioned office, Prakash had been working on a report at his desk. I looked around while I waited. A varnished board to my right displayed the names of the administrators who had served in that office, each carefully painted in white on the wood. Number twenty-two on that list, the final name, was Prakash's. I noted with pleasure and surprise that number seven had been my father, who had retired long ago. When I was still a student, he must have occupied the chair in which Prakash was now sitting. *Did I ever visit my father in this room, bringing him lunch during my trip home?* I couldn't remember.

Prakash, who had trained as an astrophysicist, wanted people to have more enlightened views about nature and society. His mission, I realized when we began talking, wasn't simply to change the popular perception of rats. It was to alter the view that most people had of a particular community almost at the bottom of the social ladder—the Musahars, known all over Bihar as the rat-eating caste. Prakash said that rats trapped in fields had long been a part of the Musahars' diet, and that there was no reason why others could not benefit from this protein-rich meat. If rats became an accepted and popular food item, and rat-farming was commercialized, the Musahars would see an automatic rise in their income. He rattled off statistics to support his theory. In 1961, the rate of literacy among the Musahars was 2.5 per cent; forty years later, it had risen to only 9 per cent. In a country and state where a significant percentage of people went hungry, rats ate 30 to 40 per cent of the crops. In each rat hole excavated in a field, you could find twenty-eight to thirty pounds of grain.

I wasn't entirely convinced, but Prakash was unfazed by my scepticism. He said that even as recently as fifty years ago, chicken wasn't allowed in many homes in Patna. It was just a matter of time before rats would be 'domesticated' and eaten in homes.

'Have you eaten a rat?' I asked.

'Yes,' he said. 'In the Musahar toli[165] in Naubatpur.' He said he had gone there with his wife, a teacher, and they had been offered lunch by the family they were visiting. The rats had been fried and then cooked in a curry. The dish had been served with rice and had tasted delicious.

I had known Musahar families even in my village in Champaran. Once, when I was a boy, I had just finished bathing at the hand pump, a little distance from my grandmother's house, when a woman had approached me. Behind her had been a child wearing a ragged pair of shorts. He was younger than me, maybe seven or eight years old. I remembered very clearly that the woman was tall, had curly hair and wore a mustard-coloured saree. She had asked me politely when I was going to return to Patna. My father had said we were to leave in an hour.

'Can't you take him with you?' she had asked me.

165 A small settlement of a particular community

I had seen the woman before, but I couldn't remember speaking to her. The boy, meanwhile, had been trying to hide behind his mother.

The woman had spoken again because I had said nothing. 'He will play with you. He will do all the work that needs to be done in the house. Take him with you. There is not enough here for him to eat.'

I had gone back to the house and pointed out the woman to my mother, or maybe it was an aunt. I was told that she was a Musahar. She had wanted her son to be a servant in our home in Patna. We were upper-caste, and I had been told that my grandmother would not allow a Musahar into the house.

The day after I met Vijoy Prakash, I went to our village with my father. Earlier, the journey used to take several hours, but I had been told that it now took half the time because of a new bypass that had been built to promote tourism to nearby Buddhist sites, such as the stupa near Kesaria. (In Bihar, no one tells you the distance between two places in kilometres. This is because everything depends on the condition of the roads, and so distance is always discussed in terms of time.) Of course, there were delays. A long line of trucks was idling on the side of the road. The highway had been blocked by angry youth protesting the death of a man injured in an accident. The victim had been taken to a nearby government hospital, but no doctor had shown up for work for several days. Ultimately, the man had succumbed to his wounds. The protesters had made a truck driver park his vehicle sideways on the road and, for good measure, had also blocked the path of approaching vehicles with a log and some broken furniture.

We had no option except to turn back, but even this was not allowed. At first, I showed sympathy to the gathered youth, but then I took out my press card and threatened them with severe consequences if we were not allowed to card. They relented after a while, and we took narrow rural roads around the blockade, re-emerging on the highway after about half an hour.

I was returning to my ancestral home for the first time since my grandmother's death, which was more than a decade ago. On the small platform with the tulsi plant, which my grandmother watered each morning, someone had placed freshly plucked hibiscus. But other than that small touch, a look of decay pervaded the house. I walked through the empty corridors and looked at the locked doors of the now-uninhabited rooms where I had spent all my holidays. Suddenly, alone in an empty hall, I began to weep. I missed my grandmother's voice, or maybe just my childhood. In any case, I didn't linger. I had come here on a small anthropological mission, not to surrender to nostalgia. I wanted a Musahar to show me how he caught a rat.

Sinhasan, a middle-aged man I remembered from my youth, was working on the construction of a hospital near the house, which our family was funding. It was to be named after my grandmother. My father had made the journey to check on its progress. Sinhasan didn't want to inconvenience me in any way. He said I could sit in the shade; he would go into the fields, catch the rats and bring them to me.

'No,' I said. 'You don't understand. I want to observe how you catch them.'

Sinhasan called out to two other men, also Musahars, and we started walking. One of the men was carrying a kudaal for digging. The monsoon rains had left the ground so soft that my shoes sank in the mud. Sinhasan said that it was easier to catch rats before the rains, early in the summer, when the wheat had ripened and was still standing in the fields. 'Rats make holes and save a lot of grain for their young ones. They are hopping around at that time, and we catch and cook them right here,' he said.

'How do they taste?' I asked.

'Good,' he said.

'Like chicken?'

Sinhasan paused for a second and then said, 'Murgi se zyada tayyar hai (It is better than chicken).'

At the edge of a field, where it was comparatively dry, the men stopped. They had seen a little mound of freshly dug earth. The man with the kudaal was named Phuldeo. He showed me a few scattered grains lying underfoot and began to dig using the hoe. The day was so hot and humid that within a minute or two, sweat was dripping off Phuldeo's nose and chin. The shallow trench he was digging was about two feet wide. By the time he was done, it was four feet long. I saw that Sinhasan and the third man, whose name was Chaprasi, had positioned themselves on either side of the trench. Both men were around forty and had thin, sinewy limbs. They looked sturdy but had adopted such a relaxed stance that I got a bit worried. When I asked if the rat would get away, Sinhasan smiled and brushed aside my concerns.

Phuldeo said he could see the rat hole. Two more heaves of the kudaal, and he bent down. The rat's snout was visible. With a quick flick of his hand, he caught it. Phuldeo held it up and I saw its lower incisors, long and curved. They were a dirty yellow, the colour of old toenails. Sinhasan said, 'If it doesn't cut with those teeth night and day, those teeth will go right through its head. It can eat through brick. Even when it's sleeping, its mouth keeps moving.'

I said that I wanted to take a picture. At that moment, while Phuldeo tried to give me a better view of the rat's head, it bit him on the finger. Blood spurted out. I took pictures of the tiny ears, the luxuriant hair around its nose, and, above those dirty yellow teeth, the glinting black eyes.

We let the rat return to the field. My Musahar informants told me that, in the right season, they ate rat meat about three or four times a week. Four or five rats were enough for a meal. *How did they cook the meat?* Over a small fire, the hair was first burnt. Then, a small incision was made in the belly to remove the entrails. After this, spices were rubbed into the meat, and then it was fried.

I had one last question for Sinhasan. A senior bureaucrat in Patna had said to me that people were judged based on what they ate. The reason Musahars were looked down upon in Bihar was because they ate rats. The official believed that if we all began to think about rats in a more positive way, we would no longer think of Musahars as a lower caste. Did this make sense to them? Did they share the official's optimism?

Sinhasan didn't have to consider this question for too long. He said, 'Only if everyone else is already of the same view as the official. Then, yes, people's sense of caste will change. Otherwise, no.' Sinhasan was being polite. He was careful not to throw the question back in my face.

High-minded abstractions weren't among his pressing concerns. In another five minutes, he was going to return to work, mixing mortar to build the front wall of the hospital. For the day's labour, he would be paid 150 rupees. A generation ago, there would have been work only on the landlord's fields. Now there were small industries, too, and payment was made in cash. But the conditions of work, and even the chances of finding it, were dismal. For those on the bottom of the social ladder, there was only harsh physical labour.

The other two men, balanced on bamboo beams behind Sinhasan, flinging water on the bricks and then cementing them, were also Dalits—literally 'the oppressed', the name adopted by those who used to be the untouchables in the Hindu caste system. In the distance, on the patio of my old ancestral home, upper-caste men were sitting on cots. They were poor, too, eking out a living as farmers, but none of them was ever likely to do manual work like Sinhasan. One of them, wearing a lungi, his bare feet cracked, had followed me when I had been talking to Sinhasan. This man had told me that he had eaten roasted rat meat when he had been a boy playing in the fields. Age had brought in an awareness of his social status and he had stopped going near the Musahars. He knew the consequences of breaking taboos. 'Shikaayat ho jaayi (People would complain),' he said.

The Goon

Dhananjay Shrotriya

(Translated from the Magahi by Vivek Perampurna)

After walking just a few steps, Minti slowed down. She craned her neck to steal a glance at Dina, who was perched on a small mound. Their eyes met, and she hurriedly started walking again. A little ahead, she stopped, turning around as if looking for something she had dropped. She stole a few more glances at Dina. When Dina stared back, she felt her youthfulness sweep through her body. But she could not keep her eyes on him for long and ran away.

Dina was dressed immaculately in a white vest, lungi and a broad muslin towel wrapped around his shoulders. Given his charming persona, Minti found it hard to believe that he was the goon people said he was. She continued walking. *How is it possible? A fine lad like him, a goon? No, my heart doesn't believe it. But why would my sister lie about it? There is no smoke without fire … anyway, what is it to me? I need to hurry up. Sister must be waiting for me. Guddu must be in tears, waiting for the jaggery.*

As she entered the house, her sister inquired, 'Where did you go to buy jaggery? Which shop? The baby has been crying so much!'

'There was none left at Somar Shaw's shop,' Minti replied. 'I had to go to the shop on the other side of the village.'

'Oh, so you had to go all the way to the other side?' quipped Rampukar, Minti's brother-in-law, entering the house. 'Well, please bring me a pack of cigarettes too, from that side.'

Minti felt a little apprehensive looking at him. She wondered if he had seen her somewhere on the way, but then she said, 'Go fetch your cigarettes yourself. I am going for a bath.'

'Where?' Rampukar asked, grinning under his tash.

'Sister! Look at him!' Minti complained to her sister and scampered off at the first opportunity.

'Hey, I am not blind. He is turning old and looks like an old fogey,' said Minti's sister, looking at her husband from the corner of her eyes.

'Oh! So now I am old? I am only forty! Wait till the night falls and I will show you how old I am!'

'Oh, that's right. I know tonight you will be seized by the spirit of the great wrestler Gama. Anyway, why are you always picking on her? Young girls are delicate, like glass bangles. One gentle knock and ...' her voice trailed off.

'Just let it go. If you are jealous of me, let's send Minti off to her home. There is hardly a soul in the village who does not envy me. Only yesterday Binesar was asking me, "Rampukar, is life fun?" As if I don't understand what "fun" he was talking about,' he said, gazing at his wife. 'But they are not wrong. When you have two ravishing beauties at home, people will talk.'

'Now don't try to flatter me,' she said and then added, 'but she has indeed grown up to be really pretty.'

★

Dina got up from the mound, but his legs felt heavy, like rocks. He wished he could just go back home and sleep, lose himself in his dreams. He went back to his small hut and resigned himself to bed. Soon, he was fast asleep, his old life reeling before his eyes. In those days, he was not Dina. He was Dinesh, a brilliant student pursuing zoology from Patna

Science College. In his village, every young man aspired to become either a professor or a doctor after matriculation. But fate works in mysterious ways. Once, Dina had come home for the summer vacation, to spend time with his friends. He was returning from the fields, a book in his hand and a couple of raw mangoes tied in a cotton cloth. Suddenly, a hand had come over his eyes from behind. He felt the tender pressure on his back and on his eyes. He knew it was a girl.

'Who is it? Let me go!' Dina had said in an annoyed voice.

'First tell me, who am I?' a sweet voice had asked.

'Listen, Kamali, I have told you so many times not to mess with me, but you never listen.' Dina was a little irritated. 'This is the last time, I am warning you. The consequences will be bad if you continue to meddle with me.'

Dina had thrown her arms off and walked away.

Kamali was the daughter of Binesar Babu, the richest man in the village. No girl in the village could match her beauty. They were all inferior to her. And she always made advances at Dina. And justifiably so, for no one could match Dina's handsome looks and talent. Kamali, finding it hard to accept Dina's snub, was seething with rage like a wounded cobra. She decided to teach him a lesson.

One day, the quiet evening was suddenly beset with pandemonium. Sticks and machetes were drawn out. There were a couple of gun fires, but no one knew what the commotion was about. Shortly, the police arrived. The villagers were taken aback when they heard that Rajesar Master's son, Dina, had been arrested. He was accused of trying to rape the daughter of the wealthiest man of the village. It was hard to believe.

The people refused to believe it. 'My heart doesn't believe it. A man like Dina!' one of them had said.

'Why not? Who knows what transpires in someone's mind? He is young, and I have heard he was studying human anatomy in Patna Science College.'

'God! Now only *you* can save this village!'

Everyone had their own opinion.

Rajesar Master had tried his best, but he hadn't been able to save his son. The magistrate was considerate with Dina, given that there was no prior case against him, and had sentenced him to only six months of rigorous imprisonment. When Dina was released after serving his sentence, he was no longer the same person. Those who had stood witness for Binesar Babu ran away in fear. Binesar himself turned away if he saw Dina coming. When his biker friends would ride into the village, the women would hurriedly lock themselves in their homes out of fear.

Binesar Babu had attempted to establish his dominance again, but now Dina controlled fishing at the two ponds in the village. Binesar was getting restless. Sometimes the tyres of his tractors would be discovered in the culvert, and sometimes he would find the walls of his house graffitied with cow dung. He hardly had a day of peace. But he was not one to give in easily. He had got Dina jailed four or five times on minor charges.

For the villagers, Dina was a veteran criminal who couldn't be subdued by anyone. Rajesar Master, meanwhile, took solace in the fact that at least no one could trouble his son with fake charges now, and he also knew that his son would not torment an innocent soul. Impervious to their parents' trashing, young brats from the village would always be eager to learn how to use guns from Dina. If a young girl crossed paths with Dina, she would turn ashen with fright.

For over a year, Binesar Babu had been trying to get his daughter married, but he was mortally afraid of Dina. Also, the spectre of being ridiculed by the villagers loomed over his heart. Finally, with an anxious heart, he fixed her marriage.

★

Minti's brother-in-law, Rampukar Babu, had no girl child in his family; so his house was Minti's home during the summer, when her college was closed. She was feeling restless. She glanced towards the door in anticipation, wondering if someone was looking for her.

She remembered what had happened the previous day. Someone had called out to her gently; there had been a sweetness in his voice. She had turned around, only to find Dina standing there. Her heart had been pounding like a blacksmith's forge blower. She had swiftly swept the surroundings with her eyes to check if someone was around, hoping that her brother-in-law was not on his way back.

'No, not today,' she had whispered, without meaning her denial.

'I won't do anything else,' Dina had pleaded. Gripping her harder, he had said, 'Just one kiss.'

'I won't let you do anything, go ask my sister for my hand…'

'Okay, but did your sister tell you anything? Or Rampukar Bhaiya?'

'Yes, he did. He said that he will marry me off to you in the same pandal as Binesar Babu's daughter,' Minti said coyly.

'God bless his family!' Dina had said and given her a tight embrace. Minti had felt a fire raging in her whole body. She had extricated herself and playfully punched his chest. She had then rested her head against his shoulders and said in a low voice, 'I will go now.'

'Where?' Dina had asked.

'To Binesar Babu's house. To sing ditties for his daughter's wedding,' she had said, rolling her beautiful eyes.

Dina had laughed. He had let go only after she promised him another rendezvous the next day. The air had become fragrant with freshly bloomed love.

The area in the vicinity of Binesar Babu's house was resplendent with flicker lights and buntings. The groom and his party were to arrive for the wedding ceremony the next day. The whole house was bustling with guests. For years, there had not been such a grand wedding in the village.

The village folk had left after dinner. Suddenly, gunshots were heard all around. Binesar Babu's house was capped in thick smoke. The earth was littered with broken glass spangles. Everyone thought it was Dina and his gang raiding the house. The chaos continued for half an hour. Then a voice was heard on a megaphone: 'Brothers, we have no enmity with any of you. Our job here is done. We are holding some of your men as hostages, and we will release them once we are out of the village. So, grant us safe passage. If you try to act smart, these men will lose their lives!'

The bandits had rounded up all the jewellery, cash and other valuables, and wanted to leave. All of Binesar Babu's family was lined up against the wall, their arms raised. The bandits made Binesar Babu, his two sons and the bride, Kamali, lead the pack. The village fell into a dead silence.

Suddenly, a shot was fired, aimed at the head of one of the bandits. Before anyone could realize what was happening, another shot eliminated a second bandit.

'Listen, all of you! This is Dina's village. The village's pride is Dina's pride. All of you are within my range. If you value your life, I suggest you go your way and leave everything behind,' a voice was heard from somewhere in the dark.

In just a moment, the tables had turned. Throwing away their loot, the bandits ran helter-skelter. Within minutes, the whole village had gathered around the house. They stood stunned. Rajesar Master, anticipating trouble, had come out with a stick in his hand and was calling out for Dina.

Dina emerged like an angel. Binesar Babu felt a deep sense of shame. With folded hands, he looked at Dina and broke down. 'Dina, my son, please forgive me. I spoilt your life with my vileness, and you staked your own life to save mine.'

He then fell on Rajesar Master's feet. 'Rajesarji, please forgive me. I have wronged you.'

Rajesar Master helped him up. 'I don't care if you wronged me. My worry is, who will marry my son now. It doesn't matter if he couldn't become a doctor or an engineer. But I don't have many children. I have only one son, and even he has been branded a goon!'

'Who calls Dina a goon? I will get him married. And that, too, to a girl of his choice. One who is a student of zoology,' Rampukar Babu interjected.

'But who is she?' Rajesar Master asked, surprised.

'Don't you know, uncle? The whole village knows that Dina is dying to marry Minti and become my brother-in-law, and you are clueless,' Rampukar Babu said, looking at Dina.

Dina looked around innocently, as if he had nothing to do with the whole affair. The atmosphere lightened up. Somewhere in the crowd, Kamali was digging in the earth with her toe. Dina caught Minti's eyes. He felt like he had stumbled upon a hidden treasure. And Minti felt like she had plunged into a bed of roses.

Dashrath Baba

Arun Harliwal

(Translated from the Magahi by Abhay K.)

An inner voice
prompted you to thrust
your chisel
into the chest of the mountain,
holding it in one hand
and a hammer in the other,
hitting the chisel hard,
so it pierced the eardrums of the sky,
and the chest of this demon
was ripped apart.

Slowly, gently, silently,
keep going steadily,
carve the path,
break this insurmountable wall,
connect village to village, man to man.

Worry you must not,
you won't cease to exist,
even if you leave your body behind.

O Dashrath Baba!
Today, everyone is amazed,
seeing your work,
the whole world is startled,
even the emperor is ashamed.

The sound of your chisel and hammer
will echo for ages,
it's another matter
this indifferent regime has turned deaf.

Baba,
May labour and love live long!
May love for labour live long!

The Scam

Tabish Khair

A little turd sits outside the metro exit closest to Jantar Mantar and offers to polish your shoes when you leave the cool, clean interior of the underground for the smog and heat of the pucca-baked roads. You say no, having no time for turds of that sort and because your boy-servant has already polished your shoes twice this morning, once of his own volition and once because you were not satisfied. So, yes, you say no. But with a plonk the little turd deposits a real piece of turd on your shoes. Oh, you do not see him do it, but where else does real turd come from if not from little turds like him?

'See, see, saar,' says the turd, speaking 'Ingliss' to you because he can see that you are the type—not phoren but polished. 'See, see, saar,' he says. 'Ssuu durrty (So dirty).'

The little turd has made a mistake. Just because you are polished does not mean that you only speak 'Ingliss'. You slap him on the head, twice. It is a language he understands. You thrust your shoe out to him and say in a mix of Hindi, 'Ingliss' and Punjabi: 'Saaf karo, abhi saaf karo shoes, harami (Clean the shoes, clean them right now, bastard).'

To this, you add a few choice gaalis[166] in Punjabi, which need not be put down on paper. If you had not thrown in those gaalis, the little turd might have raised a racket. But he is convinced that he has made a mistake. He was fooled by your patina, like those Spanish adventurers were once fooled by the shine of the copper on the Indians in America. What glittered on you was not gold. The little turd realizes his mistake. He is a quick learner. You have convinced him in two expressive local languages: Punjabi and 'Slapperi'. He wipes your shoes with a rueful pout. Then, as you turn to leave, he cannot resist the question. He is still intrigued. He needs to place you. Perhaps he maintains a record of his mistakes. He is a professional, just as much as you or anyone else in Delhi these days. So, he asks you with a comic salaam, still in 'Ingliss', 'Vaat you do, saab, vaat job-vob, saar (What do you do, sir, what job)?'

You have won this battle. You are in an expansive, forgiving mood. You decide to answer him and mention your profession.

'Repoder? Jurnaalis (Reporter? Journalist)?' he asks. Then he shakes his head, as if those words explain his mistake. 'Jurnaalis,' he repeats. 'Jurnaalis. Repoder.'

★

The street outside Jantar Mantar is a favourite haunt of journalists. Next to the eighteenth-century observatory are broad pavements, which often host impromptu protest groups. Sometimes for months. There is one occupied by the victims of the Bhopal gas leak. They have been sitting there, on and off, for a few years, down to five or six people now, mostly ignored by the journalists. A much larger group, bathed in flashlights, belongs to the Narmada Bachao Andolan. They are an intermittent fixture on this road. Because their champions include celebrities like Arundhati Roy, they attract media attention occasionally.

---

166 Abuses

Actually, they are the reason why that little turd, doing his su-paalis-and-turd-on-shoe scam, made such an error of judgement when staff reporter Syed Malik of the *Times of India* exited from the metro. Malik has long harboured a crush on Arundhati Roy. Hence, he had dressed up with extra care this summer morning. He had also left his Bullet behind to avoid the blackening traffic fumes before doing his round of the Narmada Bachao Andolan protest meet. Not that it was going to be noticed. The famous Roy was there, but she was too uninterested to give interviews, let alone be whisked away for a fawning chat in one of those three-, four-, five- and probably-more-star hotels around the corner.

So, after jotting down the day's press declaration in his spiral notebook, and after pocketing the day's press release, 'Repoder' Malik heads for one of the four-star hotels on his own. The Sangharsh Morcha has announced a press meet there, and now that Syed is there, he might as well look in, collect the releases and, hopefully, guzzle down a cold beer or two. On the way, he notices that a new tent has come up at the corner of Jantar Mantar. It bears the obligatory banner, stating 'Justice Delayed Is Justice Denied' in English. There is no one under the tent—a rickety affair, big enough to harbour only four or five people at the most—so 'Repoder' Malik cannot inquire about the nature of the justice that has been delayed or denied, though it is doubtful that he would have stopped to do so anyway.

Past the revolving glass doors of the hotel, in the air-conditioned and potted interior, Syed spots the table reserved for Sangharsh Morcha's press meet. Not many journalists seemed to have turned up. Apart from Syed, there are only two other reporters, one of whom is the editor of his own newspaper and who, it is rumoured, subsists on the beer and snacks offered at such meets. Handouts are circulated, appropriate noises are made over soda and lemonade—it appears that the Sangharsh Morcha has a Gandhian aversion to alcohol, which might also explain the low turnout of reporters. Just when Syed is about to sneak away from a rather drab press meet, the room is visibly brightened by the entry of two women.

They are two very different women. Syed knows one of them: Preeti, who works for one, or probably more, of those internationally visible NGOs. The other is a sturdy blonde woman wearing a kurta and jeans. Preeti is wearing a kurta and jeans, too, but while the blonde looks tired and sweaty, Preeti, like all women of her refined class (at least to Syed's working-middle-class eyes), never looks ruffled or unkempt. Syed has seen women like Preeti step out into the forty-five-degree heat in July without a single bead of sweat on their foreheads and without any sign of a damp spot under their armpits. He suspects that their air-conditioned cars offer part of the answer to the riddle of their unruffled coolness, but there are moments when he feels that they are another breed, a superior subspecies that has evolved beyond bodily fluids and signs of discomfort.

Preeti spots Syed and, ignoring the others, launches into the kind of direct speech that, Syed suspects, is also part of the evolutionary progress of her subspecies. 'For god's sake, Syed,' she says, 'what are you reporter-veporters doing here in this fake palace? There are two dharnas just outside, near Jantar Mantar.'

'Been there, Preeti,' says Syed.

'Not the Narmada one,' she says, after all, she is too radical to espouse specific causes, 'there is another one. From near some Tikri village in Bihar, where there has been a caste atrocity that was not reported by you guys.'

'If it has not been reported, it has not happened.'

'Oh yeah?' asks a woman sitting there with her cute little son. 'They have experienced it. Father killed, uncles chased away … but just two? A woman and a child?'

Both Preeti and her foreign friend nod in affirmation.

'It's a scam, then,' announces Syed. 'Look, Preeti, these days you cannot have a caste atrocity without a couple of politicians turning up to squeeze the last drop of political mileage out of it. If it's just a couple of people, it is a scam. Another way of begging…'

'Oh, you are so cynical,' says the foreigner in a vaguely European accent.

'Not cynical; reporter, staff reporter,' contributes Preeti and finally introduces Syed to her friend. A visiting journalist from Denmark, her name is Tina, but it is spelled with an 'e'—Tine.

'Why don't you check it out?' Tine asks Syed.

'Check what out?'

'Your scam.'

'Waste of time.'

'Or are you afraid of being proven wrong?'

'I am not wrong.'

'Check it out, then. They are just outside anyway. And you are yourself from Bihar, aren't you?'

'What if I am right?'

'I will buy you dinner.'

'Where?'

'Chor Bizarre.'

'Deal?'

'Deal.'

'Good. Preeti, you are the witness. Let's go.'

⋆

The Press Club on Raisina Road, not that far from Jantar Mantar, is sometimes called the Depressed Club. Its whitewashed colonial façade has worn thin, its floor is stained by tired feet, there are bleak notices and cuttings on the bulletin boards in the drafty corridor, the lawn outside shows only a hint of grass, the tables are piled with dirty plates, broken chairs are all around, and a slight smell of urine emanates from the toilet next to the main entrance.

There, that evening, seated at a corner table, wreathed in a miasma, which consists largely but not only of cigarette smoke, we find 'Repoder' Malik, Preeti and Tine. Plates of kebabs and beer have been ordered—there's gin and lime for Preeti—and the conversation is going strong. It is still hovering around the scam protest, though, which—on inspection—had turned out to be that rickety tent with the banner in English: 'Justice Delayed Is Justice Denied.'

'I told you it was a scam,' said Syed.

'How do you know?' asks Tine.

'I recognized the boy with the woman. He runs a shoe polish scam there. Tosses rubbish on your shoes, so that you have to pay him to polish them.'

'So?'

'So!'

'So, it proves that he does something for a living. They said they have been there for months, petitioning every person they possibly could. They showed us the petitions and letters that they had actually paid people to write for them.'

'Another way to beg.'

'Oh, Preeti, are your journalists always so cynical?'

'Only the men, Tine. Only the men.'

'Come on, Preeti. You know I am right. Tine doesn't know the place, but you know how these things happen.'

'I am not sure I do, Syed.'

'What do you mean?'

'Look, that woman had a plausible story. Small village in Bihar. Land dispute. Husband killed, murdered one night on the way back from work. Police not interested in clearing the matter. Dismissing it as the kind of thing that happens to people who belong to the so-called denotified tribes. Uncles frightened into moving away. Land forcibly occupied. The woman tries to get justice, finally takes whatever she has and comes to Delhi with all her papers. Sounds plausible to me. She's a plucky tribal woman, definitely seems to be.'

'She is not a village woman from Bihar, and that boy is too slick. He has grown up here on the streets.'

'You would be surprised at how quickly kids pick up habits and words.'

'Still, I bet you my bottom dollar. It's a scam.'

'Why don't you go to Bihar and check it out?' asks Tine suddenly.

'Check it out? The woman's village does not even have a name. "Near Tikri village", she says. Even if I could locate Tikri village—'

'Take them with you,' says Preeti. 'We will come along. I will raise the money for it.'

'I'll have to take leave, Preeti.'

'Take leave, Syed.'

'Take leave, Syed, will you please?' Tine adds, looking soulfully at him with her speckled greenish-blue eyes.

'What a waste! Okay, if you ladies insist. Let me see ...'

*

Time does not fly around Jantar Mantar. That is the magic of such places. The buildings change, billboards change; the streets change their beggars, protestors, pedestrians and cars. But all change is for the same. Time simply repeats itself, again and again.

'Jantar mantar,' say children. Abracadabra. And whoosh! Something happens. Plastic flowers turn into a dove; a rabbit is pulled out of a hat. 'Jantar mantar,' murmur old women in villages; they talk in whispers because they are talking of devious doings, black magic and sorcery. 'Jantar mantar,' say foreign-educated doctors in the big cities; they are referring to the hocus-pocus of the quacks, vaids and hakims who still cater to the rural poor and either heal them or kill them.

But Jantar Mantar in Delhi is a sprawling ancient observatory. Today, it is used to observe nothing. It is useless. Around it have risen useful buildings: offices and hotels, mostly. These buildings change but still manage to remain the same. 'Useful' people walk around here: reporters, politicians, businessmen, doctors and bureaucrats. People who change but are still always the same.

So why should anyone be surprised if, a month from the time we last saw him agreeing to go to Bihar, we see 'Repoder' Malik walking out of the same metro exit where he had encountered the turd, the boy who—along with his mother—Syed, Preeti and Tine had escorted back to Bihar just a few weeks ago? Maybe 'Repoder' Malik has changed, or perhaps he is still the same.

In any case, he is looking around. He has been doing this almost every day since all of them returned from Bihar. He looks around for the turd, for he knows that the little boy must have returned to Delhi. After all, scams have their fixed scenarios; tricksters their territory.

'Repoder' Malik walks slowly, darting quick glances to the left and right, thinking of that lightning trip to Bihar. He is not sure what happened there, but he will not concede this uncertainty to himself.

The woman and the boy had refused to go back to Bihar; Preeti and Tine had to convince them with assurances of safety and gifts of money. It had been like that all the way to Gaya, by train, and then to the village of Tikri by taxi. The woman and the boy had wheedled a minor fortune out of the two women. Syed had expected that; it had confirmed his suspicions. But he had not anticipated the certainty with which the woman had led them to Tikri and then two kilometres out to a small village and a plot of land, which she claimed was the disputed property.

That is when it had all happened, and Syed was not very certain even now about what it was. It had been late, the summer evening had been steamy, the wind had dropped. Tine had turned pink and a few beads of sweat had appeared on Preeti's neck. Both of them had been conservatively clad—a reflection of their notions of rural Bihar—in cotton salwar-kameez.

The plot they had stood on had been rocky; it had not looked worth fighting over to Syed. The woman and her son, the turd, were pointing out things like the palm trees that demarcated one end of the field, the huts—thatched, hunched--of their village in a far corner, and the small hillock that marked the other end of the field. A fly kept buzzing around Preeti, evading her attempts to fend it away with her dupatta, which she had draped loosely around her shoulders. Tine had long discarded her dupatta, displaying a rather low-cut kameez that, Syed felt, was less conservative than most shirts and T-shirts.

As the woman rambled on—the usual lament about how the land was taken away from her, how her husband was murdered, how the police did not listen to her—a group of men appeared on the hillock. They became visible as if by magic—*jantar mantar*, Syed almost thought—burly, impassive men, standing against the reddening sky, leaning on their staffs. They could very well have been a group of villagers on their way back from work, attracted by the sight of a taxi and three obviously urban-types, one of them a firang, a foreigner.

But that is not what the woman and her son, the turd, thought. Syed was not sure. Suddenly, there was a cry of fear from the boy and the woman started cursing and weeping. The boy said, 'Run, Ma, run! They said they would kill us if we came back. Run!'

With that, both of them ran in the opposite direction, towards the palm trees and the brambles and the jungle behind them. Syed shouted, but they did not stop. Preeti and Tine had not even had the time to react. When Syed had looked up at the hillock, the men who had been standing there were gone, too.

They had waited an hour, until it got dark. The taxi driver had insisted on going back, with or without them. They had returned the next day. They had spoken to the local police, who denied any land dispute or the occurrence of any murder.

'What woman and son?' the thana inspector had asked. Syed's press card had turned the police obliging and polite. The inspector had taken the three outsiders to the nameless village, foetid with garbage lying next to mud huts that had holes in their thatched roofs, and called out to an old man. 'Come out! Hey you, Dhanarwa!'

When the man had stubbled, limped and coughed his way out of the low hut, the inspector had said to Syed, 'Sir, describe the woman and her son to him. He is the headman; he knows everyone.'

Syed had done as he was asked to do; Preeti had added a word or two of detail. The description done, the inspector had addressed the old man in a gruff tone. 'So, do you know this woman and the boy?'

The old man had shaken his head silently. A crow had cawed and perched on the sagging roof of a hut behind them: with its dagger-like beak, it had started to dismember a small rodent that it held in its talons.

'Speak up. Has someone cut your tongue off? Speak up. Not to me, you dolt. Tell sir and the madams here,' the inspector had barked.

'No, huzoor,'[167] the old man had said.

'You do not know the woman?' the inspector had asked again.

'No, huzoor.'

'Or the boy?'

'No, huzoor.'

The inspector had turned to Syed, Preeti and Tine, the three now sweating profusely in the hardening sunlight. 'See, sir,' he had said, 'see, madam, what did I tell you? 420. The woman was a 420. A chaloo[168] fraud. You should lodge a case with us. We will catch them for you.'

On the way back the next day, as the train shuddered on the old tracks, Syed had his doubts. He was familiar with such interrogations by police officers. The way they asked questions often determined the answers. And though he laughed away Tine's offer to buy him dinner

167 A title of respect for a person
168 Cunning

at Chor Bizarre on their return to Delhi—'I lost the bet,' she had said—Syed still could not settle the matter in his mind.

However, Preeti and Tine had been converted. They spent much of their waking hours on the way back to Delhi calculating the money they had paid to the woman and her boy, the turd. By the time the train reached Aligarh, they had agreed on the exact sum of Rs 5,941.

But Syed wasn't convinced. Not even after they reached Delhi. And that is why now, even weeks later, when Preeti and Tine had already turned the experience into slightly different anecdotes for friends, 'Repoder' Malik walked past the Jantar Mantar area, on the lookout for the little turd. Under the tall, gleaming buildings, on the broad sidewalks with protest banners, past this useless observatory, always darting glances here and there, he walked around the place that changed and yet remained the same, always looking, looking and looking.

A Night As an Orphan

Kumar Mukul

(Translated from the Hindi by Anupama Garg and Chaitali Pandya)

The moon followed me like a greedy dog; it pounced on my soul as if it were a piece of bread. I was being torn apart. This was my night as an orphan, a night spent in the courtyard of the Hanuman temple under the candescent light of the lamp posts.

This wasn't an era where vast stretches of land were available for runaways. There used to be forests, riverbanks and mountains, but they had all been declared as nature reserves.

Now, concrete jungles abound with people, like thick foliage competing for sunlight. People keep slipping over the moss of their own pain. But at that moment, my existential crisis took precedence over all worldly concerns. Initially, I had protested, but since I didn't own the house, I had walked out on ethical grounds.

'He must have said, "You are dependent on me for your livelihood." What else could he have said? All fathers say this,' said Alok Da as he tried to convince me to return home.

'Go, tell him that this body is also his. And that I have not been raised out of pleasure but out of his anxiety for the future,' I replied.

I knew I wouldn't be able to return immediately. Yet, I promised Alok Da that I would. I convinced him and headed to the railway station. In my imagination, I was already back home, but just the thought of returning had started tiring me. I had some money, so I thought of booking a hotel room. But it didn't make sense to waste money like this.

I loitered around aimlessly. Even the familiar station platform looked different today. Perhaps my need to find lodging there influenced my perception.

It was Vishwakarma[169] puja today. There was a statue of Vishwakarma in the railway station compound, too. The children performing disco–bhangra hailed from the families of sweepers and coolies. A young Muslim man was also clapping in sync with their rhythm. For some time, I watched them dance, wary of the pickpockets. Just then, a few policemen passed by. Some of them were in uniform, and some were in plain clothes. One of them showered a few coins on the boys who were dancing, and a few coins landed at the feet of the deity. Next came a military man with an air of indifference. He made his obeisance to the deity and left.

I moved ahead. I spotted many people sleeping outside the A.H. Wheeler shop, but it was stuffy there. Outside, people slept in a small park. I considered sleeping there, but the thought of the mosquitoes there made me drag my feet towards the temple. I was hungry. I had some five to seven rupees in change. I wanted to ensure that I did not spend more than the change I had on me before I reached home. So, I ate two boiled eggs for three rupees, drank water from the nearby chaat shop, and then went and sat on the scalariform bench in the temple premises. There were a lot of people sleeping cramped up in its courtyard.

---

169 A Hindu god, the divine architect

A middle-aged man came and sat next to me. He said to me, 'How can people fall asleep here?'

'Yes, it's difficult, but somehow people manage,' I said, suspicious of the conversation, wondering if the man was a pickpocket. In no time, hopping like a monkey, he went to the other side.

Just then, a man sitting behind me remarked, 'Did you notice that this man is only interacting with young men?' I did not understand what he was trying to imply, so he explained. 'Well, he is a pimp. Why would he care where people sleep? He simply goes about finding his prey through the night.'

I was tired and sleepy. There wasn't enough space to even stretch my legs. So, to me, that old man seemed to be a symbol of compassion.

The guard on night duty was moving around, clearing the crowd with his baton. It was 11.30 p.m., nearly time for the temple doors to close. As the last prayer for the day was offered with the accompaniment of gongs and bells, the gates of the temple were shut. First the main gate, then the small gate. The red digital signboard, which until now displayed couplets of Tulsidas, went blank. Even God went to sleep. The guard started prodding his baton at some people who looked like mendicants, trying to wake them up. 'Shoo! Off you go to the platform!' he said to them.

I suspected quite a few of these people to be pickpockets. Perhaps some of them were small traders. I wondered if they had asked the guard to wake them up.

The guard walked up to me. 'Why are you sitting? Can't find a place to sleep? See, it's illegal to sit next to a sleeping man. You seem to be a decent man. It is for the safety of people like you that I have shooed the others away. Go there and lie down!'

By the time I made an effort to get up, he had already moved away.

People around me started debating the validity of such a law. Everyone arrived at the conclusion that such a law did, in fact, exist.

'But do we appear to be thieves? On the contrary, because of them we have to keep vigil.'

Just then someone shouted, 'Thief! Thief!' There was mayhem. A lot of people woke up. Someone was sighted on the street, trying to escape. A dark-skinned old man in rags was caught stealing a pair of chappals.[170] In the chaos, I found an empty spot. I used my handbag as a pillow and tried to sleep. After sleeping for half an hour on the marble floor, I woke up feeling refreshed. The moon rose from behind the pillar. It seemed to be quite slow today, as if keeping an eye on me.

Vexed, I started reflecting on the circumstances under which I had left home. All the incidents came alive. My father, sister, brother-in-law, mother, wife and me, everyone had been screaming and shouting. I had been yelling at them. *Oh, how uncivilized was that!* In a fit of rage, I had pushed my parents over.

Oh, thank god my hands are safe! I am not cursed. In Kali Yuga, curses don't influence our lives. How my father had been in utter bewilderment at my outspokenness, at my insolence! He had just concluded his worshipping ritual; the incense stick had still been in his hand when I had displayed my indignance. I had humiliated him in a pious moment. He had looked on—helpless, dumbfounded. The blood in his eyes had made his vision blur. In those moments of fierce anger, he had looked completely vulnerable and helpless.

But what about all those years of emotional trauma that I had undergone? I had started imagining myself as an orphan a long time ago. On the other hand was my unrestrained laughter, moistened by the affection of an older couple in my neighbourhood. They never called me 'son', but seeing them I would leap like a calf; their affection would flutter in their teary eyes just like a cow flickers its tail upon seeing her young one. Then there were Monu's small but real demands; the quiet observation that Golu would subject me to; the way Babli

170 A pair of sandals

would boldly call me eccentric and the way Gudiya would refuse to divulge the details of an upcoming event that she was excited about. In that case, to appease my reckless thought of orphanhood, should I abandon my world consisting of my parents , siblings and wife? All my miseries start disappearing when I remember the look of helplessness in my father's eyes.

Father, Father, Father. Son, Son, Son. One is a seed, the other is a tree. *Open your heart to me! Expand your heart so I can sprout.* Suddenly, I was shaken out of my reverie. I got up and went to the ticket counter to buy a platform ticket, so I could stroll on the platform for two hours. But it was already 2 a.m. The counter was closed. There were no trains scheduled for arrival or departure. Even the Wheeler shop had shut down. Outside it, there was a man sitting with books spread out before him. Some women with radiant faces, along with their clients, kept coming and going. I returned to my spot. It was still vacant.

At 4 a.m., I woke up and started looking for an autorickshaw. It was almost an hour before I found one. Dawn was breaking. I told myself that this was not the right time to return home. *What would people think?* They would assume that I spent the night somewhere and was now running back home. So, I got down at the zoo. A lot of people were out for their morning walks; some were jogging. I sat on a bench and saw the sun's rays breaking through the sky, the darkness seeking refuge in the trees. Finally, it was daybreak. I started walking. I noticed kids playing football in the polo ground and was tempted to join them, but then I trudged along. A young man was feeding grass to a doe. I, too, stroked the doe's back and pulled out some grass to feed it. It didn't merely want to be caressed without being fed. Finally, I reached the main road. Like a reassuring pat, the sun was rising from behind my back.

Father was strolling in the park near our home. He walked towards me. I thought I would quietly walk away if he said anything. Then his vulnerable face flashed in front of my eyes. He had come closer now. We looked at each other.

He paused and asked, 'Where have you been?' Tears welled up in my eyes. I quietly began to walk with him. He said all sorts of things, but I did not utter a word. We were approaching our home now. The neighbours would be thinking that my father had gone looking for me and had found me. I was thinking, too. *I had lost my father and his love, and now I have found him again. Will I be able to find my mother, siblings and wife as well?*

The neighbour in the house opposite ours feigned indifference, as if she'd been happy when I had run away and was upset now that I had returned. My young neighbour was looking at me awkwardly. I smiled at him and asked about his well-being.

Everyone was all smiles at home. I walked straight into my bedroom and saw my wife in tears. Of course, I was interrogated. After resting for a while, I went straight into the bathroom. It seemed like nothing had happened. I took a bath, ate and went to sleep. I woke up with a yawn and stretched like a baby in a crib.

Lieutenant Hudson

Ratneshwar

(Translated from the Hindi by Chaitali Pandya)

As soon as Gopu fell at Lieutenant Hudson's feet, seeking forgiveness, the lieutenant kicked him hard. Gopu, like a deflated football, rolled over and stopped nearly five feet away. His mouth, which usually oozed blood because of his decayed teeth, started bleeding profusely.

That day, he had been unable to find any undigested foodgrains in the horse scat or the cow dung. Shobhan, Gopu's father who couldn't bear to see his child go hungry, had dared to steal a fistful of gram from Lieutenant Hudson's kitchen. He was caught just as he was about to slip out through the back door. To make him pay for his crime, Lieutenant Hudson had played a game of fire with him. Shobhan was made to run barefoot on burning coal, holding his child in his arms.

Hudson shouted, 'You swine! Play the game of fire, and I shall feed you.'

'No, sir,' Gopu pleaded earnestly with his hands folded. 'We don't want any food, sir,' he said in convulsive gasps and sought pardon on his father's behalf.

Shobhan's eyes continued to bleed. He was so brutally beaten up that he could not even plead for the well-being of his child. A series of gunstock blows had broken his spine. His eyes had been blown out with hot skewers. He was nearing his end. It is said that a labourer who does not feel hungry is the best labourer in the world.

★

The more Diya read through these pages of history, the more she got agitated. Bitterness overwhelmed her. Distress and pain spread over her features, reading these descriptions of British savagery. In retrospect, she wondered how a man could be so barbarous.

Even my senses were stirred by this account, but I unwittingly said, 'This happens to be a true story, and history is witness to this utmost barbarity. Do you know, Diya, a man can go to any extent to realize his selfish motives, even at the cost of him becoming a cold-blooded brute?'

Reviving from her bitter state of mind, Diya, who was undertaking research on 'Development of Indian resources from 1857 to 1947 CE', said, 'Our mentor, Dr R.K. Sinha, told us that the year 1877 is infamous in Indian history as a period of helplessness, torture and hunger. In Delhi and its neighbouring areas alone, more than one lakh people had died due to famine and the apathy of the authorities, whereas the death count for the entire nation was more than four million. On the one hand, millions of Indians were dying of hunger, on the other, millions of rupees were spent in jubilation when Queen Victoria was conferred the title of Kesar-E-Hind.'

Getting bored of the pages of history, I said, 'When will your research end? Your mentor ... sometimes I feel it's me, your husband, who will become the subject matter of your research.'

Feeling a little at ease, Diya mumbled, 'All right, Sampurna! I won't bother you any more.'

★

The mattock hit something hard. Harbhu cleared the soil around it and was horrified at what he saw there. 'Oh … bones!' he exclaimed. A look of stupefaction had taken over his face.

Ramesh, the manager, bellowed, 'Why are you standing there? Were you dreaming that you would chance upon a treasure chest?'

'No, sahib … there are bones over here.'

'So how does that matter? Dig them out, bloody idiot! You are merely a labourer and you go on fussing about inconsequential stuff.'

'Sahib, I am taking them out! Why are you swearing?'

Harbhu's mattock was at work once again. In no time, a full human skeleton was unearthed. Harbhu was petrified at the sight. The skull, its protruding teeth, neck, chest and its two hands—to Harbhu it seemed as if the skeleton would come alive any moment and clasp him. He let out a cry of horror.

All the workers gathered around and began discussing the skeleton. God knows whose grave this was! Just then, Muniya's eyes fell on the locket hanging around the skeleton's neck. He immediately got down and took it off. He dusted it and, upon close examination, found a fish-like figure on the pendant. Other labourers, too, examined the locket curiously.

At that instant, Patiya crossed her fingers in pure innocence and said, 'We have become impure! Oh, no! My religion has been defiled.'

'Shut up! Don't just blabber,' chided Radhe. Patiya was crestfallen.

Soon after, the manager appeared. 'What are you all doing there? Is there a monkey dancing?'

'Sahib, we found a skeleton here,' said Radhe in a loud voice.

'A skeleton!' The sight of a full skeleton sent a chill down the manager's spine. But regaining his composure, because he had to get the work done, he shouted with a slight tremble, 'Is it your father's remains? Move away! Get back to work.'

The men, filled with rage, grimaced and got down to work. Harbhu and Diri pulled the skeleton out of the pit. A little while later, it became apparent that the workers had excavated a graveyard. There was a heap of skeletons.

Radhe abandoned the work. The other workers, too, were in a state of bewilderment. None of them knew what to do. More than disgust, fear pervaded their minds. All sorts of thoughts crossed their minds. Someone narrated an incident about ghosts; the other gave an account of having seen ghosts dancing around there. Everyone had a different story to tell.

★

In fact, just five days ago, there had been more activity than usual on Hanuman Road, on account of the foundation stone-laying ceremony on a vacant plot of land that belonged to the Delhi Development Authority (DDA). Hundreds of millionaires had gathered there. They desired to own an apartment on this nearly three lakh square feet of land. Hanuman Road, which was located exactly behind Connaught Circus, between Baba Kharak Singh Road and Parliament Road, was also flanked by Gurudwara Bangla Sahib and the Young Men's Christian Association (YMCA) building. In the past few days, the newspapers had been carrying advertisements of Baba Malhotra Constructions. Several people had already booked an apartment by paying an advance. The cost of a 2,400 square metre-apartment was Rs 12 crore.

★

The danger lies not in the fact that our soul doubts the existence of bread, but in the fact that it can make itself think that it is not hungry. It can do this only by lying, because the reality of its hunger is truth and not a matter of faith.

Someone shouted, banging the door loudly, 'Engineer Sahib! Engineer Sahib!'

I was startled and, in a state of fright, Samuel Beckett's *Waiting for Godot* fell from my hand. At first, I failed to understand what was happening and why someone was banging on the door instead of ringing the doorbell. I got to the living room and opened the front door to find the manager Ramesh standing there.

'What happened, Ramesh?'

'Sir, the police have raided the plot and seized it. They got hold of the skeletons while they were being loaded in the truck.'

'Tell me in detail. What happened exactly?'

'Sir, the skeletons were unearthed some time after the digging began. The work was going on at a good pace, as per the plan. But no sooner had they reached the depth of four feet that ... the rest is history! Skeletons and more skeletons! I even telephoned Shaukat Ali, one of my acquaintances, who flatly denied the existence of any Muslim burial ground there.'

'Was it a former cemetery of the Christians?'

'If that were the case, sir, the DDA wouldn't have allotted the land in the first place. Besides, it would certainly have the details of the land. Otherwise, why would they choose to develop this sensitive piece of land?'

'Could it be a conspiracy hatched by Agrawal Constructions?'

'No, sir. I don't think so! So many skeletons in just one day of digging? The soil had hardened and bushes had grown over it. I don't believe the skeletons were buried there recently.'

'Then how come so many skeletons were found there?'

'I have no idea, sir! But we had made arrangements for them to be disposed of and to hush up the matter. I don't know how, at the last moment, the police were tipped off.'

'Maybe some labourer or someone else...'

'Possibly! No, I mean I doubt it, because I have been on-site day and night.'

'How did you get to know that the police had arrived?'

★

'Stop!' Everyone was startled when they heard an authoritative voice. After loading the skeletons, the truck was headed in the direction of the gurudwara. Suddenly, at Hanuman Road, several police cars intercepted the truck. Heavy footsteps marched towards the truck. The police had surrounded the truck as if they were on some mission to combat terrorists.

'Get off the truck.'

The driver surrendered without any resistance. The labourers, too, got off the truck immediately.

'Sir, these are human skeletons!' one of the constables exclaimed.

⋆

'I watched the drama unfold from a distance and then walked away. Had I not done that, they would have arrested me as well. But now the question before us is, what is to be done?' asked the anxious manager.

'Well, you call up the managing director, Mr Malhotra, and give him an account of what has happened. We will meet tomorrow in the office.'

'Okay, sir!' he said, and walked away with hurried steps.

When I turned around after closing the door, I found Diya standing in the hallway. 'Oh, darling! Sorry! I disturbed your sleep.'

'What's the matter about the skeletons, Sampurna?' She appeared to be ill at ease and her face revealed signs of distress.

'I have no idea. Whatever it is, we will only come to know tomorrow. Manu is sleeping, isn't he?'

'Would it have been so quiet if he were awake?' Diya, who was fretful, didn't wish to spend the rest of the night indulging in frivolous conversation. Her sleepy eyes were half-open, but they exuded vivacity. They walked towards the bedroom, holding hands. After all, as it is said, he who has a loving wife is the luckiest.

The whole nineteenth century had erred, for they believed that by walking straight ahead, they would fly someday. I don't know when I fell asleep while reading Samuel Beckett, only to wake up to the touch of Diya's lips. I took her in my arms.

'Sampurna! Let me go. And get up fast! Your tea is ready and even Manu is up.'

'Can tea be more pleasurable than being in your embrace? Do you know, Diya, the biggest truth in this world is our love, for our love is the world.'

'Okay, now get up! Enough of your philosophy! The newspaper is waiting for you.'

Rubbing my eyes, I took a look at the newspaper. The bottom of the front page caught my eye.

63 Human Skeletons Excavated at Construction Site

Sitaram Yadav
New Delhi, 16 February

As many as sixty-three human skeletons were found during the foundation-digging for a multi-storey building at Hanuman Road in Connaught Place. Following a tip-off, the police seized the truck and arrested the truck driver for sneaking out the skeletons.

The Delhi Development Authority (DDA) had recently leased out the land for ninety years to Baba Malhotra Constructions for the construction of a multi-storey building. According to our sources, the DDA planned to construct a multi-storey building on this land, but due to reasons unknown, the land was handed over to a private builder.

The skeletons found range from children to adults. So far, no evidence has been found, nor have there been any claims that there once existed a graveyard on this land. During the excavation, a few silver chains were found on the skeletons, which were later recovered from the homes of the workers. Police have also recovered a bangle. Both the pendant and the bangle supposedly have pictures of Mithila-style paintings.

All the skeletons have been sent to the forensic laboratory. A team consisting of experts of the archaeology department, historians and doctors has been appointed to help in the investigation process.

Delhi's Urban Development minister has said that he is waiting for the investigation report, based on which further action will be taken.

I had hardly finished reading the news when Diya put Manu on my lap. I lifted Manu and tossed him up in the air as he let out squeals of joy.

'Diya, we will make our son an actor, a great actor!'

'Ha! Such silly thoughts can only occur to you.'

★

As part of the investigation, through the carbon-dating process, by adding cobalt to the G.M. counter, the radiation of each individual skeleton was detected. Dr Bhalla and Dr Sengupta conducted the radio-carbon dating, after which Dr Bhalla confirmed that these skeletons dated back to a period roughly between 1856 and 1878 CE.

Dr Sushma was storing the details of the report of each skeleton on the computer. Each skeleton was assigned a number. They were finally grouped based on the age and the cause of death.

★

'Okay, Diya, bye.'

'But, Sampurna, I need to buy some books.'

'Which books?'

'*White Mughals* by William Dalrymple.'

'I see. You need it for your research!'

'Yes, and I also have to go to the professor's house.'

'Okay, I will come back early in the evening. We can then visit the World Book Fair at Pragati Maidan,' I said, and left for work.

'Oh god, Delhi traffic!' I mumbled as the car stopped at a signal. In an autorickshaw nearby, a song was playing on Radio Mirchi: *Paan khaye saiyan hamaro, malmal ke kurte par chheent lal-lal, haye-haye malmal ka kurta...*[171]

I instantly remarked, 'He must be a Bihari!' On the periphery of GK-1, a residential locality, just before the Moolchand flyover, one more flyover was coming up. Some labourers working at the site caught my attention. One look at them and I made up my mind that they were certainly Biharis. A fleeting thought crossed my mind. *Delhi is known as the city of flyovers. These flyovers, buildings, avenues and roads, all are constructed by Biharis. It seems as though Biharis have become a metaphor for the labourers.*

Meanwhile, Dr Bhalla continued with the investigation. After a detailed examination, it was concluded that all the skeletons were that of workmen, or labourers. Through a DNA-typing procedure, it was also revealed that they hailed from Bihar's Mithila–Bhojpur and Uttar Pradesh's Benares–Gorakhpur regions.

An examination of one of the skeletons—a woman's—revealed that she had been shot in the head. On the frontal bone, there was something illegibly impressed. When efforts were made to read it with the help of chemicals and X-ray, the word 'whore' was found inscribed on the skull. As a punishment, her forehead must have been so ruthlessly tattooed that it left a mark on her frontal bone.

While examining the pulp from the cavity of the teeth, Dr Sengupta asserted, 'Many children died due to dental diseases. They caught infections and died due to lack of timely dental treatment, and hunger.

---

171 A famous song from the film *Teesri Kasam* (1966)

The bone marrow count has revealed that hunger was the cause of death among several children.'

After hearing Dr Sengupta's account, Dr Bhalla mentioned the child skeleton, numbered thirteen. 'He died neither due to a dental disease nor due to hunger. His DNA test shows symptoms of Lyme disease. Or maybe he died of malaria.'

Bone diseases were Dr Sushma's area of study. There were eleven skeletons whose arm bones were either chafed or seemed to have peeled off. This was an indication of osteoporosis, a disease that mainly occurs in people who are persistently malnourished.

Dr Sengupta was conducting his studies on thirteen skeletons whose skulls were battered. Through examination and X-rays, it was gathered that because of carrying very heavy loads on their heads, the bones of their skulls appeared to have been worn out. Among those skeletons, there were two whose spines were also broken. The reason for their deaths was similar.

⋆

Diya was marking important points for her reference after consulting several history books.

Lord Dalhousie's reform programme was already in progress. In 1858, the administrative powers were transferred from the East India Company to the British crown. In Delhi, in 1859, measures were being undertaken to set up electrical cables, followed by the setting up of the railway line in 1860.

On 12 May 1857, the rebel sepoys had taken control over Delhi. Ever since 1856, labourers had started coming, or were being brought, to Delhi because survey and groundwork for the setting up of railway and electric lines, along with the development of postal, social, administrative, military and educational services, had begun. Due to the lack of labour force, labourers were brought in from Mithila, Bhojpur, Gorakhpur and Benares.

For the British, it was essential to regain control over Delhi to boost their morale. An army was called from Punjab and stationed in Delhi. Indian soldiers fought an intense battle. Labourers brought in for Delhi's development work helped these soldiers. But eventually, in September 1857, the British recaptured Delhi. The titular king, Bahadur Shah Zafar, was apprehended. Lieutenant Hudson unleashed vengeance on the residents of Delhi, the rebel sepoys and the labourers.

Shobhan was probably the first labourer, or one can say he was the first Bihari labourer to have come to Delhi, who was later so badly beaten up that his spinal cord ruptured, resulting in his death. Shobhan's skull, too, carried the ruthlessly impressed tattoo, which still bore the vaguely imprinted words: 'Shobhan is a thief.' The bones of his feet appeared to be scorched. Investigation also revealed that his eyes had been blown out using hot iron skewers. *Was he the same Shobhan whose brutal murder was recorded in the pages of history?*

⋆

Sampurna's cell phone rings.

'Hello.'

'Sir, this is Ramesh.'

'Yes, Ramesh, tell me.'

'Sir, there's some strange situation here at the site.'

'What happened?'

'Thousands of labourers have gathered here. They have been here since morning. Some of them are crying bitterly, as if they have lost their own parents. Hundreds of them have taken off their shirts and are lying flat on the ground, as if the soil were powdered sandalwood and they were assimilating it. Sir, most importantly, along with the Bihari labourers who have gathered here, there are others who have joined them from Uttar Pradesh, Rajasthan, Haryana and the hilly areas.'

'But why have they come there?' I inquired, surprised.

'Sir, I have no idea! They probably heard the news and that's why they are here. Sir, there are also cultural workers, officers, activists and journalists here.'

'Haven't the police arrived yet?'

'Sir, the police are here! Though the land has been sealed, the Rapid Action Force (RAF) has also been deployed at the scene.'

'Okay, I will be there.'

After the call, the first words I said were, 'That's why Bihar is so backward. These scoundrels don't seem to have any work but to protest and chant "zindabad". Phew! A large sum has been invested on this land. I've already had an argument with the M.D. After all, the entire responsibility of the construction rests on my shoulders.'

From Pant Marg, as I headed towards Gol Dak Khana, I could see the large crowd. At Hanuman Road, there were several O.B. vans parked. I parked my car there and started walking towards the construction site. A little ahead, I spotted Ramesh conversing with some people.

'Ramesh, is everything under control here?'

He nodded his head and grimaced. 'The situation seems to be serious. Anyway, the investigation team is here and you should meet them once.'

'Yes. Where are they?'

'They are near the construction site. Let's go and meet them there itself.'

No sooner had we begun to talk with the investigation team than two or three journalists approached us. I wasn't keen on speaking to them, so they addressed the members of the investigation team.

I signalled Ramesh and we moved back a little. We began talking and, as we approached the almond tree across the road, the crowd went berserk. When I turned around, I witnessed a scuffle between the police and the labourers.

The RAF personnel had tried to drive away the labourers from the seized land because the investigation team was having trouble doing its job. But the crowd wouldn't budge. It seemed that the labourers had vowed not to move. The crowd had taken to stone pelting to display its resistance; the RAF had fired in retaliation. A wild stampede had broken out.

I shuddered. I took to my heels and tried to escape, but I stumbled upon something and fell. And then I was crushed under the crowd.

People were running helter-skelter. If someone fell, getting up was just impossible. There was a blood-soaked body nearby, riddled with bullets. I, too, was drenched in the blood oozing out of it. Both my hands were stained with blood; there was some on my face, too. There were more bodies around. The big, round eyes of the dead stared at me. Lieutenant Hudson's army was dragging the corpses and throwing them into the truck as if they were the noisome carcasses of dogs.

This historical character of Lieutenant Hudson, whom Diya had mentioned, where had he appeared from? *Oh, that's my face! No, that's not possible. How can my face resemble Hudson's?* Diya's voice seemed to be echoing in my ears: Hudson! Hudson! Hudson! I bent my head and closed my ears with both hands, but the voice grew louder, like beating drums. My eyelids drooped from all the bitterness and uneasiness. My face turned towards the sky with a dispassionate expression.

'No! Not me!' I screamed and woke up to find myself lying on a hospital bed. Diya was looking at me in astonishment.

You Too Must Forgive Me

Kiran Kumari Sharma

(Translated from the Magahi by Abhay K.)

The evening crept up like a black cat in an empty corner of a house. Laxmi, the maid, had not shown up yet. My temper was close to boiling point. *When is she going to come*? I kept looking towards the door and then craned my neck to see the pile of unwashed utensils. *Had the saucepan been clean, I would have made myself a cup of tea.*

And then she appeared, almost like the crescent moon. I called out to her the moment I spotted her, 'Laxmi, come here!'

'Yes, madam.'

'Don't you want to work any more?' My tone was stern.

'Have I done something wrong, madam?' Laxmi asked, her eyes and mouth wide open.

'Your demeanour has changed in the last few days. You come early in the morning and hastily complete your chores. Then you come late in the evening and again leave in a jiffy. Do you even sweep the place these days? All day long, flies keep hovering over the unwashed utensils. If you don't want to work, please let me know. If I offer money, many others will agree to work readily!'

Laxmi was stunned. She was mum for a while and then she picked up the broom. She swept and mopped the floor. She washed the utensils and arranged them. She continued with her work as if I had not reproached her, without any signs of resentment, without even a word in counterargument.

My mind drifted from Laxmi to the chilly weather. I said out loud, 'I have never felt so cold.' The radio had announced that Patna's temperature had come down three degrees. 'Don't you feel a chill in your bones? My body's getting numb. I don't feel like getting up in the morning. The cold in Pausha pierces the bones.' And then I wondered, *what did I just say*?

Whether Laxmi heard me or not, I don't know, but she finished her work quickly and walked towards the door quietly. Usually, we sat together, shared our joys and sorrows, and drank tea together. Today, I purposely did not remind her. I wanted to see if she would.

But Laxmi did not say a word. She did not seem to want to stay for tea. Perhaps she had taken my words to heart. She must be thinking that I had gone crazy. In such a situation, asking for tea would be like rubbing salt on a wound. But I could not stop myself. I called out to her, 'Please go after having tea.'

Laxmi stopped. Feeling guilty, she turned back and burst into tears. 'Madam, you're my bread and butter. Since the day my husband went to jail, you've given me shelter. Please don't abandon me. Where will I go? Who will help me? I don't feel cold otherwise, but if I catch a cold, it will be I who will suffer, not my husband. He must be comfortably smoking pipes even in jail. I'm the one who is actually serving the sentence, madam. My mother-in-law was a real gem. I had borrowed some money for her last rites. I have been working at a construction site to repay the debt. The thekedar wants us to report for work at 7 a.m. I was late for two days, so he cut my wages by twenty rupees.'

My body shivered, not because of the cold but because of her painful story. The tea tasted bitter. *It is true, the taste lies not in food but in the mind. Laxmi would be better off as a widow than as a married woman.* Her husband had come out of the jail to perform his mother's last rites. The vigour she had exuded then had been worth admiring. Glimpses of sorrow and joy had continuously flitted over her face.

Today, on her face was a thick layer of perennial pain and in her voice was a deep ocean of sorrow. Her eyes were full of tears. I shuddered seeing her in this condition. I remembered the day when Laxmi's husband was taken to jail. Her mother-in-law had wept bitterly for her daughter-in-law. 'How will Laxmi live? Not even a fortnight has passed. I had warned Laxmi's father not to get his daughter married to this indolent. He is a thief and a flirt. He was born to taint the family's reputation. But her half-witted father did not listen to me. After Laxmi's mother's death, her father married another woman, following which daughter became a burden for him. On the new wife's advice, he married his beautiful daughter off to this thief. Now who will suffer the fate that has befallen her? Oh god! For this moon-faced beauty Laxmi, there is no comfort either at her parents' home or at her in-laws'. With whom will she live now?' she had lamented.

Though her mother-in-law's heart had been torn apart, Laxmi had stayed strong. She had wiped her mother-in-law's tears and comforted her. 'I am your son. He was your daughter-in-law. He has left, but I will not leave you. I will feed you even if I have to work as a maid. I will not leave any stone unturned to meet your needs. I will not run away to my parents' home. There I have my stepmother, here I have my own mother. We, mother and daughter, will live together. These days of sorrow will pass,' Laxmi had consoled her mother-in-law.

Laxmi's heart was not ripped apart by my harsh words today. A person can bear the indignity of the world, but insults from loved ones can be unbearable. While stepping out of the gate, she wiped her tears and said, 'Please forgive me, madam.'

Laxmi left. With teary eyes, I stared at her slippers, the straps of which were broken. Leaving aside her work at the construction site, she had found time to come to my house.

Yashodhara had Rahul,[172] *a reason to live. Who does Laxmi have? She is all alone. For whom would she live? She would have been blessed many times in the past, when she must have sought blessings from her elders: 'May your husband live long, may you have children, may you grow, prosper manifold, from one to twenty-one.' But forget about twenty-one, she could not even become two. She had her mother-in-law, a reason to live, but even she has passed away. How would she bear the pain? And here I am, adding to her misery by blaming her of shirking her responsibilities.* My mind was completely occupied with thoughts about Laxmi. My ears started ringing with her words: 'Please forgive me, madam.'

And suddenly, these words flowed out of me: 'Oh, Laxmi, you too must forgive me.'

172 Yashodhara was the wife of Buddha; Rahul was their son

Transformation

Kavita

(Translated from the Hindi by Manisha Chaudhry)

After bidding farewell to Ma, who has just entered a new world, I am on my way back. Life sometimes brings us to a point where our roles are exchanged. Today, I was at such a point in my life.

For every journey, there is a parallel journey. *I'm returning after leaving Ma in a new world, then why is Ma travelling with me? Why has my journey, which I undertook while going to meet her, become a part of this return journey? We are both on our respective journeys; Ma is going back, and I am moving forward. What is wrong? Don't the earth and the planets revolve on their own axes? Rivers also change course, then why expect Ma to remain unchanged? Why must she not move on at this turning point in her life? All of us have taken steps forward on our respective journeys, but Ma must remain still and rooted as she waits for us. Ma is not a mountain, and mountains too erode with time. Like all humans, she feels happy and sad, fear and pain, disgust and anger, even as we forget something that is so self-evident. Even then, all of us wish that Ma should remain unmoving, as still as a mountain.*

When I was a child, she would narrate to me the story of the early days of creation. Bacteria, worms and insects, water and land, the earth and the sky and the plants--God must have created humans after that. All these had their own moments and their own courses. At that time, the sun and the moon decided to exchange their roles and characters. The moon would be free of its cool temperament and the sun would no longer have to bear the terrible heat every day. The next day would surely be miraculous for them as they would have moved far from the humdrum of their lives. In a new life, there would only be pleasure ahead.

But this exchange was disastrous for all of creation. People suffered from the unbearable heat every night; they were unable to sleep. The day induced sleep and all work came to a standstill. A day passed, then another. The change seemed permanent. This little exchange of roles brought on hurricanes and earthquakes. All notions of day and night, hunger and thirst, life and death began to lose their meaning. It was as if God had cursed them.

Ma, how could you forget this story? You would recite Kabir's inversions, their meaning would find expression in your life, and now you go and invert everything? Ma, you were like an ocean. You knew that the crashing waves in the ocean of your life would not dash against the breakers, but that they would cause a tsunami in our lives. That's exactly what happened. You moved on and our world was rocked to the core.

I really missed you Ma, missed you so terribly. Anuj had sensed this and would often say, 'Call Ma. Find out how she is doing.' How could I dishonour his generosity by telling him that if I called, it would only further my vulnerability? My bounds and incapacities would emerge, with their mouths wide open, ready to devour me. What if I found that Ma was ill?

That night, the phone rang incessantly. My fear held my palms captive. *Who could it be at this hour?* Anuj woke up. 'Pick up the phone, Appu.' Now that he was by my side, I steeled myself for any eventuality.

'Hello.'

'Is that Appu?'

'Yes, this is Appu. Bhabhi,[173] at this hour, what is the matter?'

The trembling within showed up all over my body and in my voice. Anuj sat up.

'What is it?'

'Nothing much, but you must take the first train tomorrow and come here.'

The first train … I felt a lump in my throat. 'Bhabhi. I hope Ma is well. When did you get there?'

'Ma is all right. The entire family is here. You must come tomorrow.'

No further inquiries were possible as the phone was disconnected. I sat down with a heavy heart as Anuj put his arms around me. 'What happened, Appu?'

'I don't know. She says that Ma is fine but that I must go tomorrow. Is that possible, Anuj?'

'Oh, they haven't visited home for so long and must have all planned this trip together. So, they asked you to come, too. Why worry so much?'

In the morning, Anuj somehow packed for me and, as he put me on the train, said, 'Come back soon, Appu. You know how difficult it is for me to stay without you even for a day.' The train moved and Anuj's hands, holding on to mine through the window, pulled away first before he slowly receded into the background. As soon as he vanished from sight, the image of Ma appeared. *What could have happened to her that everybody had gathered there and I hadn't been informed?* I scolded myself fiercely, my eyes blurring. *It is inauspicious to cry like this. Nothing has happened to Ma, or else Bhabhi would have told me.*

Bhabhi! Even though she had been in the same city, she had been living in her mother's rabbit warren of a house for a year, not with Ma. And my brother, Ma's favourite younger son, hadn't said a word. There was no place for her in her older son's house in any case. The sons felt that it was

173 Sister-in-law, brother's wife or husband's brother's wife

better this way, but it did not mean that they did not love Ma. Whenever they came, they employed new servants to ensure her comfort. They would give her lots of money and buy all kinds of things for the house. All for her and her well-being, wasn't it? But did that take care of her loneliness?

Once, I had called up and the phone rang for a long time. *Why isn't anybody answering the phone ... one ... two ... four rings.* I was just about to disconnect when I heard a faint voice at the other end.

'Hello ... who is it?' It was Ma.

'It's Appu. Why is your voice sounding so weak? Why weren't you picking up the phone? What happened?'

'I fell down in the courtyard this morning.'

'You fell? Why didn't you call me? Are you alright? Have you fractured your bone?'

'No, it is just a mild sprain. I couldn't get up from bed. That is why I took so long to answer the phone.'

'Have you been to a doctor?'

'Who will take me? I paid the neighbour's sweeper to apply turmeric and lime. It'll get better soon'

'The neighbour's sweeper? Where is Deby, your servant?'

'Oh, he ran away a long time ago. He even stole that watch of your father's—the one kept near his photograph—and some money.'

'Did you file a complaint? And your part-time maid?'

'She left two months ago saying her granddaughter was getting married, and that she may not return as her daughter will be alone after the marriage.'

Mothers care so deeply for their daughters, I thought to myself, *and daughters* ... Ma was still speaking.

'Ma, what did you eat?'

'The neighbour brought some khichdi.[174] Half of it is still left. I'll eat when I feel like eating.'

---

174 A dish made of rice and lentils

Would Anuj let me go to my mother? But why ask? Ma doesn't like me leaving Anuj behind and staying with her. But never has he said, 'Let us bring Ma here. She can stay with us for a few days.' Not once. *If Anuj loves her so much, why doesn't he understand? Doesn't he remember that my brothers had opposed our marriage?* If we got married, it was only because of Ma's staunch support. Anuj's middling job and his ordinary looks had been a bone of contention for my brothers. And the biggest stumbling block had been that he was my choice. What will people say, they had asked, 'Just because she didn't have a father, three brothers couldn't find a suitable match for their only sister.'

Ma was the one who had stood firm. 'Everyone is free to think whatever they like. I have respected the dreams and desires of all my children. Just like my sons, my daughter Apoorva has the right to make her own choices in life. I will stand by her,' she had said.

Ma, who always disliked tasteless food, how would she swallow that stale khichdi? Laughter, colour and taste were an intrinsic part of her life, but they had all vanished now. Ma used to dislike sarees in pale colours, but since Papa's death, she had only worn white sarees. Fish had been her favourite food, but now she was a vegetarian. Even in her daughter-in-law's bland offerings, she'd manage to infuse taste with a little curd here or a dash of pickle or chutney there.

I furtively wiped my teary eyes. *If any of the passengers see me crying, what will they think? I just want Ma to be fine. I will bring back all her lost pleasures, her forgotten delights and all the promises I'd made to her.*

I am flooded with memories. After my wedding, when I went to meet her for the first time, I had many honeymoon photographs. She had said to me before sundown, 'Let me see them first. Others can see them later, but I won't be able to see much without sunlight.' Ma had had a cataract for years. But nobody had thought of surgery. She still kept stitching and embroidering intricate patterns, even if she got a bad headache later. Despite a bad case of gout, she still did the household chores and walked without any support.

I'd often complain and say, 'Why don't you just sit quietly? Let others know that you are suffering. If you just keep on bearing the pain silently, how will they find out? Just resign from your responsibilities and see who takes over.'

Ma would reply calmly, 'I am getting older, so aches and pains are bound to be there. If I just sit around and do nothing, my body will rust and I'll be dependent even for a glass of water. All these afflictions are meant to warn you that old age is about to come swooping down.'

Perhaps these arguments had been futile. The years passed by. Ma began to limp more prominently. Her eyes were getting worse, too, but we brothers and sisters had stopped taking note. We had begun to see these changes as a part of her personality.

So, we were talking about my pictures ... Ma spread out a durrie in the courtyard and laid the pictures around her. She looked at each one with great attention, noticing everything. Her interest was childlike. She said, 'People must be getting drenched when the waves come. I wonder how it feels!'

It was as if she was talking to herself. Her remarks, her innocent queries echoed in my mind. 'These mountains look small in these photographs. How do they look when you are close to them?' Ma's soliloquy had continued.

I slid back into the voice of my childhood and said, 'I'll take you there, Ma. This time, you must come with me and ...' The yawning distance between what I wanted and what I could do was all too real. My joy and my precious memories weighed me down with shame. Ma had never been to big cities, never seen big rivers, never watched breakers in an ocean, never touched a mountain ... and now I felt sad and helpless. Why couldn't I fulfil my childhood promise of flying a big, big plane and taking her everywhere?

I had just entered a new, dreamy phase of my life. I slipped in and out of the visions of my future home with Anuj. *Where was the time to complete my education, so that I could keep my promise to Ma?* This happens when you are in love. Old promises fade away in the face of new ones.

If I confided in Anuj in a moment of sadness, he would say, 'What sort of brothers do you have? They have such fine jobs; they should take Ma on a trip. She is getting old now, so if nothing else, at least they could take her on a pilgrimage.' As if the responsibility of Ma's happiness rested solely upon her sons.

Why had I been thinking about Ma so often for the past few days? I understood the reason only after I got to her place. Ma had stirred in her sleep and the quilt had slipped off her face and the bed. Her face looked like that of an innocent child who was dreaming. *After Papa's death, when had her face looked so calm?* I switched off the light.

I alighted quietly from the train and took a rickshaw. Even though I had come here after a long time, why did it feel as if everything was just the same? Everything was so familiar, nothing seemed to have changed. It felt the same way with Ma. As if I had always been with her.

I tightened my fists over the worms of anxiety, refusing to acknowledge them. The neighbourhood appeared to be quiet, and so did our house. I alighted from the rickshaw quietly. *No, if there was bad news, the house would not be so quiet. No crowd, no movement, no voices.* But the silence was also disquieting. *There were so many people in the house: Ma, Bade Bhaiya, Badi Bhabhi, their daughter Nisha, Manjhale Bhaiya, Manjhali Bhabhi, Chhote Bhaiya, Chhoti Bhabhi, and still not a sound?* I opened the gate. Bade Bhaiya[175] came to the door. 'Come, Apoorva. Hope your journey was comfortable. We've all been waiting for you.'

I take note of how much Bade Bhaiya resembles my father. Greying at the temples, a certain heaviness in his frame, the same eyes. Even his voice sounds the same. He never used to look like my father; this change is sudden.

175 Elder brother

Ma was not in the sitting room. I bowed down uneasily to pay my respects to all the elders. 'Bhabhi, Ma?' I asked.

'Ma is in the kitchen.'

A wave of relief took over me, but then there was an odd feeling. *I have arrived and there is no sign of Ma to hug me joyfully.* 'I'll go and meet Ma. Give me two minutes,' I said as I made my way towards the kitchen.

Bhaiya's grim face and deep voice arrested my feet. 'Apoorva, you can meet Ma and talk to her. That is why we have called you here. But first listen to what we have to say.'

'Tell me.' I did my best to conceal the sarcasm in my voice. I thought Ma was ill and they wanted to take her along with them, but Ma's bitter memories did not let her agree. *They want me to persuade Ma. They are convinced that Ma listens to me, but what would I say to her? And how?*

'Appu, are you listening? I was saying that Ma wants to get married,' Bhaiya emphasized on the word 'married'. It hit me like a hammer on my head. I felt a strange sensation, one that wrenched me out of my reverie.

'What?'

'Yes, Ma is going to get married … and I … all of us don't see why she needs to do this. Let her spend her last years in peace and comfort. In a few years, she'll be marrying off her grandchildren.'

'Ma's gone senile,' murmured Chhoti[176] Bhabhi. 'All of you live elsewhere, so you won't be affected. We live in the same town. We'll lose face.'

I was in a state of shock. 'Whose marriage?' I asked to confirm.

'Her marriage, who else?' Bade Bhaiya and Chhote Bhaiya spoke in unison: 'She is sure to listen to you. Talk her out of this. If she feels lonely here, our wives will take turns to stay with her for four months each. Or if she is willing to stay with us, that is even better.'

---

176 Younger

I thought Ma had initiated a new game to get her children back into her life, so that the silence clawing at her existence would be replaced with sound. *Why not join her game quietly*? 'So, your wives will stay here, but what about the children?' I asked.

'Well, they can't be expected to give up their schooling. And there are no good schools here. But we'll surely bring them over during the holidays.'

'Will you be able to look after the children without your respective wives for four months?'

'Yes. What choice do we have? At least we'll be able to save our honour. If Ma gets married at this age, it would mean loss of face for all of us.'

'If Ma wants to get married now, it is because she is lonely, not because she can't control her desires, Bhaiya. Whatever dreams we had, Ma fulfilled them. She stood by each of us in all our decisions. Today, when she is all alone and has never complained about it, she has expressed only one desire. Will this be our response? How many years does she have left? Maybe fifteen. If she spends these years happily, and we too don't have to worry about her well-being because she won't be alone, I see no harm.'

'At an age when people go on pilgrimages or turn to religion, for a woman with grandchildren to marry … I've never heard of something so bizarre … Papa's soul will be in pain.'

'I don't know if there is a soul or not, but if there is, then it must have been equally hurt to see that the children she doted upon have turned away from her. You can't live your life only with memories. Perhaps Papa's soul will be at peace to see that Ma is well, that there is somebody with her to share her joys and sorrows,' I said, amazed to feel the heat of anger on my face.

I had confronted my elder brothers. Bhabhi had walked away quietly. Perhaps I should not have spoken with such bitterness. I noticed that the pain on the face of Chhote Bhaiya had lessened, though he still looked disturbed. There was a tinge of uncertainty when he spoke, as if he were considering my words.

'If Pitaji were here, we would have been preparing to celebrate their golden wedding anniversary. And if we celebrated it according to the custom, it would be like a wedding, with all the ceremonies. We would not have resented that. Ma has completed all her duties, and now she has only asked for some years for herself. That, too, of her own life,' he said.

My younger brother—Pappu—seemed to be arguing with himself. I was glad that my voice had influenced one of them at least. When we were younger, he would always listen to me; our views would often be similar. The two of us were more emotional and sensitive. That is why we did not go as far in life as the two older brothers. His wife, however, didn't value this quality of him caring for others as much. When my two older brothers were aiming high, he stayed on to support and look after Ma, while he continued to study. Bhabhi would be amused and irritated with him by turns. According to her, he was a fool and she was suffering the consequences.

'If, for a moment, we imagine Papa in Ma's place, we might have been willing to consider the idea. But Ma? Never. And who is the man? What does he do? Where did she meet him? Will someone tell me?' said Bade Bhaiya.

'The question is not who he is and what he is like. The question is that Ma is getting married. Only if you agree to that will these things matter,' said I.

'Pappu has always been a fool, but you too, Apoorva? You people do whatever you deem fit, but I have no part to play in this drama. I'll leave tomorrow morning,' thundered Bade Bhaiya.

If there had been a train today, he would have left immediately, I thought to myself.

'Me too ...' said Manjhale Bhaiya quietly. So, my middle brother will not stay either, which leaves just my younger brother and me.

Chhoti Bhabhi said, 'I'm leaving for my mother's house. You stay here and do whatever you need to, for Ma's wedding. But don't come back to me or to my children after that.'

I know now that he will not stay here either. His children are his weakness. He left Ma and went with his wife, despite all her taunts and insults, because of his children. So, only I was left. The play was nearing its climax.

I put on a serious expression and moved towards the kitchen, keeping the bubble of laughter contained in my stomach. If I laugh now, it'll shake the whole house and ruin the whole game.

I put my arms around Ma's shoulders as she made urad puri, Bade Bhaiya's favourite. *Your sons are fools. They can't see through their mother's simple, wily ways.*

Ma turns to face me, her eyes and voice speaking in unison. 'I know, Appu, even if nobody stands by me, I am sure you will...'

'Ma, you don't have to pretend with me,' I laughed.

'I am not pretending or acting. Are you supporting me because you think I'm acting? I've decided and, for the first time, it is about me. Let's see which of my children stand by me.' Ma's voice was calm and steady. 'Go, give this plate to Bade.'

Bade Bhaiya pushed the plate aside. 'Stop with all these gestures. I'm going to a friend's place with my family. I'll take the train tomorrow.'

Ma heard this, but she didn't try to stop Bade Bhaiya or pacify him. *Is she telling the truth? She knows how wilful Bade Bhaiya is. But why has Nisha moved right behind Ma?* 'I don't want to go,' Nisha said.

Bade Bhaiya tried to pull her away, but she didn't budge. Then, suddenly, he lost patience, his hand moved and landed on his beloved, delicate daughter's face.

Ma's eyes welled up. The girl was no longer a child, and her father had raised his hand on her! She entreated Nisha to go, but Nisha pretended not to hear. She moved, not towards the door but to her room, where she locked herself in. Bhabhi, Nisha's mother, started crying. 'If something happens to my daughter … if she does something foolish in anger…'

'She'll do nothing. Let her rot. I will not call her … you come,' Bade Bhaiya said and dragged Bhabhi away.

I must take courage from this girl. She had hardly stayed with Ma, yet she has such unconditional love for her. Ma gave birth to me and brought me up. And hadn't I thought on the way here that I would give back Ma her lost happiness? Now that I have a chance…

Is my heart in tune with my mind? My brother's pain finds a trembling echo in me … My father, from the photo frame, had set my heart racing. How can Ma replace him? We also own that part of her past. Even if she chooses to take that path, why should we? How would we find a father in a stranger's face? My heart, too, twisted and turned with the hurt I saw on my brothers' faces.

I had already thought of the worst. *What if Ma had really not been here when I came? I would have slowly made peace with her absence. Then why can't I do the same for her happiness?* I tried to pacify my heart.

Just then, the phone rang. Nisha picked it up. 'Bua,[177] it's Phuphaji.'[178]

'What happened?' asked Anuj when Nisha handed over the phone to me.

'Nothing…'

'Then why did they call you suddenly?'

'Ma is getting married…'

'And what are you doing in all of this?'

'I'll come after the wedding, Anuj.'

'All of you are insane! What about your brothers? They made such a huge fuss when we were to get married.'

'Bade Bhaiya has left.'

177 Paternal aunt, father's sister
178 Paternal aunt's husband

'Bade Bhaiya has left!' repeated Anuj angrily. 'And you are staying for the wedding ... I respected her so much!'

'You only respected her; you didn't love her like a mother.'

'What are you saying? She is like a mother.'

'Yes, "like" a mother, not "a" mother.'

'You have no right to talk to me like that, Apoorva. If you love me, you'll return tomorrow.'

'Aren't you forgetting something? Our love wouldn't have blossomed had it not been for Ma. And I love Ma, Anuj, just like I love you. Perhaps more than you.'

Anuj was speechless. The dust devil of his anger rose again. 'There is no need to come back after that wedding.'

The phone went silent. Just like the limit of Anuj's love, which he poured over me day and night. *How fragile was its thread that it snapped at the first instance of resistance?*

I placated myself thinking that Anuj had said it in the heat of the moment. His anger would evaporate soon. We were all in my father's room. Pappu had slept. Ma opened her old wooden chest and started tidying it.

Ma said, 'He is a doctor; he treated me on the two occasions when I fell.' Then she asked if we would like to meet him. No? Would we talk to him on the phone?

'No, Ma. If you've chosen him, he must be a good man. Why else would you have taken such a big decision?'

Was this evidence of my distrust in him? A stubborn refusal to let anyone take Papa's place? The faint fragrance emanating from the trunk was very familiar, very personal. A lot like Ma, like this house and like Papa's memories. I felt like I was losing something precious. Maika, a mother's house, existed because of Ma's presence ... and she was going away. Her eyes were wet, too, as if she was doubting if she was doing the right thing. Was Ma also facing a dilemma, like every woman, every girl? Was she tense?

I held on to Ma's hand through the night. Everything that was familiar was getting left behind.

Nisha put her head on Ma's shoulder and I held on to her wrists. We were no longer women from three generations. We were certainly not grandmother, granddaughter and aunt. We were just three women, three sisters, three friends. Time removed the barriers around us as it stood mutely in the corner, looking on. Perhaps time also felt these moments were historic, as our silence spoke to each other; it had a lot to say. *When did Nisha grow up?* We never really knew. *When a woman grows up, who knows?*

*

Ma locked up her room and handed over the keys to me.

'Why me?'

'Just like that … the whole house is vacant. If she wanted, Chhoti, the youngest daughter-in-law, could have stayed here, but I know she will not leave her mother's place. Now even more so … and even if somebody comes, this room will stay locked. I have the keys, and now you too … in case we return.' Ma said nothing more.

Nisha was brimming with enthusiasm. She found bangles and sarees in pastel shades for her dadi.

Ma, slightly abashedly, said, 'All this doesn't suit my age.'

The phone rang again. I expected it to be Anuj. Nisha was on the phone. 'Yes, I'll come, Papa. Just until tomorrow … you send Uncle.'

Would Anuj forgive as Bade Bhaiya did? He loved me a lot, but Bade Bhaiya was a father figure and Anuj a husband. *I had called on his mobile repeatedly, why hadn't he answered my calls?*

I had called the landline, too. Anuj's nephew picked up the call. 'Aunty, this is Rishabh. Uncle is not at home but he's given me the keys … I'm watching the match … Any message for him?'

'Tell him I'm coming back tomorrow. He should come to the station, or else …' My voice choked up and I disconnected the phone without completing my sentence. *Was Anuj really not there? Or was it just an excuse?*

I put together some grains of rice, fresh grass and vermilion in Ma's aanchal and knotted it with prayers for her happiness. Ma had done the same for me.

★

Ma left. Nisha and I left as well.

There was a great tumult in my heart as the train pulled in at the station. I didn't have the courage to peep out. *What if Anuj was not there?*

The keys Ma gave me jangled in my purse in response. *Why did she give these to me? Had she understood what was going on … and still? Would I have to make my way back to that locked room, to her loneliness? Like the sun and the moon, had Ma and I exchanged roles?*

A Rainy Day at Jhapsi Mahato's Tea Stall

Pankhuri Sinha

(Translated from the Hindi by Pankhuri Sinha and Abhay K.)

On a rainy day
everybody had different windows,
different viewpoints, thoughts all along.

Life and death depended
on an inch less or more of rising water.

People, confined in their homes, thought
the town must have drowned, submerged.

They rang each other up, asked about and around,
thankful, at least the phone lines worked.

The shops were all closed
on the second day of heavy rains.

Many from the neighbourhood had gathered
at Jhapsi Mahato's tea stall.

Goats, dogs, people with opposing political views,
critiquing, lambasting a dysfunctional municipality,
and those sitting in their homes were reminiscing
the open spaces that once existed,
the history of the houses in the neighbourhood
—the old and the new—
and when they were built.

And after endless debates,
they travelled back to the ponds of yore,
abound with jalkumbhi,[179]
the flowers one rarely sees these days.

They had carefully located
the exact spots where the ponds once existed,
now filled up to make way for the new houses.

On the steps of the old houses,
water played hide-and-seek,
rose up and down,
threatening to get in, knocking ferociously,
an inch closer,
or the length of a finger.

Once again, after the evening rain,
the town's skyline rose,
rising above the lives of its people,
towering over its inhabitants.

179 Water hyacinth

Oh, how many stories did that rainy evening have!
And the old inhabitants were recounting them all
stories of homes flourishing and doomed,
people alive and dead,
and inside Jhapsi Mahato's thatched tea stall,
the dripping water was fanning the hearth's flame!

Nalanda Poems

Abhay K.

The Day of Massacre at Nalanda

Bakhtiyar and his men
play buzkashi[180] in my alleys today

monks are being burnt alive, and
those who try to escape are beheaded

Dharmagunj—the nine-storeyed library
has burst into flames

smoke and ash from the burning books
have turned the day into night

180 A traditional Central Asian sport in which horse-mounted players attempt to place a goat or calf carcass in a goal

The sun has disappeared from the sky today
and even my bricks bleed

the sacred chants that once sanctified Magadha
have turned into shrieks of a failing humanity.

The light of the world is fading today
to face the ravages of time alone

abandoned, scorned, forgotten
or perhaps, to be reborn into many Nalandas.

The Rise of Nalanda

Forlorn under the red earth
buried for centuries
I rise today like a phoenix
eight hundred years later
from the ashes of my burnt books.

I open my arms today to embrace you
whoever you are, from wherever you are
come, walk into my enlightened fold
as once Buddha and Mahavira did
seeking shelter in my groves

I remember Hiuen Tsang and Faxian—
the saint-seekers from the East
I hear footsteps of Aryabhata and Charaka
in my ancient compound today,
you too come; come as I rise again.

Acknowledgements

I am deeply grateful to Chaitali Pandya for carefully reading the manuscript and offering her valuable suggestions. I would like to thank my literary agent Kanishka Gupta, and Prema Govindan, my commissioning editor at HarperCollins India, for their continuous support throughout the process of the publication of this book. A special thanks to all the authors and translators for generously offering their work for this anthology. Without them, this book would not have been possible. I also want to express my gratitude to all those who have generously endorsed the book. I take full responsibility for any error that has inadvertently crept into the book.

PERMISSIONS ACKNOWLEDGEMENTS

All the works included in this book have been voluntarily contributed by the authors and/or the translators. Permission to include these has been granted by the respective authors, translators, editors and publishers. While every effort has been made to trace individual copyright holders, if—because of an inability to trace the present copyright owners—any copyright material is included for which permission has not been specifically sought, apologies are tendered in advance to the proprietors and publishers concerned. Some copyright holders could not be traced. If any have been inadvertently overlooked, I will be glad to make the necessary amendments at the first opportunity.

'Free, Fabulously Free' by Mutta, taken from *Therigatha*, translated from the Pali by Abhay K. and Gabriel Rosenstock and used with the permission of the translators.

'Peace at Last' by Sumangalmata, taken from *Therigatha,* translated from the Pali by Abhay K. and Gabriel Rosenstock and used with the permission of the translators.

'Selections from *Chanakya Niti*' by Kautilya, translated from the Sanskrit by Abhay K. and used with the permission of the translator.

'Selections from the *Kama Sutra*', from *Kama Sutra* by Vatsyayana, translated from the Sanskrit by Abhay K. and used with the permission of the translator.

'Two Poems' by Dharmakirti, translated from the Sanskrit by Abhay K. and used with the permission of the translator.

'Selected Dohas from *Mahamudra*' by Sarhapa, originally translated from the Prakrit by Pandita Vairocanaraksita, are available in the public domain. The details of the translator into the English language are not available.

'Two Poems' by Vidyapati, translated from the Maithili by Abhay K. and used with the permission of the translator.

'Selected Poems' of Abdul-Qādir Bēdil, translated from the Persian by Nasim Fekrat and used with the permission of the translator.

The whole text of *The Travels of Dean Mahomed* is available in the public domain.

'An Epistle to the Right Hon'ble Alfred Lord Tennyson', by Avadh Behari Lall, available in the public domain.

'My Feet Are Tired of Walking', by Mahendar Misir, translated from the Bhojpuri by Abhay K. and used with the permission of the translator.

'Bridegroom', by Bhikhari Thakur, translated from the Bhojpuri by Abhay K. and used with the permission of the translator.

'Batohiya', by Raghuveer Narayan, translated from the Bhojpuri by Abhay K. and used with the permission of the translator.

'The Untouchable's Complaint', by Heera Dom, translated from the Bhojpuri by Abhay K. and used with the permission of the translator.

'The Key', by Acharya Shivpujan Sahay, translated from the Hindi by Mangal Murty and used with the permission of the translator.

'Budhia', by Rambriksh Benipuri translated from the Hindi by Mangal Murty and used with the permission of the translator.

'Selected Couplets', by Bedil Azimabadi, translated from Urdu by Abhay K. and used with the permission of the translator.

'Selection from the Third Canto of *Rashmirathi*', by Ramdhari Singh Dinkar, translated from the Hindi by Abhay K. and used with the permission of the translator.

'Famine and After', by Nagarjun, translated from the Hindi by Nalini Taneja and used with the permission of the translator.

'The Messenger', by Phanishwar Nath Renu, translated from the Hindi by Rakhshanda Jalil and used with the permission of the translator.

'The Invisible Bond', by Surendra Mohan Prasad, translated from the Bajjika by Abhay Kumar, Jay Ram Singh and Chaitali Pandya, and used with the permission of Varunendra Mohan and the translators.

'The Business of Donation', by Mathura Prasad Naveen, translated from the Magahi by Abhay K. and used with the permission of the translator.

'The Night of Full Moon', by Surendra Prasad Tarun, translated from the Magahi by Abhay K. and used with the permission of the translator.

'Fish', by Rajkamal Chaudhary, first published in *Mithila Mihir* (1966), translated from the Maithili by Vidyanand Jha and used with the permission of Nilmadhav Chaudhary and the translator.

'Babu', by Kalam Haidari, translated from the Urdu by Syed Sarwar Hussain and used with the permission of the translator.

'Deliverance', by Lalit, translated from the Maithili by Vidyanand Jha and used with the permission of Dr Padmakar Mishra and the translator.

'Today's Yudhisthir' by Ravindra Kumar, translated from the Magahi by Abhay K. and used with the permission of the translator.

Bereavement', by R. Ishari Arshad, translated from the Magahi by Abhay K. and used with the permission of the translator.

'A Song of Sorrow', by Harishchandra Priyadarshi, translated from Magahi by Abhay K. and used by permission of Abhay K.

'A Hindu Parrot', by Pandey Surendra, translated from the Bhojpuri by Gautam Chaubey and used with the permission of the author and the translator.

'Chilled to the Bone', by Mithilesh, translated from the Magahi by Asif Jalal and Abhay K. and used with the permission of the author and the translators.

'A Bowl of Sattu', by Chandramohan Pradhan, translated from the Hindi by Ram Bhagwan Singh and Chaitali Pandya, and used with the permission of the author and the translators.

'Nameless Relationship', by Mridula Sinha, translated from the Hindi by Ram Bhagwan Singh and Chaitali Pandya, and used with the permission of the author and the translators.

'The Dressing Table', by Shamoil Ahmad, translated from the Urdu by N.C. Sinha and used with the permission of the author and the translator.

'Through the Prism of Time', by Ramdhari Singh Diwakar, translated from the Hindi by Chaitali Pandya and used with the permission of the author and the translator.

'Cover Me in a Shroud', by Usha Kiran Khan, translated from the Hindi by Ram Bhagwan Singh and Chaitali Pandya, and used with the permission of the author and the translators.

'Girls on Rooftops', by Alok Dhanwa, translated from the Hindi by Anonymous and used with the permission of the author.

'A Twist of Fate', by Hussain Ul Haque, translated from the Urdu by Huma Mirza. This translation first appeared in the volume titled *Preeto & Other Stories: The Male Gaze in Urdu*, edited and introduced by

Rakhshanda Jalil and published by Niyogi Books (New Delhi, 2019). It has been reproduced here with the kind courtesy of the volume editor.

'Damul', by Shaiwal, translated from the Hindi by Ram Bhagwan Singh and Chaitali Pandya and used with the permission of the author and the translators.

'The Turning', by Aniruddha Prasad Vimal, translated from the Angika by Vivek Perampurna and used with the permission of the author and the translator.

'Journey in a Burnt Boat', by Abdus Samad, translated from the Urdu by Syed Sarwar Hussain and used with the permission of the author and the translator.

'Jugaad', by Prem Kumar Mani, translated from the Hindi by Bindu Singh and used with the permission of the author and the translator.

'Deception', by Ashok, from the collection *Daddy Gaam* (2017), translated from the Maithili by Vidyanand Jha and used with the permission of the author and the translator.

'The Whirlpool', by Nagendra Sharma Bandhu, translated from the Magahi by Vivek Perampurna and used with the permission of the author and the translator.

'The City of Gaya', by Arun Kamal, translated from the Hindi by the author himself, and used with the permission of the author.

'Kosi', by Narayanji, translated from the Maithili by Vidyanand Jha and used with the permission of the author and the translator.

'Fellowmen', by Avdhesh Preet, translated from the Hindi by Chaitali Pandya and used with the permission of the author and the translator.

'The Witness', by Vibha Rani, translated from the Maithili by Vidyanand Jha and used with the permission of the author and the translator. It was first published in Maithili as 'Rahathu Sakshi Chhath Ghaat' in *Sandhan* (October 1998, Patna).

'Amrapali', by Anamika, translated from the Hindi by Abhay K. and used with the permission of the author and the translator.

'Two Poems' by Savita Singh, translated from the Hindi by Medha Singh and used with the permission of the author and the translator.

'Pablo Neruda in Gaya', by Ashwani Kumar, used with the author's permission.

'The Rat's Guide', by Amitava Kumar, first appeared in *Harper's Magazine* (2014) and has been used here with the author's permission.

'The Goon', by Dhananjay Shrotriya, translated from the Magahi by Vivek Perampurna and used with the permission of the author and the translator.

'Dashrath Baba', by Arun Harliwal, translated from the Magahi by Abhay K. and used with the permission of the author and the translator.

'The Scam', by Tabish Khair, was first published in *Delhi Noir* (edited by Hirsh Sawhney, 2009). It has been used here with the author's permission.

'A Night As an Orphan', by Kumar Mukul, translated from the Hindi by Anupama Garg and Chaitali Pandya, and and used with the permission of the author and the translators.

'Lieutenant Hudson', by Ratneshwar, translated from the Hindi by Chaitali Pandya and used with the permission of the author and the translator.

'You Too Must Forgive Me', by Kiran Kumari Sharma, translated from the Magahi by Abhay K. and used with the permission of the author and the translator.

'Transformation', by Kavita, translated from the Hindi by Manisha Chaudhry. It was first published in *Her Piece of Sky* (edited by Deepa Agarwal), published by Zubaan Books (2011). It has been reprinted with the permission of the author, the translators and the publishers.

'A Rainy Day at Jhapsi Mahato's Tea Stall', by Pankhuri Sinha, translated from the Hindi by Pankhuri Sinha and Abhay K. and used with the permission of the author and the translator.

'The Nalanda Poems', by Abhay K., have been used with the permission of the author.

About the Contributors

AUTHORS

Mutta (sixth century BCE) was an elder nun who contributed poems to *Therigatha*, one of the first poetry anthologies in the world.

Sumangalmata (sixth century BCE) was an elder nun who also contributed poems to *Therigatha*.

Kautilya (375-283 BCE) was an ancient Indian teacher, philosopher, economist, jurist and royal adviser to Chandragupta Maurya in Pataliputra (modern-day Patna). He authored *Arthashastra*, the ancient Indian political treatise.

Vatsyayana (second–third century) was an ancient Indian philosopher who authored *Kama Sutra*. He lived in Pataliputra.

Dharmakirti (sixth–seventh century) was an influential Indian Buddhist philosopher who worked in Nalanda. He was one of the key scholars of epistemology (pramāṇa) in Buddhist philosophy, and is associated with the Yogācāra and Sautrāntika schools.

Sarhapa (eighth century) is considered the first poet in the Hindi language. He was born in Saharsa, Bihar, and his real name was

Rahulbhadra. He has numerous books to his credit, such as *Dohakosha* and *Mahamudra*, among others.

Vidyapati (1352–1448), also known by the sobriquet Maithil Kavi Kokil (the 'poet-cuckoo' of Maithili), was a Maithili and Sanskrit poet, composer, writer, courtier and royal priest. He was a devotee of Shiva, but he also wrote love songs and devotional Vaishnava songs.

Abdul-Qādir Bēdil (1642–1720) was an Indian Sufi saint and an Indo-Persian poet. He was born in Azimabad, which is present-day Patna. He mostly wrote ghazals and ruba'is (quatrains). The author of sixteen books of poetry, he is one of the prominent poets of the Indian school of poetry in Persian literature, and has carved a niche for himself with his unique style.

Dean Mahomed (1759–1851), born in Patna, was a traveller, surgeon, entrepreneur, and one of the most notable early non-European immigrants to the West. He was the first Indian to publish a book in English.

Avadh Behari Lall (1866–1921) was a poet from Gaya, Bihar. His poetry collections include *The Irish Home Rule Bill: A Poetic Pamphlet* (1893); *Behar and Other Poems* (1898); *An Elegy on the Late Right Hon'ble William Ewart Gladstone, M.P.* (1898); *An Ode on the Coronation Durbar at Delhi* (1903) and 'A Poem on the Coronation of Their Majesties King George V and Queen Mary as Emperor and Empress of India' (1911).

Mahendar Misir (1866–1946) was a Bhojpuri poet who is also called 'purbiya samrat' (the master of Purbi). He has written hundreds of Purbi poems.

Bhikhari Thakur (1887–1971) was a poet, playwright, lyricist, actor, folk dancer, folk singer and social activist, widely regarded as the greatest writer in the Bhojpuri language and the most popular folk writer of Purvanchal and Bihar.

Raghuveer Narayan (1884–1955), or Raghubir Narayan, was a Bhojpuri and English poet, and a freedom fighter. His Bhojpuri poem 'Batohiya' gained popularity equivalent to 'Vande Mataram' and is considered as the national song of India in Bhojpuri language.

Heera Dom (1885–not known) was a Bhojpuri poet from Danapur, Bihar, who contributed to Dalit literature. He is credited with crafting the first poem about the Dalits. The poem, 'Acchut Kee Shiqayat', was printed in *Saraswati* (Allahabad, 1914).

Acharya Shivpujan Sahay (1893–1963) was a noted Hindi and Bhojpuri novelist, editor and prose writer. He contributed to pioneering modern trends in Hindi poetry and fiction.

Rambriksh Benipuri (1899–1968) hailed from Muzaffarpur in Bihar. He was an acclaimed playwright, essayist and short-story writer.

Bedil Azimabadi (1907–1982) was born in Arrah, Bihar. His real name was Abdul Mannan. He has several poetry collections to his credit.

Ramdhari Singh Dinkar (1908–74) was a Hindi poet, essayist, patriot and academic from Simaria, Bihar. He is considered one of the most important modern Hindi poets. His poetry exudes veer rasa (heroic emotion) and he has been hailed as a Rashtrakavi (national poet) on account of his inspiring patriotic compositions.

Nagarjun (1911–98) was Vaidyanath Mishra's pen name. He was a Hindi and Maithili poet who authored a number of novels, short stories, literary biographies and travelogues. Also known as Janakavi, the people's poet, he is regarded as the most prominent proponent of modernity in Maithili.

Phanishwar Nath Renu (1921–77) was one of the most successful and influential writers of modern Hindi literature from Araria, Bihar, in the post-Premchand era. He is the author of *Maila Aanchal* which, after Premchand's *Godaan*, is regarded as the most significant Hindi novel.

Surendra Mohan Prasad (1925–2005) was born in Muzaffarpur, Bihar. He taught Hindi at Mithila Mahila College, Darbhanga. He has several short stories and poetry collections to his credit.

Mathura Prasad Naveen (1928–2011) was a Magahi poet. Associated with the progressive literature movement, he was born in Barahiya in Lakhisarai district, Bihar. He was a member of the Progressive Writers' Association. His songs have been used in various movements and rallies.

Surendra Prasad Tarun (1928–2016) was born in Nalanda district of Bihar. He published a number of poetry collections in Magahi, including *Magah ke Phul* and *Baj Rahal Bansuri*. He also served as the minister of state for education of Bihar.

Rajkamal Chaudhary (1929–67) was a writer from Muraliganj, Bihar. He has several novels, short story and poetry collections to his credit.

Kalam Haidari (1930–94) was born in Munger, Bihar, as Kalamul Haq. He was an Urdu short-story writer, journalist and literary critic. A staunch leftist and secularist, he launched and edited tone-setting, progressive Urdu weeklies and monthlies such as *Morcha*, *Bodh Dharti* and *Aahang* from Gaya, where he spent most of his adult life. He also published several collections of short stories.

Lalit (1932–83), or Lalitesh Mishra, was born in Chanpura in Bihar's Madhubani district. His published works include forty-seven short stories, two novels and dozens of essays.

Ravindra Kumar (1933–2006) was born in Kaghzi Mohalla in Biharsharif, which comes under Bihar's Nalanda district. He studied at Nalanda Collegiate, Nalanda College and Patna Science College. He reached new heights with his short-story writing skills in Magahi. His collection of Magahi short stories, *Ajab Rang Bole*, was published by the Magahi Sangh.

R. Ishari Arshad (1934–2014) from Biharsharif, Nalanda, is the author of several books in Magahi and Urdu.

Harishchandra Priyadarshi (b.1935) from Biharsharif, Nalanda, is a well-known poet and lyricist in Magahi.

Pandey Surendra (b.1935) was born in Saran, Bihar. He studied art in Cleveland, USA, and wrote a book on the art of bronze casting. He also has a poetry collection to his credit.

Mithilesh (b.1937) is a well-known Magahi writer and editor. He was born in Khakhari village (Kashi Chak) of Bihar's Nawada district, and now lives and works in Warisaliganj. He has authored several short stories and poems. His short-story collection, *Kankan Sora*, is an acclaimed work of Magahi literature.

Chandramohan Pradhan (b.1941) is a writer from Muzaffarpur, Bihar. He has published numerous short stories in Hindi.

Mridula Sinha (1942–2020) was born in Muzaffarpur, Bihar. Her published works include several short stories and novels. She also served as the first woman Governor of Goa.

Shamoil Ahmad (b.1943) was born in Bhagalpur, Bihar. He writes in Urdu and Hindi, and has five novels and five short-story collections to his credit. He received the International Award from Almi Majlis Farogh Urdu, Doha, for promoting Urdu in 2012. He lives in Patna.

Ramdhari Singh Diwakar (b.1945) was born in Araria district of Bihar. He is the author of several short-story collections, novels and critically acclaimed works.

Usha Kiran Khan (b.1945) writes in Hindi and Maithili. A retired academic historian, she received the Sahitya Akademi Award for the Maithili novel *Bhamati: Ek Avismarniya Prem Katha.*

Alok Dhanwa (b.1948) is a well-known poet from Munger district of Bihar. A recipient of many awards, he has authored a poetry collection titled *Duniya Roj Banti Hai.*

Hussain Ul Haque (b.1949) was born in Sasaram, Bihar, and is the author of twenty books, including six collections of Urdu short stories and three novels. He received the Sahitya Akademi Award in Urdu (2020) for his novel *Amawas Mein Khwab.*

Shaiwal (b.1950) is a native of Barh, Bihar. He shot to fame when he wrote the script for Prakash Jha's movie *Damul*, which eventually bagged the National Award for Best Film in 1984. He followed it up with a gripping story in 1997, for the Madhuri Dixit-starrer *Mrityudand*, which depicted the plight of widows in Bihar.

Aniruddha Prasad Vimal (b.1950) was born in Banka, Bihar. He writes in Angika and Hindi, and has a number of published plays, poetry and short-story collections to his credit.

Abdus Samad (b.1952) was born in Nalanda. He is a writer of short stories and acclaimed novels. He received the Sahitya Akademi Award in 1990 for his novel *Do Gaz Zameen.*

Prem Kumar Mani (b.1953) is a short-story writer from Patna. He is a journalist and a writer who has to his credit a novel, four collections of short stories, two essay collections and a biography of Jyoti Phule. He has received several awards, including the Srikant Verma Smriti Puraskar for his essays as well as the Vishesh Sahitya Seva Samman.

Ashok (b.1953) is a noted Maithili writer from Lohna, Madhubani. Mostly known for his short stories, he has a number of poems and critically acclaimed works to his credit.

Nagendra Sharma Bandhu (b.1953) was born in Balipur village of Bihar's Lakhisarai district. He currently lives and works in Warisaliganj, Nawada. His short-story collection, *Gurgeth*, is well-known in Magahi literary circles.

Arun Kamal (b.1954) is a well-known poet from Rohtas district, Bihar. He received the Sahitya Akademi Award in Hindi (1998) for his poetry collection *Naye Ilake Mein.*

Narayanji (b.1956) is a well-known Maithili poet with four collections to his credit. He has also published a collection of short stories, *Chitra*, from which the story in this book has been taken. He lives in a village and painstakingly documents the changing nature of Maithil society in his work.

Avdhesh Preet (b.1958) is a noted Hindi writer. He has received several awards, including the Phanishwar Nath Renu Award in 2003. He lives and works in Patna.

Vibha Rani (b.1959) is a writer, playwright, folk-art performer and a film, TV and theatre actor. She has written over seventeen plays—including, *Doosra Aadmi*, *Peer Parayee*, *Aye Priye Tere Liye*, *Life Is Not a Dream*, *Balchanda*, *Main Krishna Krishn Ki*, *Ek Nayi Menka* and *Bhikharin*—thirty books, two films and a TV serial. She won the Katha Award for Creative Fiction in 1999, for her short story, 'The Witness'.

Anamika (b.1961) from Muzaffarpur, Bihar, is a prominent contemporary Indian poet, social worker and novelist who writes in Hindi, and a critic who writes in English. She has eight collections of poetry, five novels and four critically acclaimed works to her credit. She is the recipient of the Sahitya Akademi Award (2020) in Hindi literature.

Savita Singh (b.1962) was born in Arrah, Bihar. She is a political theorist and a feminist poet who writes in Hindi and English, and has three collections to her credit. Her poetry has been translated into several languages and won many awards. At present, she is a professor at the School of Gender and Development Studies, IGNOU.

Ashwani Kumar (b.1963) was born in Bihar. He is a poet, author and professor at Tata Institute of Social Sciences. Widely published, anthologized and translated into several Indian languages, he is the author of several poetry collections and a book, *Community Warriors: State, Peasants, and Caste Armies in Bihar* (2006).

Amitava Kumar (b.1963) from Arrah is an Indian writer and journalist. A professor of English on the Helen D. Lockwood Chair at Vassar College (USA), he has several published novels to his credit.

Dhananjay Shrotriya (b.1965) is from Pranawan (Sarmera), Nalanda. He is the editor of numerous books and literary journals. He has edited the Magahi–Hindi Dictionary and also published a Magahi literary journal from Delhi.

Arun Harliwal (b.1965) from Gaya is the author of several poetry collections in Magahi, including *Kahan Gel Gaon*.

Tabish Khair (b.1966) from Gaya is an Indian English author and associate professor in the Department of English, University of Aarhus, Denmark. He has several poetry collections and novels to his credit.

Kumar Mukul (b.1966) is a short-story writer, poet, journalist and editor from Bihar. He has three published poetry collections to his credit, among other publications.

Ratneshwar (b.1967) is a novelist, journalist and art director. He has nineteen books to his credit, including the bestselling novel *Rekhna Meri Jaan*. He has received the Bharatendu Harishchandra Award in 1998 and the Navlekhan Award in 1994.

Dr Kiran Kumari Sharma (b.1967) teaches Magahi at Magadh University, Gaya. She has published a number of short stories and poems in various literary journals.

Kavita (b.1973) is known for her short stories based on the lives of women. She is the author of seven published collections of short stories and a recipient of the Amritlal Nagar Award.

Pankhuri Sinha (b.1975) is a bilingual poet from Bihar. She is the author of several poetry collections, both in English and Hindi. An award-winning writer, she has two published short-story collections in Hindi. Her work has been translated in over twenty-five languages.

Abhay K. (b.1980) is a poet, diplomat, translator and editor.

TRANSLATORS

Pandita Vairocanaraksita was a twelfth-century scholar and monk, originally from south India. He studied *Mahamudra* at Nalanda.

Mangal Murty (b.1939) is a noted writer and translator. He was a professor of English at the Magadh University and later served as the professor of American literature and linguistics at Taiz University in Yemen.

Ram Bhagwan Singh (b.1941) is a retired professor of English who taught at Ranchi University. He is a bilingual writer, translator, critic, book reviewer and radio presenter. He has eighteen books to his credit.

N.C. Sinha (b.1950) from Purnia, Bihar, is a writer and translator of many books. He lives in Patna.

Nalini Taneja (b.1951) is a professor at Delhi University. She translates works of Hindi to English.

Dr Syed Sarawar Hussain (b.1955), from Patna, is an associate professor at the College of Languages and Translation, King Saud University, Riyadh. He has also published eight books, which include books on literary criticism and translations of Urdu short stories and novels.

Manisha Chaudhry (b.1962) is an editor and translator fluent in Hindi and English. Her books have been published by Kali for Women, Oxford University Press (OUP), Zubaan Books, Niyogi Books and Pratham Books. She is the co-founder of Manam Books.

Rakhshanda Jalil (b.1963) is a Delhi-based writer, translator and literary historian. She has published over twenty books and fifty academic papers. She is best known for her work on the Progressive Writers' Movement.

Vidyanand Jha (b.1965) is a poet who has been writing in Maithili for the last four decades, with two collections to his credit. He is also a literary translator whose works have been published in various anthologies. He received the Katha Award for translation in 1998.

Huma Mirza (b.1972) studied English literature at the Aligarh Muslim University. She is an author, editor, translator, film-maker and social worker. She has translated numerous articles and short stories besides her father's work on Progressive Writers Movement.

Asif Jalal (b.1974) hails from Gaya, Bihar, and has written several short stories based on his experiences and translates from Magahi, the language spoken in his native town.

Jay Ram Singh (b.1975) works at the Department of Official Language under the Government of India. He writes in many languages, including Bajjika.

Vivek Perampurna (b.1976) has been rooted in his native tongue, Magahi, and loves to write and translate. He is also a painter who held his solo exhibition at Jehangir Art Gallery, Mumbai.

Chaitali Pandya (b.1979) is a French teacher based in Mumbai. She has undertaken several proofreading works and translates from and into English, French, Hindi and Gujarati.

Bindu Singh (b.1984) is an assistant professor of English at Mahila Mahavidyalaya, Banaras Hindu University, Varanasi. She teaches British and American literature to undergraduates and postgraduates. She enjoys reading and translating short stories from Hindi to English.

Gautam Choubey's (b.1986) translation of *Phoolsunghi* is the first-ever English translation of a Bhojpuri novel. He is currently working on a *History of Bhojpuri Literature*, an anthology titled *Code 302: Greatest Bhojpuri Stories Ever Told* and a monograph, *Using Gandhi*. He teaches English at Delhi University.

Medha Singh (b.1992) is a poet, editor and translator. She is the editor of *Berfrois* (London) and has authored two books. Her first poetry collection was titled *Ecdysis*. The second, a work of translation from the French, was titled *I Will Bring My Time: Love Letters* by S.H. Raza.

Abhay Kumar (b.1999) is a student at the Banaras Hindu University, pursuing a master's degree in English literature. He writes in Bajjika and English. He is also the founder and editor of *Bajjikanchal.*

Anupama Garg is a writer and poet who works as a communication strategist.

Nasim Fekrat is a blogger and journalist who has worked for various media outlets. He is a two-time winner of the Freedom of Expression Award.

About the Editor

Abhay K. (b.1980, Nalanda, Bihar) is the author of a dozen poetry books, including *Celestial, Stray Poems, Monsoon, The Magic of Madagascar* and *The Alphabets of Latin America*. He is also the editor of *The Bloomsbury Book of Great Indian Love Poems, Capitals, New Brazilian Poems* and *The Bloomsbury Anthology of Great Indian Poems*. His poems have appeared in over a hundred literary magazines, including the *Poetry Salzburg Review* and *Asia Literary Review*. His 'Earth Anthem' has been translated into over 150 languages. He received the SAARC Literary Award (2013) and was invited to record his poems at the Library of Congress, Washington, DC, in 2018. His translations of Kalidasa's *Meghaduta* and *Ritusamhara* from the Sanskrit won him the KLF Poetry Book of the Year Award (2020–21).

For more about him, visit www.abhayk.com.